518.59922

the Jesus thief

The Jesus Thief

A NOVEL

J R Lankford

Great Reads Books LLC

Published by Great Reads Books LLC
P. O. Box 2112
Bellaire, TX 77402
http://www.greatreadsbooks.com

ISBN 0-9718694-1-3
LCCN 2002105990

Manufactured in the United States of America

To those I love …

Author's Note

In 1988, a scientific team took samples from The Shroud of Turin, a 14 by 3-1/2 foot piece of ancient, handmade linen purported to be the burial cloth of Christ. The samples were subjected to radiocarbon tests in labs in Arizona, Oxford, and Zurich. All three labs dated the Shroud's linen between AD 1260 - 1390.

It seemed that the most famous winding sheet in the world was, after all, one of the many fake Christian relics produced in Europe around this time— few of which had ever been near Jerusalem, much less the crucified body of Jesus Christ.

Unconvinced, two Shroud experts subsequently announced, "We believe the Shroud has been patched … with material from the sixteenth century."

Was the carbon dating done on part patch, part Shroud, skewing the results?

The historical record could indeed imply that portions removed from the edges—perhaps as early as the reign of Charles IV of Bohemia—were later replaced or repaired, commingling first century and sixteenth century threads in the corner from which the radiocarbon test samples came. A renowned textile expert examined a sample and said, "There is no question that there is different material on each side … It is definitely a patch."

In 2002, chemical analysis confirmed these experts were right.

The authenticity of the Shroud became more plausible, but its Pontifical Custodians have not so far rejoiced, having newly removed all patches from the Holy Cloth.

Unless and until the Church approves new tests, the faithful must rely on results from the previous scientific investigation. The 1978 Shroud of Turin Research Project said in its Final Report: "We can conclude for now that the Shroud image is that of a real human form of a scourged, crucified man. It is not the product of an artist. The bloodstains are composed of hemoglobin and also give a positive test for serum albumin. The image is an ongoing mystery."

Meanwhile, one part of the puzzle seems to have been solved. Two highly regarded scientists associated with universities in Jerusalem and North Carolina studied pollen samples taken from the Shroud and concluded their source was a plant that grows in Israel, Jordan, and Sinai and nowhere else on earth.

Chapter 1

Wednesday p.m., January 12—Turin, Italy

For the better part of his forty-two years, Dr. Felix Rossi had wanted to be here in the Capella Della Sacra Sindone, the chapel at the top of the stairs in the Duomo, Turin's Renaissance cathedral, when priests came to open the tabernacle. Only six times before in the twentieth century had it happened and rarely in the presence of anyone but the priests. He'd wanted to stand beneath Guarini's famous glass-paned dome as the sun cast dazzling kaleidoscopes of brilliance down through the tabernacle's iron gates. The day had, at last, arrived.

In awe he waited with Father Bartolo, black marble beneath their feet, a white marble balustrade surrounding them, angels at each end. Everywhere in this chapel its designer, Guarini, had put statues of angels. For over four hundred years they had been here—blowing trumpets, playing harps, flying on spread wings, hovering in a frozen watch as they guarded Christianity's most famous relic. Sunlight flashed off the pair of gold Cherubs above the gates and the two Archangels leaning on their staffs as if to regard only him. In the brilliant light, Felix Rossi could barely see, but he couldn't look away. He would remember this moment until he died.

No one spoke as two priests climbed on the altar to open the tabernacle's iron gates and withdraw a silver casket. In 1509, Marguerite of Austria commissioned it for its special purpose on condition that a daily mass be said for her. Five feet long, one foot square, and encrusted with jewels, it was tied with red ribbon and sealed with red wax.

Within it lay the Shroud of Turin.

Slowly, carefully, they handed it down to Felix, who for this occasion represented science, and to Father Bartolo who represented faith—an often-uneasy alliance, but not today. Felix had quietly assembled the team of experts that waited to examine the Holy Shroud. It had undergone two previous scientific investigations—one in 1978, one in 1988. His would be the third.

Through a new Pontifical Custodian of the Shroud, the Church had picked him, over objections from a bishop who thought Felix's looks drew too much notice from young women. The Custodian had pointed out Felix's dual Harvard MD-PhD in medicine and microbiology, his much-recognized and objective scientific approach, that he was Catholic, devout, and philanthropic toward the church. The bishop was overruled. In exchange, Felix asked only for secrecy regarding his work on the Shroud, though it was the focus of his life.

But with his dreams about to come true, he looked away from the silver casket and felt the coldness of the marble room, smelled the suffocating residue of centuries of burning incense, its smoke rising from the cathedral to help the prayers of the faithful climb.

For this ceremony, the cardinal wore the red biretta on his head, had dressed in a red cassock, a knee-length white surplice atop. He lifted high a silver crucifix and said, "In nomine Patris, et Filii, et Spiritus Sancti Amen," then crossed himself. The others did the same. Felix was slow to move his hand and did so mechanically, hoping no one noticed. Then eight priests in black cassocks and white surplices made a double line behind the cardinal.

Nodding to old Bartolo, Felix lowered his end of the casket to bear the greater portion of its weight. He and Bartolo came down the two steps from the balustrade and rounded the altar, following the priests. Until 1865 this had been the chapel of the Dukes of Savoy—who became Italy's royal family—and an entrance to the palace's west wing remained. There, in the sacristy, the scientists would work.

Cameras flashed when they stepped into the long, gilded hallway. The photos wouldn't appear in the press because these were church photographers, making a record for the scientists and the priests. A woman among them flushed when she caught Felix's gaze and without thought, he angled his head and let his black hair fall in his eyes so he wouldn't see her—as if he'd taken vows with the priests. He wanted nothing to distract him from the dignity of this procession, though Felix knew something already had.

On the surface it was as planned—he in his white lab coat, Father Bartolo in black, the silence broken only by the slow, measured tread of their feet and the whine of cameras. From the solemnity of the few trusted observers in the hall, the casket might have held a man who died yesterday, not an image on an ancient linen cloth.

They entered the sacristy and conversations stopped.

Felix and Father Bartolo placed the casket on a long wooden table. Then Felix went to stand with his scientific team, all of them dressed in white lab coats and surgical gloves. They stood deferentially aside and made room for him. He was their superior in science, unswerving in his faith.

Not one of them would guess he was a Jew.

Until two hours ago, Felix himself hadn't known. The word rang in his mind—the sound of it, the idea of it—and made all else recede.

He watched the priests cut the crimson ribbon, open the casket, and remove what appeared to be a bolt of crimson taffeta. When they unwound it, a faintly dank scent arose. Lifted, the taffeta revealed the Holy Shroud of Turin, its linen the color of milk-laced tea.

For a moment no one moved.

The scientists, the observers against the walls, the priests about the room, the Poor Clare nuns who'd stitched the Shroud's special backing and would remove it, all seemed transfixed by this Sacred Linen on which so few had ever directly gazed.

Felix paid no attention to the quiet prayer being said:

O Blessed Face of my kind Savior
  by the tender love
  and piercing sorrow
  of Our Lady as she beheld You in
  Your cruel Passion,
  grant us to share in this
  intense sorrow and love
  so as to fulfill the holy will
  of God to the utmost

In his mind, he was back in his suite at the Turin Palace Hotel two hours earlier. His sister, Frances, was calling from New York to tell him Enea, their aunt, their last living relative, had died from her long illness. Before she passed away, she'd given Frances a key and a locked box full of letters—one addressed to him in his father's hand. Stumbling over the Italian, Frances read a few over the phone—letters to their parents from relatives in Italy they'd never heard of, unmailed responses written by their mother in Italian. Over and over he heard the words *Ebreo*, Italian for Hebrew, Nazi and *sinagoga*. Felix had paced in confusion, listening to descriptions of old passports with their parents' photos, but the passports carried an unfamiliar surname: Fubini. Eventually, Frances said the obvious aloud. Their parents had left Italy to escape the Nazis during the war because they were Jews. Why did they hide this fact? They'd come from Turin, this very town.

As the scientists went to work around him, uncovering their sterile instruments, Felix noticed that his friend, Father Bartolo, remained at the end of the table. He was a kind, frail priest who ought to be in bed. This morning, Felix had examined him in his cell and encouraged him to stay there, but Felix had known only death would keep Bartolo away. The priest's beliefs were simple—Jesus, God's Son, had lain under this Shroud. Bartolo's gaze was always fixed on his own inner light of truth unless something caught his interest. Then his eyes locked on and followed. Presently they were focused on Felix. Max also watched. He was a Jewish scientist Felix had picked for the team and because of his credentials the church had quickly approved. Max lived in Turin and had taken Felix home last night to share in Max's joy as the family named a new daughter in a touching ceremony full of music, poetry, candles, and Hebrew prayers.

Felix felt self-conscious under their gazes, as if two Gods vied for him through them. Who was he now, if not a man for whom Christ's passion had been the guiding symbol of his life?

Felix Rossi, his heart aching, moved from the tapestried wall where he'd stood. He approached the wooden table, preparing to look down on the face he loved.

Chapter 2

same Wednesday, in the morning—New York

When the wind blew the Graham Smith hat off Maggie Johnson's head and rolled it down the empty upper Fifth Avenue sidewalk, she thought she'd just about die. It had taken six months of saving, three more of waiting, to own it. Graham Smith made hats for royalty, for aristocrats to wear to Ascot. He made hats for the Queen. Now he'd made one for Maggie Johnson of Harlem, New York, too. At the moment, it was blowing down the street.

In spite of the spectacle she knew she was making, Maggie yanked off her winter white heels, dyed to match the silk in the hat. She ran after it like a track star, fearful it would blow across the street into Central Park. Luckily, the hat stopped under the canopy that stretched from Dr. Rossi's building to the curb. The red carpet had slowed it down. Maggie grabbed it, dropped her shoes, and stepped back into them, inspecting the hat. It seemed unharmed. She put it carefully on her head, one gloved hand holding the wide brim, the other holding the ostrich feathers in place.

Sam the doorman emerged in his long green coat and hat, looking her up and down, his ruddy Irish face grinning. He swung the heavy door wide by its brass handle.

"Maggie, my girl," he said, teasing. "You must be off to the races with the Queen in that lovely hat. Where did you ever find it?"

Angry and embarrassed that he'd probably seen her sprinting down the sidewalk, she rushed past him. Her hand skimmed the brass railing as she went down the carpeted marble stairs, then through the lower lobby to the elevators. On her left was an old mural from some Italian palace. It showed rich folks out hunting with their dogs. In front of her were floor-to-ceiling mirrors. Waving one hand to cool herself, she smoothed her winter white dress and made sure her hat was straight, remembering not to primp because of the security cameras. She'd heard even the tenants forgot and gave the limo drivers and guards in back a laugh sometimes. But it pleased her to see how the ostrich feathers floated above her short hair as she walked and the white complimented her dark sienna skin—not espresso or latte like they were always calling black skin in books. She'd matched her arm to color swatches and found out. Maggie knew she was no beauty, except maybe for her eyes, but at the moment she looked years younger than thirty-five. Of course, she hadn't meant to wear this outfit here. Not until she was on the subway, on her way to church, did she remember that she hadn't cleaned Dr. Rossi's lab. While he was gone, she only had to do it on Wednesday, but the week had flown by in a snap.

"Confess," Sam said, following her. "This hat's from London, isn't it?"

Maggie had hoped Sam would be on his break and that she could slip in without the hat being seen by anyone inclined to ask where she'd bought it and why. Ignoring him, she pushed the elevator button, fumbling in her purse for the keys, but feeling triumph. When it came to hats, nothing could outdo a Graham Smith. Maggie read *Vogue*, so she knew.

He reached down and touched a feather and she glared up at him. If he hadn't had such big shoulders, Sam could have been somebody's stand-in for long shots in a movie. His nose wasn't straight enough for him to be the star and there were faded scars around his neck that looked ragged like they came from brawls. She'd always thought he'd make a perfect Irish wrestler. He wore his dark brown hair clipped and going in all directions like the kids did.

Sam spoke French and Italian. He said he'd learned them in the merchant marine in his youth and Maggie believed him. She'd once overheard him swearing up a storm. He was a "man's man" type who probably swept foolish women off their feet with his rakish smile.

"Sam Duffy, take your phalanges off my hat!" Maggie snapped, proud that she remembered the medical term for fingers. It didn't surprise her to glimpse the outline of a holstered gun under his long coat, given how filthy rich the building's nine tenants were, each occupying an entire floor—and given how John Lennon died across the park. All in all, Sam was not your ordinary doorman. The tenants liked having him around. Usually she did, too. Not now.

"Pardonne moi, madame," Sam said and swept his hand away. "But it's got to be from England. I've never seen a hat like that anywhere else."

"It's from the selfsame place, Sam, thank you very much. And I don't want to hear none of your jokes. Okay?"

"Me? Joke? Before such a chapeau? Turn around. Let me see it. What are you so dressed up for, anyway?"

Maggie's gaze flew up to the domed chandelier in irritation. Romans 5:2-4, said "tribulation worketh patience and patience, experience; and experience, hope." Sam was helping her learn patience by getting on her nerves. She decided to be firm. "Sam, I don't have no time to play. I'm in a hurry!"

She saw a hurt look flash in his eyes and decided to say a little more. "My church is having an important function today and I've got to be there."

He looked surprised. "Off to church with you, then! Clean tomorrow. It won't matter. The good doctor's not even here and I haven't seen his sister this week. You can't work dressed like that, anyway." He scrutinized her. "Do you know you have runs all up your stockings?"

Maggie humphed, opened her large purse, and half lifted a package of pantyhose.

"I see," he said.

The elevator dinged behind them and she stepped inside the car. "I'm paid to clean the lab on Wednesdays when he's gone, Sam, dressed up or not. Lord willing, Wednesday is when I'm gonna clean." She punched the code for the eighth floor into the elevator keypad.

He shook his head as if she were hopeless.

Maggie exited into the foyer in front of Dr. Rossi's suite. In recesses on either side of his double doors were two intricately patterned blue and yellow vases Dr. Rossi said were antiques from Deruta, Italy. She unlocked the doors and entered. When she flicked a switch, light played on the wide corridor's arched ceiling, gently illuminated paintings, a softwood floor with parquet trim, and a slim Persian carpet. Midway down the corridor in a cubbyhole hung a seventeenth century crucifix made of heavy silver, the most beautiful she'd ever seen. Below and padded in red velvet was the ebony *prie dieu* on which Dr. Rossi and his sister knelt and prayed. Maggie always felt like she was in a palace, just walking down this hall. She passed rooms on her right and left and, because she thought she'd heard a sound, stopped at the solarium.

"Hello? Anybody here?" she called.

It was the only room where she'd ever heard sounds from the penthouse upstairs, which was occupied by a Mr. Brown.

Not that she was a snoop, of course. She was only curious, like anyone would be if they'd seen what she had over the years when she was downstairs in the basement emptying trash. Maggie had found that if she stepped up on one of the metal equipment housings, she could see through a crack in the wall between everyone else's garage and his. She'd seen no less than two United States presidents—one current, one an ex—a couple Arabs in their Rolexes and robes, a Supreme Court judge, senators, congressmen, and a Chinese-looking guy, most of them hat-in-hand and grinning, shaking hands goodbye as they got off Mr. Brown's private elevator, got in their limousines, and left his private garage. No fanfare. Nothing in the papers about their ever being here. It didn't seem right to her that important people should always be arriving in secret and one at a time. She'd tried to pump Sam for information, but when it came to the tenants, Sam was a living sphinx.

Maggie entered the solarium and crossed the short hallway created by the greenhouse installed for Miss Rossi's flowers. She'd had rare Moth Orchids shipped in from Asia and they were blooming in long white-to-pink sprays. Maggie passed them and went to the farthest corner of the solarium where the wrought iron furniture was. From there, she could see the penthouse upstairs, or at least a corner of its brick terrace. She took off her hat and pretended she was enjoying the lush, green view of Central Park. Maggie grew excited when she glimpsed the tip of a red hat. Either it was a tall woman, she decided, or one of those big shots in the Catholic Church.

Hearing nothing else, she returned to the hall and went to Dr. Rossi's lab at the end, getting out her key to the metal door.

Inside she took off her hat and placed it on the long table below the full-sized, framed replica of the Shroud of Turin. Dr. Rossi bought it when he was just seventeen and went on a pilgrimage to Rome. Frances said he found the Scala Santa, the twenty-eight steps of Tyrian marble taken from Pontius Pilate's headquarters in Palestine. Jesus must have gone up them on the day he was condemned. Dr. Rossi had ascended them on his knees, like the other faithful, stopping on each one to say its special prayer. He'd brought this copy of the Shroud home with him and told his father he wanted to be a priest, but his father wouldn't hear of it. For days they'd fought while his mother and Frances cried. The father won in the end, but Dr. Rossi had hung this up and lived like a priest his whole life, anyway.

To Maggie it seemed indecent to display Jesus' broken body like that, but she whispered, "Forgive us, Lord," like she always did when she saw it. She took off her white gloves and put on a long-sleeved lab coat. She pulled on medical grade latex gloves, just as a precaution. All she needed was to dust. In his absence, there would be no spills or broken test tubes, no biohazard waste.

Hurriedly, she wiped the familiar black surfaces: the glass-fronted cabinets and stainless steel shelves, the white lab refrigerator, his laminar flow hood, gleaming microscopes of different kinds, his scales and meters and racks of waiting test tubes—everything the latest and the best for his research. She knew most of his equipment because her first job in New York had been at Harlem Hospital. Once he'd had a lab at Mount Sinai but when he was refused space for a controversial project, he up and installed a lab right here. Must have had his lawyer grease palms to get the permits. Must have paid big to run the plumbing and such from his Dad's old medical office up here.

She was dusting the desk when her hand sent a notebook flying. It bounced on the tile floor and clicked as it opened, as if it had been locked. She reached to pick it up and was shocked to see her name entered on what appeared to be a list. Maggie drew the page closer, and then slapped the book shut.

"Look at me, snooping," she said out loud.

The word *Journal* was printed on the cover. She'd seen the notebook, or others like it, in the lab from time to time.

Maggie put it down and finished her dusting. Then she looked at her watch, glanced across at her Graham Smith hat, and sat down at the desk.

"Jesus, forgive me for what I'm going to do," she said.

She opened the journal to the page with her name and read the line. It said:

9. Let Maggie go before proceeding.

Chapter 3

Turin, Italy

It never failed to move Felix, this image on the cloth, viewed with scorn or veneration by millions over centuries. The first photograph in 1898 had, in negative, revealed a lifelike portrait. Even with the naked eye, the image could easily be discerned. Medical opinion agreed on this: the fourteen-foot cloth had once enclosed a corpse.

Folded crosswise in the middle, the cloth had been draped over the head of the corpse so that half had covered the back of the body. The half on which Felix gazed had covered the front. A man had died and been draped in it, surrounded by plants and flowers, their images as visible as his.

He died by first century Roman crucifixion or by a murder intended to simulate it, thus producing a fraudulent relic. How a medieval forger would know to contradict existing crucifixion art by placing nail wounds at the wrist, not the palm, hadn't been explained by those who believed the Shroud a fake. Only recently did archaeologists learn wrist nailing was the Roman practice.

Arguments arose in response to each bit of data science produced, but the faithful did not sway and neither did Felix. His mind stayed objective for the sake of the work, but not his heart.

How could it?

Here had lain a man, of approximately five foot eleven, long hair falling to his shoulders. He wore a forked beard, a mustache, had a pigtail in back. He weighed roughly a hundred and seventy pounds. His body was well nourished and had no abnormalities except those inflicted before he died.

Felix knew each one by heart.

An injury to the forehead that caused bleeding, the heavy stain of it visible down the left side of the gaunt Semitic face. Multiple blood stains in the hair at the scalp, one stain forking toward the right eyebrow and right ear, others extending in back to the scalp covering the occipital area. The right eyelid torn and the right cheek enlarged, as if from a cudgel blow. Striations on the left cheek, as in cuts from a headlong fall. The bridge of the nose misaligned, as if broken. Rivulets of blood flowing downward on the face and forming clots at the left eyelid, the left nostril, and on the upper and lower lips. The clots appeared natural, red corpuscles concentrated at the edges and a small light serum area within. On the right shoulder a deeply abraded area. Apparent multiple contusions to both knees, multiple cuts on one kneecap consistent with repeated stumbles. The left wrist placed over the right and containing a large puncture wound that would have damaged median nerve branches, producing causalgia—pain of the highest intensity that can be felt. Down both arms from these wounds, horizontal blood flows. On the back portion, the bloody imprint of a punctured right foot and a paler imprint of the left foot, placed on the right instep. Beneath all these injuries, front and back and from shoulder to calves, were small dumbbell shaped marks consistent with flogging, their directions implying two multi-thonged studded whips applied at once. Perhaps 120 lashes. Possibly more. Between the fifth and sixth ribs, an ovoid puncture to the right chest accompanied by a flow of blood downward and onto the lower back. This last would have been fatal had it occurred when the man was alive.

Death occurred with arms outstretched as was evident from the blood flows. Rigor mortis froze the feet in position and made the body stiff, which meant the image had been deposited four to twenty-four hours after death. Medical opinion differed on whether there were dislocations at the right shoulder and elbow. If so, it could mean whoever wrapped him had to break the arms so the hands could be folded over the pelvis.

Only stubbornness could keep a viewer from seeing what this was. A record of a living man's suffering. How the three-dimensional image was imprinted on the cloth, no one knew. Some said by slow bacterial action on the blood and venous fluids. Some said by energies associated with resurrection. To Felix, the how was less important than the fact of its existence—its pollen and plants from Jerusalem, its anatomical perfection and foreshortened bent knees beyond the knowledge or mastery of artists of the time.

Felix trembled before the image. For a moment he thought he would weep. Who could it be but the Lord? Who but Jesus? The Romans had crucified many, but did all victims wear a crown of thorns? Did a lance pierce their right chests as recorded in the Bible? Since childhood, Felix had yearned to undo this crime—willing though its victim—to cleanse this blessed blood, to save this Lamb led to slaughter from the Temple.

Since he was nine and first saw this face, he'd ached to undo this crime.

He felt a hand on his shoulder and looked up. It was Father Bartolo. Looking into the old priest's eyes, full of compassion, Felix knew what he'd been feeling—something of which he'd thought himself incapable, something he knew to be a sin—he who practiced tolerance. It was the residue of hatred absorbed long ago in Sunday school when Christian children were taught the Jews murdered Christ. He knew better, as any Catholic did. Vatican II had stated in 1965, "what happened in his passion cannot be blamed upon all the Jews then living, without distinction, nor upon the Jews of today." Modern biblical scholarship had gone further and disproved any basis for blame. Still, here was this feeling—he didn't want to be related to them. This feeling shamed and confused him. Desperately he wished it away. Why had his parents lied? How cleanse the double guilt he felt for being a Jew and feeling ashamed of it?

"Siete malato Dottor Rossi?" Bartolo asked.

A realization dawned. As a Jew he had a greater reason to carry out his plan. "No Padre sto bene."

He could take command of his new identity and accomplish what he'd daydreamed and prepared for—telling himself at each stage he would never actually carry it out because it was unrealistic, blasphemous. He'd drafted protocols and practiced endlessly in his lab simply for the challenge. He'd sought to be here only to view and test the Shroud. He'd kept his participation from the press only to protect his career. Shroud science was weird science to some.

Now he felt compelled to accomplish his dream—as if God himself had unlocked the box in New York and revealed the letters Frances read.

If he carried out the plan, he could leave Turin tomorrow instead of waiting out the week. He could give the excuse of a death in the family, turn the investigation over to the second man in charge, take the cramped, unreasonably expensive, but fast Concorde from Paris to New York and be with Frances in the morning.

His excitement rose at the possibilities. Afraid of discovery and equally fearful of success, Felix bowed his head to avoid Bartolo's gaze and began his work. He stopped as the Poor Clare nuns reached his position, unstitching the Shroud's backing, called The Holland Cloth. Then he and Father Bartolo unfolded the Shroud full length. As the others worked around him, Felix placed his microscope carefully here and there, his breathing heavier than normal, his palms moist beneath his surgical gloves. The microscope had a feature no one in the gilded room knew of but him. He'd designed it with this day in mind—

telling himself he'd never use it.

Felix waited for the moment he'd imagined a thousand times, wondering if he would actually go through with it. His chance came when Father Bartolo turned from the table as if to take a seat.

Staring through the eyepiece, Felix placed the microscope over the largest bloodstain, the one that flowed when the Roman soldier used his lance to pierce the chest. He adjusted the magnification until the bloodstained threads stood out.

Felix pushed a lever, his heart pounding. A thin razor with a hook at its end appeared. He held his breath. He cut two of the darkest threads, then moved down three centimeters and cut them again. He lifted his head, wiped his eyes on his sleeve, and saw Father Bartolo talking with one of the other priests. Felix bent over the microscope. When the razor retracted, the threads came too, carrying hundreds of blood cells that Felix was sure contained the DNA of the Son of God.

Breathlessly, he lifted his precious theft.

The Jews had not killed Christ.

But, God willing, a Jew would bring him back to the world.

Chapter 4

Fifth Avenue, New York

Three times Maggie read the line that said Dr. Rossi planned to let her go. Go where? He couldn't mean fire her.

She felt the words had pulled her heart out.

For five years, Dr. Rossi had shown, or pretended, genuine concern for her. She'd cleaned his lab part time at first; then the Rossis hired her full-time to take care of the whole place. Lately, because of the classes he'd arranged so she could advance in life, she was back to just the lab and a few odds and ends elsewhere. How could he fire her, knowing she still depended on him?

"Maggie, are you in here?"

It was Dr. Rossi's sister, Frances. Before Maggie could put the notebook down, Frances was in the lab, her eyes slightly puffy as if she'd cried or hadn't slept.

Frances stared at the journal in Maggie's hand.

"Is that yours," she said a little too politely, "or does it belong to Dr. Rossi?"

Sheepishly, Maggie put it on the desk. "It's Dr. Rossi's, but—"

"And you were reading it?"

Frances's face showed storm clouds when she didn't like what she saw, especially with her auburn hair slicked back on her head like it was. She was dressed in one of her chic, svelte Doncaster outfits. Not that Maggie snooped in her closets. Right now, she looked chicly scandalized.

"I didn't mean to read it. It popped open. I saw my name—" Maggie rose from the desk in agitation. "Miss Rossi, why's he going to fire me? What have I done?"

Frances's cutting gaze fell on the notebook. "Fire you? She came to the desk and picked it up. "That's ridiculous! Show me where it says that?"

Maggie stood next to her and leafed through the pages, then pointed when she found it.

"There. You see? It says, 'Let Maggie go before proceeding.'"

Frances sat down, studied the page, and drily laughed. "Human Genome Project? Nuclear cell transfer cloning? Oh, Flix," she said, using her pet name for him, "what are you daydreaming about this time?"' She slapped the book shut. "He doesn't plan to fire you. He's done this all his life."

"Done what?"

Frances looked up. "He's always been absorbed in something odd: challenges, impossible projects." She tapped her fingernails on the notebook. "Sometimes he carries them out, but usually not. It's an obsession while it lasts, but it's just a mental game. He makes lists. This one's about cloning."

"Cloning? Clone who?"

"No one, of course."

"You mean clone a person?"

"Only theoretically, Maggie."

Maggie eyed the notebook that was under Frances's hand. "But can't we just look and make sure?"

Frances frowned. "Of course not!" Then she patted Maggie's hand. "Brilliant men are often a little strange. It's just something that intrigues him. I could show you a hundred lists like this for things he never did—never remotely intended to do. He likes to try to work out the impossible in his mind, that's all."

"But why would he have to fire me?"

Frances gave Maggie a pointed look. "Maybe because cloning is controversial and he thinks you'd read his journals?"

Maggie wanted to do just that: read more of the journal to see if Frances was right. If she was going to need food stamps, she wanted to know.

Frances gazed up at the replica of the Shroud, and moved her neck as if she were drained of energy.

Again Maggie noticed her puffy eyes. "Miss Rossi, what's the matter?"

"Nothing. Well—" Frances looked toward the door. "Adeline and I have been at my Aunt Enea's. She died last night, Maggie."

For the first time since Maggie had known her, Frances looked like she would weep. Impulsively, Maggie bent and embraced her, patting her shoulder. Frances and Dr. Rossi were two of New York's mature, rich singles whose money kept them young—except he was about as far from a playboy as you could get and family was everything to her. She had been spending three and four nights a week with Aunt Enea. The periodic boyfriends who kept Frances out all night wouldn't stand a chance with her unless and until Dr. Rossi married. Maggie knew she'd never force her brother to live alone.

"Is there anything I can do? Anything at all?"

Frances sat up. "No, nothing. I thought it would be only me and Flix when she died and you know how I dreaded it—having no family left but the two of us."

Maggie could tell how upset she was, calling Dr. Rossi *Flix* to her.

"Today we've had a wonderful surprise, but I think Dr. Rossi's—"

"Don't tell me you've found relatives?"

Frances looked a little excited. "Yes, I think we have, but—well. He's upset."

"Why? Are they criminals or something?"

"No, they're not, I'm sure, but …"

"Then that's great, Miss Rossi."

Frances stood. "We'll see. Don't mention I told you. He and I need to talk. I've just popped in to put something in the safe. They heard a sound in the hall and Frances called, "Adeline, we're in here."

Maggie was staring at the journal. She felt herself flush when Frances picked it up and waved it.

"I suppose I'd better put this in the safe, too? Shame on you, Maggie."

Then Adeline was in the doorway, smiling and waving happily at Maggie. She was Frances's friend from Sarah Lawrence College. She, Frances, and Dr. Rossi had been a trio since their school days, but Dr. Rossi had only started dating Adeline about a year ago, as if blinders had suddenly fallen off his eyes. If things went well between them, Frances could let herself fall in love and have a life.

Maggie still wondered why Dr. Rossi had taken so long to notice Adeline. She was the prettiest woman Maggie had seen in person. She looked fragile, like she'd never had any fat on her body and never would. A natural blonde, her face was all cheekbone, eye socket and chin and in those deep sockets she had ash gray eyes. Maggie had been prepared to dislike Adeline when they met, but something in Adeline's spirit made you love her instantly. Everyone wanted to be around her.

She came in, reaching for a hug. "Maggie, it's been weeks since I've seen you.

How are you?"

Maggie hugged her. "Just fine. How about you?"

Adeline held her at arm's length. "Wonderful! But tell me," she said, mischief in her eyes as she glanced at the hat which was resting like a bird on the table. "Could that be yours? Where in the world did you find it?"

Maggie felt sick. Why had she discussed hats with half the population of Fifth Avenue? She wished she hadn't and particularly wished they hadn't seen this one.

"Yes, it's mine."

Adeline nodded toward the hat. "What a beauty, Maggie! Try it on for us. Please!"

Maggie sensed Adeline was also trying to cheer Frances up. She couldn't refuse and when she put the hat on and saw the glee on Adeline's face, the two of them giggled like schoolgirls.

"It's divine, you know. Really divine," Adeline said.

"It better be," Maggie blurted out. "It's a Graham Smith."

Maggie saw them exchange a swift glance of surprise. She'd made a big mistake.

Frances came nearer. "A Graham Smith? What a coup! A Graham Smith, Maggie, of all things. Did you buy it? Whatever for?"

For a moment, Maggie wished she was the lying type. "You remember Sharmina?"

"Your friend at church?"

"Yes, well." Maggie rushed the story out. "Me and Sharmina have had a hat war going on for fifteen years and she's bragged all over the congregation about a new one she ordered. We've got a special guest speaker coming in today from California and his wife has got this real nice hat boutique. Don't you see? The church is holding the biggest hat contest it's ever had and she's going to judge it and Sharmina said she'd win and—" She paused, feeling silly.

Frances lifted the hat from Maggie's head, slipped it on her own for a moment and pranced about, clowning. "Don't you worry, Maggie. Sharmina's not winning anything today." She walked over to put the hat on Adeline.

Maggie grew still inside.

"No, Frances," Adeline said, but Frances was already positioning it on Adeline's head.

"There! What a hat. Turn around in it, Adeline, let us see."

As Adeline turned, Maggie couldn't breathe. She'd bought and paid for the hat, had the receipt to prove she owned it, but it belonged to Adeline.

Adeline took it off and put it back on Maggie, looking into her eyes. Maggie felt something she would have called kinship if they'd been more alike. "You'll have a victory today," Adeline said and disappeared back into the hall.

Frances took Maggie's hands, still looking surprised but thrilled. "When Sharmina sees you wearing that, she's going to faint, I tell you. Faint!"

When Maggie didn't respond, Frances searched her face. "All right, tell me the truth—"

"I always tell the truth, Miss Rossi."

"Well …" Frances tightened her lips and raised her brows, looking at the hat.

Maggie felt so embarrassed she couldn't speak. Frances was a "horn of plenty" around her relatives, her orchids, her S-Type Jaguar, her black Andalusian stallion named King, but on all else she tried to be thrifty, declaring she refused to spend *outrageous sums on every single thing*. What must she think of Maggie's extravagance?

Frances touched her arm and made tut-tutting sounds with her tongue. "Tell me if I'm off-base, but would you like to start working here every day again?"

Maggie thought of the tuna fish casseroles she'd eaten daily for six months. "Okay," she said quietly, "but Dr. Rossi's already paying me as if I did."

"That's only for light work in the lab. Would you do the rest again as well?"

"Well, yes."

"Fine. I'll have him pay you more. Set your hours around your nursing assistant school and let me know what they are. You can start right away." Frances headed toward the door. "Have fun, today, Maggie. You deserve it. Tell me all about it tomorrow."

"Are you leaving?"

"Yes," Frances paused at the door. "Adeline and I are going to the funeral home, then I thought we'd drive out to the Landing and spend the night at the cottage. I want to get out of the city for a night."

Maggie nodded. The Rossis called their place across the Hudson on Cliffs Landing a cottage, but it was two or three times bigger than most people's homes.

When Frances left, Maggie stared at the closed door a long time. Then she went to Dr. Rossi's prep room and took off her latex gloves and her lab coat. She rolled down her torn stockings, worked a fresh pair up calves that were thinner than she'd like and hips that were more ample, took out her compact and in a ritual that wasn't conscious anymore, refreshed the little makeup she used: a touch of highlighter down the center of the nose to draw attention from wide nostrils; a similar trick on a too-lavish mouth using brown lip gloss around the rim and a blush of color within. Swipe, smear, smear and she was done. She did nothing to her eyes—medium brown with olive flecks—thankful that God had given her one gift.

She waited to leave until she was sure Frances and Adeline had gone, then she turned out lights as she walked down the Rossis' palatial corridor past the living room with the safe and the journal she couldn't read to find out if she was going to be fired. She locked the front door and pushed the button for the elevator.

It took longer than usual to arrive.

She saw the reason when the doors opened. For only an instant and for the first time ever, Maggie was face-to-face with Mr. Brown, whose private elevator must have exploded or something for him to be in theirs. He was the man from the penthouse upstairs who never came down to his private garage to greet his VIP guests, or Maggie would have peeked a good look at him before. The few times she'd glimpsed him, he'd worn a large fedora and she couldn't see his face.

The sight of him stopped her still. His head was oversized, giving the impression of an idol, instead of a man—thick hair framing his face like a platinum aura, offsetting a long nose and powerful jaw. He had prominently jointed thumbs on large chiseled hands, implying a formidable grasp. It was hard to gaze into his eyes, given the piercing dismissal of his stare. He wore clothes that at a glance revealed none were more costly.

His butler had moved to block her view, just as the doors began to open. But Maggie had glimpsed enough to come to three conclusions. She remembered faces and had never seen his in *Vogue* or *Town & Country* or *W* or any newspaper. His name was probably nothing so ordinary as Mr. Brown. Whatever his real name, he held everyone but himself in contempt, especially—at the moment—her.

"Wait, please," the butler ordered coldly and pushed the button.

The request stung her, but she nodded, looking beyond him at what she could see of Mr. Brown. When the doors closed, she realized she'd been holding her breath. Moments later the elevator returned and she got on, avoiding her reflection in the mirrors. She'd seen her homeliness when Adeline wore the Graham Smith hat, been reminded she couldn't afford it by Frances, felt humiliated to be caught trying to rise above herself, had her unimportance confirmed in Mr. Brown's gaze.

Maggie dabbed at her eyes, so Sam the doorman wouldn't see she'd cried.

Chapter 5

Thursday morning

Felix felt the Concorde slow in preparation for landing at JFK airport. He'd booked late and had to take a seat in the back, instead of the quieter front of the plane. Soon the hundred passengers would feel shuddering as the Concorde landed like an awkward swan—nose high, wings spread against the wind to halt its solitary flight, wheeled feet reaching for the approaching ground. He much preferred landings to takeoffs, though—climbing two thousand feet a minute at a speed of two hundred-eighty knots that pinned them in the small seats like astronauts in rockets. Then a low rumble when the afterburners ignited to propel them to Mach 1, then Mach 2, up above the clouds and into dark, purple space, the curvature of the earth visible outside the windows.

To his relief, he'd recognized no one on the flight so far. Concorde flyers were a relatively small club: those who not only had the nine grand for a ticket, but were also in a hurry or wanted to traverse the heavens like gods. Usually, Felix was in neither category.

He'd tried to read, but his eyes kept returning to the valise that he'd hand-carried onto the plane so the threads wouldn't undergo temperature extremes. He'd tried to sleep, but when his eyes closed he had a vision that disturbed him—a boy in a yarmulke ran, crying, through Central Park while a group of boys chased him, calling, "Jew, Jew, show us your horns!" All his life this scene had been in his mind and he'd never had the courage to ask if it was real. Had it happened? Was he the pursuer or the pursued? Now Enea had died and she was the last one who might know.

He picked up his still-blank customs declaration form, deeply conflicted. In his daydreams, he hadn't imagined this part. Honesty required that he write: two blood-soaked threads from the Shroud of Turin. However, this would result in his immediate arrest. Importing stolen cultural objects was a federal crime.

He'd thought himself home free when he retrieved the two threads from his microscope and sealed them in a sterile culture dish at his hotel. Only then had he remembered customs. For Concorde passengers, the risk of being searched was slight, he knew. What the customs form did was remind him he was sinning. He could barely believe he'd actually stolen threads from the Shroud and, however minutely, defaced what he knew to be the greatest treasure of Christendom.

The form quivered in his hand as the plane's nose rose to a high angle and the engines roared in descent. His view out the small window was obscured by the delta wings, but he felt the wheels touch down—three hours and forty-five minutes after they'd lifted off. Almost simultaneously the nose swooped low, leaving his stomach lurching. All in all, first class on a Boeing 747 beat the Concorde by a lot in his opinion.

As they rolled to the gate, he entered his name, passport number, and Fifth Avenue address on the declaration form. Then, accepting he had no option but to lie, he marked the box labeled *Nothing to Declare*, feeling deep disgrace.

Minutes after the plane stopped, nearly all passengers had disembarked. Felix crouched because the sleek plane's ceiling was low for anyone over five foot ten. With their usual attentiveness, the Air France staff returned coats and hats originally checked at the Concorde lounge in Paris. In the immigration room, Felix and other frequent overseas travelers bypassed the lines and went to the blue INSPASS machines. He inserted his ID card and placed his hand in the reader for palm print identification.

When he arrived in the customs area, bags were already being delivered from the plane. He retrieved his luggage, as did the ninety-nine other passengers. He approached the customs agent who seemed to have the friendliest face. Too late, he saw the agent was smilingly insisting that a white-haired man who wore a hand-tailored suit by Kiton of Naples open his lambskin Seeger luggage for inspection. Never mind that the luggage cost three thousand dollars. Felix knew because he owned a similar set and had half a dozen suits by Kiton.

He was thinking of changing lanes when the agent looked up and caught his eye. Felix smiled and didn't move as sweat moistened the underarms of his silk shirt. Apparently, while he and the man with the Seeger luggage were crammed in their Concorde seats, the JFK customs office went completely mad and decided to search the rich.

He looked uneasily around and saw a vaguely familiar face, which reassured him without cause. As he tried to place it—long jaw, slit of a mouth, and wavy bronze hair—the man left his line and came to Felix.

"It's Dr. Rossi, isn't it?" he said and held out his hand.

"Yes," Felix said and extended his own, trying to recall where he'd met the man. He looked to be in his late thirties and had an English accent.

"Jerome Newton with *The Times*?"

"Of course," Felix said, remembering. Newton was one of England's working aristocrats. He made a specialty of picking a field and profiling those prominent in it. He'd included Felix in an article called *The New Geneticists.* Newton had also done one called *Scientists of the Shroud* back in the mid-nineties. Felix's nervousness increased.

"Good to see you again," Felix managed, trying to keep his eye on what was happening to the white-haired man.

"A pleasure indeed. On the way home, then?" Newton asked.

Felix composed his face into a smile. "Yes, yes I am. And you?"

"On my way to the Art & Antique Fair in Palm Beach, mainly."

"It's being held again?" Felix had attended the first one and been amazed at the range of art objects for sale in a single place. That's where he'd bought the silver crucifix which hung above the prie dieu in his hall.

"Yes. Extraordinary that they've drawn the world's top dealers for a third year straight. I'm doing another group profile: *The Art Mongers of Palm Beach.* Thought I'd sod about in New York for a fortnight."

Newton was blatantly staring at the customs declaration form that Felix forgot he was holding in his hand.

"You were in Turin?" Newton asked.

Felix lowered the hand with the traitorous form and tried to sound lighthearted. "Yes. Lovely city."

Off-handedly Newton asked, "You didn't happen to be at the Duomo, did you?"

"The Duomo?"

"I think something's doing about the Shroud but they won't let regular press in."

Felix swallowed, reminding himself there was no reason for Newton to suspect him. Felix had never been publicly associated with Shroud work in any way. "Is that right?"

"Something's on there, I'm betting. I rang two Shroud scientists for routine updates and, lo and behold, both happen to be in Turin all week and unreachable."

"I doubt if it would make much of a story. Nothing ever changes with the Shroud. Believers believe; skeptics don't. Scientists argue 'facts'."

Jerome chuckled and gazed toward the front of the line. "Look at that."

The customs agent had emptied the white-haired man's first suitcase and was working on the second. Felix felt sympathy for the man who was somehow maintaining his dignity as his folded undershorts were exposed.

"You don't think they mean to well and truly search us all? Must be that art theft in Paris yesterday," Newton said. "Hope my clean grundies are on top."

He knew Newton must be wrong, but Felix glanced toward the agent, then down at the valise on the floor. The culture dish was in a reinforced compartment next to his microscope.

Jerome grinned down at the valise. "If there's contraband in there, m'lad, you could be in trouble."

Felix composed himself, looked at Jerome and didn't say a word.

"Pardon, Dr. Rossi, just a joke in poor taste." He faced the front of the line. Nodding, Felix did the same.

The agent was helping the white-haired man repack. He motioned to the next person in line, a woman simply dressed in dark clothes. Her long, straight hair reminded Felix of Gloria Steinem in the '70s. She walked to the booth, produced her passport and customs form, then Felix heard her say, "You intend to search my belongings?"

The agent coolly studied her declaration then, to Felix's horror, said in a thick New York accent, "Yes. Would you open your bag?"

The woman did, her lips pressed tight in indignation.

Jerome leaned forward. "Definitely seems we're about to be frisked."

"Seems like it," Felix said and kept dread from his voice, thinking he actually had two problems. First, getting past this agent. Second, making sure Jerome didn't see or suspect the contents of the culture dish. Jerome might inquire about the threads. As a journalist, he had the means to investigate and the motive to expose whatever he found.

He imagined the headline Jerome would write and for the first time realized the sheer insanity of what he had done. If his Petri dish were found, it would of course be inspected to make sure it didn't contain something dangerous. If he told the truth about his work, the agent might put two-and-two together. In moments, he could actually be in custody. Tomorrow his name could be in the news, his reputation and career destroyed.

His mind flashed back to yesterday. In the morning he had been himself, a man of faith and honor whose actions derived from deeply reasoned thought—though his imaginings did not. He'd considered duplicity beneath him, had never expected to actually carry out his plan. He was reasonable; it was not. One phone call had deranged him.

"It's your turn, Dr. Rossi," Jerome said. Felix looked up, startled, as the agent beckoned.

"Thanks," he said to Jerome who was studying him with open curiosity. Felix bent and picked up the valise, his suitcase, and his garment bag. Silently, he put himself in the hands of Jesus, ready to accept his fate.

"Hello," he said to the agent, a dark-haired, square-faced man who looked wholly unimpressible.

"Hello," the agent said and took Felix's proffered passport and declaration. He looked down at his luggage and read the form.

"What was the purpose of your trip?" he asked.

"Business," Felix said.

"What sort?"

"I'm a microbiologist."

"What was your business in Italy?"

Felix felt numb as he spoke. "I was at Turin's cathedral as part of a scientific team."

The man looked up. "Isn't that where they have the Shroud?"

Felix blinked. "Yes."

"You haven't seen it in person, have you?" The man's face showed the awe Felix had seen on every pilgrim to the Shroud.

"Yes, I've seen it."

The agent lowered Felix's documents. "Do you think it's real?"

"In my opinion, it's the burial cloth of Jesus Christ."

They were quiet for a moment, then the agent picked up Felix's form. "Dr. Rossi, did you stop in Paris?"

"Only to transfer to this flight."

"Which of these bags did you have with you?"

Slowly, Felix pointed to the valise. "Only this."

"There's nothing in it you didn't take overseas yourself?"

Felix paused, unable to make his mouth form an actual lie. "Just one small item connected with my work."

"Show me," the agent said.

Felix opened his valise and unsnapped the reinforced pocket that held the culture dish. In dread he pointed to it. "Just this."

The man reached inside and lifted the dish. "What's this, a Petri dish?" He held it up to the light and stared.

As Felix silently prayed, he heard a woman shout, "How dare you!" heard a smack, and looked up to see the customs agent in the next line drop a brassiere into a suitcase and rub his cheek. The woman who owned the suitcase had slapped him. Red-faced, the agent held up his palm, telling the customs police he didn't need help.

Felix's agent chuckled, then put the Petri dish back in the valise. He asked Felix, "Anything else?"

"No, nothing."

The customs agent stamped Felix's declaration form and returned his passport, giving the culture dish a quizzical final glance, as if he sensed the holiness of the threads.

"Next!" the agent called when he looked up.

Gratefully, Felix closed his valise, having abandoned all his plans for the threads. Not only would he make no use of them, he would call Father Bartolo, confess the theft, and return them to the church, where they belonged. He turned to say goodbye to Jerome Newton, then realized he must have seen the dish.

The reporter didn't look at Felix. He was busy writing on a small note pad that he tucked into the pocket of his shirt.

Chapter 6

Thursday morning—Fifth Avenue

Sam Duffy discarded his winter overcoat and went outside to enjoy the unseasonably warm January wind sweeping down Fifth Avenue. Early morning was his favorite time of day to be on duty at the door, especially in weather like this. From within the multimillion-dollar apartments and townhouses on and near the Avenue, people would come out in sweats and jogging shoes, leading their dogs across the street. There they'd mingle with stockbrokers, bums, and the messengers who delivered their diamonds from Cartier. All would breathe the same air, enjoy the trees and ponds and grass, in the city's greatest asset: Central Park.

He liked the park just as well when the weather drove them all indoors. He'd stand outside alone in blizzards, thick fogs or torrents of rain, as he'd done in his youth standing lookout watch on merchant ships, loving the wild innocence of the weather and the sea and thinking he'd never leave it.

Straight from college, he'd entered the merchant marine as a deck hand, wanting to experience that life before the new computerized container ships changed it forever, as they'd since done. While working his way up to able bodied seaman, he'd religiously taken every available moment in port to stock up on and read local papers, tour the city and talk to people, go to public trials, make friends with local cops, in particular, and listen to their stories. He'd amassed a hands-on knowledge of the ways of the world, which had since stood him in good stead.

He understood both the rich and poor, the weak and powerful, could operate in either world, but his father had been a doorman. Sam had never lost his love of simple people and honest work.

On Fifth Avenue, in the light of dawn, he could pretend life was still wholesome, people innocent—himself included.

His cell phone rang.

It was one of five drivers in the limo pool shared by all but one of the building's nine tenants. They never needed more cars. With multiple homes and vacation retreats, a third of the building was invariably not in residence here but at Argentine ranches, Tuscan villas, Swiss chalets, London town homes, or yachts moored off the Great Barrier Reef.

"Sam, I'm just on the other side of Central Park. Two, five minutes and I'll be front and center with Dr. Rossi."

"Gotcha," Sam said and hung up.

He walked to the curb and as Dr. Rossi's limo pulled up, opened the door. A tall, elegant man in his forties emerged. Slim in torso and broad in the shoulder, he had a mane of black hair that he kept well-groomed, no doubt to keep from looking any more like Lord Byron than he did. Sam could almost picture him in a waistcoat.

"Hello, Sam. It's good to be home."

"Good to have you back, Dr. Rossi."

Sam saw a woman gaze at Dr. Rossi from a passing taxi. Rossi had charisma of the teen idol kind. He and his sister could top New York's A-list if they chose. Often invited, they rarely appeared. He was a devout man of few interests—the reclusive altar boy who should have become a priest. His sister and her friend were private, too.

"Anyone here?" Rossi asked.

Sam would have offered to carry his valise, but Rossi gripped it under his arm as they walked to the door. "No, sir. Your sister's out. Maggie's coming later, I think."

"Not on a Thursday. I'm not expected back."

Sam had heard Frances Rossi talking to her friend Adeline in the lobby. He knew all about Maggie's new schedule and the hat contest with Sharmina at the church.

"I'd better leave it to the ladies to explain."

Sam held the door as Rossi entered. When the limo driver pulled off toward the tenants' garage, the quiet of Sam's morning was restored. Again he stood alone at the front doors, but now the sun was fully up, most joggers and dogs had left the park, and the Avenue was filled with cars.

He glanced across the jammed street to one of the park's tranquil old willows, its long, swaying limbs still sporting dried leaves. The wind billowed its branches as if they were shredded sails.

When a yellow city cab pulled from traffic and parked, he walked the red carpet beneath the canopy to the curb and opened the door, wondering who this was. A long-jawed, bronze-haired stranger came out, saying, "Good afternoon. Do I take it correctly that this is Dr. Rossi's address?"

"And you are?"

"Jerome Newton's the name. I'd like to see him."

Sam smiled. "Is he expecting you, sir?"

The man asked the driver to wait and closed the taxi door.

"Well, not precisely, but I thought I'd have a go at catching him in."

"Let me ring his apartment for you, sir," Sam said. Inside he picked up the lobby phone and buzzed Rossi's apartment. He knew Rossi was up there, but no one answered.

Sam hung up. "Sorry, no answer."

The man looked perplexed.

"If you'd like to wait I'll try again in a few minutes."

"Yes, thank you. I would."

Five minutes later, Sam tried the number again. This time Rossi answered. "Someone named Newton here to see you, sir."

Sam listened to Rossi's voice become agitated. "Newton? Bronze-haired guy?"

"Yes."

"He's just a reporter. Don't send him up."

"Of course, sir. I'll tell him you're not available."

When Sam delivered the news, the reporter looked surprised. "You gave him my name?"

"Yes, I did."

An unexpected reporter on unknown business was of keen interest to Sam. "You're a reporter?"

The man paused, studying him. "Yes, I am."

Sam put on a crafty smile. "Tell me what you're after and maybe I could help."

The man grinned and said, "Brilliant!" He reached into his pocket and flashed a hundred dollar bill. "Is this the going rate?"

Sam chuckled. "Depends on what you want."

"A tip off when he's about to leave the building so I can get here and talk to him. You'll know when he orders his limo, won't you?"

"You want a lot. I tell you what. Double the amount, give me some idea of what you're after so I know you're not some kook, and maybe we can make a deal."

The reporter smiled, peeled off another hundred and handed it to Sam. "I work for *The Times* of London. Dr. Rossi's brought something interesting back from Turin. I flew over with him on the Concorde and glimpsed it in his valise but I'm not sure what it is. Get me within talking distance of him and that's what I'll ask. It would be worth a great deal more to know what he does in the next few days. Where he goes. Who visits him."

Sam handed the money back to the reporter. He bent and reopened the taxi door, saying. "What if I give you two hundred dollars to move your cab from my curb so I can do my job?"

The man looked startled, then angry. He got in and the cab pulled away.

Sam headed inside to tell Rossi what the reporter wanted. Then he would observe Rossi's activities more closely in case he became of interest to Sam's real boss, which wasn't the Tenants Association.

Rossi's curious maid, the tenants, the guards and drivers, would be surprised to know what Sam did: that this building, and all the others on this block, really belonged to the man who lived in the penthouse. So did much of a dozen prosperous towns and villages strung along both coasts of the U.S., an assortment of chemical, electronic, mining and banking concerns did, and a number of politicians.

After three years at sea, Sam had been an L.A. private eye for a while, but for the last eleven years he'd worked for only one man. It had been Sam's idea to come here under the guise of a doorman to better serve his sole employer, Mr. Brown.

Chapter 7

Thursday morning—Rossi Apartment

As soon as the elevator stopped on his floor, Felix got out and collapsed against the wall, drained by the sudden release of tension in the privacy of his own foyer. Knowing the driver would deliver his bags there in a moment, Felix opened the double doors, took his valise inside, retrieved the culture dish, and walked slowly to the prie dieu nestled in its concave space in the hall. On the red velvet cushion he knelt, the Petri dish in hand, and looked up at the seventeenth century silver crucifix.

He bowed his head to ask forgiveness, but no prayer came. Instead, he thought of his father's letter. What explanation could it possibly contain? He rose and entered the living room his parents had decorated with Italian art and furniture, some from the Renaissance. A few were brilliant 1920's fakes. Over white sheers at the room's twelve-foot windows hung velvet charcoal drapes fixed with tassels. The floor tiles were eighteenth century terra cotta. They'd said the room reminded them of Italy. Felix liked it because it reminded him of church.

In an effort to update it, Frances had put a charcoal area rug on the floor, and replaced the formal couches and straight back chairs with upholstered sofas in red, gold, and black, added matching easy chairs in solid colors. It made the room more homelike, if less inspiring.

An original Modigliani hung on one wall—one of his rare landscapes with elongated trees. A copy of one of his swan-necked portraits, this one of his sister-in-law "Paulette Jourdain," hung above the fireplace. Behind it was the safe.

Felix moved the painting aside and dialed the combination. When it opened, he was surprised to find his latest journal inside. Of more interest was a carved wooden box that hadn't been there before. It was made of walnut and walnut veneers, with carved bellflowers on top, in the style of the Venetian writing desk in the guest bedroom. Frances had left it for him.

In spite of the warm day, he put a log on the fire and lit it. Though it was only ten-thirty and he rarely drank, he poured himself a brandy before sitting on one of the sofas.

It took no searching to find the letter in the box. In large, faded script the envelope said: To My Son, Felix. The date was September 1981, the year before his parents died in an auto accident on the way home from Frances's graduation.

At the sight of his father's handwriting, his feelings plunged into turmoil once again.

Beloved Son,

I don't know if you will read this long after my death or only hours from it, whether Mamma or Aunt Enea will deliver it to you. If you come upon it by accident and I am still alive, please wait to read it until I am dead. I prefer not to discuss these things again, but you are entitled to know them.

I leave it to you whether and when to share this with your sister. Now I begin the tale I wish I did not have to tell:

Your mother and I were born and raised in Italy, as you know. However, as you may know by now, I have lied to you about the specifics. We did not come from a small town, destroyed in WWII by the bombing. We came from beautiful Turin and a grand house situated on the sloping banks of the River Po, just above the Church of Gran Madre di Dio. Perhaps its black iron gates still stand. Five generations of our family lived there, but our name was not Rossi. It was Fubini. We were not Catholics, but Jews. Enclosed are the names of all the relatives we left behind—not many. If you wish to contact them, go first to my brother, Simone, if he is still alive.

Dearest Felix, I am not ashamed of my lies to you, but my heart breaks for the pain you must be feeling because of them.

Felix stopped reading and looked up at the Modigliani copy above the fireplace, at the real one on the opposite wall. He wanted to take down the painting of the swan-necked woman, which suddenly reminded him of himself: the fake Christian, sitting beneath the fake Modigliani. He returned to the letter.

I will do my best to explain.

First, you can be proud of your real family. The Fubinis were good citizens of Italy. We helped start schools and hospitals for the poor. The family insurance business still exists, Assicurazione Di Fubinis. On its wide street, Turinese took carriage rides on Sundays before the war. Though I have not spoken to your Uncle, Simone, for almost forty years, he continues to send my quarter of the business profits to our bank account.

Why did I leave him, leave Italy, leave our faith? Jews had been in Italy before the Romans. Fubinis were in Turin for centuries.

No one foresaw Auschwitz.

We Italians prize amore, la famiglia, despise la brutta figura, giving an ugly face to the world. We value honor and respect but have little use for most rules. You, yourself, commented after your first trip to Turin that, on Italy's streets, a red traffic light is only a suggestion. Italy had many foreign occupiers and each had different rules. Breaking them became a national pastime. These are the people on whom Hitler tried to impose his anti-Semitism, people who enter when a sign says, Keep Out.

In 1938 when they passed The Racial Laws, your mother and I were young lovers. Our families hoped we would marry, and in 1942 we did, but our wedding was not what we planned. By then, our Christian friends were afraid to be seen entering Turin's Great Synagogue. They came to us in private with their blessings and gifts.

Because of such kind people, most of Turin's Jews adjusted to the restrictions with little complaint, thinking they would end in their own time. However, I am a suspicious man, as you know. I had friends across Europe—old classmates from university, former patients. I heard whisperings others did not. To me, it was very serious that I could not legally treat the patients who wanted my help. Many would come and make jokes. They'd say, "I am not here to see you as a patient, I am only dropping by as your friend. While I am here, would you look at my shoulder? I will not pay you, since it is forbidden. I will only lose some money in your hand."

This is how most Italians are. Not only did they ignore Mussolini and Hitler, they bravely carried on in the way they thought right. Yes, some cooperated, some betrayed us. Most did not. I did not fear Italy's people. I feared its government.

Here, Felix, I come to the terrible part, but let me delay a little longer. Let me tell you about our joy.

Look in the brown envelope I have left and you will see a photograph. A beautiful young woman and a not completely unattractive young man stand before a small yellow villa, a bower of roses above their heads. They gaze at each other, and—in spite of the sunshine, the birds, the glorious lake beyond, in spite of the roses—they have eyes for one another alone.

Felix frowned. There had never been photographs. His father said everything had been lost in the bombing. Felix reached into the envelope and found the picture. He recognized his parents right away, so young they seemed hardly old enough to wed. His father wore a yarmulke, his mother a scarf of lace. They stood before an old-style brick and stucco villa by some far-off shore. The photo was black and white, but he imagined the stucco painted yellow as his father described. The villa had arched windows, a tiled overhanging roof, and a small front balcony supported by spiraled columns. Felix felt distant from the couple, shut out of their lives, these people whose past had been hidden in a box. The phone began to ring. He waited for it to stop and returned to the letter:

From this photograph, my son, you see the source of your good looks. Your long black lashes, thick straight hair, and pale skin are from your mother. Your sister looks more like me: handsome, perhaps, but darker and less fragile of frame.

The photograph was taken on our honeymoon. We spent it on Lake Maggiore at this villa two kilometers outside of Arona. The villa was a wedding present from her family and mine. I have not inquired if it still exists, or if anything of our old lives exists. If not, it would be a small loss compared to what was suffered in that war. Still, I do not wish to know if a bomb or a tank destroyed this lovely place where your mother and I first lived as man and wife.

On the property was a small lake house. Your mother loved its wide deck that stretched out over the water. For a happy year we often slept out in the open on this deck, or at night made fires on shore, or sailed our boat out from its porticiollo under the stars. When I returned to my practice in Turin, she asked to stay at the villa but at every excuse I was there ... so frequently my clandestine practice dwindled. She didn't like the city, wanted to live on the lake where she became an expert swimmer and sailor. It was she who planted the roses, hoping the villa would become our home.

By these roses, by this lake, she became pregnant with my son.

Felix stopped and reread, not comprehending. He was his father's only son, born in New York. His parents had been childless until late in life because his mother couldn't conceive, or so Felix had been told. Had that been another lie? Quickly he read on, his stomach taut with fear:

There was another reason I allowed your mother to stay in Arona. Secretly, I had been making plans. Over the protests of my father, I began sending my own inheritance and your mother's out of the country to Swiss banks. They were small amounts in today's terms, but considerable for 1938—enough to see us through misadventure. Several times we visited friends in Domodossola. Your mother did not know they were in the anti-fascist underground. Several times we went to the Swiss border, making friends with a particular guard. Secretly I gave him money against a future day.

Then I waited, hoping the Italy I loved, the Italy that had sheltered Jews during the Inquisition, would protect us. It did so until otto settembre, the 8th of September of 1943. Every Italian knows this day. Mussolini's government had fallen. German troops marched into Italy and occupied our country.

On that same day, the roundup of our people began. Your mother and I were at the lake house with my sister, your Aunt Enea, when we heard the phone ring in our villa above. I ignored it because we were having a disagreement. Your mother was seven months pregnant, but wanted to sail. I would not permit it and she was angry. Enea sat on the deck of the lake house, trying to help us calm down. The phone kept ringing. It stopped, then rang again, stopped then rang again.

Finally, we went up to the villa. As your mother and Enea waited under the roses, I went inside. Our local baker was on the telephone. He didn't call my name or say hello. All he said was, "Take up your hat."

It was a signal.

Many friends of Jews used it when danger was at hand. They would call on the phone and say, "Take up your hat."

I hung up immediately, reached for the wallet with our money and traveling papers, went down to your mother and your aunt, and put them in our car. We drove without stopping to Domodossola and found it full of German troops, but we waited in the woods until nightfall and knocked on the window of the priest. He put us in a hay wagon and sent us into the beautiful Valley Vigezzo where slopes become hills and hills become mountains, their peaks obscured by clouds. We reached a small town called Re only miles form the Swiss border, and stayed at the local Inn.

In the middle of the night, the Germans came.

Now we have reached the terrible part.

Felix stood, the letter trembling in his hand. He laid it down and walked about the room, picturing his mother as he'd last seen her—much older than in the photo, but beautiful to him. They were at Sarah Lawrence College. She'd hugged Frances in her graduation gown, then reached up and ruffled his hair, an intense look of pride on her face. She took their hands and said, "Always take care of each other." An hour later, the auto wreck happened and she and their father were dead.

He returned to the sofa and took another swallow of the brandy, then picked up the letter again:

Our Italian friends were in their beds, like we were. They could not get to their cars and drive us away as planned. They could not guide us through the valley or over the mountains to the border or to waiting cottages in the Alps. Your Mamma and I and your Aunt Enea ran in our nightclothes down to the stazione, the little train station. We hid in a low woodshed across the tracks.

That night, summer ended. Rain blew through the valley, followed by a cold, wet wind. When the Germans searched for us, we left our shelter and fled across a meadow then followed the railroad tracks. On foot in the wilderness, the tracks were our only guide.

My son, nothing but my love for you could make me revisit that night because I must picture the two women I loved—cold, frightened, stumbling, your mother pregnant with our first son. I must see my sister shiver, see tears on your mother's face, watch the rocks and rails cut their feet, witness terror in their eyes.

Germans rode the trains that night. They searched the tracks. Twice we escaped just in time.

Only a few kilometers from the Swiss border, the railroad crosses the top of a small hill. On either side, trestles rise from the valley floor to support the tracks. We crossed on these trestles, fearing a train would come when there was nowhere to leap but down to our deaths. We reached the hill and its small clearing, your mother in labor. There your older brother was born too soon and I had nothing to help him survive. He lived for only moments, though it seemed like hours I fought for his life. Under the clearing's tallest tree we buried him. Your Mamma bled so much I thought she'd die. In my arms I carried her across the second trestle, the icy wind in our faces, the sound of the river in our ears as it rushed over the jagged rocks below. Half dead from the cold we reached the border, where the guard I'd come to know let us pass.

From that night to this, we have not been Jews.

I pray you understand. If this could happen in Italy which I loved and which loved us, it can happen anywhere. I refused to expose your mother and our future children to danger so easily avoided.

That is all I will say of our troubles from that time. Thanks to the good Italians who love family and honor, and who so vehemently despise other peoples' rules, 90 percent of Italy's Jews survived. Their neighbors hid them and helped them. Nevertheless, seven thousand were deported to German concentration camps. Most never returned. A few hundred more were murdered in Italy itself. Some were drowned in our beautiful lakes, including the one your mother and I so loved.

I hope you are an old man when you read this, since age will help you understand.

If I have been wrong in keeping this secret, may God in his mercy punish me alone, while blessing you, my beloved son, your sister, and your mother. The truth is I love all of you more than any religion, any God, more than my own life. For you, I would risk the wrath of heaven and do the same again.

Felix put down the letter and gazed at the fake Modigliani in sorrow. Only now did he remember Modigliani was a Jew. For almost two thousand years, the world had made scapegoats of the Jews for Christ's death: the holocaust, the inquisition, the pogroms. Perhaps it would never end.

He drained his brandy glass and went to a corner of the room where the family Bible lay open on a carved stand. Felix closed the Bible, closed his eyes, and then opened the book at random. When he looked, he was staring at Exodus 2:5 and 2:6

> 5 Now the daughter of Pharaoh came down to bathe at the river, and her maidens walked beside the river; she saw the basket among the reeds and sent her maid to fetch it.
> 6 When she opened it she saw the child; and lo, the babe was crying. She took pity on him and said, "This is one of the Hebrews' children.

Felix drew in his breath. It was the story of Moses. Like Felix, Moses had been raised as a gentile, but it proved to be God's plan. As a result of being raised in Pharaoh's family, Moses had the access and the knowledge by which to set his people free.

Felix picked up the Petri dish and the threads he possessed as a result of being raised to believe in Christ. He headed for his lab, all his guilt, shame, and confusion gone.

Innocent people would keep paying for the death of Jesus Christ, unless God had given Felix the means to reverse it once and for all.

Chapter 8

Rossi apartment

His first task was to properly store the threads.

In the small prep room he hurried to put on a lab coat, wash his hands, and pull on surgical gloves. He entered his white, black, and chrome laboratory crowded with equipment, all of it in place, every tile, enamel or metal surface gleaming. Maggie's doing. He would miss her here, but from now on he'd have to clean it himself. He opened the dish under the chrome laminar flow hood and again his heart pounded as, with tiny sterile tweezers, he transferred the threads to another dish that had a grid of small holes in the lid. What would he see when he examined the two thousand year old blood of Christ?

He'd have to be patient and finalize his protocol first. He opened an incubator cabinet and placed the aerated dish on the empty turntable inside. Then he punched numbers into the keypad. Soon the cabinet would simulate the wrapped and cushioned inside of a sealed silver casket in a stone church in January in northern Italy.

When the phone rang he stared anxiously at it, wanting no interference. Seeing the call was from downstairs, he pulled off his gloves and answered. It was Sam, the doorman, saying Jerome Newton was here. Felix was so surprised; it took a moment to register. Why had Newton come? What did he think he'd seen? With conscious effort, Felix curbed an urge to panic. He knew that to accomplish this goal, any goal, he must avoid distraction and remain calm. He told Sam to send Newton away.

He sat at his desk and opened the journal Frances had put in the safe, wondering why she'd done it. She was out at Cliffs Landing, he knew. To give himself time to secure the threads and make plans, he hadn't told her he was coming home.

He began by revisiting his protocol.

January 13
Today I begin in earnest what I had only speculated on before. On the surface,
it is simple:

1. *Extract blood from the threads*
2. *Isolate cells with their nuclei intact*
3. *Culture the cells in a dish*
4. *Starve the cultured cells into the totipotent state*
5. *Extract unfertilized eggs from a donor*
6. *Remove the nucleus from the eggs*
7. *Replace each nucleus with a cultured Shroud cell to produce "fertilized" eggs*
8. *Grow the fertilized eggs in a suitable culture to the 5-day blastocyst stage*
9. *Transfer a blastocyst to the donor womb*

Except for the first entry, this was the protocol used to clone Dolly, the sheep. Steps 1, 3, 4, and 8 were procedures any microbiologist could perform. Step 5 happened daily in in-vitro fertilization labs, and Felix consulted for two in New York. His PhD was in microbiology, but his MD was in obstetrics. Blindfolded he could do it.

Nuclear transfer, as steps 6 and 7 were called, presently required skill. In secret Felix had practiced the micromanipulations on thousands of mouse eggs, pig eggs, sheep eggs At every stage, each species proved susceptible to harm in different ways, but Felix had focused on this for the last three years. While the rest of cloning science floundered, producing healthy embryos in only one or two of a hundred trials, Felix had raised his success rate to 50 percent. Of every two he tried for any species, one survived to the all-important five-day blastocyst stage.

When a private firm precipitously announced it had cloned the first human embryo, Felix had laughed. An embryo was, by definition, a fertilized egg that has implanted in a womb, or could. Those eggs had divided once or twice and then died. They had never been viable. Two other human cloning scientists announced they had pregnancies underway, but he doubted it. Felix, far ahead of the rest of cloning science in his techniques, had resisted the lure of fame— not because of the Shroud, he'd told himself, but to continue his work in peace. His results were in his journals and nowhere else. But Felix knew that one day NT would be so routine, high school students—when they weren't dissecting frogs—would perform it on cat and dog eggs.

Still, he hadn't tried to clone a human embryo and it was time to decide if he should practice. It would be easy to salvage eggs slated for destruction at an in-vitro fertilization clinic. He could enucleate them, insert cells from his own body then destroy them when they'd grown to the five-day stage. He didn't doubt it would work. He'd just have to confess what the Christian right and the Catholic Church considered a sin: destroying a pre-embryo.

Scientifically, Felix had a hard time believing life began with conception. He agreed with bioethicists that life couldn't begin before day fifteen. That's when the embryo formed the precursor to its spine and nervous system called the *primitive streak*. Without it there could be no sentience. Ironically, his parents' Judaism would have solved his ethical dilemma because both Jews and Muslims believed life began on an embryo's fortieth day. Yes, it troubled him that pre-embryos would be destroyed in the course of human cloning, but when the time came Felix knew he'd follow science, do it, and pray.

For him, Step 2 was the real hurdle.

In this case, the DNA was ancient and might have badly deteriorated. But Felix had two reasons for hope. The Shroud's linen, itself—a polymer of glucose—could have served as a binder to the DNA, stabilizing it for hundreds of years. If so, his concern would be cell death, the definition of which was open to debate. At what point does reversible cell injury become irreversible, making it impossible to culture a cell? His far less scientific but greater reason for hope was that if the resurrection happened while Jesus was in the Shroud, the same energies which restored the body to life might have preserved the blood and serum on the Shroud.

Even so, the other hurdles were significant. Conceivably, human NT could pose problems he hadn't encountered with other mammals, though he was confident of his ability to surmount them. Also, Dolly's creators had been forced to use many blastocysts to produce a single viable womb implantation. And it had taken many womb implantations to produce five live births. Of these, only one sheep clone had survived.

He would need luck and effort to improve these odds, but Felix was cautiously optimistic. Refining new genetic techniques was art as much as science and he had talent for it.

He reread his list and when he came to the last entry, "transfer a blastocyst to the donor womb," Felix paused, dropped his pencil, and lowered his head into his hands. When this was only a theoretical exercise, he hadn't lingered on the fact that a donor womb meant a real woman—an altogether different and vastly more complicated ingredient than a donor sheep.

He stood and paced. Clones needed mothers, like everyone. For Jesus to be reborn, he would have to find a modern Mary.

He sat down and began again. On a new page, he slowly, carefully listed each key step, up to and including birth.

He worked for three hours then realized he wasn't alone. Someone else was in the apartment. Frances, he assumed. He removed his lab coat and hung it in the prep room, disappointed that he hadn't had more time alone. Out in the hall, he locked the lab behind him, calling, "Frances?"

Her voice came from the kitchen. "We're in here."

When he entered, Frances and Adeline stood at the central counter with aprons on. Maggie was at the sink, loading the dishwasher. He hadn't seen Frances in an apron since the eighties. When their parents died, Frances had moved up to Boston for his last year at Harvard, and Adeline had often come up on weekends. Sometimes, she and Frances cooked. But when he graduated and they moved back home, they had their in-home meals catered, usually by Fabulous Food, its cooking rivaling that of the world's best restaurants. Occasionally, Maggie made breakfast if he kept her late and she spent the night. Frances and Adeline were obviously up to something.

"Flix, why didn't you phone and say you were coming?" Frances asked as they came across the room into his arms. "It's hard to believe Aunt Enea's actually gone," she moaned.

Soothing her, he answered, "I know. I know."

He hugged them both and smelled the light scent of Adeline's golden hair, realizing that in his heart they were so nearly the same to him—treasured sisters, except Adeline would be his wife when he proposed.

Frances raised her head. "Did you find the letter?"

To Felix, her question was a harbinger of change, of unforeseeable alterations, just when he couldn't handle them.

"Yes," he said, "but I have a favor to ask. Let's put off discussing it a while."

"But—"

He let go of them. "Please, Fran."

"Well, all right. But I'm making arrangements for the funeral. It's Monday and Enea had a few special wishes, Flix—"

He sat down at the table, turning his attention to a plate of zucchini marinating in a sauce. "Handle it however she said. I know you'll make the right decisions. Just tell me the place and time. He speared a slice of zucchini and popped it into his mouth. "Delicious!"

Adeline and Frances exchanged a furtive glance and returned to the counter. He'd known how Frances would respond. What he wouldn't do, she wouldn't do. What hurt her, hurt him. Adeline had seen their private conspiracy and had long ago slipped into it.

"Hello, Dr. Rossi," Maggie said as she closed the dishwasher. She had the disinterested expression he knew was a cover up for curiosity. "How was your trip back, sir?"

Felix remembered he'd put firing Maggie on his list of things to do if he ever really tried to clone Christ. If she sensed a secret, he knew she would pry.

"It was just fast," he said, regretfully deciding Maggie would have to go. He'd make sure she didn't suffer financially, but she couldn't be here while he worked. Frances would respect his privacy if he asked her to. Maggie wouldn't. She might not reveal his secrets, but in this case he couldn't take the chance.

"Things look wonderful in the lab, Maggie, thank you and, for the thousandth time, you don't need to 'sir' me. Now why have they put you in the kitchen?"

Frances said, "I've asked her to take care of the whole apartment, again, Flix. It's all arranged."

"Oh?" Felix said, thinking this was the offshoot of living in a house full of females. Periodically they got together and rearranged everything. However, it might be his way out.

"Well, in that case, Maggie, you can skip the lab. We're not going to work you to death. Besides, you have your studies."

Maggie looked surprised, but she nodded.

He would change the lock tomorrow, then watch her for a week to see if she became curious about what he was doing in the lab. He liked Maggie and knew Frances did, too. If he could keep her, he would.

"Flix," Frances said. "Do you know what this reminds me of?"

He looked around, nodding. It was often like this before their parents died—the whole family in the kitchen, his father reading or working on patients' charts, Frances pruning plants right on the kitchen table or playing piano in the next room, while his mother concocted something unbelievably good.

Rarely had anyone else been here. Rarely had anyone telephoned, other than his father's patients. To protect the family secret his parents had kept to themselves and lived an insular life, as if they were their own independent nation. He and Frances had absorbed their parents' reserve. How Adeline and Maggie had ever broken through, he wasn't sure.

He put down his fork. "It reminds me of the old days, too. All right, ladies. Will someone tell me what's going on?"

Frances raised a book from the counter and he was startled by its title: *Cucina Ebraica*. Only yesterday they'd learned their parents were Jews, but Frances was already embracing that heritage.

"I walked into a bookstore and there it was," she said. "Italian Hebrew cuisine. Just like Mamma and Dad must have had when they were young."

Felix looked at Adeline. "You know?"

She came and kissed his cheek, smiling. "When I saw one of the letters, Frances told me. I'm in love with a Christian Jew, it seems."

Felix wasn't prepared for this. Though he understood his father, a powerful sense of estrangement returned. He wasn't used to being thought different from the woman he planned to marry. Abruptly he rose from the table.

"I can't explore this now. We'll talk in a few days, I promise."

Frances took off her apron, watching him with a sisterly expression that meant she thought she knew best. "Come on, Flix. Let's walk in the park." It was a request he'd never refused and their code that things were urgent.

Suspiciously, the sounds of chopping immediately resumed. This walk had been planned. Sam must have told them he was here. Felix had to put his own plans in motion before events overtook him. No more scruples. He'd have to tell a few necessary lies.

"I'm sorry if I sounded harsh," he said, as they buttoned their coats on the elevator. "By the way, I met an acquaintance on the flight who'll be staying in the New York area for a while. I thought I'd let him use our place at Cliffs Landing, but I can't find my key. Do you have yours?" He was surprised at how flawlessly he'd misled his own sister, but even without Maggie in the lab, he couldn't work at home for long. He'd need complete privacy. The Landing was perfect, but he wouldn't tell Frances until the pregnancy was definite. In her concern she'd try everything to stop him, short of setting fire to his lab, but if it was too late, she'd be loyal. After the birth, he'd tell the world.

"Sure, who is he?" she asked, opening her purse and searching for her keys.

"Someone connected with the Shroud project; you don't know him."

She took a key from the ring and gave it to him. "Let me know when I can go out there again."

"Thanks. I will."

When they reached the lobby, she said, "Oh, Sam wants to see you about something." But a substitute was at the door instead of Sam.

They stepped out into the afternoon. Rather than crossing to Central Park, Frances hooked her arm through his and began walking down Fifth Avenue.

"Where are we going?" he asked.

"You'll see."

Felix scanned the faces of women they encountered on the uncrowded Avenue, trying to divine which were mothers, or had the qualities to be. His OB-gyn practice had been brief. Had he learned enough to pick the best mother for Christ? Across the street in the park he saw two riders talking to each other, their horses' heads together. Perhaps a mother and daughter. He noticed the older one listened to the younger with an expression less of interest than of emotion. He could sense her love.

Suddenly, Frances stopped and faced him. "Flix," she said. "The things we found in Enea's box aren't just yours. They're mine, too. We need to talk about this because it's going to affect us both. I already feel it changing you, and to be honest, it scares me a little."

He peered at her. "You've never been afraid of anything. Ever."

She ran her hand along her purse strap, saying nothing, and Felix became aware of the neat winter gardens encased by low wrought-iron fences on the wide sidewalk. He wished his life were as orderly.

"I think I'm afraid," she said.

"Oh, is that right?" He put his arm across her shoulder and walked her backwards in a circle until she was laughing—something he'd often done when they were young.

"All right! Stop it! Stop it!" She smiled at him. "There's something I want to show you down on 92nd."

"What is it?"

"Just come and look. Promise?"

"Promise," he said, trying to remember what was on 92nd. On the way he saw a young woman on skates, her baby before her in a stroller. He tried to remember his mother's face, but it was Frances's face he saw. She'd been mothering him since their parents died. He asked himself if Frances might be his Mary, but he couldn't imagine examining her, much less impregnating her, even artificially.

Then he saw what was on 92nd: the Jewish Museum. Frances knew he loved museums, and must have decided a visit here would help. Reluctantly, he followed her along the carved French gothic Warburg Mansion, the windows in its limestone facade converted to displays. One held a silver menorah. Another said: Culture & Continuity; The Jewish Journey. In a glass-covered marquee at the curb, a poster showed a famous painting of two women, one in a black evening gown, the other in white. The artist was John Singer Sargent whom Felix hadn't known was Jewish.

He followed Frances up the building's three wide steps, through glass doors with ornately carved wood frames and, as she bought tickets, he waited among a crowd of school children and their teachers, unsure of his feelings. He noticed the teachers seemed conscientious, but not bound in spirit to their charges like the mother on horseback. Then the obvious struck him: he should look for his clone's mother among women who loved God. He should look within the church.

They entered the museum. The first room was a testament to Jewish accomplishments in Germany before the war. Oddly, Felix found it awful evidence of how outcast the German Jews had been, as if they felt the need to prove themselves human. Why should they not have accomplishments, just like others? He followed as Frances exclaimed over things.

Then he saw something arresting at the end of the second room. It was a small painting entitled *Woman at a Writing Desk,* by Lesser Ury who died in 1931. In a chair she sat in her long skirts and white blouse, intent upon her letter, the sun bright outside her window, but not streaming in, her chair seat a lovely blue, the rug beneath her feet a warm red. How many times had he put down his Sunday paper and seen Frances like that, writing to college classmates at father's old desk. The likeness was startling. He stood admiring it, wishing it wasn't a priceless work of Jewish art, but was for sale so he could give it to Frances for her birthday.

He looked up but she had gone around the corner. He found her standing before another painting. Felix was surprised to see Lesser Ury's name beside it. How could he have created this and the other too? The painting was huge: five feet by three feet. In it, a skeletal man crouched against a mountain's blue/black rocks. His only covering was a long red cloth which swathed him from waist to ankles. His bony frame, and the long, craggy lines of his face, implied there was no difference between the rock and the man. The mountain hugged him as if it were not stone. Ury had painted human sorrow in a cold, unyielding world. Felix thought he recognized the red in the gaunt man's robe. Could it be the same red on the woman's rug? He stepped back around the corner to be sure. It was. Here the red was luxury, there privation. The blue was elegance in her chair, but desolation in the rocks. One painting was of home and love, the other was the coming Holocaust. Ury had used the same colors to contrast tenderness and the results of hate and the effect was devastating. Felix didn't want these two paintings to represent his past like they did: his family's life in New York and what had happened to his parents in the war.

He signaled to Frances he was leaving, and escaped into the lobby full of school children whose teachers must not love them, as far as he was concerned, or how could they shove them into this chasm of emotion?

Outside, Frances caught up to him and grabbed his arm. "Flix, you can't avoid this. Don't you understand? The funeral's Monday. Do you know we have an uncle, Dad's brother, alive in Italy? He's Enea's brother. Do you realize that? I got in touch with him—"

"You didn't."

"For God's sake, it's his sister who died! He was so happy to hear from me. You should have heard him. They all cried. He's coming for the funeral and so is—"

He felt surrounded, invaded. With a houseful of relatives his time wouldn't be his own. If he ignored them and stayed in the lab, it would draw attention, raise questions. He could wait until they left, but Felix had the urgent sense he mustn't delay.

"I'm sorry, but they can't stay here! Put them in a hotel. See them all you want. Don't bring them here! Dad never had them here, remember? We need to talk things through before we do things like this. Believe me, this is the wrong time to open our lives to strangers!"

He left her and quickly returned to the apartment where he went to the solarium, trying to calm his mind to work. He looked down at Central Park, easily the biggest perk of living on Museum Mile, the stretch of Fifth Avenue that bordered it on the east. The park had been the playground of their childhood. Every corner of it he knew, every pond, boulder, statue, and flowerbed. Often he stood here, watching as Frances rode King, her Andalusian, and Adeline rode her Arabian, Moonless. For a moment, Felix yearned for the contentment he'd experienced at those times.

He felt arms wrap around him from behind, and he reached back to touch Adeline.

"I'm sorry if I said anything out of order, Felix. I didn't realize how upset you were. It doesn't matter," she said. "Really it doesn't. I mean, some things do matter in life. Whether you're an honest person or not. Whether you help or hurt others. Being Christian or Jewish doesn't. It just doesn't."

He turned around to her. "If you thought it didn't matter," he said and kissed her forehead, "would you be trying so hard to convince me?"

"Darling, I'm only trying to untie those knots you're all tied up in. It's obvious something's wrong. Where is Frances?"

"She's coming."

"And Maggie doesn't know what to make of us."

Felix felt embarrassed to have a witness to their private turmoil, even Maggie. He felt confused by Adeline's instant acceptance of a heritage he was having trouble with. In her pale beauty she looked like an angel. Their relationship reflected their religious beliefs, because they'd made love only once. He often wished they had respected the covenant of marriage and waited, though nowadays few did. But one beautiful night in this very room he'd succumbed and so had she. Since then they'd been a couple. He planned to propose to her on the anniversary of their first official date, suggest they dispense with an engagement and have a private church ceremony right away. They were meant for each other. Instead of having sex, they spent hours discussing God. Felix's passion was for Jesus Christ and hers for his message of mercy. She'd considered entering a convent as a child. He'd wanted to be a priest.

When they weren't riding, she and Frances spent their time on charities, sometimes odd ones. Adeline found them. She was constantly in search of ways to help people, to do the greatest good with her money and her time, both of which she gave unstintingly. Of the saints, her favorite was St. Colette, a French girl who, orphaned at seventeen, gave her entire inheritance to the poor, became a nun and went into seclusion until God revealed her destiny. She founded seventeen new convents, motivated by her visions of the Passion. It was said she prophesied the specifics of her own death.

Adeline squeezed his hands in reassurance. "Felix, how strong is your faith in God?"

He touched her hair. "You know the answer."

"Then don't question this. Believe God has his reasons for the way he is unfolding your life."

Felix stared at her, knowing the reason, remembering the passage he'd been led to on Moses, remembering his journal, and how he could make no progress without a woman, someone worthy to mother the Son of God. Someone of profound faith. Someone unafraid. Someone as near to being an angel as human women got. She was standing before him.

Could he ask her? Would she say yes? Was this the destiny God intended— for the woman he'd imagined could one day hold his own son in her arms?

Felix stepped away from her and walked toward the orchids Frances loved to grow. From there he watched as the lowering sun bathed Adeline in light, and he pictured her pregnant with a holy child, he and Frances at her side. They'd do it together, the three of them bonded as they'd been since school.

He went to Adeline and held her in what felt like a goodbye to the life he'd planned for them. He put his cheek to hers. "Let's go out tonight, Adeline," he whispered in her ear. "I need to be alone with you."

Chapter 9

Thursday afternoon—Fifth Avenue

Sam had tried to call Dr. Rossi about the reporter, but he hadn't answered his phone. When Frances Rossi came with Adeline Hamilton, he'd sent a message to Rossi through them, but apparently they'd forgotten to deliver it. Probably a lot was going on with the Rossis just returned, and their aunt having died.

He phoned to be relieved at the front door, went into the building and descended the stairs to the sunken lobby, taking a shortcut through the chandelier-hung ballroom to the area they all called The Barracks. It consisted of an apartment for the building engineer, a common room for the drivers, doormen and security guard, and a much larger apartment for Sam, who supervised everyone. His place had once been the medical office for Dr. Rossi senior, Felix Rossi's father. Now the spacious rooms were Sam's—they and everything in The Barracks paid for by the Tenants Association.

He looked into the common room. The security guard was alternately scanning the front, back, and lobby monitors, and listening to a morning talk show which the two drivers on duty watched. Behind one of the sleep cubicles, a third driver snored. Two others were off duty. Sam called, "You can erase the pickup for Dr. Rossi from the schedule board, guys; he's been here for hours."

"Sure, Sam," one of them replied.

Sam moved down the corridor and unlocked the door to Mr. Brown's private basement garage. Mr. Brown's schedule was never on the board. It wasn't written down at all. He descended the stairs to a wooden canopy with a red carpet beneath it, extending to Brown's private elevator. At the far wall was Brown's car collection: a white Porsche Brown had driven only once, two black Lincoln Town Cars to disguise himself as just another rich person in New York on the few occasions he went out, and a Rolls Silver Seraph he'd never used. On the night Rolls unveiled the Seraph in the Scottish Highland, they'd worn their tartans, played bagpipes, and drunk Old Pulteney single malt, or so Sam had heard. Not much in the way of cars for a man like Brown. He'd once told Sam he had little interest in them.

Sam put on his hat and waited below the polished canopy. In moments he heard a horn blow, pushed a button to activate the garage door, and another on the intercom.

The butler answered. Sam said, "He's here."

The garage door lifted and admitted a black limo. It stopped at the canopy and Sam opened the back door.

"Good morning, Mr. Secretary."

He held the door for the U.S. Secretary of State, while the driver opened the trunk and retrieved his overnight bag.

Sam took it and followed the Secretary down the red carpet to the elevator. When it came, they stepped inside.

"How was your flight up, Mr. Secretary?"

He sighed. "It doesn't matter."

Sam knew the Secretary's wife had died in a freak auto accident last year. Though he exuded confidence in public, in private he still seemed a defeated man.

The Secretary looked down at the manila envelope in his hands. "Doesn't Brown ever get to you, Sam?"

Instead of answering, Sam changed the subject to the glorious weather, until the elevator reached the ninth floor penthouse. When the doors opened, there was Mr. Brown.

Brown's demeanor got to Sam, all right, like it did to everyone. He'd read J. P. Morgan had a similar effect on people, his eyes glaring so intently, it felt like being in the headlights of an approaching train. Though he usually wore gray trousers and a simple shirt with no tie, and the luxury that surrounded him was on a tasteful scale, everyone who saw Brown behaved as if he were God.

The Secretary's head dipped as he shook hands.

The butler entered and took the Secretary's overnight bag and Brown said, "Wait, Sam. I have an errand for you."

"Yes, sir." As Sam stepped back into the lobby, he heard Brown ask, "Did you bring the draft cease fire this time?"

The Secretary replied, "Yes, yes of course," his voice tight.

Sam made a point of not wondering why some of Brown's visitors found him this intimidating.

He sat in a comfortable chair in Mr. Brown's foyer, quietly humming Too-ra loo-ra-loo-ral to himself. As he hummed, he watched the butler return and take the elevator down then watched the numbers rise from seven to eight to nine. The doors opened. Out stepped the butler, followed by a woman he'd seen once or twice before, her soft chestnut hair cascading onto an animal's black fur—or an exceptionally good fake. A glance at her walk had told him she was a dancer—among the thousands aspiring to fame in New York, and not the first he'd seen here. Her musical was, no doubt, financed—and her fabulous coat supplied—by Mr. Brown. Sam inspected her as she passed. The Secretary of State would be entertained tonight. Sam envied him.

Moments later, the butler reappeared and led Sam to the library. That's where Mr. Brown liked to meet with favored guests and those in his employ. Sam suspected every other room but Brown's own bedroom was bugged or videotaped. He knew the main guest bedroom was. When the woman took off her fur and danced on the Secretary's happy body, Brown would have a record, in case of need.

Sam took a seat on a tan leather couch, thinking of the ordinary stakeout in his L.A. private detecting days that led him here. He'd been hired by a rich housewife to follow her husband and get evidence of adultery she could use in court. The husband turned out to be balling two young actresses who roomed together and happened to like men, as well as each other. The night Sam found them they were all in the girls' bed enjoying themselves. What Sam didn't know was the wife had followed him, planning to blow husband and lover off the earth.

While Sam took pictures, the wife was busy aiming a gun. The first shot got the husband in the left shoulder. Sam reached her before the second shot and took the gun away. Without publicity, he got the husband to his doctor, the wife to her therapist, and advised the two girls to move and leave no forwarding address.

For a year after, Sam had a stream of weird, difficult, and lucrative cases, in each of which he satisfied the client. One day he got a big check in the mail, a ticket to New York, and a request to show up for an interview where he learned he'd had only one client all year: a Mr. Brown, whose rebellious sister had been one of the two girls. Apparently she'd told her brother, who'd given Sam the anonymous test he'd passed. He was put on Brown's security payroll where he'd remained for eleven years doing various kinds of interesting work, usually aboveboard but sometimes a little below, at a salary that would suit a minor prince.

A voice boomed from the hallway. "Sam, there you are!"

Brown entered and sat in the high-backed chair next to a computer that gave access to supposedly classified government websites. Ancient and modern maps hung behind him on the wall. With no preliminaries Brown tossed a thick, sealed envelope on the table in front of Sam. "This goes to our friend at the consulate. You're expected there in exactly one hour."

"Yes, sir," he said, not surprised by the envelope's destination. Two African countries had recently started a new war across their borders, and the U.S. was helping broker a cease-fire. Brown was no doubt sending the one he favored advance notice of the proposed terms.

Sam tucked the envelope inside his jacket as Brown looked off skeptically toward his library: five rows of standing bookshelves, each unit clearly labeled with a continent's name and the countries within it, or a period of history.

"You should read more," Brown said, as if thinking about something not in a book.

Sam rose, went to one shelf and saw Pliny the Elder's *Historia Naturalis*, Quintius Curtius Rufus's, the *History of Alexander* and Plutarch's *Lives*. On another were Lao Tze's the *Tao-te-ching*, the *Art of War* by Sun Tzu, a volume of Li Po's poems, and the records of Ssu-ma Ch'ien. From India there was the *Ramayana*, the *Vedas*, and the *Mahayana Sutras*. Naturally, the *Bible*, the *Torah*, the *Qur'an*, were there. Combined with all else he knew of Brown, this library in which it was possible to browse the thought, art, religion, and history of every known society, told Sam when he first saw it that a captain worth serving was at the helm. Over and over he'd seen Brown look into the future, instructed by the past, and fix what he didn't like before it happened.

"What do you think of the world, Sam?"

"Me?" Sam selected Machiavelli's *The Prince*. He'd never actually read it, because he suspected he already knew what it advised. "Well, I first saw the world as a sailor, as you know. To tell the truth, it didn't look that different than a merchant ship to me: men living and working in close quarters, no way to get off, sailing dangerous seas. Without a captain, a hierarchy, and a decent set of rules, the pressures would make seamen destroy each other before the ship reached port."

"You think the same is true elsewhere in life?"

"Yes."

Brown stood, delivering his version of an *approving father* smile which consisted of less piercing intimidation. Sam liked and admired Brown, if from a necessary distance.

"Everything fine in the building?" Brown asked.

"A reporter came by asking for Dr. Rossi earlier today."

Brown's smile ended. "A reporter? What about?"

"Something about his work, I think."

"Find out. Let me know." He glanced toward the door, meaning he had no time for more talk and Sam should leave.

Sam took the elevator down and, through the open front door, saw Frances Rossi and her friend, Adeline, waiting like statues for a limo. Going shopping, he assumed. He paused to watch them, struck as usual by the immobility they shared with most of the ladies in the building. It was as if someone had told upper class women not to move if they could help it. Frances seemed unfit for this restriction. Every now and then she'd behave like her horse, King, and actually use her muscles in public. He'd noticed Adeline, on the other hand, had mastered inertia. For long periods she wouldn't budge, then something would touch her: a sound, a word. She'd unfreeze like melted ice and flow into a new position that expressed her changed state of mind. Then, for a long time, ice again.

More than once he'd idly fantasized simply seeing these women move.

He remembered leaving his cell phone at Mr. Brown's, went back up and retrieved it, and was unhappy to see the elevator slow for the eighth floor on the way down. He'd taken the public elevator without thought.

As the doors began to open he glimpsed Maggie, the Rossis' maid, blatantly peering to see who was coming down from the penthouse. He grinned and quickly squeezed into the front corner of the car where she wouldn't see him right away.

"Curious are you, Maggie, my girl?" he said.

She jerked at the sound of his voice and stumbled as she came into the car. Sam caught her before she fell. It always cheered him to see Maggie, her big doe eyes usually fascinated by something that wasn't precisely her business. She never gossiped, as far as he knew, but she definitely wanted to know everything.

She felt helpless in his arms, staring up at him and looking vexed, her hand over her heart. He smiled, thinking of how proudly she'd worn that hat—like an African queen. It crossed his mind to kiss her then he wondered where that thought came from.

"What are you trying to do, scare me to death?" she said and disengaged from him as the doors closed.

"As if I could," Sam answered, still smiling at her. He wondered how much money she'd wasted on the hat. His mother had been like that—went without food after his father died so he could have fashionable clothes to wear to the fine school she maneuvered him into. He'd since hated seeing a poor, good woman impoverish herself on clothes to feel of value. Maggie was one of the good ones.

She lowered her voice. "Anyway, I was looking for you."

"Really? He still had fifty minutes to get to the consulate and it was only twenty minutes away. He pushed the elevator stop button and tried to look serious, inspecting her plain but honest face and liking it.

She said, "I heard you wanted to talk to Dr. Rossi, and I thought you could just as easily tell me about it and not disturb him."

Sam grinned. He'd been considering how to have a private chat with her on just this subject, and had almost decided to ask her down to his place, though no one from the building ever came there—only his women visitors who used the private entrance from the street, not the lobby. Now the problem was solved.

"Is that right? Did Rossi send you?"

"Not exactly."

"You mean not at all?"

She looked exasperated. "Sam Duffy, there's enough going on in that house without you adding anything. What is it you want with Dr. Rossi?"

Sam nodded at her protectiveness. There was more loyalty than servility in it, though Maggie did a five-star imitation of being servile when she chose. At least he hoped it was an imitation. The idea that she might feel herself truly beneath others troubled him when he thought about it.

He leaned back against the brass railing. "Before I answer, don't you even want to say hello to me, Lass?"

"I'm not a lass." She paused as if regretting being rude. "Hello, Sam." She gave him a plastic smile.

It caused him a twinge of hurt because he liked Maggie, and had been trying to be her friend for years. He saw the kind heart under her toughness, and it made him want to protect her, though he knew she was in no danger here. He didn't really blame her for not responding. How could she know that his experience as a seaman had made race, religion, sexual preference and such permanently unimportant to him. In the close quarters of merchant ships at sea, harmony among the crew was the highest good, the worst evil was anything that destroyed it. If you weren't already tolerant, as a mariner you learned to be. But Maggie was having none of his Irish friendship, so he settled for teasing her.

"Hello, Maggie. I have a confession to make."

She looked at him with interest.

"I overheard Frances Rossi and her friend, Adeline, talking about the hat contest at your church with Sharmina. How did it go?"

In a motion which implied it had gone so-so, Maggie looked bored and shrugged one shoulder, but he knew the hat must have been a success.

"It was just a hat, just nonsense."

"Nonsense?" He couldn't believe Maggie, whose hat mania was well known, had described her prized possession as nonsense.

"Your Graham Smith? Yes, I heard that, too. Maggie, you must be running a fever. Now tell me. What did Sharmina say, or was she speechless?"

Maggie looked up to the ceiling as if she'd decided to indulge a child. "I walked in, if you must know; sat in my usual place—on the aisle, third row. People noticed, I suppose. A couple of them said 'lovely' and such. Five minutes before the service, there was Sharmina staring down at my hat, the whole church staring at her. She never said a word. Next thing I knew she'd gone home, or so they told me, and missed the contest. I won, but I can't say I beat her since she wasn't there. Satisfied?"

Sam laughed. "What a coward! Forgot all about the Lord, did she? You threw the first cork and she gave up then and there."

Maggie looked at him in surprise. "Throw the cork? You play darts, Sam Duffy?"

He put his hands on his hips. "Better than any Irishman in New York. Do you?"

"I do. And pretty good, if you really want to know."

He laughed. "Then put your money where your mouth is, woman! He looked at his watch. "Tonight. Six o'clock. I'll take you to Molly Malone's. The McSorley's on me."

She stared at him as if he'd lost his mind.

"I've asked something sinful, have I? All right, never-you-mind. We'll get married first then play darts. How's that?"

Maggie rolled her eyes. "You think I'm going to some pub with you, Sam? You want to play darts, you can come up to the rec room at my church, is what you can do. Back to what we were talking about before somebody calls this elevator?" she said, no delight on her face, which disappointed Sam. He'd love to play a game of darts with Maggie, and he'd looked forward to enjoying her triumph with the hat.

"No darts, no wedding? You're a hard woman, Maggie." He gazed into her olive-brown eyes, wondering if she knew they were beautiful. Then he cleared his throat. "Okay, then tell me. Why would a reporter suddenly take an interest in your Dr. Rossi's work?"

She sighed. "Is that all? Lots of them take an interest in his work. Don't you read the papers? And you wanted to come up and bother him about that?"

He leaned slightly forward. "Not exactly. Why would one try to bribe me to learn what Rossi brought from Turin?"

"Bribe you?" She looked shocked and a little thrilled.

"Yes. A reporter tried to bribe me. He wanted to know what Rossi had in his valise. What do you make of that, Maggie?"

She leaned back against the opposite railing and shook her head. "That's a mystery. Only one thing's changed that I know of. It's something personal, not something I can tell you. I can't believe a reporter would be interested in it, though."

Sam studied her. Another thing he liked about Maggie was that if she couldn't tell the truth, she said nothing at all.

"Just personal?" he said. "You never know. These days, they'll print anything."

Maggie nodded, still gazing in the air; then she seemed to remember the point of her mission. "Sam, do me a favor, would you? Don't tell Rossi about it today, all right? Give the man a chance to settle back into his house, to talk to his sister and his fiancée."

"His fiancée? They're really a pair?" Sam realized this tidbit could win him a few bets with the limo drivers if he were so inclined, which he wasn't.

Maggie eyed him as if he were a rascal. "Well, they're not officially engaged just yet but everybody knows they'll get married. By the way, what were you up to at Mr. Brown's?"

"Rossi's business is private, but not the other tenants', huh?"

"All right, all right," she said and faced the elevator doors, looking nonchalant.

Reluctantly, Sam released the stop button, wishing he could continue fencing with guileless Maggie, instead of returning to the cunning world. "Just an envelope delivery, curious Maggie," he said.

Chapter 10

Thursday night—Rossi apartment

In the shadows of his darkened lab Felix slowly paced. Already dressed for dinner, he wore the black wool serge suit Adeline liked and the richly patterned Stefano Ricci tie under his lab coat, cap and mask. He knew Adeline waited in a guest room that had become her own room here. Frances, who was pleased to hear they would be going out, told him Adeline would be wearing a new black sheath and he'd dressed to match it.

In the lab, a single light shone on the cause of his delay: he'd prepared the threads from the Shroud of Turin.

Unable to resist, he'd extracted the blood using the mildest possible solution, the gentlest centrifuge settings, and had a sample ready on his Atomic Force Microscope. He must only walk over and take a glance. Then he'd know whether his project had any hope of success.

He might see intact cells containing the full genetic code in a DNA strand's double helix, its two sides joined by roughly three billion base pairs, like a twisting ladder and its rungs. He needed white blood cells because red ones had no nucleus and no DNA. Or he might see many fragmented DNA strands missing a few hundred base pairs here, another few hundred there. He hoped for either. What he didn't want to see, what would stop his project at once, was DNA so degraded only fragments of a few hundred base pairs in length remained.

Felix lingered in the shadows.

Why couldn't he look? Why couldn't he walk five feet and look

He felt impotent and afraid, fingering through the lab coat the signature buttons of his Brioni suit. He'd willingly trade it for one good cell. If the DNA was terribly degraded, all his money couldn't restore it. His plan, his dream would end. No, his heart would break if the DNA wasn't there.

He paced to the door, took a breath, then went straight to the microscope and peered through the lens at the image being magnified several million times. At first his vision wouldn't focus, he was so aware of the holiness of what he had. Felix closed his eyes then looked again. He saw large-celled fungi and bacteria and among them fragments of smaller red blood cells, recognizable by their biconcave shape. He saw not a single white blood cell, fragmented or intact.

Panicked, he set the scope for an automatic scan of the entire sample. Felix saw no useable cells or DNA.

He heard a buzz and went to the intercom at the door.

"Yes?"

"Flix, Adeline says to tell you she's almost ready."

"All right. Give me a minute more."

The scan had finished and there was nothing. Perhaps the solution had separated, and he wasn't viewing a representative part. He lifted the test tube containing the rest of the solution and poured it into a large, sterile Petri dish that he covered and placed in the scope's special vacuum mount. He could observe as the dish was being sampled by the scope. It seemed ages that he peered, seeing nothing useable, his heart sinking, feeling foolish that he'd even hoped. Then a large cluster of neutrophils came into focus, many apparently intact. They were a special kind of white blood cell present in pus in large amounts. "My God," he whispered and brought his hand to his mouth, realizing these cells must have gathered in the wounds of Christ.

Fighting tears, Felix whispered a prayer, "Eternal Father, I offer Thee the Wounds of Our Lord Jesus Christ to heal the wounds of our souls. Amen." Then he sat back in the lab chair and breathed out in relief.

He heard the door buzzer again, then, "Flix, what are you doing? You're going to miss your dinner reservation, for heavens' sake!"

Jubilantly he rushed to the intercom and replied, "Coming, sister dear!"

Carefully he removed the Petri dish and, holding it gently, put it in the incubator at ambient conditions that would keep it exactly as it was until he returned.

He opened the lab door and there was Frances, dressed in a caftan for an evening at home, her favorite blue pointed Dipinti slippers on her feet.

"What are you so happy about?" she said.

He kissed her cheek. "Nothing, nothing. And I'm sorry about earlier in the museum."

"You should be." Her eyebrows rose in a comic wounded look.

"You're a gem. No, you're wonderful. Let's talk in the morning."

Then Adeline came into the hall, looking breathtaking in her sleeveless sheath, three thin straps at each shoulder. Her hair was up, wisps falling down her neck. Strands of diamonds dangled from her ears and she wore a large onyx and diamond ring. She smiled when Felix took her arm.

Frances surveyed them, outright approval on her face. "Do you two have any idea how good you look together?"

"No, but do tell us," he said.

"You look like movie stars," Frances said, smiling. "I ought to despise you both!"

Adeline laughed.

"Well, then, plain Jane," he said, teasing because he regarded Frances as beautiful. "Let us leave so our fans can worship us." He chucked her chin as he passed.

Downstairs, Sam had their limo waiting. Felix took Adeline to it. "Just a second," he said then walked back to the door with Sam.

"You wanted to see me about something?" Felix asked.

Sam looked toward Adeline. "Nothing that needs to keep a lady waiting. Will you be in tomorrow?"

"Yes, I will."

"I'll find you. Enjoy your evening, Dr. Rossi."

Felix nodded and returned to the limo, not minding that January's coldness had returned and that he was shivering because he hadn't worn a coat, only a scarf. Adeline had wrapped herself in her warm shahtoosh or "ring shawl," the precious garment he'd bought for her in Nepal for a justifiably astronomical fifteen grand. At the time, he hadn't known the Tibetan antelope, from whose beard the wool came, was being killed in droves by poachers so they could smuggle the wool to Nepal. When he read Zhaba Duojie, the endangered antelopes' chief protector, had been killed, Felix felt terrible and made a donation to Doujie's family and conservationist group. Adeline knew none of this. She hadn't asked and he'd never told her the shawl's real price. To her, it was just an especially fine Pashmina.

"*One if by land, Two if by sea*," he said to the driver.

"Yes, sir, Dr. Rossi," the driver replied and pulled onto the Avenue, heading south toward the Village.

Adeline leaned over and kissed his cheek. "Thank you," she said.

"For what?"

"For everything. For taking me out tonight, for being you, for this shawl. She nestled against him and put her hand in his.

As quickly as he'd decided what to ask her this evening, he now wondered if he'd been insane. She loved him. He loved her. He should be asking someone else.

"You know, I prayed before we left tonight," she said in a quiet voice.

"Did you?"

"Yes. I felt it was important to put myself, ourselves, in God's hands. To reiterate in prayer that the life I want for myself, and for us, is the life God would have us live."

He found her conversation remarkable, as if she were reading his thoughts. He gripped her hand, reassured, and looked ahead into the shining New York night.

Around them were the headlights and taillights of taxis, limos and cars. On their right he saw the dark park's bright lanterns passing. On poles arcing over the road, streetlights and traffic lights blazed. Below on the Avenue, which sloped south before them, the lit floors of skyscrapers turned them into gleaming grids. Felix's eye caught the distant sign above the building at 666 Fifth Avenue, between 52nd and 53rd. Its three huge, red neon number sixes had converted the building's infamous address into a publicity gimmick. Felix had always secretly hated having to see these numbers—the mark of the anti-Christ, the beast in Revelation—every time he drove down his own street.

Tonight it seemed a threatening portent. As if in confirmation, their driver grumbled as he looked out the rear mirror.

"What is it?" Felix asked.

"That car behind us has practically been in my trunk for three blocks. Can't see the plates. Probably a New Jersey driver."

Felix turned, imagining the devil at the wheel behind. Seeing nothing of the kind, he gripped Adeline's hand and reminded himself of the miracles of coincidence that had already occurred: the cloning research he'd done without realizing he would actually need it, the timely call from Frances that prompted him to use his only moments of access to the Shroud, the customs agent at the airport, and, against all odds, the haunting cluster of neutrophils he'd just seen in the microscope. Perhaps not as dramatic as God turning Moses' staff into a snake, but wondrous nonetheless.

As they pulled into a quiet West Village side street, Felix realized his whole destiny might await him here. He'd chosen this restaurant because Adeline loved it and he liked it, too. Originally, it had been the stables and carriage house of Aaron Burr's home. Purchased and opened by the flamboyant Armand J. Braiger almost thirty years ago, *One if by land, Two if by sea* had remained delightful, drawing them frequently back even as trendier restaurants came and went. Its whitewashed exterior and the raised white letters of its name, its simple window frames, were easy to miss if you didn't know it was there. Inside, all was elegance and ambiance and charm.

He opened the black enameled door for Adeline and they stepped into a cozy entrance and bar. Two fireplaces with wooden mantels and brass gridirons were on the right, set into exposed brick walls. At the paned-glass windows, a pianist played a baby grand.

They walked past the fireplaces and the striped upholstered sofas and approached the maitre d's tall desk. He came to greet them.

"Dr. Rossi, Madame. Welcome back. We have your usual table. Those immediately around it will be empty tonight." He surreptitiously winked at Felix who had requested whatever privacy they could arrange.

Felix walked behind Adeline as she followed the maitre d' through the restaurant's main room. Here, most of the original second floor had been cut away to provide high ceilings. Railings had been placed across the open doors of the remaining upper rooms. Diners above could look below and those seated below could look up. He never sat in these areas. They were for people who wanted to be seen. He didn't. When eyes didn't follow them to their table, he was relieved.

They passed American folk art hung on oak paneling set into the bricks; a red and blue stained glass window; tall, spectacular floral groupings; and pristine white tables, their crystal and silver glimmering in candlelight. They stopped by the viewing garden next to French doors with white draped and shirred window treatments. The maitre d' seated Adeline then lit the single candle in its pewter holder. On the damask table linen, as Adeline had once informed him, everything was real: the silver, the china, the perfect pink rosebuds in their silver bucket vase. The table behind them was empty, as was the table in front and the one directly across the aisle. As he sat down, Felix slipped the maitre d' an extra hundred-dollar bill.

The maitre d' left them with menus: *prix fixe*, like most New York restaurants of its class. They could dine for the modest price of fifty-nine dollars each for a first course, entree and dessert of their choice. At the venerable *River Cafe* it would be seventy apiece, at the fabulous *Daniel* eighty-five. Neither offered the seclusion he wanted tonight. Wine or cocktails were extra, as was the lobster salad, the prime rib, or a soufflé for dessert. He never paid the bills directly. They arrived with all the rest, once a month.

"Darling, they have turbot in parchment tonight," Adeline said. "I'll have that and a lemon soufflé."

"What would you like for a first course?" he asked.

"You know me. If there's mushroom soup, I'll always have it." Her gray eyes shimmered in the candlelight, distracting him from the speech he was rehearsing in his mind.

He put the menu down. "I'll have the same."

He placed their order with the waiter and selected a wine, noticing the sound of a sliding chair. When he turned he saw a man had occupied the table one row away. He was sitting with his back to them. Felix judged he was too far to hear their conversation.

"Adeline?" he began, pulling his chair close and lowering his voice.

She moved closer, too. "Yes, darling?"

"I want to talk with you about something important."

She smiled and looked seriously at him.

"I need to warn you. It will sound strange at first."

She looked perplexed. "Strange?"

"Yes, very. I'm hoping it will make sense by the time I finish."

"What is it? You can tell me anything."

"First, will you pray with me?"

"Of course."

They made the sign of the cross and bowed their heads and when Felix began in a hushed voice, Adeline joined him:

"I, Felix—"

"I, Adeline—"

"give myself and consecrate to the Sacred Heart of our Lord Jesus Christ my person and my life, my actions, pains, and sufferings, so that I may be unwilling to make use of any part of my being save to honor, love, and glorify the Sacred Heart. This is my unchanging purpose, namely, to be all His, and to do all things for the love of Him, at the same time renouncing with all my heart whatever is displeasing to Him."

Impulsively, Felix stopped, reached across the table and took her hands in his. Carefully, methodically, he began to explain what had happened. He started with the moment Frances had called him in Turin.

Though he looked at Adeline while he talked, at times he didn't really see her face. He saw the Shroud, saw the blood, which became his mother's blood, saw images of wounds, which became his brother's infant body. Twice he stopped because he just couldn't speak.

Adeline paid such close attention, she seemed to be memorizing his words. Encouraged, he told the whole story, up to and including tonight. When he paused, he realized they were holding onto each other as if letting go meant they'd fall.

He saw her swallow, her gaze fixed on his face. He'd saved the part concerning her for last.

He kissed her hands and whispered, "Who is my Mary, if not you?"

"What?" She breathed the word like a prayer.

"Will you be the mother, Adeline?"

She opened her mouth but said nothing. Instead, two bright trickles spilled down the center of her cheeks.

She was crying. "Don't," he said, because he hadn't expected this and didn't know what it meant.

Quickly her tears overflowed and a sharp sob came from her mouth. She tried to pull her hands away, but he was afraid, now, and wouldn't release her.

"Don't cry, don't cry," he said, his voice rising with her sobs. They came unstoppable and unrehearsed, like a baby's. He shot from his seat, still holding her hands, knowing too late what an awful mistake he'd made. Then she was in his arms, her head on his chest, her costly shahtoosh trampled underfoot, and the maitre d' was there, saying something Felix didn't understand. But the French doors opened and then they were outside, alone in the viewing garden, being viewed by other diners as if they were actors in a movie.

"Adeline, Adeline," he repeated. He tried to lift her face from his chest but she seemed to slide lower, bending over, burying her wet face in the jacket of his suit, her slight torso rising and falling in a losing effort to stop her sobs.

Chapter 11

Rossi apartment

When Maggie saw the cookbook Miss Rossi had bought, when she and Adeline announced they'd gone shopping on their own, put on aprons, talked about secret letters and chopped vegetables, Maggie knew things had changed in the Rossi household. It was Maggie who usually took a limo to Harlem's Fairway Uptown to fetch their smoked salmon, caviar, bagels and such. But when Dr. Rossi said he didn't need her in the lab and Adeline announced she was in love with a Jew, Maggie wondered if she ought to spend the night. She might not have a job by the morning, if things could change this fast.

She pictured her journey home. Downstairs to Fifth Avenue, wait for the 96th Street cross town bus west—because there were no subways east of Central park, west of Lexington, and north of 63rd where most of the rich lived. Get off at Broadway and wait for the number three subway north to Harlem. Ride that to the end of the line. A different world. Twenty-nine minutes away.

Walk one block; go through an arched tunnel covered in graffiti to an inner courtyard with scraggly trees and bushes. She might have to pass some drug dealers. Climb the dark stairs; enter a large apartment with ceilings just as high as those here. Her building had been a model for ones like the Dakota, except the Dakota hadn't fallen into disrepair.

Or she could get off two stops early at 135th Street where the colorful Black

Manhattan mosaic was. Martin Luther King, Marcus Garvey, Satchmo playing his horn. Walk south from Harlem Hospital and the Schomburg Library, down to 131st and turn right into a street full of churches, most converted brownstones. Hers wasn't. It was made of stone. It had a big neon cross, visible at night when sin was most likely.

At her church was where she'd first heard of Dr. Rossi and that he was looking for a maid with laboratory experience. Maggie campaigned her minister shamelessly for an interview, using his favorite biscuits as persuasion and a jar of the homemade cranberry sauce he loved.

When she first came to the Rossis' apartment, she could hardly believe this place—or the lovely little room behind the kitchen that they soon said was hers when she liked. Maggie hadn't let herself stay overnight too much, because she wanted them to know she had a home. Tonight she had a reason to stay, and she believed God helped those who helped themselves.

As he left for dinner, she'd recognized Dr. Rossi's jubilant expression. He could never hide it. It meant something exciting had happened in his work. Now was the time to learn why he'd suddenly shut her out.

She moved about the house, dusting invisible dust, and waiting for Miss Rossi's delivery to arrive from Balducci's. When it did, she set it out on one of their beautiful hand-painted trays, and took it to the living room where Miss Rossi sat by the fireplace reading a bunch of faded old letters, her slippered feet up on the coffee table. Maggie assumed these were the letters from their Jewish relatives Miss Rossi and Adeline had been talking about outside of Dr. Rossi's hearing.

"Here, isn't this lovely?" Maggie said and put the tray down.

Frances lowered her letter, saying, "I can never resist these," and picked up a fat cream cheese and crab roll with her fingers. She bit into it and sighed. "Oh! There ought to be a law."

"Do you need anything else, Miss Rossi?"

"No, Maggie. And I don't want you spending the night here just to wait on me hand and foot like this. You're welcome to stay, of course, but I don't intend to turn you into a slave." Frances stopped and looked horrified.

"That's all right," Maggie said, smiling. "I know I'm no slave. We used to be." She turned her palms over and back. "Nowadays we're just minorities."

"I can't believe I of all people said that."

"Don't worry about it, but since you brought it up, how does it feel?"

"How does what feel?"

"Being a minority. Does it feel any different?"

Frances looked up toward a painting as if considering. "It doesn't feel the least bit different. In fact, I don't care at all. I feel like myself."

"Me too," Maggie winked. "Now you know our secret."

Frances laughed and lifted a saucer from her tray. "Have a crab ball, Maggie. Sit down here with me for once and let's talk. I'm sure I could use some advice."

Maggie stalled. "Uh. In a minute. I've got work to do before I relax."

"Oh, sit down," Frances said. "Put your feet up. It's not a crime."

"In a minute, in a minute. I'll be back." Maggie rushed from the room and stood listening, out of sight. She waited until she heard only the fire crackling and pages being turned. Then she tiptoed back through the kitchen, out into the hall, and down the Persian carpet to the lab.

At the door, she reached into her pocket and took out the key Dr. Rossi hadn't yet asked her to return. Holding her breath in fear, she depressed the lab's intercom button and, searching in her apron pocket for something to hold it down, found a paper clip and wedged it in place. This way she could hear if someone came down the hall. Only then did she unlock the door, inch it open, then close it behind her. Maggie flicked on a low light and raced to the desk. Nowhere did she see any journals.

She opened the center drawer where she'd often seen him put them. Only journals with old dates were there. She searched the side drawers and didn't find a current journal. Had he learned about her snooping and hidden it?

As Maggie rose to search the rest of the lab, she stopped in shocked surprise at the sound of Dr. Rossi and Adeline returning so soon after they'd left. He was loudly asking her to stay and Adeline was just as loudly refusing. Maggie could hardly believe what she was hearing. Then Adeline accused him of lying that the limo couldn't drive her straight home. She said she didn't want to wait any longer. She was going back downstairs and have Sam get her a cab, but apparently Dr. Rossi was blocking the front door. Then she heard Frances in the hall, asking what was wrong. Adeline screamed that nothing was wrong at all.

Maggie felt as panicked as Adeline sounded. Here she was, trapped in Dr. Rossi's lab when he'd said he didn't want her here. She wrung her hands as she listened over the intercom. They must have lowered their voices because all she heard was mumbling for a moment, then Dr. Rossi shouted, "Leave us alone!" to his sister, and then Miss Rossi went somewhere and slammed a door. Maggie heard that just fine.

Then Adeline must have sat on the hall floor because Maggie heard crying, but from a lower angle, and Dr. Rossi pleading and apologizing—probably on his knees, Maggie thought.

What had he done? Not in the whole five years she'd worked here had there ever been a scene like this. She knew that some men weren't able to go a full twenty-four hours without causing upset, but Dr. Rossi wasn't like that.

Maggie listened and prayed he wouldn't think of coming to the lab.

"I didn't mean to hurt you. I had no idea you felt this way," he was saying.

Adeline burst into tears and he pleaded with her not to cry.

She moaned, "I'm a woman, a flesh and blood woman!"

"I know."

"No you don't! You know nothing about me!"

Maggie wondered what could possibly have happened.

"Of course I do." Dr. Rossi spoke as if he were reasoning with Adeline, who responded as if she were mollified, though Maggie didn't believe she was. Maggie was right because suddenly Adeline announced, "I don't agree! And I refuse to carry some … some … clone! I want to carry our son! I want us to get married and for you to make me pregnant with your son! Yours, Felix! I haven't just loved you since that time we made love. I've loved you since we were in school. All along I hoped you'd give up living like a monk. You're not a priest, Felix! I know you wanted to be, but you're not."

It was silent in the hall, probably because Dr. Rossi was in shock. Maggie certainly was. She never would have guessed Adeline had loved him all this time, but Maggie was more concerned about the mention of a clone—the thing his journal said would make him fire her.

Maggie left the door and rushed about the lab, checking every surface, every cabinet, every drawer and finding nothing. "Jesus, if you mean for me to know what's going on so I can help and maybe keep my job, let me find it, won't you?"

She was about to give up, when she saw something atop a monitor mounted on the wall in a corner of the room. She reached up. It was his journal. Adding an apology for speaking sharply to the Lord, she grabbed the book and raced back to the door, trying to hear if anyone was coming. The hall was silent, which disturbed her.

Unable to resist, she inched open the metal door until there was the barest crack, enough to see Adeline and Dr. Rossi kissing outside his bedroom door. Actually, Adeline was doing the kissing and Dr. Rossi was trying to hold her off.

"We can't," he said "We have to wait. You'll have our son, Adeline, I promise, but it can't be now. I must do this, I must. I hope you'll understand."

Breathing hard, Adeline stepped back from him. Maggie let the door close and started rifling through the journal as she listened.

"You're serious?" Adeline said. "Instead of loving me, you want to save the Jews?" She started crying again but instead of consoling her, Dr. Rossi talked in a strained voice.

"Now that I know what happened to my parents, I see why every Jew I've ever met has been a walking barometer, cautiously sensing the atmosphere of the non-Jewish world, knowing it can turn poisonous for him. You can't be sure of being forever safe, here or anywhere. It can mean discrimination. What am I saying? It can mean hounding. It can mean torture. It can mean blood. It can mean death. It can mean—"

Maggie heard a slap, then silence. Had he hit her? No, he wouldn't. Adeline must have done it. Maggie would have hit him, too. He was beginning to sound hysterical.

Maggie found the new pages in the journal, and as she scanned them, heard Miss Rossi's voice in the hall again. She sounded depressed, as if she'd lost a dream.

"Can I make a suggestion?"

Maggie heard deep sighs.

"Flix, Adeline. I don't want to pry, but whatever the trouble is, I'm sure it will look better in the morning. Maybe we should all turn in for the night."

They must have moved toward the front door because Maggie couldn't hear them well. They were all speaking in civilized tones. She did hear the front door close and Dr. Rossi say goodnight to his sister.

Maggie was thinking of where to hide if he came to the lab.

She listened for a long time and, hearing nothing, took the journal to his desk and sat down. He'd begun another list with a clearer step-by-step procedure, followed by pages of details but Maggie couldn't understand all the scientific terms. He'd written about donor eggs and donor wombs—not of animals like Dolly the sheep, apparently, given what Adeline had said. What Maggie didn't understand was his mention of threads. What threads? Why were they full of blood?

Maggie opened the big medical dictionary on his desk and, looking up practically every other word, stumbled through pages of his journal about in-vitro fertilization and DNA. Was he trying to clone a person with genes different from those God gave it?

She read his notes about gestation, which listed what he'd have to do at different points. Maggie looked it up and it was pregnancy, as she thought. He had reminders all the way up to the ninth month. She went back and reread the first paragraph about the threads, then looking up, caught sight of his replica of the Shroud.

He'd been in Turin.

"Oh Lord, oh Lord!" Maggie whispered, horrified. She raced through the journal, rereading every mention of the threads. Where had they come from?

Gradually, different memories came together in her mind, along with things she'd only half known. The reporter Sam mentioned, curious about what Dr. Rossi brought from Turin. Adeline's tears. What Dr. Rossi said about Jews. How close he was to the church, how he had priests who were friends and one was in Turin. How deeply he believed in the Shroud.

It couldn't be.

Maggie looked up at the replica of the Shroud.

It couldn't be.

She put the journal into the center drawer, turned out the lights, and after listening at the door, slipped back into the hall and removed the paper clip from the intercom. She locked the lab behind her and went to the empty living room where she put out the fire, fluffed sofa pillows, and picked up the painted tray. In the kitchen they never used, she put Miss Rossi's saucer in the Fisher & Paykel dishwasher that came special-made all the way from Australia, washed the crystal wine glass by hand, and put the wine and the crab balls away.

Then she went to the room they'd given her. It had its own bath. It had maroon print wallpaper and the loveliest woven wicker bed, piled with frilly pillows. Maggie knelt on the rug, clenched her hands, and stretched her dark arms out on the pink and maroon comforter.

"Jesus," she prayed. "Watch over Dr. Rossi. He's a little crazy but he's really a good man. Cradle him in your arms, like you've cradled me. Give him wisdom. Help him do your will. Keep Satan from him. Lead him right if he's on the wrong path. If he isn't—" She bowed her head, at a loss for what to say, Bible verses racing nonstop through her mind. She felt dizzy and afraid. "If he's not on the wrong path," she whispered, "if he's doing your will," she paused, her hands trembling, "give him grace, give him your favor; in your eyes, let him find grace."

Chapter 12

Friday morning—The Barracks

Sam put down the newspaper. Overnight there'd been a massacre in Africa. He'd just read about it in *The New York Times*. It involved the two countries that had recently gone to war. The aggressor was the side he'd taken the draft cease fire to for Mr. Brown. Apparently, they hadn't liked the terms.

He left his apartment and walked down the hall to the common room in The Barracks, wishing he hadn't seen the photo of the two dead kids. To Sam's way of thinking, when two kids had their heads cut open by machetes, troops should already be on the way, but he was used to the fact that he thought more like a European than an American.

"Hey, how're ya doing?" he said to the guard on duty and the two limo drivers dozing with their feet up on the table.

They mumbled responses. It was still early.

He grabbed a cup and poured himself coffee. By the time the cup was full, Africa was no longer on his mind. He checked the schedule board to see that everything looked all right, and then started planning his day off: a trip upstate to see a man about a motorcycle he'd wanted for over twenty years and, if he could get back in time, an evening at the Jersey docks.

It was a really bad habit left over from his sailing days. The only female companionship many seamen ever got were the whores who met the merchant ships in every port. Sam loved all kinds of women, could land almost any available one he liked, except society broads. He was a too beefy New York Irish type for them. But he'd never gotten over his first real loves, honest-to-God sailors' whores. Dangerous as hell. Sam spent most of his free evenings with his cronies at a bar called Molly Malone's, but since leaving the U.S. merchant marine eighteen years ago, he found he couldn't last much more than six months without an exciting carnal visit to the docks—even if he was seeing a woman. It had been seven, and Sam was restless.

Over the years, he'd watched the New York ports close, saw the old Brooklyn piers go down just off the BQE until there was only one sailors' bar left, hanging on like a ghost as the area got gentrified. When it finally closed, he switched to Jersey, nursing fond memories of the Atlantic Avenue bars that the cops were in almost every night. He yearned to stroll on a pitching deck as if he still had sea legs or at least take a walk beside the water and swap yarns with sailors in the few remaining bars on shore. The seamen were almost all foreign, now, because most ships sailed under cheaper foreign flags. For communication, his French and Italian got him by. Then he'd pick a lady primed for a man who hadn't had a woman in weeks.

The thought was so tempting, he considered forgetting his trip upstate to make sure he could get to the docks. Then he decided he'd waited long enough to own a 1979 T140D Triumph Bonneville Special. It would give him pleasure longer, anyway.

He made his way to the lobby and looked around, as if he were checking his own home before he left. He started up the steps to the door and spotted the beautiful legs of a dancer. He looked up and recognized the woman who'd visited the Secretary of State at Mr. Brown's yesterday. Today she wore a different fur, a gray one, and she looked so good Sam envied the Secretary of State even more.

"Good morning," he said.

She paused when she reached him. "You're Sam, aren't you?

He grinned, his feet moving toward her without instruction.

"Now how did you know my name?"

"I heard the butler say it yesterday."

"I was in a doorman's uniform. I'm surprised you recognize me."

She laughed. "It's obvious there's more to you than doors. Am I right?"

She held her hand out as if Sam should give her his arm. He did.

He escorted her down into the lobby. "Maybe you think so because there's more to you than dancing. Am I right?"

She dropped her jaw and widened her big hazel eyes at him, implying he knew the answer.

"Shall I call up to Mr. Brown's for you?" he asked.

"No." She sat on a cushioned marble bench. "I'm a little early. Keep me company."

Sam looked up at the lobby monitors. He knew the boys were watching him and the woman, hooting and placing bets on what would happen. He hoped he wouldn't disappoint them.

She patted the cushion and he sat down, sure he'd sized her up.

"Do you enjoy it?" he said.

She met his gaze. "Usually. Not yesterday. He's a bastard, you know."

"Who?" he said, concerned.

She looked down at the cream carpet. "You know who I mean."

"I'm sorry. Is he still up there?"

"Sure is," she said and crossed one gorgeous leg over the other. "He's angry I'm alive and his wife's not."

Sam leaned forward, resting his forearms on his thighs. "Don't go back," he said, lowering his voice.

She patted his hand. "Nah. Got to. The rent, you know."

He liked what he saw in her face. She was smart, nice, knew all about men, probably loved the act of copulation, and was just into money a lot. Definitely his kind of broad. "How much do you need?" he said.

She gave him a pitying look. "Five grand."

Sam whistled. "You must be awfully damn good."

"That's the price I set to come back. Believe me, it should have been higher."

Sam didn't want to hear about it, like he hadn't wanted to see those two dead kids in the paper. He knew what men could do to women, what the world could do to people, and sometimes he was a part of it. He couldn't help her. The motorcycle was rapidly returning to first place.

He stood to leave, but she took his hand and said, "Sam, nothing says his highness has to be the first man in."

"Really?"

They smiled at each other, her eyes part mischief, part revenge.

He knew the guys in the back fell off their chairs when she grabbed his hand, but Sam was past caring. He guided her by the elbow into the ballroom, heading for the empty kitchen which had no security cameras since there was nothing to steal, and only one way in and out. Before the door closed behind them, Sam took off her coat and almost fell over backward. She was naked except for her heels and a sheer thong—a seduction that never got old. He stared at the two reasons she hadn't made it as a dancer, but had been a success with the Secretary of State. Her breasts were amazing: large but high and perfectly shaped. They didn't look fake. He'd never seen knockers like that in the Rockettes line. And if she danced in a musical, the music would be overlooked.

He put his hands around them, his thumbs on the plump nipples, and pressed his body to hers. Fifteen strenuous minutes later, Sam bent quivering at a counter, her legs around his waist, his face between her breasts. She hadn't come, but he sure as hell had. Sam wouldn't be visiting the Jersey docks tonight.

When his cell phone rang, he didn't move his body as he retrieved the phone from his jacket pocket. He wanted to stay like this awhile.

"Yes?"

It was his substitute at the front door. "Did you see someone come in, looking for Mr. Brown?" The substitute didn't disguise the amusement in his voice.

"Yeah, yeah."

"Well, they're waiting for her upstairs. Are you gonna take her up?"

Sam sighed and ran his tongue around her nipple. "Yeah, I'll take her up."

He almost grew aroused again, remembering the wild moment when she'd almost come—she'd seemed to fight it. He'd lost it and felt good as hell. Clicking the phone off, he put his fingers between her thighs, but she pulled away.

"I've got to give that to him."

Sam understood. A woman who could orgasm from regular sex was damned exciting. Suck her tits, fondle things, stick it in and sock it to her, and she'd honest-to-god come all over your throbbing cock. The best whores could do it. That's why they cost more. It was one of the things he was addicted to about them. Fakers could be fun, could be sweet, but Sam and men like the Secretary craved the real thing.

Moments later they were in the lobby, Sam having frantically dressed while she scooted across the ballroom to the john. As the elevator doors shut, he kept trying to slip his hands under her coat but she pushed him away, smiling and curling her tongue at him.

"Are we going to get to do this again?" he said.

"I sure as hell hope so."

They kissed until the elevator slowed. When the doors opened, there was Mr. Brown, staring at them, his butler behind him.

"I see you found her," he said and reached for the woman's arm.

Only then did Sam realize he didn't know her name, where she lived. Nothing except she could darned well be the greatest lay in New York.

He watched Mr. Brown pass her off to the butler who examined her from head to toe, arranged her hair, opened and closed her coat, and led her into the apartment.

Sam could do nothing. When she was out of sight, his attention returned to Mr. Brown. They'd never had a dispute so he didn't know how Brown would react. As always, the man looked like an earthly version of God Almighty, staring down at someone insignificant, to whom he'd chosen to be reasonably kind.

"What's the story with Rossi and the reporter?" Brown asked.

Sam looked calmly back at Brown, though he was actually a bit scared. "Still working on it. The maid doesn't know."

"Get on it, Sam. I won't be blind-sided by anything in this building."

Sam nodded and stepped back into the elevator.

"One more thing," Brown said.

"Yes?"

"Don't hump the help."

Sam froze.

After a moment, Brown leaned inside the elevator and pushed the lobby button for Sam.

Chapter 13

Friday morning—Rossi apartment

Felix paused outside the kitchen, as tantalized by the rare smell of frying meat, as he was unsure of what it meant. Had Maggie cooked, or was Frances still campaigning? Worse still, she knew he and Adeline had quarreled last night, though he doubted Adeline would tell Frances why. For the first time, he saw the downside of being in love with Frances's best friend. He had to stay on good terms with both to have peace in his home.

He took a deep breath and entered the kitchen.

Frances was at the stove, her new apron on. She looked up and said, "Don't worry. It's safe. I won't ask questions."

She lifted two fat links with a spatula and plumped them on a plate with a mound of marvelous-looking scrambled eggs.

"If you want to tell me, Flix, that's fine. If not, fine." She put the plate on the table next to folded blue cloth napkins he'd never seen "I didn't eavesdrop and I won't ask Adeline what happened, or let her tell me if you'd rather I didn't. It's us, Flix." She pointed one thumb at her chest and the other at him in a comic gesture. "I want you to know that."

Felix hugged her.

"I know. I'm the best sister on earth. Sit. Eat."

"Just a bite. I've got a lot to do." He looked uncertainly at a mound of something next to the eggs. "Is this another Jewish recipe?"

"Sausage, apples?" She dropped the spatula into the sink. "Flix, you are threatening to be ridic—"

A ringing phone interrupted them.

"I'll get it!" Maggie yelled from her room beside the kitchen.

They looked at each other.

"Do you suppose she heard us?" he said.

Frances shrugged. "Maggie's the sane one around here at the moment." She poured coffee and brought it to him as he bowed his head and said grace, "Bless us Oh Lord, and these thy gifts, which we are about to receive from thy bounty, through Christ, Our Lord. Amen."

He bit into the sausage and Frances continued, "When it comes to you and Adeline, I won't interfere. What we need to discuss, Flix, whether you're ready or not, is Enea's funeral."

Felix put his fork down, knowing what she really meant. "We're not having strangers here."

Frances glared at him. "Our uncle and our cousin aren't strangers. We'll be welcoming family into our home. And I'm not Enea, remember? She might have let Dad boss her because he was her brother, but I'm not her and you're not Dad."

"No, I'm not. But I'm going to honor his wishes. He wanted me to manage this. Why else do you think he wrote the letter to me and not both of us?"

"It's my life, too."

His instincts were still telling him to avoid delay, especially since he had to find a surrogate mother. Quietly, Felix said, "They can't stay here. Fran, I'm sorry."

"That's your final position?"

"For now? Yes, it is."

"Now is the only time that counts!" Frances took off her apron, threw it in the trash and left the room.

He looked down at his plate, wondering what Moses did with his sister when he was getting the tablets off the mount and parting the waters.

He picked up his fork, but Frances suddenly returned, snatched up his plate, and dumped the contents in the sink. Without looking at him, she stormed away again.

"Dr. Rossi?"

He looked up and there was Maggie, her gaze kind. Why, he couldn't imagine. He must have sounded like an ogre, but he had to put his attention on the threads, not on entertaining a houseful of new relatives.

"Dr Rossi?"

That quickly, Felix had forgotten she was there. "Maggie, I hope we didn't disturb you last night or this morning. We're having troubles, family troubles. They'll be settled soon."

She stared at him, a strange expression on her face.

"What did you need, Maggie?"

"Oh! Sam's on the phone. The doorman? He's saying it might be urgent, so it probably is. He wants to come up."

Felix tried to imagine what emergency could cause the doorman to visit for the first time since they'd lived in the building. In his paranoia he thought of the threads, then dismissed that idea.

"I'll see him in the solarium."

On the way, he passed Frances's room, saw she was putting on perfume, and wondered if she was meeting a male friend. Since breaking up with her college boyfriend after their parents died, she never confided, and he never asked, about the men who sometimes picked her up and kept her out all night. She looked unhappy and he felt sorry to have upset her.

"Are you going out?" he called.

She turned her back to him and didn't reply.

From the solarium he heard the front door slam and knew it was Frances leaving. Again he felt besieged because he should have been in the lab already. He looked down into the park and saw a blonde woman riding hard on the bridle path just north of the reservoir. She disappeared under the spreading limbs of London Plane, the park's oldest tree, and then reappeared. For a moment he thought it was Adeline, but decided it was not.

"Dr. Rossi, here's Sam,"

He turned and saw Maggie leading Sam in past the orchids.

"Hello, Sam, come in. May we offer you a cup of coffee?"

Sam glanced at Maggie. "I don't want to put you to any trouble."

"No trouble," Maggie said as she left.

Felix sat on the wrought-iron sofa's cushioned seat and pointed Sam to a matching chair, the sun streaming in as if to clear up the day's confusion.

"You said it was urgent, Sam?"

"It may be."

Felix listened as Sam described his worst fear. The reporter who'd been here wanted to know what he'd brought from Turin and who he would see in the next few days. That meant Jerome Newton was trying to build a story.

"Unbelievable," Felix said out loud.

"What shall I say if he comes back, sir?"

"Well—"

"If you tell me what he's after, I could try to steer him off track, maybe keep more reporters from coming. I know you don't want press here at the building. None of the tenants do."

Felix focused sharply on Sam, who wore too innocent an expression, given that he'd just delivered a barely-veiled threat. Anyone who drew press here for too long would be asked to leave the building. The tenants wanted privacy.

Then Maggie arrived with the coffee. Instead of giving it to Sam, she spoke sharply to him.

"Sam, Dr. Rossi's busy! If he's got anything to tell you, I'm sure he'll let you know. You can go on back down to the door, now."

Sam was obviously taken aback. He, tall and solid, stood and gazed down at smaller Maggie with his mouth ajar.

Disturbed by her interference, Felix said, "Maggie, that's uncalled for!"

Sam, who had been looking mildly irritated, quickly changed. "Uh, Dr. Rossi, don't be mad at Maggie. It's my fault. She's right. I probably shouldn't be taking up your time."

"Thanks, but I would prefer that Maggie not—"

Maggie ignored Felix. She said to Sam, "No, you shouldn't be taking up his time. Dr. Rossi's busy. Go on, now, Sam. Thanks for coming up."

"Maggie, that's enough! I'll thank you not to—" Felix began.

Sam interrupted. "Don't talk to her like that."

When Felix's and Maggie's eyebrows flew up, Sam resumed apologizing and backing to the door. "Sorry, Dr. Rossi. I forgot my place. Like I said, it's me, not her. Don't be angry with Maggie. She's just looking out for you. I'll leave. I shouldn't have barged in like this."

As Sam moved toward the door, she pursued him into the hall, coffee cup in hand. Felix followed her, unsure of what was going on.

Maggie looked back and pointed toward the living room. "Adeline's here to see you, Dr. Rossi," she said, sweetly and obligingly. She continued ushering Sam out the door.

Felix didn't know why she'd done it, but he decided to be grateful. Since his return from Turin, unanticipated events were piling up, while the most precious blood on earth lay in solution in his lab, waiting for him.

"Thank you, Maggie," he said and went to the living room, unable to guess at Adeline's state of mind this morning.

She was in her riding clothes: boots, tan jodhpurs as pale as her hair, a navy blue hunt coat, white shirt, her helmet beside her. It had been Adeline, after all, in the park. He felt uncomfortable that he hadn't recognized her.

"What did you do with Moonless?" he asked. She boarded her black Arabian across the park on W. 89th at The Claremont Riding Academy, with Frances's Andalusian, King.

"I rode with one of the academy people. He walked Moonless back."

"I see." Felix sat across from her, his foot on the low coffee table, waiting for her to open the conversation. He didn't know what to say, except to offer another apology.

Instead of speaking, she reached over and touched his shoe with her boot tip.

He smiled at her. "I suppose I'll never seem normal to you again."

She said, "Probably not," but she smiled and he was glad. It felt awkward to know how she'd felt all these years, that she'd dreamed of his child growing in her body, had yearned for it and he hadn't known. He'd thought they were alike. He felt blind, wondering what else he didn't see.

"Did you rest last night?" he asked.

"No, I didn't really sleep. Did you?"

"No."

She retrieved folded pages from within her jacket and put them on the table. "I thought I'd better educate myself so I went on the Internet."

He picked the pages up.

"It says human cloning is going to be made illegal in this country, Felix."

"Well, it hasn't been yet." He looked seriously at her. "Michigan banned it. Not New York. The U.N. adopted a policy that it ought to be banned, but it hasn't been here in the U.S."

"But the President—"

"Clinton put a five-year moratorium on federal funding of cloning research. That's all. Not private research. Bush has a task force working on it. Reproductive cloning hasn't been outlawed. Yes it might be, but at this moment Congress is still debating."

"Apparently, after the first human embryo was cloned—"

"That one was a farce," Felix said with contempt. "They were pre-embryos that died almost at once. They hadn't divided more than twice and weren't remotely mature. They couldn't have been implanted. They were never viable."

"Nevertheless, Congress is overwhelmingly opposed to reproductive cloning. Only therapeutic cloning is in debate. Some doctors think that if a sick patient is cloned and the embryo's stem cells are harvested, the cells can be used to grow new tissue and organs the patient's body won't reject. Is that right?"

"Yes."

"They're even debating that much—the moral issue of creating life simply to destroy it and save the DNA donor."

"I won't be destroying life," he said, deciding not to mention the multiple pre-embryos he'd have to create to increase his chances. Adeline wasn't a scientist. She didn't care when the primitive streak was formed. To her, life began at conception.

"Felix, why do you even think the clone would be Christ? People are more than their genes."

"Half of these particular genes came from God, Adeline. Maybe all of them did. Maybe The Virgin Mary carried the first clone. I've thought that a long time, in fact. What could God's genes produce but God?"

She stared at him. "Darling, you must be aware that the Pontifical Academy for Life will take a position against human cloning. Maybe it already has."

He rolled his eyes. "Of course it will. But I'm a scientist, and in this I disagree with the Pope. If it could, the Vatican would curtail most of microbiology's contribution to human reproduction. It opposes birth control. Yet, without it, the average woman would have a baby every year. The church closes its eyes to the need to feed and clothe these children it wants born. It ignores the maternal deaths that occur when women's bodies are worn down by constant birth. How could God want more hungry children with fewer mothers? In this our church has failed us, Adeline. It has forced us to think for ourselves. I have. I wish you would, too."

"What about birth defects? Every successful cloning experiment seems to have first produced horribly deformed animals. If—"

"Adeline, my work is not slipshod. I've studied this problem. I feel I know how to avoid it."

"Goodness, Felix! Aren't you even a little afraid of triggering Armageddon? The Apocalypse? That's what's supposed to follow a Second Coming, if you remember!"

Felix gazed at her, disappointed. "Enlightened biblical scholarship rejects the apocalyptic sayings attributed to Jesus and so do I. I thought you did as well. You've actually attended the Jesus Seminar, read everything in the field. Most likely it was the disciples who said all that, not him."

"Most likely, yes, Felix. Yes! That isn't the same as being sure, though, is it? What about the rights of the person being cloned?"

He looked away. That subject he'd been avoiding.

She cleared her throat. "I found this paper from the *Texas Law Review*. It seems to be a fair and honest evaluation, all the pros and cons and issues. It says if human cloning is allowed, agreement of the parties will be central."

"Yes, I know all that."

"Felix." She put her boot down to lean forward and look in his eyes. "Everyone seems to agree that even if reproductive cloning were allowed, legal consent of the DNA donor would be absolutely fundamental, that you can't clone people without permission. With few exceptions, what they'll surely outlaw is cloning the dead since the dead can't give consent! Perhaps they'd allow cloning a child, but surely only with the parents' permission."

Felix rose and walked to the window. He stood between the charcoal drapes and looked up at the morning sun, filtering through the sheers. For a long time he stood there, hoping God would speak into the silence of his heart. His feelings were in limbo. Ethically, she was right. But did human ethics limit God's work on earth? God would surely stop him if He didn't want Jesus reborn.

"There's a reporter sniffing around," he said.

"A reporter?"

"Someone I know. He happened to be there when I went through customs. He's with *The Times* of London"

"Not a London paper. They're worse than ours. They hound people."

"Yes."

"Felix, you've got to stop! Please. Tell me you'll stop!"

He sensed her request was a final one. As he turned around thinking of Jerome Newton, he visualized the reporter's face and his wavy bronze hair. Then he remembered how Adeline had suffered in the restaurant last night. It was his fault, he knew, still it made him angry that her heartbreak had entertained those watching them in the viewing garden. The two images came together. Adeline sobbing. Jerome Newton's wavy bronze hair. Felix had seen it again last night. At the restaurant. One row behind. The man sitting with his back to them had been Jerome Newton. How?

Felix remembered.

As they'd neared 666 Fifth Avenue, as he watched its ominous red neon sign, the limo driver had said: *That car behind us has practically been in my trunk for three blocks*. Had Newton waited out of sight and followed them? Even so, he'd been too far away to hear. Or had he?

"No, Adeline, even if human cloning is banned tomorrow, I won't stop. Jesus wasn't human like you and I. He was divine. I'm so sorry. I hope one day you'll either forgive me or understand. I can't stop. I have to hurry, now."

Adeline whispered, "You realize I don't feel obliged to keep your secret?"

Felix studied her hurt face. "I pray you will."

Adeline's expression went blank, her lovely gray eyes withdrawn, her gentle spirit that had loved him so, gone where he couldn't follow.

Chapter 14

Friday midmorning—Turin, Italy

It was a cold morning in Turin, Italy. Father Bartolo pulled up the collar of his black priest's coat and rose, his bony knees aching. Since last night, the silver casket had been back behind the iron gates in the altar's black marble tabernacle. The scientists would be here another few days, conferring, but life in the Duomo had resumed as the church awaited the outcome of the new tests. More photographs, more pollen samples, more of any test that didn't deface the Shroud. Results were due in a year. He knew they wouldn't settle anything.

Every morning Bartolo came here to the Capella Della Sacra Sindone, the chapel at the top of the stairs in the Duomo. He came to pray beneath the Holy Shroud and ask God to reveal its secret. He wanted to know the truth— whether from a scientist or a holy revelation, he didn't care. Before he died, he wanted to know. Had Jesus, The Savior, really lain beneath this cloth? Was the image of Him? Were these His scars, His wounds, His blood? On the day Bartolo died, would the face on the Shroud be the one he saw—ever living, crowned in glory, hands held forth in love?

Every morning Bartolo wept here, surrounded by Guarini's angels, wishing they were real. He yearned to be where they were, there with Jesus. Then he'd never again perform Last Rites at the bedside of a child and hold its inconsolable father, hold its mother, because words could not reach them. He'd never have to kneel and pray with an imprisoned man and watch his tears fall too late to save him. Most of all, he wouldn't have to face the doubts of those who would believe if Bartolo could only convince them that God lives. That He made us. On His feet we walk. Into His arms we fall. His is the wing by which the dying rise.

For this last reason more than the rest, Father Bartolo prayed the Holy Shroud was real. He wanted the scientists to prove it was the burial cloth of Christ. At first he'd been surprised at their hesitancy, their caution. Then he'd been deeply disappointed. But finally bold ones had taken the initiative and proved the carbon datings might be wrong. Then the Church itself had reacted with hesitancy and caution, refusing to let Dr. Felix Rossi's team cut more samples from the Shroud. On that day his disappointment had been so deep, Father Bartolo stayed in his bed, took no confessions, heard no prayers, said no masses.

Slowly, he descended the black marble stairs that led from the chapel. Down in the Duomo, he walked the center aisle of the Latin cross, genuflected at the back and dipped his fingers in holy water before he left.

In the Piazza Castello, he waited for a boy who was peddling nearer on a bike.

"Buongiorno, padre. Come sta?" the boy shouted and threw Bartolo a copy of *The Times* of London.

"Buongiorno! Bene grazie!" Bartolo replied and looked up at the beautiful sky. "Che bella giornata!"

"Si, si. Ciao caio."

"Ciao!" Bartolo waved, tucked the paper under his arm and looked off toward the snowy pre-Alpine hills. Then he went to eat the good breakfast cooked by the Poor Clare nuns.

Chapter 15

Friday morning—Felix's lab

When Felix unlocked his lab at the end of the hall it was past 10:00 a.m. Adeline had stayed, trying to dissuade him, until just moments ago.

He closed the door behind him, looked at the Shroud replica on the wall, at the expensive equipment that surrounded him. Was it only a coincidence that Mount Sinai had refused him space for all his projects, forcing him to build his own lab?

He let himself think of what he'd lost in the last forty-eight hours. Adeline's love. His sister's trust. Leadership of the team he'd assembled in Turin. Peace of mind.

The idea of suffering didn't bother him because Jesus had suffered. What bothered him was the fear he might fail. Jesus hadn't.

He said the words that came to mind, "Yea though I walk through the valley of the shadow of death, I shall fear no evil for thou art with me."

Someone knocked on the door. He pushed the intercom button.

"Yes?"

"It's Maggie, Dr. Rossi."

"Maggie, I'm—"

"I've got something for you."

Felix opened the door and she stood there with a breakfast tray. It made him realize he was famished. He followed her to the kitchen and quickly ate every bite as Maggie hovered, wiping surfaces. He thanked her sincerely and rushed back to the lab.

In the prep room he put on a clean lab coat, a mask, a hair cap and washed his hands, then he went straight to the incubator and opened it. There was the solution, just as he had left it.

His thoughts scrambled in his eagerness to begin. Once he extracted and cultured the blood cells, he'd have only a certain window of time. Cells couldn't remain in culture forever. Everything else should be in place before he began. He should order equipment now for their place at Cliffs Landing, which was where he'd work with the mother.

He closed the incubator, removed his gloves and sat at his desk, thinking of how he had no mother for the clone and finding one could be the hardest part. He knew better than to expect Adeline to change her mind, though he hoped she would. His next option was the church. He and Frances attended mass at The Church of St. Thomas More. He knew several young women in their parish—or, rather, they seemed to know him. One in particular might be suitable, but at the moment he couldn't think of her name. If he went to every mass and church activity for a week, he'd see her or perhaps find someone else. Maybe something would click. If not, he'd have to explore with his lawyer the idea of hiring a surrogate mother. At least he knew they existed. He decided to get the church schedule and plan all else around it.

But if the Shroud DNA wasn't perfect, it could take weeks to repair and he had no guarantee of success. Without useable DNA, everything else was pointless.

He opened the middle drawer and withdrew his journal, something bothering him. He glanced at the journal, at his pens, at the phone books, the catalogs and the phone, knowing something was wrong, but not seeing what it was. Maybe his nerves were over exercised. Maybe he was starting to feel jet lagged.

He went to the prep room sink and filled a beaker with water, thinking of the accident when he was nine. After being hit by a car he'd lain unconscious for days, but he woke with an impression of drinking water from a straw. He'd learned his mother, believing water cures all ills, had stayed at his bed, trying to make him sip water from a straw. In times of sickness or stress, he still did. He returned to his desk with a stomach full of water, renewed faith in the DNA, and a determination to stop wasting time.

First he arranged to visit an in-vitro fertilization lab to obtain eggs slated for destruction, but if he ran out of time, he could skip this step. He didn't feel the need to practice. He felt certain he could create a viable embryo if he had good DNA. He called his church and got the schedule, went through the catalogs and circled the equipment he would need. He called the company that had installed his lab and his father's medical office. Yes, they'd remain on notice to come out to Cliffs Landing when he called. He phoned his lawyer to arrange the necessary permits.

It took less than thirty minutes. He had an hour before the 12:15 p.m. mass. There'd be another at 5:30 p.m. He would go to both.

Felix pulled up his surgical mask, preparing to begin by separating the whole blood cells from cell fragments using fractionation, a method that sorted by density and size. It would take forty-five minutes for the necessary gradients to form. He could finish in time for the noon mass.

Again there was a knock on the lab door.

He went to the intercom, deciding to put up a *Do Not Disturb* sign.

"Who is it?

"It's Maggie."

"Maggie, I've already said I'm busy. Unless it's urgent, I'll talk to you later."

"Please let me in, Dr. Rossi."

"Is it urgent or not?"

"Please!"

He swung the door open. Maggie stood there, looking worried and uncertain, gloves on her hands as if she meant to clean. He pulled down his mask.

"Maggie, for heaven's sake, I've asked you not to disturb me! What's the matter?"

She wrung her hands. "I—"

"What? What? I'm very busy."

She squeezed her eyes shut, suddenly trembling. "I know what you're doing."

"What?" he said, not grasping what she meant.

"I know," she whispered. "You're trying to clone Jesus."

Felix pulled her inside the lab, regretting he hadn't fired her yesterday.

"And just what makes you think such a thing?"

Maggie was breathing hard, both hands over heart. "I'm a snoop. I can't help it."

"A snoop?" Then he realized what had been wrong at the desk. He'd left his journal out last night, not in the desk drawer. Someone had moved it. He slapped his cheek and groaned, "Maggie, Maggie, don't do this. Please!"

"Dr. Rossi, it's all right," she said, wringing her hands again. "Nobody else knows. Just you and me and Adeline. She might not help, but I bet she won't tell. And I can keep a secret through this life and the next, if I've got to."

"You are wrong about this, Maggie!"

She continued in a hurried, gasping voice, as if she hadn't heard him.

"And what kind of trouble can that reporter cause, except making a nuisance out of himself? What can he say? He doesn't really know anything. He doesn't have a lick of proof. Don't they still need at least a little proof to print things? All you have to do is not give him any. He's got to know you could sue him if he named you. As for Sam, leave him to me. I'll see he minds his business."

Felix shook his head. "Maggie, I don't understand you. Why did you come into my lab and read my journal? Why are you here now?"

She stepped closer, tears springing to her eyes. Felix thought if one more woman cried in his presence he'd go mad.

"I'm the one."

"What?"

"Let me do it. I know I can."

Felix's mouth gaped open in shock. He surveyed the woman before him as if for the first time. Her skin was richly dark—a burnt sienna—her hair short. Her features were quite plain, at least by Anglo-Saxon beauty standards. She had the physique of whatever African tribe's blood was in her veins—wiry arms, thin legs, strong thighs, anthropoid hips, an ample behind. The only notable thing about her were the brown eyes now pleading with him.

"Even if I pretended to know what you're talking about—" he began, but her look stopped him. She'd read his journal; he couldn't lie. As Maggie folded her slim arms he wondered how old she was, and then dismissed the thought.

"You think God is dumb or something?" she continued, gulping air. "You think he doesn't have any better sense than to let me see this stuff, since I'm like I am?"

Felix looked toward the door, wishing he could magically transport through it, but there was no escape.

"What is it that you are, Maggie?"

"I'm the one."

He propped his chin in his hands and closed his eyes.

"I'm the one because I don't care what happens. I don't care if you mess up and give me some disease. I don't care what people will say. I don't care. I'll sign any papers you want to prove it—"

He grew angry. "Stop this! I want you to stop this!"

"Why? Because I'm black?" She went to his desk and picked up one of his journals. They had all his notes, discoveries, wild guesses. They had his fears and yearnings on page after page. If she'd read them, she knew things Frances didn't, even what had happened when he was nine.

"It might not make a difference who the woman is. You wrote that here yourself." Her tears overflowed and he felt for her. She was a woman pleading for a child—no different than Adeline had been last night. "Maybe nobody's got to worry he'll have my kinky hair. If all he needs is health, love, strength and common sense from a mother, I've got them four things, Dr. Rossi."

"Maggie, listen, I—I'm not really doing this, I'm just, just—"

"Excuse me, but you are lying, Dr. Rossi."

He laughed, though he felt sorrow in his heart. "You have no idea what you're asking. Even if I were doing what you say, no one would believe—"

"That a sister is carrying Jesus? None of your people you mean. Mine won't have any problem with it, assuming they believe it could happen in the first place. I've been trying to think like Jesus would, Dr. Rossi. Who would he pick? Who would he? Adeline's beautiful and Adeline's good. No doubt about it. But would Jesus pick her for a mother? She's rich as sin. She doesn't have a care in the world except how you been acting. She's got everything, in fact. But his first mother wasn't like that. Wouldn't Jesus be looking for somebody like Mary? A woman who's an outcast like the Jews were in them days? They don't treat Jews like that over here. It's blacks this country kicks around." She pointed to herself.

"It's likely Mary was from the House of David and not especially outcast."

"You mean Luke 1:32? That's just a maybe. In Luke 1:47-48 she said with her own mouth, 'My spirit hath rejoiced in God my Saviour. For he hath regarded the low estate of his handmaiden.' I'm of low estate, too, Dr. Rossi!"

Listening to Maggie, he saw an image of ex-husbands or ex-lovers popping up and demanding payment. Just as quickly he felt guilty for his thought.

She pressed the advantage she thought she had. "Right now, you ain't *got* nobody else. Not a soul."

He never liked it when she started saying, "ain't."

When he didn't answer, she came gently to him, pulling off her plastic gloves as she did. To him, the motion seemed symbolic since the gloves protected her from accidental contact with dangerous things as she cleaned. She held his gaze all the while, reached out and took his hand and put it to her cheek.

"Sir, you are blessed and so am I. We've been chosen, don't you see that?"

He recognized the sudden intimacy between them. It was from the residue of grace God had left in the world. Felix had felt it all his life. Until last night, he'd thought Adeline did, too.

Maggie wasn't crying now. Her face showed no fear. "I don't care if I die, Dr. Rossi. If Jesus wants to come among us, let him come by me."

Chapter 16

Friday afternoon—Sam's apartment

When Sam left the Rossis' apartment, his already high opinion of Maggie had increased. She'd obviously listened to the conversation Rossi and he had in the solarium. He would have enjoyed verbally sparring with her, but he couldn't let her risk her job just to herd his Irish butt out the door where it belonged. Rossi, a rich man used to having his way, might not realize he shouldn't fire his mouthy maid, but give her a raise. It had annoyed Sam when Rossi started berating her. Rossi was book smart, but probably stupid about a lot of real life.

Maggie wasn't. Sam couldn't afford to further rouse her suspicions. He'd have to take the route he'd tried to avoid.

Once again, his purchase of a '79 T140D Bonneville Special would have to wait. There'd be no trip upstate today. He returned to his apartment, went to the kitchen and opened a small pantry door. He removed a plastic screw cap beneath a shelf, revealing a hidden keyhole in which he inserted a special key. A door swung open, shelves and all. He entered and flicked on the light.

Monitors like those in the common room were lined up on a desk, gathering dust, except these weren't trained on the public areas or used by the building guards. They were linked to hidden pinhole cameras. There was a multichannel amplifier, linked to tiny hidden mikes, though he wasn't sure all of them still worked. No one else but Brown knew this room existed and no one had access but Sam.

When Mr. Brown bought the building ten years earlier, he'd ordered new electronic smoke detectors installed in nearly every room of every apartment on every floor except his own, to cover what he was really doing. Cameras and bugs were almost everywhere, so hidden you'd have to tear out the building wiring to find them. Sam had supervised their installation and set up this secret room to monitor them. It wasn't the first time he'd wired a building for surveillance.

He'd bugged his whole house when he was just a kid, concentrating on his older sister's bedroom. He ran wires from the basement and installed speakers, telling the family he was bringing music in, which was true. He hadn't mentioned the speakers could double as microphones. Listening to his sister and her friends, Sam had learned the truth about them. They talked about love all the time, unaware the boys they considered dreamy, only dreamed of getting in their pants. After a while he felt ashamed and three months after he put them in, took out all the bugs.

Now the shamed feeling returned. Brown didn't know he'd used this setup only once. He thought Sam spied on the tenants frequently. Sam didn't. When he needed information on innocent people, he got it in less underhanded ways. He hadn't been a voyeur since he'd listened in on his sister and her friends.

He sat at his hidden surveillance desk, dusting it off and imagining what Maggie would say if she could see it. Her snooping was nothing compared to this. Mr. Brown might have lived in a private, gated mansion like the ones he had in Malta and the Caribbean, or in one of the large townhouses he owned in the area. Instead he hid in plain sight—among ordinary rich people, in an ordinary building, on a well-known street in New York—because he had the means to know what every tenant did. Not using this room was Sam's only disloyalty to Brown.

Sam switched on the monitor for Rossi's apartment, wiped dust off the screen and clicked through the rooms. Rossi wasn't in the solarium, the library, the living room, dining room, kitchen, the pantry, Maggie's room, his sister's room, his room, or the guest room. He must be in his lab, the one place other than Sam's apartment and the ballroom kitchen that didn't have secret surveillance because they had to be inspected by the city. He switched to the hall and laughed out loud. Maggie was tiptoeing down it. She stopped at the last door, and put her ear against it.

It hadn't escaped Sam's attention that she hadn't gone home since Rossi arrived. That alone told him something was going on.

His cell phone rang. It was Brown's butler calling to say Sam was wanted in the penthouse.

"Yes, I'll be right up," he said.

As he got off the elevator and entered Brown's foyer, he looked for any sign of his dancer. He'd wanted to ask the boys downstairs to keep an eye out, but he knew they'd tell if Brown inquired. They always did what he wanted. In various ways, Brown had made it clear to building staff that he didn't enjoy the word, *no*, unless he himself was saying it.

"This way," the butler said. He looked irritated with Sam, probably for humping their dancer—Brown's gift to the Secretary of State. The butler was a perfectionist, which for Brown must have outweighed the fact he was a pain.

Brown stood at one of the library shelves, a book open in one large hand, the other resting thoughtfully in his platinum hair.

"Come in, Sam. Have you read Aeschylus?"

Sam shook his head and sat down, recognizing Brown's philosophical mode. It meant he wanted something big to begin, end or change. Because it was important, he would frame its introduction with the learning of the ages. Sam felt like he was waiting for an oracle to speak.

"Aeschylus was the first of the great Greek tragedians. One of his most famous tragedies is called *Prometheus Bound*. You know the story of Prometheus?"

"I learned it in school but it doesn't come to mind."

"In Greek myth, he was the Titan who stole fire from heaven and gave it to man as a gift. Zeus, king of the gods, was displeased. He punished Prometheus by chaining him to a rock where every day an eagle feasted on his ever-renewing liver. He was told:

> And every hour shall bring its weight of woe
> To wear thy heart away; for yet unborn
> Is he who shall release thee from thy pain.
> This is thy wage for loving humankind.
> For, being a God, thou dared'st the Gods' ill will,
> Preferring, to exceeding honour, Man.

Brown's eyes narrowed in amusement. "Stealing from the gods carries a gruesome penalty."

Sam almost flinched, thinking of the dancer. Then he relaxed. Brown wasn't needlessly heavy-handed.

Brown put down his book and picked up another. "Sadly, Greek and Roman classics such as this were lost to the west after the Roman Empire fell. Any idea who preserved them, Sam?"

"Not really."

"The Semitic people. The Arabs and the Jews. Christian Europe rarely acknowledges they owe the Renaissance, which ended their Dark Ages, to the Arabs and the Jews. Without them, English poets like Percy Shelley wouldn't have been the classicists they were. Shelley recast Aeschylus's lost play, *Prometheus Unbound*, in a great poem of his own of the same name. In it, Prometheus and mankind triumph over the gods.

> We have passed Age's icy caves,
> And Manhood's dark and tossing waves,
> And Youth's smooth ocean, smiling to betray:
> Beyond the glassy gulfs we flee
> Of shadow-peopled Infancy,
> Through Death and Birth, to a diviner day;

Sam stared. He didn't have a clue where this was going.

Brown went to his desk, picked up the folded section of a newspaper and tossed it on the table by Sam's chair and said, "Through Death and Birth, to a diviner day."

Sam picked it up and read the circled paragraph in the London Times:

Cloning in America

Want to be the mother of Julius Caesar? How about Mozart? Buddha? Go to America. According to those ever-handy reliable sources, a distinguished scientist who lives across the pond has deluded himself into thinking he has authentic DNA from perhaps the most influential figure in all of history and—not joking here—plans to clone him. Come on, America. Pretend you're a civilized country, for once. Ban reproductive human cloning and stick to therapeutic cloning like the rest of us. We British aren't keen on doing George Washington again. Do you relish another go with Al Capone?

Sam looked up at Mr. Brown and thought he saw real fear in his eyes.

"*The Times* doesn't often get it wrong, even when indulging in typical British sarcasm."

"Yeah, I know."

"Is someone stealing fire from heaven, trying to topple Zeus from his throne? Trying to give man what once belonged to gods? If it's true, find out who."

Sam didn't need to be told to stop playing doorman for a while and revert to private detective, using the resources of one of their dummy corporations, as required. Exactly what Brown would do with the information, Sam didn't know and would never ask. Mr. Brown was the captain, and a good one. He decided where to sail the ship. Sam only had to steer it and he was good at that.

"Consider it done."

Brown tossed Sam another sealed envelope. "For our friend at the consulate again."

Sam pocketed it. "Yes, sir."

"How was she?"

"Who?" Sam asked, startled.

"The girl. How was she?"

Sam blew out air and looked away. "Great. Maybe the best."

"What did she say about the Secretary?"

He looked at Brown and saw it was a serious question. "She said he was a bastard."

Brown picked up his book again. "Smart girl. You know, I've always envied and loathed Percy Shelley's father. To have such an excellent talent in your care and then crush it because of stupidity and misplaced morals. If he'd had a better father, Shelley wouldn't have gone sailing in a storm and killed himself."

"That's what he did?"

"Yes. He wrote:

> There are mincing women, mewing, …
> Of their own virtue, and pursuing
> Their gentler sisters to that ruin,
> Without which—what were chastity?

"I have a fondness for whores, too," Sam said.

"Shelley died on the afternoon of July 8, 1822. He was twenty-nine. Just twenty-nine. His father was responsible. He was a bad steward. That's what comes of bad stewardship, Sam."

Brown raised his eyes and stared directly into Sam's, something he rarely did. His message was clear. The dancer was one of many things in the world under his stewardship.

Sam stood. "I'll be going if that's all."

"That's all." Brown returned to reading Percy Shelley's poems.

Alone in the elevator, Sam whistled Too-ra loo-ra-loo-ral to himself, thinking of the splendid fifteen minutes he'd had with the dancer and never would again.

————

When Sam left, Brown's eye fell on his least favorite lines of Shelley's *Alastor*:

> Mother of this unfathomable world!
> … I have made my bed
> In charnels and on coffins, where black death
> Keeps record of the trophies won from thee,
> Hoping to still these obstinate questionings
> Of thee and thine, by forcing some lone ghost,
> Thy messenger, to render up the tale
> Of what we are.

He snorted contemptuously. "Well, black death, if you are keeping a record of the trophies I have won, hell must be running out of ink."

Closing Shelley's collected works, he put it back in its spot on the shelf labeled English Romantics. In his entire life, Brown couldn't remember feeling afraid so he had nothing with which to compare the inner hollowness, the sense of dread, that he'd masked when talking to Sam.

He thought of his Chestnut-haired dancer and wished for her company, which surprised him. He wasn't a man weak for women. Still he sat down, tapped on a monitor and watched as she entertained Congressman Dunlop in the guest bedroom. It involved no touching. Unlike the Secretary of State, the Congressman was married. He wanted to be able to tell his wife he hadn't screwed another woman. Her job was to stand over him, naked, and amuse herself as a fully clothed Dunlop watched and did the same. Today Brown had overridden that order.

As Dunlop approached the point of no return, the dancer did as she'd been told and lowered herself onto him. Dunlop didn't resist. He couldn't. He was weak. Brown would now have video of the event, which was surprisingly prolonged in spite of the fact that Dunlop paused to cry. His dancer was poignant in her concern, but relentless. Good girl.

The video would very likely never be seen. Dunlop would continue to be pampered and cajoled, but Brown would make sure he sensed a hidden threat. Brown might have greater need of Dunlop soon.

He turned the monitor off and opened a drawer that contained the source of his unease. A folder. Leather-bound. In gold letters: *Death Scopes*. A name invented by the astrologer who'd written them at his father's bidding thirty years ago and covered herself by warning that they weren't always correct. He'd felt contempt for his father's willingness to submit to another's mind, but his father had said knowledge of death was as vital as knowledge of life to those who would be powerful. That's why princes and kings from time immemorial had consulted the stars.

Brown informed his father that he didn't believe in beliefs, especially superstitions. His father's success was his own, not due to the stars. Corporations that made mergers, politicians who announced their candidacies, only when an astrologer told them to were deluded.

Death Scopes were, of course, ridiculous.

The astrologer had reported that Uranus, bringer of sudden electrifying events, was the ruler of his father's 8th house of death. It was in his 9th house of foreigners and foreign countries and in a water sign. He would drown in a foreign country. Brown had sneered at the prediction until his father's yacht was struck by lightning and floundered off the coast of Malta in a rare Mediterranean storm, drowning him.

The astrologer had also written a description of Brown's personality:

With your Sun and Mars in Leo in the 4th house of home: you are a king who will boldly reign from the privacy of your own castle. With all planets but two below the horizon: your activities will be unknown to the world.

This was obviously correct, as were other of the astrologer's conclusions: *You will take a comfort close to fondness in those who work for you, as if they were extensions of yourself. You will feel the need to be fair to them and of use to the world. A threat to national security will be felt as personal. You will assist the country more than once.* He had.

Your feelings, instincts and decision-making work in automatic harmony. You take all perceptions personally and have a swift and imaginative mind. Your thoughts are penetrating, probing, fearless. You seek to control outcomes but not from fear since you experience inner peace, clarity of mind and intent.

All this was true.

You enjoy owning beautiful things but forming true bonds with others does not come naturally. Also true.

The most powerful and portentous aspect of your birthchart is the exact Jupiter/Saturn conjunction ninety degrees from your Sun. This makes you cautious, conservative, contemptuous of excess, aiming to preserve a substantial material inheritance. In some sense, on this earth, I daresay you want to be the only God. In this you will succeed, to some extent.

Incredible.

He was a rational modern man, but it had been a strain to ignore his *Death Scope*, given the accuracy of this part, on top of his father's death. Brown had, indeed, consciously modeled himself on the God of the Bible. He'd created a private kingdom for the joy of doing so, taking care to deny others access to his power. When strings were to be pulled, he pulled them. There was no hierarchy that could be wrested from his control. Those who did his bidding were personal disciples—privileged, coddled and very well paid. With rare exceptions—the butler, Sam, his dancer—they knew only him, not each other. Even these three had minimal contact until Sam entertained himself in the ballroom kitchen. His dancer had volunteered the information in response to the merest question, affirming his trust in her. Good girl.

Brown controlled them all through their gratitude and the awe he intentionally inspired. Like the God of the Bible he did virtually no smiting— and not on American shores, unless it was unavoidable. People remembered smiting, resented it and rebelled. Brown's severest interventions appeared natural, or like acts of God.

In all things, he practiced what his father had called the meritorious minimal. Just like the astrologer said.

Brown turned to his Death Scope.

With no apparent fear of being thought a fool, the astrologer had asserted as follows: *The Star of Bethlehem had just risen above the horizon when you were born. It is the Jupiter/Saturn conjunction in your chart. Wise men from the east saw the one of their time as a symbol of the birth of a king. It occurred in Pisces, associated with the Jews. At your birth, the conjunction was reoccurring—as it does every twenty years. However for you it is in the sign of Taurus and rules your*

8th house of death from the 12th house of hidden things, including assassins.

It is possible you will die outdoors on dry land at the hand of an assassin worthy of respect who is motivated by the birth, or rebirth, of a king. Strangely, since the 12th house is the natural home of Pisces, the sign of the Jews, it may— literally or figuratively—be the same king the wise men sought.

Brown had been in his late twenties at the time. He'd laughed, told his father he'd keep an eye out for the Second Coming and ignored the *Death Scope* until his father drowned.

Now this.

He closed the folder and locked it away with the article, *Cloning in America,* from *The Times*. It said the person being cloned was perhaps the most influential figure in all of history. Brown knew who that was. Did *The Times?*

Chapter 17

Monday p.m.—Church of St. Thomas More, New York

A small sea of black-clad bodies, now and then crowned by fashionable hats, moved through the high wrought-iron gates, up the graceful granite steps and through the arched mahogany doors of The Church of St. Thomas More. Its location off Museum Mile between Park Avenue and Madison meant its parishioners were the elite of Catholic New York.

Inside, their church was just like them.

Above the altar a single exquisite stained-glass window, a simple carved crucifix below, the altar plainly adorned, pews of solid wood, polished square tiles on the floor, a few statues and wood carvings of saints, beautiful flowers gently arranged, a small organ with good sound. Nothing fancy, nothing showy. Everything simple, tasteful, elegant and, in quality, rich as sin.

At the moment, Frances Rossi didn't feel a sense of belonging. She sat in the front row next to an uncle and a cousin she'd met only yesterday. Felix, aware of her frosty anger, sat at the far end next to Maggie. Behind them was Adeline, whom Frances, until now, hadn't seen or spoken to in three days.

At first Frances had been overjoyed at the discovery of her hidden heritage and its prospect of relatives untold, because it offered the kind of family experience she'd always longed for. More. More people who looked like them, talked and thought like them. More who belonged to that trusted inner circle to which she'd seen two outsiders admitted in her whole lifetime and one was Adeline. The other was Maggie, the maid, though Felix hadn't always seemed to realize that. Even she hadn't intentionally been admitted. Maggie had arrived there spontaneously somehow and Frances was glad. It was often lonely in the privacy of the Rossi family.

These past three days had been the loneliest of all. Just when she'd found the larger family she'd dreamed of but hadn't known, Frances had somehow lost the smaller one she'd always had. For the past three days, Adeline claimed to have previous commitments, and Felix had grown invisible. He stayed locked up in his lab. Instead of keeping Maggie out like he'd said, she was locked in with him. Maggie emerged on Sunday to go to her Baptist church and home for a change of clothes. Otherwise, she came out only to sleep or order food for them. She looked engrossed, but unhappy. Dust was piling up in every room.

Once when Frances banged on the door and demanded an explanation, it was Maggie, not Felix, who answered saying, *Dr. Rossi is very busy, Miss Rossi. He knows you want to help him. I wish he'd let me help more, too, but he won't. Don't feel he doesn't love you because he does.*

The indignity of having her maid—never mind that it was Maggie—cryptically explaining her brother's absence was so unexpectedly humiliating, Frances didn't go near the lab again.

Before, he'd gone to mass only on Sundays. Now Felix went twice a day, saying only. "Hi, going to mass," as he left. Once she followed and saw him stalking women outside the church as if he were trolling in a bar. That's when she'd first called Adeline, to no avail.

He'd done the same this morning, right near Enea's casket, buttonholing for a good twenty minutes Sylvia Canady who lived on Park Avenue just up from The Dalton School where in their childhood she and Flix were taught via Helen Parkhurst's Dalton Plan. It emphasized taking control of your life.

Worst of all for Frances was being alone at the airport when Uncle Simone Fubini and his daughter, Cousin Letizia, arrived in America for Enea's funeral. Felix should have been there to greet the man who looked just like their father: a tall, slim man square at the shoulders, with expressive hands; deep-set compassionate eyes in a round, almost elfin face. He cried as he held her in his arms. Cousin Letizia—who knew a little English—translated their broken words of joy, then added tears and hugs of her own. Looking at Letizia had been like looking into a sister's face. The same auburn hair. The Rossi nose.

There'd been silence when they pulled up to a hotel—a fine hotel, but not the home where Uncle Simone's niece and nephew lived. Frances had seen the flash of pain on Uncle Simone's face. It hinted at a past of trials beyond her comprehension and made her ashamed to have a brother who refused to hold this uncle in his arms.

Only just now had they met. On the church steps, Felix recognized Uncle Simone without an introduction, either because he looked so much like their father or because of the yarmulke he wore. Apparently feeling obligated, he'd walked up and said, "I'm Felix. Very sorry about your sister. We loved her."

Now Enea lay before them in her coffin. She would never know how awful Felix had been to their relatives. Their father's favorite rosary lay in her hands. Enea had lived as a Catholic and asked for a Catholic funeral. Once committed, always committed. That's how Rossis were.

Frances had made a commitment, too. Something for Uncle Simone, to help him with his grief. Felix didn't know and she was glad. In her opinion, he needed a shock. She had arranged it with their pastor who had already organized a number of Catholic-Jewish conferences, trying to heal two thousand years of mistrust between their faiths. The pastor had been sympathetic to her plight. She'd also asked him to speak to Felix, but he'd said it was better to let Felix come to him.

Uncle Simone patted her hand as they neared the end of the service, and the pastor announced, "We will have a special ceremony in honor of those who have joined us from afar."

Uncle Simone rose and went to the front. He draped a prayer cloth he called a tallit around his neck, and stood beside his sister's coffin. A rabbi came forward, bowed, and tore the right side of Simone's shirt.

She glanced at Felix, who turned and stared at her with hurt confusion in his eyes. Served him right.

In the back, men in yarmulkes and prayer cloths stood, because this couldn't be done without a minyan—ten adult Jewish males. She'd borrowed them from the Park Avenue Synagogue and been touched at how readily they'd agreed to pray, even in a Catholic church, when she told them the story of Enea, Simone and his daughter. It helped that the church and the synagogue had already held a number of interfaith marriage ceremonies. In New York they happened all the time.

Uncle Simone had asked for the privilege of reciting the ancient Jewish prayer for mourners, the Kaddish, as his duty and last honor to the sister he'd lost so long ago.

In a deep, resonant voice, Uncle Simone chanted in Hebrew while Cousin Letizia whispered the translation she must have practiced in advance, "Glorified and sanctified be God's great name throughout the world, which He has created according to His will."

The beauty of the chanted prayer as it echoed in the church shot tears to Frances's eyes. In the silence, Uncle Simone's strong voice broke. He wiped unembarrassed tears away and continued.

"May He establish His kingdom in your lifetime and during your days, and within the life of the entire House of Israel, speedily and soon; and say, Amen."

The minyan responded:

"May His great name be blessed forever and to all eternity."

Frances suddenly longed for her lost heritage. Through her tears, she saw surprise on many faces and didn't care. She heard rustling and the creak of benches as the congregation turned, heard whispers around her as they realized that if this Jewish man was their aunt's brother, then Felix and Frances must be Jewish, too, at least i part. Heads turned in their direction, but Felix hadn't looked at them. He kept his eyes on Frances as they listened to Uncle Simone's reverent voice and his ancient prayer.

When he finished, Uncle Simone returned to his seat, and the congregation knelt to pray. Frances cast a triumphant glance down the row toward her brother, expecting to see anger on his face. Instead, he and Maggie prayed as if Enea's loss had so utterly shattered them, only by the grace of God could they ever expect wholeness again.

Frances made a decision. When the funeral was over, she would go back home, knock on the door at the end of the hall, bang on it, shout, start a fire. Whatever it took, she'd get into that goddamned lab.

Chapter 18

Church of St. Thomas More

Maggie stood outside the Church of St. Thomas More saying goodbye to the Rossis' relatives from Italy. She wished she hadn't worn her Graham Smith hat to the funeral. She'd done it to honor Enea Rossi Evans because it was the best hat she had, but nobody else had worn one thing that wasn't black. Black suits, dresses, shoes, socks, stockings, pocketbooks, gloves, coats, and hats. Half the men even wore black shirts. It was funny, in a way. All the white folks had worn 100 percent black, and the one black person wore the only white. Maggie wanted to take the hat off but feared it would be crushed in the crowd if it didn't stay on her head.

"Our enjoy meet of you," their cousin, Letizia, said in the worst English Maggie had ever heard. Maggie started to reply when she saw Dr. Rossi rushing away.

"Excuse me, everyone."

She hurried after him and whispered, "Dr. Rossi! Go on back there with your sister, and talk to your relatives like you should! Ain't you going to the graveyard?"

He stopped. "Enea knew I loved her because of how I treated her when she was alive. She isn't in that coffin, anyway, and I've said my goodbyes. I'm leaving and you should, too! We have work to do, remember?"

"Humph!" she said. "You mean you have work to do. It don't seem to concern me except for taking notes, making calls, and cleaning up. I'm glad to help, but—"

"Not here, Maggie, for goodness sake. We're leaving."

Maggie watched him continue toward Fifth Avenue while Sylvia Canady stared at the well-bred, handsome scientist who'd asked her what she thought of surrogate motherhood and if it was something she would ever do. Maggie had overheard the conversation. She caught up and walked beside him, looking longingly across the street toward Central Park.

"Dr. Rossi, can't we walk in the park for a minute before we shut ourselves back up in the lab? You're burdening yourself more than Pharaoh burdened the Hebrews. Me, too."

He looked irritated, then sighed. "For a minute."

They crossed the street and walked until they reached 96th. "Do you know the name of this gate?" he asked as they came to an entrance in the park's gray stone walls.

"Nope, what is it?"

"It's Woodmen's Gate. The park has eighteen named gates. The one north of us on 102nd is called Girl's Gate. Opposite it on Central Park West, there's Boy's Gate at 100th."

"Is that right?" She looked up at Dr. Rossi whose eyes seemed focused on the past.

"What other gates are there, Dr. Rossi?"

"Inventors' Gate, Merchants' Gate, Women's Gate. Stranger's Gate across the park on 106th."

"A park that welcomes strangers. That's nice."

"This was our playground, Frances and I. We'd skate outside on Wollman Rink in winter, New York towering around us, and we still do, now and then. We sailed our boats when it was warm." He laughed. "Sometimes we sneaked into the Zoo just to prove we could, or spied on outdoor diners at the Tavern on the Green. We used to walk like Egyptians when we played at Cleopatra's Needle behind the Metropolitan Museum. We'd pretend the hieroglyphs on the stone stele spelled out our names. Christian names." He paused. "Now I know a Jewish man named Felix, a Jewish woman called Frances."

Maggie tried to imagine growing up on Fifth Avenue. She'd been working on it so long she almost could. What a contrast with her own life in Macon, Georgia, then in Harlem. If she'd been born down here, she would have stayed put, too, like they had.

He led Maggie across East Drive until they arrived at the bridle path that circled North Meadow's soccer fields. Just northeast of The Reservoir, they came to a large tree.

"It's London Plane," he said, "a hybrid sycamore believed the oldest tree in the park."

They walked on the bridle path beneath it, Dr. Rossi gazing up at its high, gray limbs. Maggie watched him, wondering what he was going through. She tried to imagine it happening to her—praying her heart out to Jesus since she was a child then learning she came from people who thought Jesus was just a rabbi. She'd feel betrayed.

"We're almost there," he said. "We're almost there. Just one more day, I think. Then I'll have the cultures I need. When it's time, I'll transfer the cells to a new medium which will starve them into the totipotent state."

"Don't it feel funny, having all those copies of Christ's cells in a dish?"

He looked down at his hands. "Sometimes it does. They aren't alive, though. Not yet."

"Are you considering, like you promised?"

His response to her impassioned plea had been only that. He said he'd think about letting her be the mother of Christ. In the meantime, would she help him with the work and—most of all—say nothing to anyone about it; not now or ever, unless he gave permission? Maggie had offered to swear on the Bible that she would.

"Yes, I'm thinking about it, Maggie. By the way, I never asked. There's still no husband or boyfriend to be consulted?"

"No and no."

"All right, but don't get your hopes up."

She hung her head. "I don't see why—"

He leaned against the old tree's thick trunk. "Mitochondrial DNA. It's why, in a perfect world, you shouldn't be the mother."

"What is it?" she said, alarmed.

He made an oval with his forefingers and thumbs. "Picture an egg. It has a yolk and white surrounding it?"

"Yes."

"Pretend that's a woman's egg. What I'm going to do is remove the yolk, or the nucleus. That's where 99 percent of the DNA is, in that nucleus. I'm going to replace the nucleus with a blood cell from the Shroud, which I've treated so it will behave like a new nucleus."

"Don't tell me," Maggie said sadly, already guessing his point. "The other 1 percent of the DNA isn't in the yolk. It's in the white part of the egg."

He smiled at her and looked impressed. "Yes, 1 percent of the DNA is in the white part, the cytoplasm. It can only come from the woman who contributes the egg. That's why it's technically impossible to fully clone an adult man from his own cells. To clone a man, you need to start with an egg from a female relative because it carries the family's mitochondrial DNA in the white part, the cytoplasm. It's passed from mother to daughter to daughter. The male doesn't pass it on because the male has no eggs."

"Yeah, so I heard, but—"

"I don't mean to offend you, Maggie, but the fact is that Jesus didn't have African mitochondrial DNA. Science doesn't yet know exactly how it affects nuclear DNA so it may not matter in the least, but—" He started walking back toward Woodmen's Gate, Maggie rushing after him.

"Then why were you asking women at your church like Sylvia Canady? Why did you ask Adeline? Jesus wasn't Irish, either, and he certainly wasn't English, like Adeline's genes are."

"With Adeline I wasn't thinking. As for Sylvia, I remembered a woman at church came from a family of Conversos, but I didn't remember who, so I had to talk to several. It's Sylvia Canady. Her father is Irish Catholic, but her mother's family are Conversos, Spanish Jews who converted to Catholicism rather than face death in the Inquisition."

"Oh."

"Her mitochondria is very likely Semitic."

"Well, if you hadn't been so mean to your relatives, maybe you could have asked your cousin."

"A woman who lives in a foreign country and doesn't speak English? At least Sylvia's here."

"Well, what did she say about being a surrogate mother?"

"Before or after she laughed at me and asked if I was ill?"

Maggie patted his arm. "Can't do much, can it, if it's only 1 percent, besides, Jesus had to have a little black in him. Plenty of Arabs are dark and they're Semites. Didn't people start in Africa, then spread into the Middle East? The Bible says he had hair like wool, you know."

"Jesus did not have wooly hair!"

She stepped in front of him. "Do you want me to show you where it says so in the Bible?"

He frowned. "Revelation 1:14. It says hair as white as wool, not hair like wool."

Maggie felt her eyes start to water. She whispered, "Are you just scared he'll be ugly like me?"

She saw he didn't respond because he'd stopped listening.

"Mary was a Semitic woman," he said. "All right, I'll do it. I'm going over to the Park Avenue Synagogue."

"Oh, sure!" she said and sniffed. "You're going to find a rich Jewish woman who wants to be the mother of Jesus. Dr. Rossi, I'm beginning to think you never really read your Bible."

"Why not?" he said. "I'm Jewish! According to them, anyway. They say if your mother's a Jew, then you're a Jew. My mother was a Jew. You'd almost think they'd figured out mitochondrial DNA. I'd ask Frances if she weren't my sister and if I didn't think she'd have me committed."

"Dr. Rossi, I know you're still confused about all this, but believe me, you're not Jewish like people in the Bible. Jews were scattered across the face of the earth. I'm not educated, but I can read, and I spend my free time reading anything that's got to do with God and the Bible."

Felix looked skeptical. "When you're not reading *Vogue*, you mean."

"All right, when I'm not reading *Vogue*. Do you know they found that Cohen 'priest' gene in all kinds of people, even an African tribe. Jews mixed with other races, just like Africans did here. Our genes are all over this land in people who look like me and people who think they're white. So are the Jews's. I could even be part Jewish, Dr. Rossi. You're a little bit more. So what? The thing is, anybody might be. If somebody claims they're only this race or that, I say put 'em under one of your microscopes, and there's a better than even chance they're mixed. I know. I read about it. Your mother was a Catholic woman, Dr. Rossi. You're not Jewish if you don't want to be."

He looked at her as if she'd said something indecipherable.

Because Maggie pleaded, they strolled through the park a little longer before returning to the building. Again Sam was nowhere in sight. Maggie hadn't seen him since she chased him from the solarium on Friday, and now it was Monday. His backup was at the door. As Dr. Rossi started in, she said, "And if it's only 1 percent—"

"Ssshhhh," he said, his finger flying to his mouth.

In the lobby, waiting for the elevator, stood Frances with Uncle Simone and Cousin Letizia.

Chapter 19

Monday afternoon—Rossi apartment

Uncle Simone and Cousin Letizia barely had coffee cups in their hands before Dr. Rossi excused himself and fled to the lab. Maggie watched him go, urgently wanting to follow.

Frances glared from one of the new red, black, and gold couches. "Go with Dr. Rossi, Maggie, if you must."

"Miss Rossi, it's just that—"

"Go ahead," she said. Her lips were pressed so thin, her expression was so irate, that Maggie didn't budge.

"Go, I said!" Frances repeated harshly, making Maggie jump.

Uncle Simone sat on the low stool he'd requested. He motioned to Letizia and whispered in her ear when she bent down. She stood and said, "Very are we often leaving now."

"No!" Frances shot to her feet, her tone emphatic, her finger pointing to the charcoal carpet. "No! Stay here!"

Letizia sat down, looking confused.

Maggie was dismayed when Frances grabbed her arm and moved her toward the hall, saying, "Please stay!" to Uncle Simone and Letizia.

Once out of the room, Frances said. "If you want to work here another minute, Maggie Johnson, you'll do just as I say. Understand?"

Maggie understood. The jig was up. There was no stopping Frances now. Maggie followed her to the end of the hall.

"Ask him to open the door!" Frances demanded in a whisper.

Maggie took a deep breath, let it out and knocked, calling, "Dr. Rossi, it's me, Maggie."

A moment later he opened the door, and Frances barged in, Maggie following, her hands to her face as she mouthed an apology.

Maggie stayed at the door, and watched Frances and Dr. Rossi take positions against opposite walls, as if a bell would ring and they'd come out fighting.

It was Frances who spoke first. "For almost a week I've watched you behave like an ass. It's over! First, you're going to tell me what you two are up to. I know it has something to do with Adeline. I know that's why she's disappeared. That alone tells me you're doing something wrong. Second, Felix—" Frances flung her arm toward the door. "You are coming back into that living room and treating those people like our relatives! They want us to sit Shivah with them!"

"And exactly how is that done?"

"You've already seen part of it. Maggie had to cover up all the mirrors; we had to wash our hands when we got back; and Uncle Simone has to sit on a low stool. They want boiled eggs. It's—" Frances waved her arms. "I don't know what else, but I'm going to do it. Next we all might have to cook, I think. You know perfectly well that the Jews have a special way of mourning, so you'll do it, too. Hate them if you want, but you're not going to mistreat them to their faces. I won't stand for it another second!"

The way brother and sister stood, staring helplessly at each other, Maggie knew this was the most serious fight they'd ever had.

"And how," he said, "do you propose to make me comply with these demands?"

The phone rang, but they all ignored it.

In a quiet voice, Frances said, "I'll leave here if you don't."

Suddenly Dr. Rossi looked woeful, like a little boy abandoned, but he said, "Fine. Your decision," and Frances looked as if he'd struck her.

"May I say something?" Maggie asked, one hand on her heart because the tension and sadness upset her. When they didn't respond, she went ahead, speaking louder. "Miss Rossi, you're wrong to pry into Dr. Rossi's work. Dr. Rossi, you're wrong to mistreat your relatives. Would Jesus do that?" Maggie blinked and swallowed and felt she'd suffocate, speaking to the Rossis like that.

Neither responded. Dr. Rossi simply nodded for Maggie to answer the ringing phone and she did. It was Adeline and she sounded upset.

Maggie listened then announced, "Adeline says you should turn the TV on. Right away. She says you've got to turn it on right now."

He said, "I don't have one in here. What channel?"

"CNN."

"Thanks Miss Hamilton," Maggie said and hung up. She rushed to follow Dr. Rossi and Frances out of the lab into his bedroom, which was the next door across the hall. There he grabbed the TV remote and sat by Frances on the bed, while Maggie stood at the door looking in. A panel discussion called *Cloning in America* was being aired.

"Oh no, oh no," Maggie whispered.

Dr. Rossi sounded disgusted. "It's the rabid red head."

It was his least favorite of the talking heads. Usually she opposed everything he supported.

"The question is," she said, spreading bony manicured hands in the air and baring prominent front teeth in a snarl. "How do we even know it's true? The reporter won't name the scientist or identify the historical figure he supposedly intends to clone. Given this—"

Another journalist tried to interrupt, but the rabid red head wouldn't let him step on her words.

"—given this, given this!" she continued. "It's too soon for you bleeding heart, save-the-world do-gooders to start calling for government interference in yet another aspect of our lives and choke another industry before it even gets off the ground—"

Her opponent got a word in. "What industry? The people-copying industry?"

The red head sputtered then launched a counterattack. "You know very well there's serious medical research underway by legitimate people. I don't mean reproductive cloning. I don't mean trying to duplicate a person. I mean therapeutic cloning. If I'm sick and they take a cell of mine to get stem cells to treat me—all right, what's wrong with that? I mean there's no sperm here, so it's not a regular embryo. What you have is an empty egg and someone's cell, all right? A skin cell or something. They're not *real* embryos, for heavens' sake. Now this scientist, if he exists, needs to have his head examined for trying to bring a dead person back to life and—"

The host went to commercial as the rabid red head snarled, and Frances gazed at her brother as if she didn't know who he was.

"Why does Adeline think this would interest you, Felix?"

He was still staring at the screen.

"Felix?" Frances said, "Why does she think—"

A breaking news story interrupted the commercial. "CNN has just learned that *The Times* of London reporter in the American cloning story, Jerome Newton, has had a suit filed against him in the English courts alleging he got his information by stealing the private papers of—"

Dr. Rossi clicked off the television and looked at Maggie, who knew what he would say before he spoke. Already she was thanking God.

"There's probably not much time left, Maggie. If you still want to, let's go ahead. It may be now or never."

Frances looked back and forth at them, her mouth trembling. "Do what? What are you talking about?"

Her brother faced her. "I stole DNA from the Shroud of Turin. I have an opportunity to clone Jesus Christ. Maggie has offered to carry the child, to be the mother. She and I plan to bring Christ back."

Maggie went to a chair and dropped into it, whispering, "Thank you, Lord."

Slowly, Frances shook her head as if to dislodge what she'd heard. "What? What? What are you saying? You can't be saying—"

He went to a window and stood there, looking out at the day. "I won't let you stop me, Frances."

Maggie understood his new composure. She felt the same because her course was also set—however hard the road, however lonely.

"Felix! Flix!" Frances sounded near hysteria. "Tell me you don't mean this."

"I do."

"You're being an idiot, an idiot! Good God! Don't you realize it could just be a story, Felix! Just a story! Every word in the Bible isn't true, for goodness sake. Maybe some are. Maybe most. Others aren't. How do you know which ones? How do you know the real Jesus was really crucified at all? Or that he laid under that cloth? People believe it, but it hasn't been proven as a historical fact. What about Buddhism? What about Islam? What about Judaism? How do we even know which religion is based on fact? I have beliefs, just like you. Proof is another thing. It hasn't been proven the crucifixion even happened, Felix. It could be a story, for God's sake, just a story!"

He turned to her. "No, it isn't. In the Roman historian, Tacitus's, *Annals* there is a sentence—"

"A sentence?" she insisted. "Were you there? Was I there? No! Nobody takes Bible stories that seriously anymore, Felix. Nobody. You have no way of knowing whose DNA you have. It could be anybody's. A priest's, a pilgrim's, a nun's, even a criminal's."

"Don't worry, Miss Rossi," Maggie said. "God's been with me every day of my life. He's guided every step I took. He won't let Dr. Rossi put no criminal in me. If that's who it is, something will go wrong. If it works, the child's Jesus. That's what I believe."

Dr. Rossi looked at Maggie with admiration, but Frances's eyes were wild with fear. "You two are, are … brainless!" she shouted. "How many people even go to church like you two anymore?"

"That's true," Maggie said. "Every Sunday in my church the preacher climbs the pulpit and talks to mostly women and children and precious few of them. Can't hardly find a man there at all. You know why? Because religions won't change. We got six billion people already, and the Pope's out telling Catholics to have billions more. People got common sense. They know better than that. The Jews are still carrying on about eating pork chops and Trick or Treating on Halloween. So is the Christian right. I mean, do you really think an all-loving, all-knowing, omnipotent God is worried about Trick or Treat?"

He looked confused. "Then why are you doing this, Maggie?"

"Because I think we need him to come back. Religions have stood still but their congregations haven't. People have moved on and, Dr. Rossi, I'm telling you that's God's plan. It was him that made us thinkers, him that made us curious. Take a baby in diapers, put him alone in a room with a box, and the baby's gonna crawl to that box and see what's in it."

"Yes, you're right," he said, smiling at her. "Preach on, Maggie."

"That's why I don't think Jesus meant for us to stand still based on how things were two thousand years ago. It wasn't even him that started Christianity. Anybody who takes the trouble will learn it was mostly Paul who started it, and he never even met Jesus Christ! It took three hundred years for them to come up with the Bible. When they did, they threw out the oldest gospels and a lot of the truth, if you ask me."

"Which gospels?" Frances demanded.

"The gospel according to Thomas, for instance. I read it. It's the oldest one of all. I studied all about those Dead Sea Scrolls and Gnostic Gospels. According to Thomas, Jesus said, 'The Kingdom of the Father is spread out upon the earth, and men do not see it.' As soon as I read that, I knew in my bones Jesus really said those words. But look what awful things we've done and still do in His name. That's why I want to help Him come back, take a look around, and give us an update. Something to go on for the next two thousand years. If I can do that, Dr. Rossi, any troubles I have in the process won't be a hill of beans to me. There's nothing better I could do with my life."

"Simple as that," Frances muttered. "They've cloned a sheep, let's clone the Shepherd?"

"Then you don't believe what the Bible says about the Second Coming?" Felix asked Maggie.

"I don't know and I wish I did. But I can't picture gentle Jesus throwing poor lost souls in a lake of fire just because they'd messed up some in life. Everybody messes up, near as I can tell. I wouldn't put 'em in no lake of fire, no matter what, and I figure Jesus has got to be at least as nice as me."

Felix went to her and took her hand. "We need to leave for Cliffs Landing. I'll call and make sure things are ready. We'll pack and leave tomorrow. No one knows we have a place out there except Adeline. We can trust her. She won't tell and neither will you, Frances, right?" He looked hopefully at her.

Frances had her fist pressed to her mouth as if she'd scream in fright. "Felix, you need to slow down. We have to discuss this. You can't clone a dead person. There must be ethics; there must be laws. There must be … danger to the clone! Do you want a crippled Christ? You're not thinking!"

"I've already had most of this conversation with Adeline," he said.

Frances cried out, "Well, you haven't had it with me!"

Maggie sat down beside her. "Miss Rossi, it's all right. You've got to believe me. Now I know how Mary felt. To be a plain, poor woman and then somebody says you'll give birth to the Son of God. I know why Mary didn't mind. She could help send a message that everyone's special to him. Even women who don't have Graham Smith hats. I was being silly. What matters is that God's been by my side all my life, which means he's by your brother's side or I wouldn't be here. Don't worry."

"Yes, don't worry," he said, glancing up at Maggie as if she'd said something strange. Then he stared at his sister. "Oh, but Maggie! We forgot! Frances is a Semitic woman. She's a better match. Frances, I don't relish the idea of being your obstetrician, but hear me out before you say no, I—"

Maggie's heart flip-flopped.

"You're insane!" Frances whispered, backing away.

Seeing her reaction and probably remembering he'd lost Adeline like this, he said, "No. All right, then. No. Maggie wants to do it, so she should. Don't worry about us, Frances. We'll check back with you every day."

Frances took her fist down from her mouth, and Maggie thought she would burst into tears.

"You fools!" Frances said, raising her voice. "What can I say to stop you?"

Felix turned fiercely on her, "Nothing!"

Maggie could hear their breathing as they stared at each other, facing the loss of a bond they'd treasured all their lives.

Felix turned away and took Maggie's arm then they heard Frances say, "Do you think I'll let you go out there and do this utterly stupid, stupid, brainless thing alone?"

Dr. Rossi ran and hugged his sister and Maggie knew he'd wanted Frances's help all along.

They heard the front door close.

"Oh no!" Frances whispered.

When they rushed out to the foyer, Uncle Simone and Cousin Letizia had already taken the elevator down.

Chapter 20

Tuesday midday—Henry Hudson Parkway, New York

Sam had taken an early flight out of London's Heathrow Airport and landed in Newark at 11:10 a.m., grateful to have missed New York's morning traffic jam. In his taxi on the way from the airport, he felt satisfied with what he'd accomplished. One phone call, one visit, a trunkful of money, and a case was now pending in England's Royal Courts of Justice, filed by a junior barrister of flexible ethics at the prestigious firm of Thames Walk Chambers.

The plaintiff? Dr. Abrams, a formerly respected scientist who more recently could be found in his local pub, not his lab. The defendant? Jerome Newton.

Sam chuckled.

He'd had no trouble learning that Newton was an idly employed member of the upper crust fighting boredom, more decorative than esteemed. Not particularly noble. Not particularly valued by his newspaper. The charge against him? Breaking and entering. Stealing confidential documents on which Newton based his *Cloning in America* story.

Jerome Newton had stolen nothing, of course, but to defend himself he'd have to reveal his real source and, in the process, the name of the American scientist in question. Newton, who'd been in New York, had scurried back to London when the case was filed. Sam was confident an expensive High Court trial would soon prove unattractive to him, compared to whispering a name in the junior barrister's ear at Thames Walk Chambers.

Any day, any moment, Sam expected a call.

He relaxed in the cab and enjoyed the view. Soon they were speeding by his second favorite park in the city, Riverside. At its 79th Street Boat Basin he would often walk next to the water and smell the salt air, but his favorite spot was the Soldiers and Sailors Monument on the hill at 89th. He'd stroll the park's promenade to reach it. Then, from the base of the monument's white marble columns, he enjoyed a splendid view of the charming park, the Hudson River, and the New Jersey waterfront on the opposite side. There, a fetching lady who thought he'd drunk too much had tried to roll him last year. She didn't get what she wanted. Sam did.

"Aaah! Traffic," the Pakistani driver said as they lurched to a stop.

Sam watched a ribbon of cloud drift across the pale sky, and because his body was jet-lagged, he dozed. He woke as the cab sped onto the 96th Street Transverse running east-west through Central Park. Rubbing his eyes, he reached for his wallet as they drew close to his building on Fifth Avenue. A dark SUV sat in front—obviously brand spanking new because it had a ten-day temporary permit taped inside the rear window. When they got closer Sam saw it was a Range Rover. He wondered who was in it, but he couldn't see through the back windows. It moved and the cab pulled up to the curb. One of the boys from the back appeared at the lobby door as Sam came from the taxi.

"Hi, Sam, how was your trip?" he said.

"It was fine. Everything okay in the building?"

"Yeah."

"Who was that in the Rover?" Sam asked as he went to his own entrance, steps away.

"The Range Rover? I don't know. I just came on duty. You have to ask—"

"Yeah, yeah." Sam would check with his substitute later.

He opened the door to his apartment and went inside, dropped his suitcase, and took off his coat. He retrieved today's *New York Times* and took it to the john, turning to see the inside pages. There it was again, from the enemy of the country of his envelope deliveries: photos of African kids with their heads cut open by machetes. Except this time it wasn't two. It looked like somebody had fertilized a whole field with their bodies. Sam read the article, feeling sick. Where the hell were the good guys? Why weren't they on their horses, charging to the rescue? Where were the guys in the damned white hats?

Chapter 21

Tuesday afternoon—Henry Hudson Parkway, New York

Maggie hadn't expected mothering the Son of God would make her rich.

She sat in the back seat of the Rossis' new Range Rover which Frances said was Niagara Gray with Lightstone Leather upholstery, but to Maggie the seats were tan and the car was charcoal. Until today, Dr. Rossi claimed he didn't need a car. Since they'd be gone nine months, this Range Rover had appeared.

Even in the back, the seats were comfortable, but the car felt solid. It was like riding in a cross between a limo and a tank.

In the cargo area behind her were four boxes of things from Dr. Rossi's lab and several suitcases, including his Seeger luggage and Miss Rossi's made-to-order natural cowhide Glaser bags. One cloth suitcase held Maggie's few things from their apartment. She hadn't gone home to get anything, had no parakeet or cat to tend, no relatives to notify. Dr. Rossi said he'd help her figure out what to tell her friend, Sharmina. Then he sat her down in front of Frances and said he'd consulted the family attorney who had served them since before their parents died. For starters, Felix had handed her two charge cards, said her salary would be doubled, and the attorney would deposit fifty thousand dollars into her checking account, as soon as she was pregnant. Next, the attorney would draw up two sets of papers. One was Rossi's promise to co-adopt. The other gave Maggie a life annuity if she delivered in the next fifteen months.

She was rich.

Dr. Rossi thought things were settled, but Maggie knew they weren't. He'd mentioned a final, troubling condition. She had to be in excellent health. The lab didn't have the equipment he needed to examine her, so he would do it when they got to the Landing.

As the Range Rover drove north on the Hudson River Parkway, Maggie was having a silent talk with God about her blood pressure. It went up now and then, probably because she hadn't stopped eating fried foods like the doctor told her to.

Maggie asked for a miracle as she watched the river pass. If God would just keep her blood pressure down for the exam, she promised to never eat a fried pork chop, fried chicken breast, or fried corn-on-the-cob again. She'd even give up fried biscuits.

They passed 125th Street and were officially in Harlem. Soon Maggie's river view was obscured by the Riverbank State Park, which had been built over a dump. When Harlem residents complained, the city encased it in concrete, painted it, and put a basketball court on top. Now the dump disguised as a playground made her aware of what she was leaving behind. No more drug dealers to pass on the way home. No more scrimping to buy a nice hat. The only thing she'd miss about Harlem was Sharmina, her church, and the way everybody said hello to one another on the streets—even the dangerous drug dealers. Maggie realized her baby might one day save them, and she was glad.

They turned onto the George Washington Bridge, and approached the lofty cliffs of the Jersey shore. Running all along the river, the cliffs had given the Palisades Parkway its name. They took the tree-lined road north to the New York/New Jersey border where they would cross back into New York State. It would take less than thirty minutes door-to-door.

Dr. Rossi glanced right to the river and said, "The Indians used to call the Hudson the Shatemuc. It means the river that runs in two directions or the river that goes two ways. It has two high and two low tides—one rising, one falling. At each, the current changes direction."

Maggie saw a deer streak across between the cars in a brown and white blur. It vanished into the forest on the opposite side. Her journey might be risky, like the deer's. Like the Shatemuc she was changing direction, one she hoped would not reverse. The next time she crossed the Shatemuc she wanted to be holding her baby in her arms.

She closed her eyes and prayed until she felt the Rover slow to take the Cliffs Landing exit. The Rossis usually brought her out to clean and cook on the weekends they spent here. Remembering something, she moved to the right window and looked for the sign she knew was there. It said Skunk Hollow and had dates commemorating a little village of coloreds and whites that had thrived here a hundred years ago. There'd been a church, and it had a colored minister, Uncle Billy Thompson. Maggie resolved to find the ruins of Skunk Hollow on the walks she'd probably have to take when she was pregnant—assuming she passed Dr. Rossi's tests.

He slowed as usual as they approached the Presbyterian Church. The minister stood on the lawn, and Frances waved at him. The church was in the middle of Cliffs Landing. Just like a hundred years ago in Skunk Hollow, it was the center of village life. If folks here had to come together, they usually did it in this white steepled building that had a sign saying everyone was welcome. It wasn't her own church on 131st, but it was a good substitute.

They passed it, and turned right where the road split in three directions, and wound down unexpected hollows, and up ridges held back by old stone walls.

Most of the lanes ended at the Hudson or ran along the ridge above it. Glimpsed between the trees were Cliffs Landings' rustic homes, some the size of mansions.

Soon enough they rumbled down Lawford Lane then turned left into a driveway obscured by gnarled trees. They drove along a graveled path, and stopped at what looked like a low stone wall. It was actually the side of the house, most of which sloped down a hillside. A path of big round stones led along the front. A door opened and out came the caretaker. Dr. Rossi had phoned him before they left.

"There you are," the old man said. He put on a canvas cap and started buttoning his blue squall jacket.

"Hello, George," Dr. Rossi called. "Everything all right?"

"Yep! Got the place warmed up and ready for you. Everything's been delivered and installed. They finished the cleanup this morning. Need any help with your luggage?"

"No, don't think we do," Dr. Rossi said.

George walked past the Range Rover, tipping his cap to Frances and Maggie. They didn't offer a ride because he wouldn't accept. George liked to walk.

"Appreciate it, George. Stop back when you get a chance," Dr. Rossi said.

George answered, "Thanks, believe I will," but he wouldn't. It was just how people at the Landing talked. Old residents casually invited each other by, but no one was rude enough to come unannounced.

Together they carried the suitcases into the foyer. It had a stone wall on one side, wood on the other, and an ironwork lantern hanging from the gabled ceiling on a chain. Felix went back for the boxes, while Maggie and Frances crossed the foyer's hooked rug and turned left. They went down two polished wood steps into the living room. Anyone who hadn't been here would think they'd detoured back outside into the woods. From floor to eighteen-foot ceiling, the living room's rear wall was solid glass.

The room itself was huge. At the far end sat a baby grand next to steps that rose to an open library. Closer in, a black stovepipe climbed to the ceiling above a round freestanding fireplace. At this end was a teakwood bar, which matched the room's teakwood ceiling and teakwood trim. There were casual groupings of easy chairs and sofas.

Nothing could compare to the view.

Wide and spindly trunks of moss and ivy-covered trees created an expanse of forest and sky that was breathtaking, no matter how often Maggie saw it. The trees grew down to the cliffs above the shore. Beyond the cliffs the Hudson flowed. She couldn't imagine what this house must have cost. She was just glad she had gotten to visit over the years. Now it would be her home.

"They won't find us here?" she said.

"Of course not! Well, not without a great deal of effort," Frances replied. "Technically, the house is still in Enea's name, though the family used it. We've never entertained out here—not that we did much of that in New York. So unless you've told someone about it—"

"Me? You said not to, so I haven't."

"Well, then. No one knows it's here. And why would anyone search for us, anyway? If that reporter really knew anything, I assume he would have told. He didn't. No one else knows Felix had anything to do with the Shroud or that the Shroud has anything to do with the cloning. You can help Felix be a mad scientist in complete privacy."

Maggie thought it was best not to reply.

As they carried luggage from the foyer into the hall, they passed the dining room and the glass door to the magnificent rock terrace, which in spring and summer became the Rossis' outdoor living room. They deposited suitcases in the art deco master suite Frances occupied. It had a luxurious bathroom suite and another fabulous view. They left Felix's bags in his smaller rooms, done in sleek bachelor leathers, blacks and browns.

Maggie's room was on the lower level which, she discovered, had been transformed. One room that used to hold billiards and ping-pong tables now looked like an obstetrician's office, except for a curtained area to the left. Isolated by glass walls at the far end was a smaller version of Dr. Rossi's lab.

Felix beckoned them in and opened an adjoining door.

"This is your room, Maggie."

There was the white wrought-iron bed she always slept in when she was here. A white rocking chair and a small floral-patterned sofa had been added. A new wall unit held a stereo, television, knickknacks, and books on pregnancy and childbirth. Near it was a white table and chairs. The room had three other exits. One led to the laundry room beneath the steps. The other opened through French doors onto a white-pebbled outdoor garden, its walls overgrown with ivy, a heated fishpond at its center.

"This is mine?" Maggie said.

Felix nodded, looking out of place in the feminine surroundings. He opened the third door and held it for her.

She walked past him into a powder-blue nursery and tapped a mobile of angels, which hung above the white crib. They bobbed up and down on translucent wings.

The basement was now a single interconnected suite. Everything ready. Everything new. In one room he'd make the baby; in another he'd deliver it. In the other rooms, Maggie and her precious child would sleep.

"It's lovely, Flix," Frances said. "How did you ever do it?"

"I've had a decorator and crews out here practically round the clock for five days."

He left and, a few moments later, returned with a striped hospital gown, handing it to Maggie. "We'll be in the lab. Come in when you're ready."

This was it.

Looking at the fishpond out in her new garden, Maggie reassured herself as she undressed. She went to the bathroom, brushed her teeth, and showered for the exam. With the gown on, she got down on her knees and lingered over a prayer, asking the Lord for low blood pressure.

Chapter 22

Tuesday afternoon—Cliffs Landing

Felix removed sterilized instruments from his autoclave, while Frances in a white lab coat stood at the obstetrics room door, her arms folded. So far she had refused to come in.

"You realize I've actually been in an Ob-gyn office recently," she said. "How long since you were?"

Felix exhaled. As usual, Frances had seen to the heart of things. He hadn't personally managed a pregnancy to term in years, but he often served as an expert consultant. His MD focus on Ob-gyn had nicely complemented his PhD work in Molecular Genetics. He'd done his residency at Mount Sinai and afterward did clinical research at NYU, and he remained on the staff of both. For a while he'd had a small Ob-gyn practice in his Dad's old office. All in all, his preparedness was that of an obstetrician with superior training, special skill at in-vitro fertilization, and less-than-average exposure to patients. He'd have to brush up on some things, but he felt competent to proceed.

"I'm not exactly out of touch. Will you come in and help me?"

"I'm no nurse, Flix," she said looking away.

"All you need to do is pay attention to Maggie. Calm her, reassure her, provide companionship. Tell me if you notice anything troubling. I'll be watching, too, of course. Later you can go on walks with her and such. You can see she takes her vitamins."

Frances sniffed and gazed around. "Good thing the Vatican can't see this. Why do they think you disappeared from the Shroud work, anyway?"

"Enea's death."

"How sweet."

Felix hung his head. "I didn't say it. Bartolo assumed I was too distraught to run the team. Someone else took over but I keep in touch enough not to raise questions."

"Flix, why on earth are you so confident this will work? Have you produced a human embryo before and not told me?"

"Mouse embryos, sheep, pigs. A monkey embryo."

"Should that impress me?"

Felix knew he couldn't show any doubt. "Yes. I let them grow before I destroyed them. I tested them. They were healthy. I can do it. Will you help?"

"I'll think about it." She turned to leave.

"Frances, I need you here when I examine her, especially the first time. It's going to be awkward enough."

"Like I said, Flix—"

"Yes, you're not a nurse, but you're a woman. There should be another woman here at least." Felix retrieved a clipboard, went to Frances, and put it in her hands. "You can take her medical history. Ask the questions and record her answers."

Frances looked at the clipboard. "You want me to ask all this before you examine her?"

"No, no. Let's be informal. We have time."

She didn't say yes, but she didn't leave. She stood in the doorway, patting the clipboard against her knee. They were used to being together, used to helping each other. What he wouldn't do, she wouldn't do. What hurt her, hurt him. It had always been like that. Felix was counting on it now.

He'd worked on the cells for a week, growing them in different media, examining them, experimenting, taking notes. The DNA was as ready as it would ever be.

"I'll develop a daily exercise regimen and a diet, of course," he said. "That's for later, though. For now, you only have to be here for her exams so she's comfortable."

Still Frances didn't come in.

Felix moved about the room, re-inventorying supplies, turning equipment off and on, glancing back toward her now and then. Besides the autoclave, he had a neonatal center which could double as an incubator, a portable EKG, a portable ultrasound, defibrillators, oxygen, and everything he could think of that was normally in an emergency or delivery room. Behind a door with a thick window, basic radiology equipment had been installed.

Sterilized instruments were on a rollaway tray, covered by a sterile cloth. Maggie need only come out and they could begin.

He paused as he passed Maggie's door. "Why do you think she's taking so long?"

"Fear, embarrassment, second thoughts. I know I'd be having them all."

"Maybe you could go and—"

Frances slapped the clipboard against the doorframe. "Absolutely not! Maggie has every right to make up her own mind as slowly as she likes and even change it. Down to the last second, understand?"

Felix nodded, feeling nervous. "Yes, down to the last second. But what do you think—"

They heard the knob turn on Maggie's door. It opened and there she stood, wearing the gown—visibly trembling.

"Oh Maggie!" Frances cried and rushed to her. "You don't have to do it. You don't!"

"I'm a little scared, I admit." She looked at Felix. "Where do you want me?"

"Don't be afraid, Maggie." He took her other hand. "I'll be as careful as I possibly can."

"Okay, where do you want me?"

"Come. First, let's get your weight and height." He and Frances walked her to the scale, and Maggie stepped on it.

"If it's a pound over 135, don't tell me."

Felix slid the weights across the beams. "132. How's that?"

"Not bad, I guess."

With relief, he saw Frances record the weight.

He raised the height rod and asked her to turn around. "Five foot seven on the dot."

Maggie stepped down and asked. "Where now?"

He pointed to the open striped yellow and white curtains, a pale yellow birthing bed behind. It had a wooden headboard and side rails that could be swung away when not needed, adjustable stirrups that could be made to disappear. The bed could be raised or lowered, and the sectioned mattress put in full recline or full chair, dropping the front for delivery of the baby. At the moment it was in the chair position.

"I thought we'd use it as our examination table. Then you'd be used to it by the time—"

Quickly, Maggie sat on the birthing bed, Frances taking position beside her with the clipboard.

He slipped a blood pressure monitor cuff on her wrist and noticed Maggie start trembling again. "Let's get your temperature and pressure. Then we'll take a medical history."

Frances said, "Shall I hold your other hand?"

"Thanks, Miss Rossi."

"Just relax, now," Felix said. He slipped a digital thermometer into her mouth and went to rewash his hands at the sink and pull on surgical gloves, knowing he must exude a doctor's confidence and authority so Maggie would feel reassured.

He sat on a rollaway stool in front of the bed and smiled. "Try to relax, everything's fine."

Frances bent to his ear and whispered, "When do I begin her history?"

Maggie said, "Don't be whispering before we even start. What is it?"

"Nothing," he said to Maggie. He looked at the pressure monitor cuff and noticed her pulse was 86, her pressure 138 over 90, close to Stage 1 Hypertension, but Felix knew just the prospect of a physical exam made many patients tense. "Try not to be nervous. This is the easy part."

"To tell the truth, I'm surprised I haven't fainted. I guess that's why my blood pressure's high. Just ignore it, Dr. Rossi. It'll come down."

Frances said, "Felix, let's wait."

"No! Please." Maggie looked dismayed. "Let's at least do this part. Yes, I'm nervous, but look." She closed her eyes and took a few slow breaths.

Felix watched her diastolic pressure decline a bit. "Good. I'll draw your blood, first, and start a hematology analysis. Then if you'll give us a urine sample, we can get a urinalysis going, too. All right?"

"Why? What are you looking for?" Maggie asked.

"The normal thing. Diseases—"

"I don't have any."

"Good. Anything in your system like—"

"I don't take any medicines or drugs, Dr. Rossi."

"Well, perhaps birth control. We'll have to see what kind and—"

"Nope. I don't take birth control."

"Well, surely—"

"Doctor gave them to me, but what am I going to take them for? I don't have a man."

"Listen to me, Maggie. I have to run blood tests and a urinalysis. We'll check your heart, your lungs, your thyroid. We'll do a neurological and a pelvic exam. We'll do a pap smear and a couple of other cultures. We need to test for tuberculosis and, for our purposes, HIV. It's all routine."

Maggie clasped her hands as if she were begging. "I tell you, I'm not sick. I don't have any diseases. Not one! Never had an operation. There's nothing in my blood stream that God didn't put there." She looked at the blood pressure monitor on her wrist. "See? All this is making me very nervous. Can't we skip some of it?"

Felix took her hand. "Maggie, some conditions have no obvious symptoms and they could damage both you and the baby."

She looked solemn. "Oh."

"Just relax. As I said before, this is the easy part."

She looked more frightened and asked, "What's the hard part?"

In pointedly neutral tones, he said, "I have to retrieve your eggs, remember?"

"Oh, right. How?"

"Normally, a woman produces one egg a month. We'll make your body produce several eggs at once. It's a procedure that takes about three weeks. I'll give you injections. We'll monitor your body's response with blood tests and ultrasound. When you're ready, I'll give you a final injection to ripen the eggs. Then, exactly thirty-seven hours later I'll retrieve them."

"Am I going to be awake when you do?"

"I have a friend here in the Landing who's an anesthesiologist. We could bring him in to give you intravenous sedation or an epidural block."

"Is it safe to bring somebody else in?"

"Yes, that's the problem. We'll focus on this more as we go along."

"How do you get the eggs out of me?"

"I'll pass a needle through your vagina to the follicles and draw out your eggs. The ultrasound will guide me. It's not really risky, just more involved. Today, we're only doing a normal exam."

"One more thing," Maggie said when he reached for a syringe to draw her blood. "How long after you get the eggs can you … you know. Give me the baby?"

"Not right away. Five days, if any cells from the Shroud fuse with your eggs and turn into embryos. They might. They might not. It's possible we'll have to harvest another set of eggs. That's why we need to begin."

Maggie looked sad. "I didn't know it would be so hard."

Felix's training as a doctor had made him tell a truth he'd been avoiding. He was speaking to himself, now, as much as to her. "I can't promise it will work. There's a chance. It's about fifty-fifty, though. Actually, it's less Maggie when you consider that the embryo has to implant. That doesn't happen every time." He took a deep breath. "But, without boasting, I can say there is no one who could give you better odds. If a clone can be produced from this DNA, I'll produce it. You—we—must be realistic, though. Even my best might not be enough. There may be no child, Maggie. We should prepare ourselves for that."

He'd seen unhappy looks before on women when they learned they weren't pregnant after all, but nothing like Maggie's crushed expression. It made him remember the other danger he hadn't discussed.

"Maggie, there's something else."

She looked up. "What?"

"Theoretically, the cloning process could produce a defective fetus that doesn't survive or one that survives with a deformity—perhaps a terrible deformity. However, I have confidence in my—"

"Shhh," Maggie said and closed her eyes, as if in prayer. Felix prayed too. He knew what he was doing, but there was still a chance things could go very wrong.

Maggie opened her eyes and smiled at him. "Don't worry, Dr. Rossi. If he lives, my baby's not going to be deformed. I feel it in my heart."

Frances had been gazing at them; now she hugged Maggie, then him. "You two are dreamers. Maggie, you think you're Mary. And Flix you think you're the Archangel Gabriel. If there's so little chance, why take these risks?"

They were silent for a moment.

Maggie looked down at Felix. "Didn't you say you need a urine sample?"

"I did."

"Where's the cup?"

When she returned with the sample, Frances took it, looking resigned. He knew his sister, though. While she helped them, she would keep trying to change their minds.

Maggie sat quietly on the birthing table as he drew blood from her plump, healthy veins, then she lay unmoving as he listened to her chest and ran an EKG. She was still so nervous she trembled now and then, especially when he looked at her blood pressure.

Frances asked questions from the form, then flushed, stopped, and looked at him, her face an embarrassed plea when she reached the section about Maggie's menstrual cycle, miscarriages, abortions, and live births. Felix nodded, indicating she could skip them for now. He'd get the information from Maggie when they were alone. As he worked, he noticed how carefully Maggie answered when Frances asked about a family history of hypertension. Instead of yes or no, she spoke in long rambling sentences, which he suspected were intended to mask the truth. He decided to monitor her blood pressure around the clock for a day. In pregnancy, hypertension could threaten mother and child.

For now, Felix took his time, using a subdued bedside manner. He checked Maggie's eyes looking especially for retinal hemorrhages. He checked her ears, and mouth, felt the glands and nodes at her neck, then checked her reflexes, letting her become accustomed to his touch. He listened to her heart and lungs. He took a twelve-lead EKG and found no evidence of disease, no rhythm or conduction disturbances. The most intimate aspects he left for last.

First he examined her abdomen to see if her internal organs were in their proper places and of normal size. He felt no swelling or displacement. She fixed her eyes on the ceiling when he felt for lumps in her breasts and compressed the nipples to see if fluid was expressed. When he raised the stirrups for her pelvic exam, the moment was even more awkward than he'd imagined. Given his relationship with Maggie, the last thing he wanted was to examine her pelvis. Frances looked like she wanted to drop through the floor.

Maggie handled the moment by scooting her bottom down to the end of the table without instruction, lifting her right leg and inserting it in the right stirrup, doing the same with the left leg in the left stirrup, and shutting her eyes. He'd be glad when they'd grown used to these exams and they weren't an embarrassment anymore.

He nodded to Frances, who stepped closer and asked Maggie if she was all right.

"Yes, Miss Rossi. I'm all right. You can go ahead, Dr. Rossi."

He turned on an exam light and asked Maggie to lift her gown. Felix sat down to visually examine her pelvis first, looking for signs of pathology: rashes, unusual growths, any malformations. Carefully he spread her labia, looking for scarring, lesions, warts. He frowned, applied jelly to one glove, inserted a finger about an inch and stopped. In shock he jerked his hand away. He rose and looked at her, disoriented, pulling off his gloves.

"What is it? What's wrong?" he heard Maggie ask.

"Felix, what's the matter?" Frances said.

He couldn't answer or say anything at all, only stare. Felix left the room and took the stairs two and three at a time, their voices and unanswered questions disappearing—not thinking, because he couldn't think, only berate himself for being so stupid.

At the top of the stairs, he heard, "Felix?" and there was Adeline, standing in the living room, her shahtoosh from Nepal draped around her shoulders. She must have arrived while they were down in the lab.

"Felix," she said. "I called and you'd left. I assumed you'd all come here. I— I wanted to say goodbye because I'm leaving the country for a while."

He stared at her.

"But before I did, I wanted to see if perhaps there was anything I could say to … I wanted to ask if—"

She came closer and it troubled him to see her hopeful eyes. She felt compelled to try again to stop him.

"Felix, what's wrong? You look terribly upset."

He couldn't talk to her. He couldn't talk.

He heard Maggie and Frances coming and felt trapped in a world of women, a place where a man shouldn't go without armor or they would shred his self-control. That's what was happening as he stood there between these women then slid down the wall to the floor. All his life he'd run from them because they were of the flesh that turned his mind from God. He'd studied the power and mystery of their bodies, but would never understand their hearts. Not Frances who had sex all the time and never fell in love. Not Adeline, who had secretly been in love with him for years. Adeline couldn't have known that as she was driving here to make a final plea, he'd have Maggie on the table. He was embarrassed by the emotion they'd revealed in him, unable to think or look them in the eye, these women.

"Felix!"

Frances took him in her arms and rubbed his hair as if he were a boy while Adeline just looked numb and Maggie stood there, afraid of what he'd say, oblivious to everything but her yearning to carry the Christ child.

"Felix! You're frightening everyone," Frances said, but she hugged him and caressed him like his mother had when they thought he would die long ago. For days his mother had stayed at his hospital bed, after the accident when he was nine, trying to make him drink from that straw. His body had been there, but his spirit rarely was. He'd been in another place.

He'd been with the man whose face was on the Shroud.

That's how he knew it was Jesus. He had recognized the face on the cloth.

"I'm sorry, Dr. Rossi," Maggie said, her voice so tragic it hurt him. "I didn't know anything was wrong with me. I didn't, Dr. Rossi. I swear I didn't."

Silently, Felix rose, shaking his head. "When did you last have sexual intercourse, Maggie?"

She looked mortified and stammered. "I—I."

Felix went and wrapped his arms around her. "You can't answer? You can't because you're as virginal as the day you were born." He lifted her face. "You were always my Mary. Why didn't you tell me, Maggie? Why didn't you tell me?"

Chapter 23

Tuesday evening—Thames Walk Chambers, London

Beneath white vaulted ceilings in the London office of Thames Walk Chambers, Jerome Newton found his late-afternoon tea break unappetizing. It had been brought round on a cart by an aproned, white-haired woman who urged chocolate-covered biscuits upon him, on the grounds she had made them herself. Staring through the triangular panes of medieval windows, he stirred his tea, which had two lumps instead of the one he'd requested.

Jerome was in the first-floor office of a still-bewigged Walter Finsbury, the junior barrister who'd filed suit against him in the Royal Courts of Justice. Finsbury had sought this private meeting and rushed to it from the Old Bailey where a former civil client of his was now on criminal trial, and this wasn't the first time.

Hodges, Jerome's attorney, was presently on his right, nearly choking on a homemade chocolate-covered biscuit.

"Well, then," Finsbury began from behind his ancient wooden desk, as he too-loudly downed a last sip of tea. "Surely we can easily come to terms?"

"Right you are," Hodges said. "For the record, my client, Jerome Newton, claims to have stolen nothing from your client: Dr Abrams, is it?"

Finsbury said, "Hmmm. That's not quite what Abrams says, is it then?"

"Bollocks!" Newton rudely replied and casually crossed his legs at the knee. "Abrams is a drunken sod who hasn't worked in years. He wouldn't have secret information about a human cloning even if it was happening on his own verandah. I'll stake my life he never had papers I or anyone else would have wanted to steal. We can come to terms when you drop the suit!"

"Drop the suit?" Finsbury said. "My client, the very distinguished Dr. Abrams, would see me disbarred first."

"What's the point of meeting, then?" Hodges said, gulping down a last bite of dry biscuit.

Finsbury leaned forward. "I'm aware that your journalistic reputation is at stake, Mr. Newton."

Jerome who was aware of this, too, scowled at Finsbury. The fact that *The Times* almost fired him last year—for twice embellishing stories with plausible, but not-quite-accurate details—was the only reason he'd come. One more episode so soon after, and only rag sheets would buy his stories at rock bottom price.

Finsbury continued, "Therefore, I prevailed upon Dr. Abrams to avoid a travesty. He's convinced you forcibly entered his premises and copied his very valuable private files, but on the off-chance there happens to be more than one madman in America trying to clone the departed great, well. I think you see my point."

Hodges chuckled. As the Newton family's attorney, he would counsel them on whether and how vigorously to defend the suit, but this was sounding like a joke. "Precisely what are you hinting at?" he said to Finsbury.

"Precisely this. Tell me to whom Newton's article referred. Show me the notes as proof. If my client's American scientist and your client's American scientist aren't the same man, we will of course withdraw our suit and, in consideration of our error, cover your expenses."

Jerome Newton laughed then spoke derisively. "You bloody swamp crawler! You think I don't recognize a dodge when I see one? You're out for information, no more, no less. You've been put up to this by another paper, trying to steal my story. I'm not telling you a thing!"

Hodges leaned to whisper in Jerome's ear, "Let's not resort to name-calling." He patted Jerome's shoulder then said to Finsbury, "Suppose, instead, you give

us the name of your cloner first. Satisfy us that your Abrams legitimately
believes he's been wronged. We'll sign a confidentiality agreement in advance,
so Abrams avoids the risk we'll divulge any secrets he thinks he has."

Finsbury snorted. "That would compromise Dr. Abrams's case against you,
wouldn't it? I assure you no other news media are involved. I'll sign a
confidentiality agreement of yours, if you like, but you must tell me your
American scientist's name first and show me your notes or we go to trial."

Hodges stood. "I need a moment to consult with Mr. Newton."

"Of course," Finsbury said.

They left Finsbury's office, passed his clerk's desk and went outside to a leafy
cobbled courtyard where Dickens might have walked, and then turned left for
a stroll along the Thames. A barge was going by, heading for Waterloo Bridge,
where tourists would gather at sunset for the famous view—east to the golden
dome of St. Paul's Cathedral, west to the ramparts of Westminster.

"This wouldn't be the first time someone's used the courts for coercion,"
Hodges said. "How vital is it that you keep your secret?"

Jerome Newton stretched and yawned, trying to cover his irritation. He
needed Hodges to believe him. "I respect the man involved, though I believe
what he's doing is utter lunacy. And—" Jerome gazed across the river at the
South Bank Centre complex full of halls, galleries, gardens, cafes, and shops.
"There's a chance—ridiculously small, but still a chance—he will succeed in
the end. Should that happen, I'll be onto a story of the ages. An incredible,
history-changing story."

"And you won't give me a hint of who's being cloned, or by whom?"

Jerome winked at him. "Not a hint, old boy."

"But you'll tell me how you got the information, if not from pilfering
Abrams's files."

Jerome smiled. "I have a hidden talent, Hodges. You're in the presence of one
of the world's best followers."

"Am I? What's your secret?"

"Passé, old boy. A minimum of two cell phones, two drivers, two cars—at
times, three. Works like a charm. Add a nearly invisible earpiece and a
microphone shaped like a pen and voila! Information. I came by it honestly, so
to speak, and I've done my duty by reporting it. I've given humanity a chance
to save itself before dead historical figures begin repopulating the world. Maybe
Genghis Khan's and Tutankhamen's DNA hasn't survived, but will someone try
to replicate Napoleon, Stalin, Abraham Lincoln, Edgar Allen Poe?"

"People are more than their genes."

"How much more? Do you relish bringing back the Marquise de Sade to
find out? However, I won't go so far as to stop the man by publishing his name
outright or risking a leak."

Hodges had been watching him closely. "Very noble of you."

"Yes. Practical, too," Jerome said. "The reason my family has stayed rich enough to retain you full-time, Hodges, is that we've never ignored the opportunity to make a new fortune. If my scientist succeeds, I'm in position to make bloody millions. Would you like to represent me in the negotiations?"

"Negotiations?"

"Surely the scientist will seek a formal agreement when I offer not to immediately publish his name."

"In exchange for?"

"In exchange for exclusive access, now and in the future—interviews and filming as the process unfolds, all for publication after the fact. In exchange for continued exclusive access to the cloned child as it grows." He laughed and gestured across the Thames, its winds presently wafting the smell of a fine curry to him. "They'll want the photos on exhibit at Royal Festival Hall, Hodges. Surely the media will shower buckets of money on whomever reports the first cloning of a dead human being, complete with video of the birth— especially when the cloned man's name would, alone, make headlines worldwide. Surely there's a book, no several, in the offing. Ones I intend to write."

"Really?"

"Hodges, the fact is, I'm weighing a potential cash bonanza against being dragged through a trial I'll ultimately win because I'm innocent. Finsbury's on a fishing expedition, I tell you; or that drunk, Abrams, made a mistake. In either case, I need you to hold them off as long as you can."

Hodges clasped his hands behind his back and watched the barge make its way to Waterloo Bridge. "In that case, Jerome, I'll recommend to the family that we fight. What say we go inside and suggest to Finsbury where to stuff his junior barrister's wig?"

Chapter 24

Tuesday night—Cliffs Landing

Maggie turned out the lights to see the moonlight on the fishpond, the rock wall, and the trees outside. Until now she had passed the time by watching *Mystery* on PBS. She'd first watched *Mystery* about a year ago and couldn't make out the British accents. But the stories were so good she kept tuning in until she understood the men who played Poirot and Sherlock Holmes just as well as she understood Columbo.

Her mind wasn't on the program, tonight. She'd been thinking of what took place today when Dr. Rossi learned she was a virgin—a condition that wasn't precisely her fault. Fourteen years ago, when she found herself twenty-one and still untouched, Maggie had definitely tried to change that. Each time, something had gone wrong.

On her first try the man got such a bad Charlie horse, Maggie had to drive him to the hospital. The second guy had chickened out when he learned she was a virgin, claiming his intentions weren't honorable so he didn't have the right to deflower her. She'd argued he did, to no avail. She and the third prospect had parked in a secluded spot, taken off her bra and were working on her panties, when the wife Maggie hadn't known about arrived.

It kept on like that until Maggie stopped trying because the failed attempts were hurting her feelings. Besides, on the days when life reminded her she had no education, wasn't really ambitious, and would never turn heads when she walked down the street, being a virgin sort of cheered her up. Nowadays, it was definitely special. She concluded either the Lord was protecting her from an unseen danger, or He had something else in mind. When she read Dr. Rossi's journal, she at last knew what it was.

Secretly, she had always felt special, even blessed, but the outside world hadn't seemed to agree.

Already that had changed.

After the exam, Frances seemed rattled. For a while she acted like she was the maid, waiting on Maggie hand and foot. It didn't last. Soon enough Frances got back to being herself, but for a long time Dr. Rossi gazed at Maggie as if she were a hallucination. Only Adeline had stayed the same. She'd said she loved them but they were all crazy to proceed with the media on their heels. Sooner or later they'd be found, even on Cliffs Landing, and since she couldn't dissuade them, she wasn't staying here for the mess. She was off to Europe, for how long she didn't know. Letizia had invited her to visit, and she probably would stop there for a while. Maggie suspected Frances was behind the visit— sending Adeline as her emissary until Frances could go herself.

Then Adeline took off her shahtoosh and gave it to Maggie. "It's a rather too precious shawl," she said, and gave Dr. Rossi a knowing look. "Take it, Maggie. Let it keep you warm through all this."

Dr. Rossi hadn't tried to stop Adeline very hard. In a way he seemed glad she was going. He had Maggie write out postcards and address them to her friend, Sharmina, then asked Adeline to mail them periodically during her trip. Adeline seemed reluctant, but he kissed her on the forehead as she left, and then went back to exclaiming how Maggie's virginity was a sign from God.

Of course she was a virgin. Too embarrassed to tell him, she had assumed he figured it out. How else could she mother Christ?

After a while Dr. Rossi seemed almost himself again. He'd finished the exam, and strapped a monitor on her wrist that continuously transmitted her blood pressure to the lab. At first it had terrified her, but since there was nothing she could do, she tried to relax, knowing it was in the Lord's hands. When Maggie went upstairs to eat the dinner of grilled and steamed foods Frances had managed to cook, Dr. Rossi stayed behind.

Now Maggie rose from her floral sofa, and went into the nursery to see if she could hear him on the other side of the wall in the lab. She heard nothing and it was getting late. Perhaps he'd forgotten she was waiting. She went back in her apartment and opened the door to the obstetrics area, then went left and looked into the lab.

Dr. Rossi sat on a stool at a counter, his head down before a computer screen on which she could barely make out a graph with two wavy lines. At first she thought he was sleeping, but soon he raised his head, his black hair in his eyes and Maggie wondered why God would give hair that gorgeous to a man. The soft, dark stubble on his face seemed like the beards boys grow to look like men.

Maggie was glad she wasn't attracted to men this pretty. If he'd looked like Sam she might have been in trouble, especially with him rummaging around her private parts.

She knocked on the glass door.

"Dr. Rossi?"

He looked toward her as if she were a mirage. Being special was nice, but she'd be glad when he snapped out of it. He rose, switched off the computer, came to the door, and flicked off the lab lights as he left.

"Well?" she said. "Do I pass?"

"The tests aren't complete, yet, but there's something I want to talk with you about."

Maggie didn't like the sound of that. "Come in and take a load off, then."

He followed to her apartment and sat on the sofa, not smiling as she'd hoped he would.

She sat in her rocking chair by the French doors. At first no one spoke, then Maggie couldn't stand the suspense.

"Dr. Rossi, please take pity on my nerves. What is it?"

He leaned over, his elbows on his knees. "The good news is that you won't need preliminary suppression drugs so we can cut seven to ten days off the schedule."

"The bad news?"

He grimaced. "You have borderline high blood pressure. It's in the upper high normal range, but it's close to Stage 1 Hypertension."

She whispered to herself, "Now don't you do this to me, Jesus." She said to

Dr. Rossi, "Normal high is still normal, right?"

"Not for pregnant women. Those with underlying chronic hypertension have a ten times greater risk of developing PIH, that's Pregnancy-Induced Hypertension. There's a 6-8 percent chance of its occurrence anyway. For hypertensive women, it's 60-80 percent."

"What does that mean?"

"PIH is a major cause of fetal and maternal death."

She gazed out at the rock walls, bathed in moonlight. "Is there anything you can do?"

He came and stood beside her. "Yes, but if I give you anti-hypertensive medication it could put the baby at risk. Maggie, you're only thirty-five. You're not overweight. You say there's no history of this in your family. Do you exercise? What in the world do you eat?"

She told him about the fried pork chops and fried biscuits and how she hated exercise.

"A change in your diet and exercise patterns might do the trick. It's been known to lower blood pressure by 9 millimeters or more."

Maggie stood and put her palms on the lapels of his lab coat. "I'll do it, Dr. Rossi! I swear! I promise! I'll walk every day."

"It would have to be at least thirty minutes a day, preferably more."

"I'll do it."

"You'd have to cut out salt. No fried foods. No liquor or coffee. Lots and lots of fruits and vegetables. Bed rest if your pressure climbs even a little."

"I'll do it, I'll do it!"

"If you take vitamins and eat garlic, plenty of garlic, and drink peppermint tea it might help. Medical research is showing these old remedies can be powerful. These particular ones can't hurt, so there's no reason not to try."

"I will. I promise!"

Felix sat on the sofa again, his elbows on his knees, his head down, his hair falling forward and hiding his face. "I'm a doctor. My oath says, 'First, do no harm.' There's still some risk."

Maggie didn't want to go back to being overlooked 99 percent of the time. She didn't want to give up on bringing Jesus back. The world needed him. She needed him. Her heart said this was meant to be.

"I told you it doesn't matter to me, even if I die, as long as the baby lives. My heart's in it. It's all I care about now. Don't people die of broken hearts? You can't sit there and tell me there's such a thing as pregnancy with no risk, because I know better. Print out the contracts, Dr. Rossi, let me sign them. You said your lawyer emailed everything, didn't you? Please. Get up. Get the forms. Miss Rossi can witness our signatures, can't she?"

"I don't know. We're supposed to read them first and get back to my attorney. He might want you to consult a lawyer of your own as well. I think there's more to it than just signing. They're supposed to be notarized, at least."

"Well, it can't hurt, can it? We can sign these now and sign something else later, too, if your lawyer wants, and I don't need to consult anybody else."

He hung his head.

"Don't we trust each other, Dr. Rossi? Isn't that the real point? I'm ready to go ahead without any kind of contract, but if your lawyer says we did it wrong we can fix it later."

He didn't budge or look at her.

"Dr. Rossi, for goodness sake. Suppose somebody finds us and tries to stop us before we start? How many times in our lives do you think we'll get the chance to clone Christ?"

He narrowed his eyes, rose, and fetched two documents and a pen. "This one is a surrogacy agreement. It says you know the source of the DNA. This one takes care of the life annuity, my promise to adopt and have joint custody with you." He went to the house intercom and buzzed Frances. Moments later she walked in, looking anxiously at the two of them.

"The tests came out all right?" she said. "You're going ahead?"

"Everything's fine, Miss Rossi."

He handed the forms to Maggie, who grabbed them as if they'd saved her. She signed them at once. He signed them. Frances signed them. He gave Maggie a copy, took the rest away, and returned holding a tray and wearing gloves.

"This is the first injection."

Worriedly, Frances clasped her hands. "You're beginning now?"

"Yes, yes," Maggie said, looking at the tray. "This is just to prime me. Don't worry, Miss Rossi."

"But I didn't think you had all the test results. Suppose some are troubling?"

"The forms say we can back out up until I'm pregnant, don't they, Dr. Rossi?"

"They do," he said. "This is a hormone called gonadotrophin. It has no real side effects because it occurs naturally in the human body. The dose I'm giving you will cause you to produce up to fifteen eggs. More, if we're lucky. By the time we're ready to harvest your eggs eight to fourteen days from now, I'll have some idea if your blood pressure is being controlled. We can begin now and make the final decision then."

"Blood pressure?" Frances said. "What blood pressure?"

Maggie's eyes were on the tray. "It's all right, Miss Rossi."

He set the tray down, inserted a needle in a vial, upended it and pulled until the syringe filled. Then he put it down and crossed himself. "We should pray first."

"Pray?" Maggie said, losing patience. "Don't you think what we're doing is the biggest prayer we could ever make?"

"Bless us, Father," he said. "Come sit on the sofa, Maggie, I need your hip."

Frances shook her head and left the room.

As she sat, Maggie lowered her pajama bottoms so he could swab her hip. She felt the needle, felt the hormone invade her flesh, then he bandaged the spot and it was over. He took the tray away and returned. Again he sat on her sofa, picked up the remote and flicked on the TV to the final minutes of Hercule Poirot.

"I'll stay with you awhile," he said.

Maggie nodded and went to the bathroom, his poetically resigned expression on her mind, like a lost astronaut floating helplessly through space. She touched the sore spot on her hip gratefully, thinking of what she'd say to make Dr. Rossi smile when she returned.

Chapter 25

Tuesday night—Sam's apartment

Sam had lost his fight to stay awake. He fell asleep on his sofa and had a surrealistic nightmare in which someone had cloned London Bridge. The replicas were installed everywhere and, all over the world, the bridges were falling down and reassembling to fall again. Whenever one tumbled into a river, dozens of African children drowned. When his cell phone rang, Sam jolted awake, breathing hard, and answered the phone.

"He's ready to see you," Brown's butler said.

Hurriedly Sam splashed water on his face, brushed his hair, and arranged his clothes. He headed to Brown's elevator, checking the time—only 8:30 p.m., 1:30 a.m. London time. Finsbury would be sleeping the sleep of the seriously-in-trouble, he hoped. How he'd fouled up the arm-twisting job Sam had handed him for Jerome Newton was a mystery.

Newton was skating on the edge with his journalism career. Nothing else he had was his—not the money because he wasn't the heir, not the title, not his social standing. These came through his uncle, the Duke. All Newton personally possessed was his job. One source had confided, "A young Winston Churchill sending dispatches from South Africa's Boer War, is how he fancies himself." Going overboard to make this true was how he'd landed on probation with *The Times*. Even a whiff of a suit about a story's source and Jerome

Newton should have given up. Why hadn't he?

It troubled Sam, just like those photos of the dead African kids. They troubled him and he wasn't sure why. The Rossis' sudden disappearance bothered him, too. He'd found out from his substitute that they had been in the Range Rover—Felix Rossi, Frances Rossi, and Maggie. Where they'd gone or why no one knew. From the hidden surveillance room, Sam had checked their apartment in the middle of the day and found it completely dark, as if they'd closed the blinds and drapes for a long absence. He thought the Rossis had a yacht moored in Spain. Maybe they'd gone there.

He got off the elevator and there was the butler, ready to lead him to the library. When Sam arrived, Mr. Brown was already there. A first.

"Was your trip successful?" Brown said when Sam appeared.

Sam stood before the desk. "Not yet."

"Sit down and tell me why." Brown motioned to the sofa.

Sam sat and explained what had so far occurred. Brown nodded, saying nothing, a sign of his confidence Sam would find a way to prevail. When they'd finished, Brown opened a desk drawer and tossed another envelope to Sam.

"For our friend at the consulate tomorrow morning, Sam."

As before, Sam pocketed the envelope. Without planning to he asked, "Not that I care, but why do you suppose they're killing the kids?" He made sure not to sound too interested.

Brown looked up at him. "Is that a serious question?"

"Yeah, I guess."

"Why do you want to know?" Brown was appraising him.

Sam hoped his answer would make Brown talk. "No particular reason. Trying to understand the African mind set, I guess."

"You didn't travel there during your seafaring days?"

"Some, not much."

"Their mind set is no different from that of the Serbians who killed children in Bosnia's marketplace for four years."

"I didn't understand that one, either."

"Really? It's fear. Fear will make anyone do anything perceived as necessary to survive. A frightened person is easily controlled. Only the fearless are free. They're rare, as it happens."

"What are the Africans afraid of?"

"The same thing we were in the last two world wars: each other. Within Africa's fifty-four nations are hundreds of separate ethnic groups. Colonialism disrupted their internal controls. This is one result."

"Well, if it keeps up, there won't be any more kids there to kill."

Brown nodded. "Don't feel sad for them. Species become extinct, so do races. There are no Phoenicians anymore, no Etruscans or Minoans. They and their cultures succumbed to nature, to themselves, or to more aggressive races. Their genes contributed to human evolution, but they're not identifiable anymore."

"You think Africans are becoming extinct?"

"Yes, eventually." Brown stood. "For now I think their numbers will just drastically decline."

Sam was stunned. "What makes you say that?"

"Drugs and violence in their poor neighborhoods here. In Africa, HIV and wars—even in the countries most beset by AIDS. In one hundred days in 1994, Rwanda's Hutus killed 800,000 Tutsis, trying to wipe Tutsi genes off the earth."

"Hitler tried that, too, but it didn't make Jews extinct."

"Africa's experiencing not just a holocaust, but an apocalypse of war, poverty, and disease. Forty million African children will be orphaned by AIDS in the next decade, though not for long since most will be infected by it, too. It's like watching the last of the dinosaurs start to crawl into their tar pits to die—a process that in this case may take less time."

Sam looked at the man he thought of as his captain, wondering what made him so cold at times.

Mr. Brown motioned Sam toward the door.

Sam left, thinking of the children in the paper with their heads chopped open and not liking Brown's grim prediction. If it was true, it didn't feel right that Brown could see it so clearly and nobody was doing anything. He wanted to talk with someone and wished Maggie were around, though he wasn't sure she trusted him enough to discuss war and AIDS in Africa. If she did know the things Mr. Brown had described, he wondered what she thought about them. Most of all, he wondered where she was. He wished he'd activated the tape system that could have recorded the goings-on in Rossi's place before they left.

Sam returned to his apartment and for probably the twentieth time, read the *Cloning in America* article in *The Times*. He wondered why the story, if true, had surfaced in a London paper and not here in *The Inquirer* or something.

Sam dropped the newspaper, suddenly remembering a reporter with a British accent asking for Dr. Rossi about a week ago. Now, Rossi had disappeared.

A coincidence?

He took out his cell phone, pressed a button, and listened as it dialed the country code for England, the city code for London, followed by Walter Finsbury's home number—never mind that over there it was 2:00 a.m. When Finsbury sleepily answered and complained about the time, Sam growled that he'd damned well better wake up, get out of bed, find a photo of Jerome Newton right away, and fax it to Sam's apartment in New York.

Sam clicked off the phone, remembering what Brown said about people controlled by fear. Sam had long thought the same. That's why he tried not to be afraid as he thought of Maggie leaving in the Range Rover with Dr. Rossi, an American scientist who, if Sam was right, had the kind of expert knowledge a person would need to make a clone.

chapter 26

Wednesday a.m.—Virgin Atlantic, London to Newark, NJ

As he flew from London Heathrow to Newark Airport, Jerome Newton kept his eye on the cabin's closed red curtain. If it opened, someone in Upper Class might see him, though chances were it wouldn't be anyone he knew. Still he didn't want to be gawked at by people who'd think what he once did when he glimpsed a passenger sitting behind first class: *It's such a pity you're poor.*

On Hodges's recommendation, the family had agreed to cover Jerome's legal defense and his expenses in America, provided they descended to a lower scale. He'd been banned from the Concorde, from first class and from Virgin Atlantic's cheaper Upper Class, as well. Jerome felt humiliated to be sitting in a Virgin Atlantic Premium Economy seat—all the more because he'd never liked Richard Branson, Virgin Atlantic's founder. He was England's P.T. Barnum, too influential to ignore. Jerome had been among the invited few on Virgin's inaugural flight, but he deplored Branson's circus tactics, and envied his net worth—unencumbered by family and trusts. And the man smiled altogether too much.

On a tiny TV screen in the gray seatback before him, Jerome watched a kid who needed a shave get on a skateboard. It was a rerun from the TV comedy series, Spaced. Someone had made a fortune by putting a girl who thought too much and a kid who didn't think at all together in a north London flat. Jerome leaned back and closed his eyes, hoping the laudable Dr. Felix Rossi did plan to outdo Richard Branson in the outrageous department.

Jerome hoped Rossi had seen the article in *The Times,* or heard about it on the news, and was frantically cloning DNA from the Shroud of Turin by now. If so, Jerome need only reveal he knew about it, then offer a deal.

He'd call Rossi the moment Virgin landed, then take a taxi straight to Museum Mile.

———

Wednesday p.m.—Sam's apartment

Sam watched, his fists clenched, as the photo of Jerome Newton came through on his fax. Though he had called Finsbury twice more about a photo, it had taken until one-thirty in the afternoon to locate one. Now it was here. Sam recognized the long jaw as soon as it appeared and the straight line that was Jerome Newton's mouth. Next came the eyes and the wavy hair. No question it was him. It couldn't be a coincidence that this reporter who had written the *Cloning in America* article about an American scientist, was trying to spy on Rossi a few days ago. Sam had gone online and pulled up articles from scientific journals to verify that it was microbiologists who were doing the cloning. Rossi was a microbiologist.

The machine disconnected and Sam picked up the fax. He'd flown to London and paid a wad of money to learn what he already knew. Without Newton he never would have put it together, though. Microbiologists were a dime a dozen. Of course Brown didn't care about the expense. He wanted an answer. Who was the American scientist cloning the dead?

Though Sam was sure he had the answer, he hesitated, but only for a second. In three years at sea he'd never disobeyed an order, nor in his eleven years with Brown. Brown was the captain. He'd know what to do. He folded Newton's photo and went out to the elevators. He entered the code for the ninth floor, his stomach churning. He felt the smooth acceleration of the expensive elevator car and stared at his troubled expression in the mirrors. He passed the fourth floor, the fifth, feeling more uncomfortable as he rose. At the seventh floor, Sam punched the stop button hard with his thumb and closed his eyes, picturing Maggie in the Rossis' Range Rover. Sam had asked for details from the substitute doorman, who revealed Rossi seemed preoccupied when they left; his sister had seemed mad, but the Rossi's maid had seemed happy as hell.

Why?

Perplexed, Sam stared at the elevator keypad, wondering what was wrong with him. Never before had he delayed fulfilling an order from Brown. Yet all he could think of was Maggie. He felt lonely as he wondered where she was. He pictured her in her Graham Smith hat, peeved by his teasing. He pictured her ushering him out of Rossi's Solarium in her apron, pictured her snooping through the halls. In the five years he'd known her, Maggie had made him remember there were still good people in the world. In the elevator, she'd felt so vulnerable when he caught her in his arms.

Sam canceled the ninth floor code.

He went back to his apartment and into the surveillance room hidden behind the pantry. The Rossis' place was still pitch dark in every room. Where were they?

He wasn't big on taking independent initiatives because, in his opinion, too many already did and not well. Sam offered what the world was short on: a man who shut up and delivered. If it weren't for his worry about Maggie, he'd be delivering Rossi to Brown right now.

He left the surveillance room. Maybe Maggie had only gone along to cook and clean. He looked up the number of a friend who could search the passenger logs of flights. Sam phoned him. During the wait, he logged onto the services that collected public records like property deeds and, for a fee, made them available on the web.

His cell phone rang.

"That fellow you were looking for is here," said his replacement at the door.

"On my way."

Sam went out to the lobby and found Jerome Newton sitting on one of the cushioned benches. The last time Sam had sat there was before his fifteen minutes with the dancer.

He put it out of his mind in favor of more important things.

Newton stood when he saw Sam. "Hi. Remember me?"

"Sure do. What're you after now?"

Sam watched Newton put on a repentant expression. "I'd like to apologize for our last encounter. Obviously, you're a man of ethics."

"No problem. What can I do for you?"

"I've been phoning Dr. Rossi for over an hour and wondered if anyone knows when he'll return."

Sam rubbed his chin. "Not soon."

"Really? Could you phone him?"

"You said Rossi had something interesting in his valise. What?"

"Why do you want to know?"

He raised his eyebrows noncommittally and watched Newton decide he was too dumb to be a threat.

"Will you phone him for me?" Newton asked.

Sam looked uncooperatively away.

"He had threads from an ancient cloth. Happy now?"

In spite of himself, Sam blinked. "Can't phone him for you, but I know where he is."

"Where?" Newton asked as if pained by the suspense.

"Out in Colorado skiing," Sam said and kept a straight face. "He rented a cabin. No phones."

Newton sighed. "Do you know when he'll be back?"

"Couple months."

Newton looked desperate. "That long? My good chap, I know you don't want to help me, but it's urgent that I get in touch with him. Really, would you—"

Sam leaned forward. "You wouldn't still happen to have that four hundred dollars? I made a little bet I can't cover and—"

Immediately, Newton pulled out his wallet. He pressed five hundred dollars into Sam's hands, along with a notepad and paper.

Sam tried to look like a man newly plunging into sin, but he felt like laughing. In a million years, Newton wouldn't guess Sam had caused his legal troubles. "Nobody ever knows I told you this, all right?"

"Of course. I'm a journalist. Anonymous sources."

Sam wrote directions to an old friend's cabin hanging off the side of a ledge—way, way up a mountain in Colorado.

Newton took it, saying. "Well, let's hope he doesn't freeze to death, nor I for that matter."

Sam patted him on the back. "If so, I'll come to your funeral."

As Newton drove away, Sam stared after him in disbelief. The only ancient cloth he'd heard of in Turin was the Shroud, supposedly Jesus' burial cloth. Was there anything on it that a fanatic could clone? Anything that would make a usually savvy, but deeply religious and openhearted Maggie suddenly abandon the good sense she had?

Chapter 27

4:45 p.m. Palisades Parkway

In a Lincoln Town Car, borrowed from the pool, Sam crossed the state line from New Jersey back into New York and stopped at the first gas station on the Palisades. It was on a center island, north and south parkway traffic dividing around it. He bought a Rockland County map and spread it on the seat of his car. It took a while to locate Cliffs Landing. He had passed it miles back.

He'd learned the Rossis hadn't taken a flight today, and, at first, he'd found no evidence of a second home. He'd been about to give up and wait for a credit card trail, when he remembered the Rossis had an aunt who'd died. He called the Church of St. Thomas More and learned her name: Enea Evans. A little more sleuthing and he'd phoned the Rockland County Land Records office. Yes, Enea Evans owned an improved four-acre lot, located on Cliffs Landing at 200 Lawford Lane. Before leaving, he'd strapped on a shoulder holster under his black leather jacket. One thing he'd learned as a private eye was never to approach the unknown unarmed.

Sam folded the map and headed south, reached the turn-off, took it, and was lost. There were virtually no street signs in Cliffs Landing, and the few names he did glimpse weren't on the map. It had no stores, no gas stations, no public buildings of any kind, only a church with its doors closed and no cars in the parking lot.

The rest were private homes. Half had cost someone an arm, a leg, and a section of the torso. The others were of modest size. Sam suspected the owners of these and their forebears had lived here a long time and probably wouldn't sell easily.

What struck him most about the place was its sense of isolation. One-car roads that turned and twisted. Moss-hung trees with spreading limbs and wizened trunks that looked as old as the country. Nothing about Cliffs Landing extended a welcome to the stranger. Nothing said: *y'all come back, now, hear?* What the Landing said was *stay away, no one's home, if you're lost, turn around and leave.* One huge place had fences all around and a big sign warning of vicious dogs. Most didn't bother with fences. The lack of street signs and visible house numbers, the narrow roads with no sidewalks, the forbidding old trees, the very air of Cliffs Landing protected them. Living here was probably delightful. Visiting was not.

Sam's Town Car lumbered conspicuously round and round, back and forth until, unexpectedly, he saw a sign that read: Lawford Lane.

He headed along it and wondered how to find 200 Lawford Lane among these trees and hidden homes.

It was getting dark. He was stiff from sitting in the car. He was hungry and needed to take a leak. Giving up, he drove to the end of Lawford Lane and parked on the grass beneath a wall. He left the road and saw thick woods stretched behind it. A perfect place to relieve himself. He didn't know why most guys loved peeing outdoors—maybe some latent instinct about marking your territory. Afterwards, he headed in the direction of the Hudson, knowing it must be downhill through these trees. The ground sloped more and more. He heard the sound of rushing water. Just in time, he remembered why the Parkway was called the Palisades.

Sam stopped only feet from what was easily a three hundred foot drop down a wall of cliffs. With ease he found the waterfall he'd heard. It cascaded down in sheets to the banks below and ran off toward the Hudson—the kind of spot every kid in Cliffs Landing must know and have visited.

He would have rested there, enjoying the waterfall and the lights coming on across the river, if he hadn't needed to find out if Maggie was here and why.

Knowing the house must be near, he moved north on the cliff until he saw a wall of rock through the trees, too symmetrical to be natural. Through his binoculars, he saw it was one of those rock, wood, and glass homes that always made him marvel. Softly he whistled. Not an artificial thing in sight. It was the kind of place nature freaks built, provided they had buckets of money. Sam doubted if much plastic had ever gotten beyond its doors. Maybe a toothbrush, an orange juice carton, but that's about it.

The place was gorgeous. It was the kind of place the Rossis would own. But why did people who built homes with walls of glass, not worry that anyone could look in? Sam crawled closer and scanned what appeared to be the living room. A woman was there. She picked up a magazine, flipped through it, and left. She looked like Frances Rossi, but he had to be sure.

He circled the house to the left and came to what was probably a garden. Ivy spiked above the enclosing wall. Sam thought it was thick enough to hide him. He hauled himself up, lay low, and peeped through the ivy at a fishpond surrounded by white pebbles.

French doors opened onto the garden. Even with binoculars he could hardly see inside. A woman sat alone in the shadows watching TV. At first, he couldn't make out who she was. He waited, needing confirmation that this was the right place and, if he could, to see what was going on. Then he'd know what to say when he knocked on the front door.

He saw a figure in the doorway. A man. When he turned on the light, Sam saw it was Felix Rossi. "You've found them, Duffy," Sam whispered, congratulating himself. Felix wore a lab coat and surgical gloves and held a covered tray. He recognized Maggie on the floral sofa. She wore slippers, pajamas, and a robe. What was Rossi up to? What right did he have to walk into her bedroom like that?

Growing angry, he watched as Rossi put the tray down, inserted a thermometer in her mouth, then looked at something clamped to her wrist. Perhaps Maggie had only gotten a cold or the flu.

This delusion was dispelled by what happened next. Rossi sat next to her. Maggie took off her robe. He uncovered the tray, picked up a needle and filled it. Then Maggie lowered her pajama bottoms, raised the top, and exposed her backside. He swabbed it and injected her with the contents of the needle, then covered the injection site with a round bandage. Whatever they were doing, Rossi handled her too casually, as if she weren't a person.

While Maggie straightened her clothes, Rossi put down the needle and dropped his head as if his heart would break.

Sam watched, enraged, as Maggie consoled him. He could tell from their attitudes Rossi wasn't even screwing her. That Sam could understand and forgive. She was nothing but a guinea pig to him. Instead of being concerned for her, he was moaning like a wimp.

Sam tried for self-control. What the hell was he doing here, anyway, hiding in the ivy? But he couldn't take his eyes off them. Where was Maggie's good-natured toughness? She'd never let people put anything over on her and that included him, so what was this?

Still it was none of his business. Maggie was grown and could make her own decisions. But she was a woman and Sam was a man. She couldn't know what he did. That men only came in two varieties: those who did their best to protect, or at least not hurt, the defenseless, and wimp-assed snotty little bastards who were a danger to everyone they knew. Every time Sam had sailed, there'd been a cowardly know-it-all aboard, and half the time he'd almost sunk the ship. It was clear that Rossi was that type.

If something happened to Maggie because of working for this jerk, Sam would feel responsible, as if he should have watched her back, helped her to keep being tough.

Maggie looked like she was pleading with Rossi. She dropped to her knees and tried to get him to raise his head.

Sam couldn't stand it any more. His blood boiled over like it had when he was young on the docks in sailors' bars—over a woman, a bet, or even a bad word, except this time he wasn't drunk and it was Maggie, his friend. He jumped down from the wall, raced across the white pebbles, and banged on the damned French doors.

Chapter 28

Wednesday evening—Cliffs Landing

Maggie screamed at the sudden, loud banging on the doors and flew to her feet. Dr. Rossi moved in front of her, shouting, "Who is it? Get away from that door!"

Maggie ran and turned off the lights then couldn't believe her eyes. "It's Sam, Dr. Rossi! Sam, the doorman!"

"What?" He went to the doors and unlocked them. "What in the world—"

Sam came through the doors, grabbed Rossi by the collar, and wrestled him to the floor as Maggie shrieked, "Sam! Stop! Help! Help!"

Footsteps thundered on the stairs, then Frances was at the door, screaming, "Stop! No! Help!"

Sam had raised his fist, but the screaming made him pause long enough for Maggie to throw herself against him before his fist could descend while Frances, still shrieking, ran to her brother and helped him scramble away.

"Sam! Sam!" Maggie shouted until the wild look left Sam's eyes.

"All right, all right," he said. "I'm through. I'm sorry. I'm through. Okay? All right?"

Frances looked terrified. "But you're Sam Duffy, the doorman!"

"Yes," Sam said, looking cornered as he hugged Maggie to him, his arm encircling her neck.

"What are you doing here?" Frances shouted. "I just can't believe this."

Sam erupted. "Yeah, babe? But you can believe your brother using Maggie for a guinea pig. That you can believe!"

"Don't you dare call me *babe*, you—"

Dr. Rossi rose to his feet. "How do you presume—"?

"No, how do you presume, you little—"

Decidedly, Maggie reached up and covered Sam's mouth. He stared down at her in surprise then gently moved her hand, grunting, "All right, all right."

The two men glared at each other. Then, Dr. Rossi, his eyes still on Sam, shrugged his shoulder as if it pained him saying, "What were you, a linebacker?"

Sam ignored him. "Maggie, are you okay?"

"Other than almost dying of a heart attack, you mean? Yes, I'm okay. Really. I'm all right. What in the world are you doing here, Sam?"

"That's an excellent question, Maggie," Dr. Rossi said.

"Yes, excellent," Frances agreed.

Maggie was astonished by Sam's sudden appearance.

"Go ahead, Mr. Duffy," Dr. Rossi began. "Give me a reason why I shouldn't call the police."

"Do what the hell you like, but call me Sam, because I'm not about to call you Dr. Rossi."

"What difference do you imagine that makes? Sam, do you realize that if you'd knocked on the front door expressing concern for Maggie, we would have talked with you just as quickly?"

"Yeah, I thought of that. It slipped my mind when I saw you inject her like a rat!"

Dr. Rossi looked out at the pebbled garden. "Oh, I see. Perhaps you can tell us why you were out there at all?" he said, obviously trying for self control.

"To ask why you've dragged Maggie into this."

Dr. Rossi flushed purple. "How could you possibly know what *this* is?"

"I know, never mind how. I've kept your location from that reporter. The one who wrote the *Cloning in America* article? He's looking for you."

Rossi looked stunned. "You mean he's come to the building again?"

"Yes."

"What did you tell him?"

"I told him you were in Colorado. He's gone after you."

Dr. Rossi gave a surprised laugh and so did Frances, though hers sounded nervous.

"Back to Maggie," Sam said.

"Apparently you haven't noticed me sitting here right next to you, Sam," Maggie said. "I can speak just fine for myself."

"Maggie, no offense, but I want to hear it from him. Why is she involved, Felix?"

"Just for the record, Sam, be explicit about what you think I'm doing if you don't mind."

"Trying to clone goddamn Christ?"

Dr. Rossi raised his hands in the air as if he were flabbergasted. "Does all of New York know?"

"Not yet."

"I see." Dr. Rossi sighed like he was making a decision. "Sam, are you religious?"

"I go to mass every Christmas and Easter."

"But you believe in God?"

"I guess. I've never seen him."

Dr. Rossi stuffed his hands in his pockets, jiggled keys and said, "I have."

Maggie heard Sam mutter, "Oh, Jesus."

"Yes." Dr. Rossi turned to him. "That's who I saw as a boy, as plain as I'm seeing you. Jesus Christ. I was telling Maggie about it when you arrived. I'd had an auto accident and he was there. To this day I remember his face. The next time I saw it, I was gazing at The Shroud of Turin."

The room was silent, Sam looking away from Dr. Rossi.

Frances said, "Not everyone will understand that story, Felix."

"I understand," Sam said. "You believe—"

"I don't believe. I know."

Sam grunted. "You have a right to your beliefs. That's not what I question. It's Maggie's—"

She punched Sam's shoulder. "Sam, don't be a meat head! Nobody can make me do what I don't want. I asked to be the one. No, I begged. Didn't I, Dr. Rossi, Miss Rossi? I begged! On my knees I begged to sign his contract and—"

"Contract?" Sam said.

Briefly, Maggie looked down. "Yes, well. Okay, I guess the lawyer did get a little upset that we moved so fast, and I guess Miss Rossi couldn't witness it after all so we made new copies and went out and got our signatures notarized today. It's official." Maggie didn't mention that she still hadn't read it. She trusted God and Dr. Rossi, not a lawyer's words.

Sam balled his fists. "No contract on this earth can force you to—"

"Not force, Sam," she said. "It's just saying what we agree to. It's what I want."

"At first I said no," Dr. Rossi continued, "but only because I didn't remember how God does work in mysterious ways. I didn't know Maggie was—" Felix stopped.

As he and Frances gazed at Maggie, the pride she'd felt in her virginity disappeared. Would Sam think she was virtuous or that no man had wanted her?

"Maggie was what?" Sam said.

"It's not for me to say." Felix moved to the French doors and looked out at the night.

"What?" Sam insisted.

"Oh, Sam!" Maggie said and covered her eyes. "It's none of your business!"

He glared at her. "Maggie was what?"

Realizing they had to make Sam understand, she whispered. "Fit to carry God's son. All right?"

"What?" Sam said.

"Fit, Sam. Fit!"

"Fit? What does that mean?"

Maggie shouted, "I'm a virgin, all right?"

She watched in fear as Sam rose, shaking his head as if incapable of speech. He reached in his jacket, brandished a gun, pushed Dr. Rossi to the wall and jammed the gun tight against his throat.

Sam shouted, "You little fucker! You motherfucker! What kind of sick damn shit is this?"

Again, Maggie and Frances jumped to their feet, screaming. They tried to pull Sam away but he didn't budge.

Maggie shouted. "Sam, stop! Stop it! You can't assault Dr. Rossi with a gun."

"I can't?"

Sam slipped the gun quickly in his pocket and crunched his fist into Rossi's jaw as Frances and Maggie shrieked. He pulled him up by the collar, blood dripping from his lip, and jammed the gun against his throat again.

"For God's sake, Maggie, for God's sake!" Sam sputtered. "I can't believe you're letting them do this to you and still you're calling them Dr. Rossi and Miss Rossi!"

Hurriedly, Maggie said, "Dr. Rossi, do you mind if I call you Felix?"

"No," he said in a hoarse voice.

Her eyes on her brother, his sister said, "Call me Frances anytime you like."

"Thank you, Frances. See, Sam? I'm not calling them that anymore."

If she hadn't been so frightened, Maggie would have been relieved. She agreed with Sam that she should be using their given names, but she hadn't known how to broach the subject. She hadn't thought of holding a gun to

Felix's head.

For an instant, no one spoke, as if they'd somehow reached a brink from which they all must jump. Standing there in the twilight, near the floral sofa, wondering whether Sam was going to blow Felix's brains out, Maggie had a revelation.

Sam Duffy loved her.

Maybe no one else ever had, but Sam did. Watching him, Maggie doubted he even knew. She wasn't white, beautiful, or sexy. Not the kind of woman she'd imagined Sam would love, but he did.

Chapter 29

It was as if they were thinking with a single mind. Sam had to curb his temper. He had to do it voluntarily. They were waiting.

Sam screwed up his mouth like he was trying not to curse. He lowered the gun, pulled out the clip, and laid both on the table. His promise to behave was clear.

Her arm around her brother's shoulder, Frances said in a brittle voice, "For what it's worth, I agree with you, Sam. I think this is all a terrible idea, a tragedy in the making, and I've done my best to talk them both out of it from the start."

Sam nodded. "You've got sense, then, Frances."

Felix wiped blood from his mouth. "You owe me an explanation of how you learned what you know! After all, it's of some interest to me."

"If and when you need to know, I'll tell you. I just came to get Maggie out of here." He turned to her. "Pack your things. We're leaving."

"I'm leaving, am I?"

"This could get dangerous. You need to leave. Pack your things."

"What are you not telling us?" Felix asked.

Sam didn't respond.

Maggie said, "Answer him, Sam Duffy, or I'm not listening to another thing you say."

Sam studied the floral sofa, sensing Maggie disbelieved the neutral mask he'd made of his face.

"Common sense," he said. "This could be dangerous."

Frances said, "You're not just a doorman. You're nothing close to being only a doorman, are you?"

Sam snorted. "Only, huh? Yes and no."

Felix was keeping his distance from Sam. They were virtually the same height, but Sam easily had fifty pounds on him—all muscle. "What does that mean?"

Sam sat down and the others followed.

"It means you should trust me when I tell you there's potential danger here. You should give up this so-called cloning project of yours. It's got to be medically dangerous for Maggie. Have you told her?"

"I know all I need to know," she said, disliking his implication that she couldn't think for herself.

"As for you, Felix," Sam continued, "I guess I can see wanting to be the first scientist to clone the dead, but a clone of Christ? Won't you be a laughing stock? Sooner or later all the press will know who you are and what you're up to. They'll find out long before any nine months is up."

"May I know how you found me?"

"Using methods any lawyer and private detective could, and a little common sense."

"I see."

"That's what you really are?" Frances said. "A private detective?"

Sam ignored her and answered Felix. "No, you don't see. The press will find you and so will others. People who don't care about a Second Coming because they never cared about the first. People who've made a point of trying to break all ten commandments."

"I see."

"You keep saying that," Sam replied. "I'm telling you that you don't."

"Why are you so sure?"

"Do you have a gun in the house?"

"No."

"Do you have a security system installed?"

"No."

"Have you swept the place for bugs?"

"No."

Sam shook his head, rose and walked to the door and back. "You people have no idea what's going to happen to you, do you?"

"What do you feel is going to happen, Sam?"

"You're out here in a glass house in the woods. If nothing else, one day you'll get out of the shower and have paparazzi standing in your bedroom, snapping photos of your naked ass. And that's just for starters." Sam gestured with a fling of his arm. "Look, every kook within a thousand miles, hell, in the world, will hop, limp, and crawl to get a look at El Nuevo Virgen Maria, expecting to be healed." He turned to Maggie. "Are you ready for that, my girl?"

"If God wills it—yes."

Sam groaned. "Look, can't you people imagine what religious extremists will do? There will be more snipers in those woods than the 1950s civil rights activists dreamed of in all their nightmares. Do you think the police at Cliffs Landing are up to that? The place will be *packed*. There'll be people selling dolls that look like Maggie and crosses and hotdogs; people who want a piece of her child—something that he touched, a lock of hair, and another and another. My God! *That's* the threat."

"Well, we'll get a security system—"

"You need a gun."

Felix pointed at the table. "That's the first and last gun that's going to be in this house."

"Listen, Rossi, if Maggie stays here—and I hope she doesn't, but if she does—you're going to have to deal with me. You might want to walk off a cliff, but I'm not going to let her do it with you."

Maggie couldn't believe what she was hearing.

At first Felix looked angry then he narrowed his eyes in thought. "In that case, perhaps you might help us. We need three weeks here. A month at the most. Then we could go anywhere, though I'd actually prefer to stay here. You don't know this town. I do."

Maggie grabbed his hand. "Oh, Sam, would you help us? Can you give us three or four weeks?"

"I'd cover the costs, pay what you ask," Felix added.

"Not that I'm going to do it, but what's the month for, Rossi?"

"That's when we'll know if there'll be a child."

"That's your concern. Mine is Maggie. I'd like to speak to her alone."

"Of course, Sam," Frances quickly said. As Felix gazed at Maggie with pleading eyes, Frances practically dragged him from the room and closed the door behind them.

Maggie sat on one end of the sofa and patted the cushion at the other end. "Sit with me."

"When a woman says that, I'm usually in trouble."

"Oh yes, you're in trouble, Sam Duffy. Sit down anyway."

He took off his jacket and his shoulder holster, looking around as if he hadn't noticed the room before. Again Maggie thought he'd make a wrestler. She pictured him in green tights, shamrocks tattooed on his biceps, and wondered why poor Felix's bones weren't broken.

He looked at the door as if to make sure it was closed, then sat where he'd been told, putting his knee up on the couch and turning to her.

"Maggie, my girl, how do I get you out of here? You're too sensible for this. You don't belong here." He pointed his thumb toward the door through which Felix and Frances had gone. "This is going to turn into a mess."

Maggie felt her eyes watering. "You don't even know me, Sam."

"You're wrong." He patted her hand. "I know you, because I know people. All kinds. I've been trying to be your friend for five years."

She moved her hand. "Get out of here, Sam."

"I don't really mean like that—though hey, I'm a man. Sex is something I try never to turn down, but that's not what I'm talking about. I mean I like you, Maggie. I really do. Some days I think you're the best thing in that building. You don't know what goes on there."

She looked up at him, her suspicions confirmed by that one sentence. She didn't know what went on in the building, but Sam did? How? There was nothing strange or scandalous happening on the first eight floors or she would have heard.

"You're talking about Mr. Brown, aren't you, Sam Duffy? Then I guess you're not really a doorman, like Frances said. Is that why you carry a gun? Is it him you really work for?"

She watched his noncommittal expression return.

"Oh, you don't have to cover up on my account. Nothing slips out of my mouth unless I want it to. Is that where all this danger's really coming from? Something to do with Brown?"

Sam spread his fingers wide in frustration. "Maggie! Danger's right under your nose. When did Felix last deliver a baby? I read his bio online. You can't put your life in his hands!"

"I'm satisfied with him. And don't bother telling me I can't be sure whose DNA it is and all. I don't want to hear it." She turned her head away.

Sam reached to her chin and turned it back, but he didn't say anything.

She sighed and said, "I guess I should tell you enough so you'll understand."

He nodded, worry in his eyes.

Maggie looked out at the night, not seeing the dark, pebbled garden, but a different night, twenty years ago. She saw the crowd that had gathered around her parents' house, shouting the Johnsons should get out of town. It might sound made up to him, sound like a soap opera, but by searching for her, barging in and threatening to blow Felix's head off for her, Sam had earned the basic facts.

"I was born in Macon, Georgia. Did I ever say?"

He shook his head.

"Well, I was. Get ready for a sob story."

"What happened?"

"We were farmers. My daddy owned 260 acres, all told, until we had three straight years of drought. Like everybody else, he asked the bank for a loan to get by, but my daddy owned rich land. Know what happened?"

"No loan."

"No loan. Foreclosure. We moved north like a lot of others with hardly anything but the clothes on our backs. A man who used to till his own land, hauled other people's garbage. It killed him in less than three years. Mama passed the year after that."

How old were you?

"Fifteen."

He stretched out his legs and leaned back as if he'd been run over. "And you were alone in New York?"

"Yes. Can you picture how hard that was?"

"How do people survive tragedy like that? The Irish have had it, too."

"I can tell you how I did."

"How?"

"By the grace of God. With the help of my friend, Sharmina, and the 131st Street Baptist Church."

Sam nodded. "What are you trying to tell me, Maggie?"

"That in the process I survived troubles you can't imagine. So I appreciate it, Sam Duffy, I appreciate it—but I don't need taking care of. I'm not some fragile little thing."

"How do you expect me to leave you here, knowing what you'll do?"

"I promised my life to God. He's the one who got me through before. He'll do it now."

"So that's it? That's why you're a virgin? That's why you want to help Felix Rossi?"

After returning his gaze for a while, she lowered her head. She'd never been a liar and wasn't starting now, especially with a man who'd come to help her. "That's what I tell myself. Some days I believe it's true. There's a name for what I am. You know what it is?"

"What?"

Her eyes welled with tears. "I'm just an old maid, Sam."

He shook his head.

"Well, it's true. I'm an old maid and a pretty ugly one, to boot."

"Maggie, you're just thirty-something, aren't you?"

"Thirty-five."

"You're not old. You're not ugly. Have you ever bothered to look at your own eyes?"

"If my eyes could walk around on their own, yeah, somebody might say I'm not bad. As it is, they're connected to all the rest of me—my plain face, short hair, skinny legs, big behind and . . . There are mirrors everywhere I go, Sam, and I'm not blind. Nobody will ever mistake me for Adeline, for instance."

"The hell with Adeline!"

"Lots of men would go there for her, that's for sure. You know my Graham Smith hat? When she put it on, I saw how the hat was meant to look!"

"So that's what got you down about it. Maggie, don't talk like this! Don't tear yourself apart. You're not what you're saying."

"You don't know me, I tell you."

"Is that so? Remember I said I'd been a sailor?"

She looked at him. "Yeah?"

He pointed to a scar on his neck. "A whore in Taiwan gave me that one."

"Oh," Maggie said and tried not to look scandalized.

"One thing I know is women. Another thing I know is most men. Now me? I'm 50 percent scoundrel, just like you always said. I love raw sex, Maggie. I'm weak to a dangerous whore." He laughed. "In fact, I recently met my female mirror. I'll probably never see her again, but she's a tomcat, just like me. I have another bad trait. I can't keep away from boozing and brawling on the docks. At least twice a year I've got to go and do it."

Maggie felt hurt, imagining his female mirror. "Well, you could try to keep away, I suppose, if you wanted to, Sam."

"I'm telling you I know people inside out, from their gutters to their penthouses and sometimes they're not different. Maggie Clarissa Johnson—"

She smiled. "You remember my middle name?"

"I know who you are."

She looked up at him suspiciously. "Who am I?"

"You're as tough as that whore in Taiwan. She didn't have your good heart. She wasn't wise, you are. You have a thousand times more guts. In that department, alone, you've got Adeline beat to hell and back. You've got your own kind of beauty. You notice everything around you. You make me laugh at myself .... You're ... I'll show you who you really are."

Sam Duffy stopped sputtering and grabbed Maggie so quickly she didn't have time to move. He put his hand on her cheek and kissed her. At first, her eyes stayed open in shock. Then she closed them and enjoyed her first feel of a man's mouth in close to fourteen years. It amazed her. It thundered through her body like a storm and made a flood of passion between her thighs. Sam Duffy did love her and, though he wasn't exactly the hero she'd always longed for and thought would never come, he was busy pretending he was.

She kissed him. Even when she thought she needed air, she kissed him. She reveled in the scrape of his stubbled chin because it was so unlike her smooth one. She inhaled his smell—his skin, his aftershave, his leather jacket, and in his sweat, the woods and the wall he'd climbed. It seemed the finest aroma on earth. She felt the muscles of his chest, his shoulders, his arms—held up her hand so she could see his bigger one engulf it. All the while he kissed her, and Maggie felt each movement of his lips as they pressed her and caressed her, his tongue like a rod of liquid fire. She felt his erection against her body and touched it—closed her eyes so she could know the beauty of its shape. She felt his hands warm her flesh in waves. Maggie collected the joy of these sensations and stored them in her body's memory. She opened her eyes and looked with love, with adoration, on the man she knew would always be her friend.

"Sam Duffy," she whispered.

He groaned into her hair and pulled her tighter.

"Sam Duffy."

He moaned, "Maggie," and pulled at her underwear.

"You have to let go, now, Sam."

"No." He held her tighter.

She stroked his hair and said, "I'm not yours, Sam, you've gotta let me go."

He gave her a frightened look and kissed her, looked into her eyes and kissed her again.

Maggie didn't respond like she had at first. She couldn't. She was being held by other hands.

Chapter 30

Thursday mid-afternoon—George Washington Bridge

Sam's car sped across the George Washington Bridge toward New York, his only regret that Maggie wasn't with him. She hadn't changed her mind and he had no big hopes she would. All Maggie did was leave him in bad shape.

Sam had lied to her a little. It hadn't seriously crossed his mind she'd be such a sweet thing to touch. When she put herself down he'd kissed her on impulse—only because he liked her so much. She'd probably hate him if she knew, but there were worse things than caring how someone felt.

He'd also been half-thinking that this might be over if she wasn't a virgin anymore. He hadn't expected having Maggie in his arms would turn out to be so great. She wasn't a four-alarm fire like his dancer, but she was 100 percent there with a man—holding him right back, kissing back, touching back, the right places, the right way. God, it had been hard to stop.

Why had she put herself in a cage—never having a man in her whole life? Why did she think she was ugly? She wasn't a classic beauty, true, or even close, but Maggie had a pleasant appearance; at least to him she did. Usually when women hated themselves something had happened to them. Sam wondered what it was. She hadn't been raped.

He'd honored her wishes and kept his hands to himself the rest of the night, though they'd stayed up and talked for hours. This morning he asked again if she intended to go through with Rossi's scheme. Maggie insisted that she did.

So Sam had gotten something done. Checked the place for bugs. Had Felix buy the best security system. They'd started installing it right before he left. Ordered treatment for the windows to make it harder to see in. Told Rossi to settle the will fast, anyway he could, get the house out of his aunt's name and into someone else's—Maggie's, for instance, since she might be risking her life for him.

Rossi had looked strange when he said that. On his next visit, Sam would explore what that look meant.

Frances Rossi was going to be a minor problem and he'd seen it coming right away. She loved her brother, but hated what he was doing. Her actions wouldn't be predictable. During most of the arguing, she'd looked like she wanted Sam to die, but he suspected it was the sort of hate easily turned to lust. Sure enough, this morning, she'd managed to let Sam catch her in a flimsy robe and nightgown. She probably hadn't done it consciously. Hormones were at work. Rossi had two women captive who ought to be in the arms of their own men.

When they'd bumped into each other this morning, Frances's eyes had bored into the front of his pants like x-rays then she'd stormed away, acting like she hated him again. She'd looked great in that flimsy gown. It made him hope a willing woman showed up in his bed pretty damned soon.

Sam's life had become complicated.

As he drove back down the Parkway, he didn't gaze over the water at the horizon or scan Riverside Park like he usually did. Sam thought of Brown who was waiting for an answer. He thought of the danger Maggie was in.

He pulled into the garage just before 3:00 p.m. For the first time in eleven years, Sam knew he was going to lie to Mr. Brown. In the big picture, Brown's intentions were benign and enlightened, Sam was sure. That didn't keep an occasional bystander from being ground to dust.

He left the keys in the pool car and let himself in The Barracks. The common room was full. Everyone seemed on duty, though they were all watching Tiger Woods line up an impossible putt, his eyes like lasers. Tiger settled in position, sank it and they roared.

"What are you guys all doing here?" Sam said as he leaned in the door.

"Opening night at the Winter Antiques Fair," one of them said.

"Oh, right."

The Winter Antiques Fair would take place at the Seventh Regiment Armory, which occupied the block between 66th and 67th on Park Avenue. The drivers and the limos got their biggest workout on major charity gala nights like this, because most of the tenants who were in town would attend.

Sam liked the huge red brick building. It still had whole floors of original nineteenth century rooms designed by Tiffany and Stanford White and such, but water leaks had caused so much damage, several rooms were closed. Tonight no one would see the leaks. They'd all be focused on the Drill Room, the biggest open interior in the city and the oldest so-called balloon shed in the country. For the sake of the East Side Settlement House, they'd pay as much as two thousand a head to get in. He wished they wouldn't just party there, but keep up the building, too. It was sad to see original plaster soaked through and fallen in rooms that had no surviving equals. So much for heritage.

He glanced at the limo schedule then headed up to the penthouse, thinking he would have seen the Rossis' names for this one if they were here where they belonged instead of off trying to bring back Jesus.

Mr. Brown took a while to arrive this time so Sam waited in the library among the shelves. Brown liked visitors to browse. He'd start conversations on what interested them.

Sam found a whole section labeled Africana and read the books' spines. Chinua Achebe's, *Things Fall Apart*, Davidson's *The Lost Cities of Africa* and works by famous African and African-American writers that Sam had been exposed to in college. The books made him feel more confident about his secret envelope deliveries to the consulate, though he hadn't seen a newspaper in the last couple of days. The next Africana shelf had books detailing black social problems here and abroad. Sam noticed one in particular, *The Bottom Rung: African American Family Life on Southern Farms,* and remembered Maggie's story. He memorized the title and author, knowing better than to reveal this interest to Brown.

He was back in his usual spot on the sofa when Mr. Brown arrived. "Hello, Sam. Lots happening. How's your project coming?"

Sam knew how to lie convincingly, but Brown knew how to dig out the truth.

"I'd say there's a 90 percent chance it's no more than a reporter's exaggeration. Worst case, raise a flag to see who salutes it kind of thing. Probably heard some wild rumor and—"

"Give me particulars."

Sam had hoped to get by without that. "The reporter is British aristocracy working for the hell of it but he wants to make a name while he's at it. Twice he's written shaky stories. *The Times* is on the verge of ditching him. Even under pressure he didn't give names and sources."

Sam had told the truth.

Brown looked unmoved. "I don't want a guess. For this I want that other 10 percent."

"It's better than a guess. I have good people in contact with him. The guy has everything to lose and nothing to gain by keeping his mouth shut. I made sure of that."

Mr. Brown peered at Sam. "Where is he now?"

Sam felt a chill. Brown ought to have accepted his word by now. No way Sam could reveal Newton was here.

"My people met with him in London night before last."

"All right. Keep at it until you're 100 percent sure. If it turns up nothing, I'll have another assignment for you."

Sam hesitated, very grateful that Brown didn't know who was being cloned, or that Rossi had access to the Shroud. He'd be suspicious of Rossi's absence. Brown had said he didn't want the scientist to do anything stupid. What did that mean?

"I could get you a who's who in cloning and an overview of what they're up to."

"No!" Brown let the book he was holding drop loudly on the desk. "I want that last 10 percent. If there's a chance someone's really cloning Lincoln or Alexander the Great or ... whoever, I want to know and soon. Keep the reporter as your top priority until you're sure. Everything else is secondary. Everything."

Something troubling flashed through Sam's mind: the story of King Herod ordering the slaughter of male children because he heard Jesus Christ had been born. What the hell was Brown worried about? Why did he care about some clone, whoever it was?

"Absolutely," Sam said in a voice he made sound willing. He regretted not asking more questions in the past eleven years.

Brown nodded and left the room. Sam went down on the public elevator, wishing the doors could somehow open and reveal Maggie, here where she belonged, nosing around.

If Brown was worried about Alexander the Great, Sam could imagine what he'd think of a clone of Jesus Christ.

He had to think. He had to imagine each course events might take so he could intervene before they veered off a cliff. It seemed that exercising logic or even the smallest caution was going to be up to him. Rossi and Maggie were off in religious la-la land. Frances would probably do whatever her brother said, even if she didn't agree. If Newton discovered where the Rossis were, he'd probably run with it. Rossi was a public figure in terms of his work. The law wouldn't shield him from publicity, as long as lies weren't being told. Protecting Maggie from the outside world would be impossible then.

When had she become so important to him?—somewhere in these five years of seeing her every day. He'd never met a woman as canny and cool as she was who hadn't picked up her smarts turning tricks or running hustles. Yet Maggie hadn't even had sex. She had a heart, though, and it could be broken. He could tell.

Sam went to his apartment, showered and changed into his uniform, relishing the thought of a few hours at the door because it settled his mind. He thought of calling out to Cliffs Landing but decided against it. He hadn't found bugs here because Brown trusted him, but if Brown became suspicious Sam had no illusions a bug would be installed.

At 4:30 p.m. he relieved his substitute, and watched the first limo pull up to take tenants to the gala. Shortly afterward, Mr. and Mrs. Amsterdam came down. He'd retired at a young age, having made millions in the art world—especially the black market art world, rumor said.

"Good evening, Mrs. Amsterdam, sir," Sam said, preceding them to the limo. He opened the door.

Mr. Amsterdam looked at his wife, but walked indifferently around to the other side as if he'd done enough by putting on a tux, forking out two grand for a ticket, and double or triple that for her voluminous dress. The doorman could help her get it in the car.

One by one they came down to the limos, the women resplendent in their designer gowns that lately weren't making them look like vampires because fashion minds had changed. Now they could be beautiful again. Their hairdos looked less like they'd all slept in barns. Tomorrow he'd see their photos in the society pages, a month later in the party sections of ritzy magazines.

Sam didn't begrudge them their splendid lives. Yes, if they'd donate the cost of the dresses, the hairdos, the tuxedos, the band, the decorations and the food, the charity would at minimum quintuple its take. But they were people, just like him. They could hurt, be lost, be wrong or right, be depressed as hell or get a kick out of living. Or they could be complete assholes like Rossi, able to make weird dreams real because they were rich. Maggie's faith in him was frightening. Rossi was dangerous.

Sam looked up toward the penthouse and admitted the truth. So was Brown.

He smiled at all the tenants until the last limo pulled away and he was finally alone at the door. In the dark of evening, he stood on the wide Fifth Avenue sidewalk which was too elegant to be full. Up here you could forget that seven million people lived in this town.

He imagined scenarios that could occur out on Cliffs Landing. Only Jerome Newton posed an immediate threat. For now, Brown had no way of even guessing about the Rossis unless he learned Newton was the reporter who'd been here. Brown seemed to have forgotten about that, though.

The distant future looked worse, particularly for Maggie, whatever scenario he picked. In none he could live with did he see himself having much sex. Bottom line: he'd have to be out at the Landing when he wasn't at work, trying to convince Maggie to stop this and, if he failed, watch out for her because one day someone would know.

Luckily, he'd always spent his free time away from the building, drinking with his buddies at Molly Malone's and enjoying Manhattan. He could be out at the Landing without rousing Brown's suspicions.

As a taxi slowed and pulled up to the awning, Sam went to the curb and prepared to open the door, but the window rolled down and there was Jerome Newton, wearing a tuxedo.

"Colorado, huh?" Newton said, grinning.

Sam made his mouth gape open in shock. "You didn't find them?"

"No, and not for a moment do I believe you're surprised."

"What happened?"

"Don't bother pretending to be sincere. I wouldn't believe you. When may I have my money back?"

Sam shrugged. "Now okay?" He reached in his wallet and returned the same five hundred dollars.

"What is your name, anyway?" Newton said.

"Hickock. Walter Hickock."

"Hickock, is it?" Newton pursed his lips. "Well, Hickock, I don't suppose I'll see you at The Winter Antiques Fair. That's where I'll be, along with most of the people you work for, I imagine. A pity you can't come. Ta-ta." Newton rolled up the window and the cab pulled away.

Sam looked after it, more worried than before. Newton should have been apoplectic and he wasn't. Mildly peeved didn't fit. Now Sam had to wonder why Jerome Newton wasn't upset.

Chapter 31

Friday morning, a week later—Cliffs Landing

"No, sir, it's just us again," Maggie whispered to the man at the security service and hung up the kitchen phone. She'd accidentally tripped an alarm again, this time by opening the kitchen door. Everything had changed in the week they'd been at Cliffs Landing and so far they hadn't gotten used to any of it. Almost every day, she or Felix or Frances did something that made the security service call. What's more, the house was only now not stinking to high heaven.

After the installers left with their soldering irons, most rooms smelled like burnt electrical wires. When another group came to treat the outside windows, a chemical so awful drowned out the burnt smell that Maggie's eyes watered, and Frances took to sneezing and swearing she couldn't breathe.

Sam said it was worth it. For the first time, they were physically secure. What he didn't know was that for three days straight, Felix had opened every door and window as soon as he left, to keep the chemicals from Maggie until the smell died down.

"Was that you?" Sam said to her from the doorway as he lowered his gun. He'd spent last night here installing extra surveillance.

"Yes, sorry to wake you."

"That's okay, got to head back for work." He didn't leave, though. He just holstered his gun and stared at her with that lurid look on his face.

"It's still early. Walk over to the Cascade with me, Maggie?"

"It's hardly light, Sam, and it's freezing cold."

"We can watch the sun come up."

She didn't want to go, but she decided not to pass up a chance to be alone with him and try to make him talk. Sam was worried about something and hiding it. She had her suspicions, given his slip about unsavory happenings at the building. In her opinion, no one who lived there could worry a man like Sam but a man like Brown.

"All right. I'll go."

They put on coats, he grabbed blankets, and they went out, their feet crunching on white pebbles. She followed Sam out of the garden and up the rise beside it, kicking up acorns from beneath the icy carpet of dead leaves. Two squirrels, heavily furred for winter, scurried across their path. Here and there they passed evergreens thick with needles, but most trees were bare, their brown trunks a maze of giant stalks, growing more distinct in the dawn.

Soon they heard the Cascade's falling water. Sam found a spot to lay out the roll of blankets he carried. Her back against a tree trunk, she sat on them away from Sam.

He was now in charge. His authority only stopped at the lab and the obstetrics room. He'd even tried to intervene there, but Maggie had heard Felix brush him off like a fly.

About everything else, Felix let Sam decide. You couldn't easily see in the windows anymore, and you couldn't sneak in the house without tripping an alarm. Maggie had a multimillion-dollar house in her name and a seventy thousand dollar car. She felt changed, but not because of this.

She didn't know if it was the hormones in the daily injections or Sam's hands all over her that first night, but the passion she'd felt with Sam returned all the time. Her body had yearnings she'd forgotten it could have. Right now, she was trying to ignore how his wool scarf settled all cozy against his neck and how his arm muscles pressed against his leather jacket.

Every morning Felix ran tests to see about her eggs and if they were ripening. Maggie could have told him without the tests. She was ripe and getting riper all the time.

As if he'd read her mind, Sam turned to her. She couldn't see his expression because his back was to the rising sun.

"How are you doing, Maggie my girl? Too cold?" She could see his breath in the chilly dawn.

"No."

"Here, let me warm you up."

He reached to her hands, slipped off her gloves, and put her palms on his face, rubbing the backs.

In the frozen morning, Maggie felt like lightning was shooting through her hands. Her small breasts had gotten plumper from the fertilization drugs. Now she felt the nipples press into her coat.

"Sam, stop it!"

He tried to put his arm around her.

"That's enough, Sam Duffy. We're walking, not sitting." She rose and headed off along the cliff, Sam laughing and scrambling after with the blankets.

"You are fresh, do you know that?" she said when he caught up.

"That I do."

Maggie stopped and looked up into his face.

"Why do you have your gun?"

"You know why."

"Nobody knows we're here. Maybe they will, but right now they don't. Why do you have that gun? What are you worried about?"

He smiled. "You."

Maggie ducked just in time to avoid a kiss.

They walked along the cliff and watched the sun rise, watched lights blink on across the river, and listened to the waterfall while Sam whistled an Irish song, Too-ra-loo something. Maggie couldn't recall the name, but it was beautiful. She took him to Skunk Hollow and they climbed to the top of the hill. He showed her where the old church's foundation must have been, next to the cemetery. Maggie imagined she could hear the black preacher, Uncle Billy Thompson, talking to his mixed congregation long ago.

Would he approve of the white man in the scarf and leather jacket, who carried a gun and tried to kiss her all the time?

Early the next morning when Sam wasn't there, Maggie was in the living room looking through the double-height wall of glass. Her menstrual cycle had been in just the right phase. If today's tests were good, as early as tonight Felix could give her the final injection that would fully ripen her eggs.

She was so thrilled, she'd been awake since 4:00 a.m.

Through the now one-way glass wall, she saw Felix walking alone in the woods, a coat over his pajamas. Either he was excited, too, or he couldn't sleep because Adeline had called yesterday. Frances had talked to her for almost an hour, explaining where things stood. When Felix heard Adeline was at their Cousin Letizia's in Italy, he said he couldn't come to the phone, but to send his love. What kind of love, Maggie couldn't guess. In her opinion, he was being awful. Maybe he held it against Adeline that she hadn't stayed to help.

Nothing else had happened in the whole time they'd been here, at least nothing Maggie knew how to think about. She'd seen Frances look too long at Sam several times and thought Sam might have once or twice looked back. Even though Maggie kept turning down Sam's advances, this hurt.

Maggie left the living room and went into the kitchen where she grabbed a mop and twice ran it dry around the dining room. No dust, no dirt.

As she saw the art deco wall clock register 6:00 a.m., she heard the faint trill of Felix's alarm clock and raced downstairs to her room. She changed into a clean hospital gown, went to the obstetrics room, and sat impatiently on the birthing bed, her hips sore from the injections.

Felix came in and yawned, his coat still on over his pajamas.

She said, "Please let today be the day."

"Good morning, Maggie, feeling all right?" He shuffled past her to the lab, brought out her chart, stuck a thermometer in her mouth, and clamped on a blood pressure monitor, hardly looking. A week of twice daily examinations and they were used to each other. By the fourth day, Frances had stopped coming, it had gotten so routine.

He took the thermometer out. "Your temperature's normal."

She looked at her wrist. "And my blood pressure's normal, too, isn't it?"

He kept looking at her chart. "It seems so, Maggie. It seems so. Certainly better than it was. You've done well."

She knew she had. She'd eaten raw garlic until her stomach burned, drunk gallons of peppermint tea. Not a grain of salt had passed her lips. She hadn't touched a frying pan.

As he washed his hands, Maggie examined the prick marks ranging down her arms. Fourteen in all. This would be the fifteenth. He put on surgical gloves, drew her blood, and took it to the lab.

"You were the first chemist, Lord," she whispered. "Bless my test results."

"Your estradiol level is in the right range," he said when he returned. "Let's check the size of the follicles."

That meant vaginal ultrasound. Maggie contained her joy and put her legs in the stirrups, her prayer changing. She'd always been a spiritual type of woman, but these days she felt as physical as the river, as the hills and ridges, as the trees and rocks of Cliffs Landing. Often the feeling was so intense she couldn't breathe, couldn't think. She felt ripe enough to burst, and these exams were becoming an ordeal in themselves. She cared nothing about Felix in a sexual way but her body's strange state was betraying her. She'd feel the mouth of her vagina contract around his finger or the vaginal ultrasound probe—a special thin one, made for virgins. She shivered at the slightest touch. Even the wind could tantalize her face, her lips. Sunlight on the river could make her cry. Let a sand martin chirp on the bank and her ears heard joy. When Sam whistled his Irish song, she wanted to hold him. Only the Lord's mercy had kept her from putting Sam's hands exactly where she ached for them to be.

"Lord, numb me," she whispered during the exam.

Felix seemed not to notice her condition or, if he did, only nodded and said everything was fine. For Maggie it was humiliating. She was sure Mary, Jesus' first mother, hadn't responded like this.

Felix finished the exam and patted her knee to say it was over.

She closed her gown and sat up, noticing the jubilant expression he could never hide when things went well. "I'm ready, aren't I?"

Felix smiled—half kid-at-Christmas, half proud father. Except for last night's dinner, he'd spent all day and most of the night here or in the lab, but if he was tired it didn't show anymore.

"Yes, Maggie. Yes, you are. The follicles are eighteen millimeters. I'll inject you with the hCG tonight. We can retrieve the eggs about a day and a half later. Everything is perfect!"

Maggie reached out in glee, and they hugged excitedly.

"All right," he said, standing straight. "Now we have a decision to make, remember? My anesthesiologist friend can come in to give you intravenous sedation or an epidural block. I can put you to sleep, but frankly I don't want to bring him in."

"And I don't want anybody else working on me, either."

"Let me explain before you make a final decision. Your blood pressure has declined, overall, but now and then it isn't where it should be. That's called labile hypertension. I think we'll eventually control it, though. The next thing is that full anesthesia has some risks, as does an epidural block."

"Yeah, I know about them."

"But for us the most significant thing may be that the eggs would be bathed in the anesthesia. It's better for the eggs if I give you a local anesthetic at the last minute and dispense with other drugs, but you'll feel it, Maggie. Can you manage?"

"I don't want anything happening to those eggs. It was hard enough to make them in the first place."

"All right, then. You're very brave. Before I forget, we can't tell Sam. We've got to do it when he's not here. He doesn't trust me. Not at all." Felix looked toward the wooden crucifix Maggie had hung over the birthing bed. "Sam's the first person in my life who has no trust in me at all. If he heard you cry out, he might come in. Anything could happen, to say nothing of the germs he'd introduce."

She wasn't thinking about Sam. "I'm really going to cry out?"

He looked sympathetic. "Yes, I'm sorry. I think you will."

She blew out air. "Maybe I should practice not screaming."

"Just practice breathing, like I showed you. I'll be as quick as I can. As soon as I harvest your eggs, I'll join cells from the Shroud with them. If it works, we can try an implant five days later. I'll be giving you other injections to keep your body prepared."

Maggie frowned. Soon it would be too late to tell him what was happening inside her. She knew she ought to. He was her doctor. She shouldn't risk keeping things from him. She swallowed and closed her eyes.

"Felix?"

"Yes?"

"Something's really, really different inside me. I've been meaning to tell you about it—"

"What?" he said. She could hear him sit down beside her on one of the rollaway stools. "What is it, Maggie?"

She kept her eyes closed. "I haven't been feeling very much like a virgin lately."

She opened her eyes when he chuckled and patted her hand.

"I could tell, but that's normal. It's a very good sign, in fact."

"It is?"

"Normally a woman's body produces more testosterone near ovulation. It helps ripen her egg and encourages her to seek or accept a partner to fertilize it. You're experiencing that as well as the heightened effects of super-ovulation drugs. I should have told you. It will subside very quickly, especially if the implantation works. Different hormones will be released in your body then."

"Ones that say: no point in sex, you're already pregnant?"

"Yes, those."

"Now, Maggie, it's time to talk about the part we've been avoiding."

She looked away, knowing what he meant.

"When I retrieve your eggs, I'll have to use a speculum."

"Okay, you can show me now. Which one is it?"

He picked up a white plastic device that looked like a spring-action duck's bill, two long prongs attached to a handle. It looked gruesome. "To put it bluntly, it's for prying a woman open down there. I'll need a full view of your cervix. It's going to be just a little uncomfortable but this is the smaller size—

it's called a virginal speculum, in fact. I'll do my best not to break your hymen."

Maggie shuddered. "No point trying to keep it. If a baby's coming out, it's got to go, anyway. In fact, go ahead and get it over with. Just break it."

"All right, if you're sure I'll do an incision."

"No! Don't cut me, just break it. That's how the Lord meant for it to go, not by slicing me up with a knife, for goodness sake. Just use the regular-sized speculum. Can't you do that?"

"Yes, I can, but it will be very uncomfortable, not only breaking your hymen but fully dilating your vaginal canal when you've never had sex." He knew from having examined her that she'd feel pain.

"How long can it hurt? A minute? It'll be easier for you to get around down there and easier when the baby comes, won't it?"

"Yes, much easier, but—"

"Then it's settled. Don't cut me, though. Just … push through. I gotta admit I never in a million years thought I'd lose it this way, though."

She stared at the speculum, sighing in distress. It was only a necessary medical device. Suddenly Felix was beside her, holding her hand, an embarrassed look on his face.

"Am I being insensitive, Maggie? Perhaps you've thought of losing your hymen in the context of love. Any woman would. If we were cloning anyone else, I'd say I'm being stupid. Your first real penetration should occur in the natural way, because it's your right."

Maggie looked at the speculum and remembered how wonderful Sam had felt that one night. Her body yearned for him and not just because of Felix's hormones. She looked back at the cross above the birthing bed and wanted to drop onto her knees and pray.

"Under other circumstances, I'd ask if there was someone you genuinely trust," he continued. "If he were willing to take very careful precautions, he could come and be with you. I want you to know I'm aware of your sacrifice."

Maggie looked down. "I don't have anybody, Felix, so don't worry about it."

"Good. Yes, you said that." He let go of her hand.

Hurriedly, he added, "No, I didn't mean it's good you have no one. I mean in that case the speculum is—" He took her hand again but seemed to be talking to himself. "Medically and emotionally this isn't the ideal way, it's true. I mean, you're not actually The Virgin Mary, you're a normal modern woman." She watched, fascinated, as Felix turned scarlet and moved away from her, fiddling with instruments and dials. She became more aware that he was wearing his pajamas. He seemed to gather courage and moved suddenly back.

"Maggie, you have a right to know what I would do in other circumstances. Instead of making you go through this, I would have been willing, no honored, to be your first—if the clone were anyone but Christ." He touched his forehead as if he'd remembered something. "Oh, I apologize. That would be fornication. Well—"

Maggie gazed at him, her eyes wide. Felix looked like a red-faced soldier trying to prove he'd report for duty. A beautiful soldier, true, but Maggie had always thought of him as boyish. He obviously didn't know how she and Sam had made out last week. She couldn't help it. She burst out laughing. She laughed so hard she rolled back on the birthing bed that served as their examination table. Maggie couldn't stop, even when she saw the anguish on his face.

"It's all right," she choked. "I don't feel cheated. I'm happy, Dr. Rossi. I mean Felix."

She tried to sit up, feeling terrible to be laughing at him, but Maggie was unable to stop. For years she'd tried to get a man to touch her, now she couldn't make the offers end—real or theoretical. Sam and Felix both saw her body was on fire and had responded. Maggie sensed there was something significant about it—something basic—a strange kind of chivalry inherent to the human male, that they should offer their services to women in this way. From now on, she'd look differently on men who tried to sleep with widows, still in tears from their husbands' funerals. Maybe they weren't dogs after all. Maybe something programmed them to take out their penises and help.

Felix went quietly to the door and left, Maggie laughing and laughing until she stumbled to her room, lay on her white wrought-iron bed, put her face in a pillow and cried.

That night when Sam came, she didn't tell him she'd received her final injection. She didn't say that in thirty-seven hours, Felix would harvest her eggs and, technically, she would no longer be a virgin. Instead they all had a gourmet dinner together, catered in from New York by Fabulous Food, whom Sam made Felix pay in cash so there wouldn't be a credit card trail. For that purpose, Sam drove Felix to his bank and back. Anyone could get credit card records, he said.

Maggie wanted to make a joke about the Rossis eating with their doorman and their maid, but she wasn't sure it would come out funny. She was surprised Sam let the evening happen. At first he'd strongly objected, but Frances kept saying she yearned for something decent to eat. It had been Sam's reluctant idea to bring in Fabulous Food. Everyone knew that if God had a caterer, it was them. More importantly, FF thought the sin of blabbing about clients was right up there with murder and rape. The FF chef in their kitchen had been dressed like a chef. The FF waiter wore black tie when he served them. Maggie's saltless bouillabaisse was, as expected, divine. When FF had gone, they all had coffee outside on the rock terrace. With the outdoor heaters, even the January air didn't bite. They looked down toward the Hudson and listened to night creatures in the woods. Beneath one of the simulated period gas lanterns on the terrace, Maggie watched Frances thank Sam for the dinner and brush seductively against him as she poured coffee in his cup.

Chapter 32

Sunday morning—Cliffs Landing

"Maggie? How long have you been up?"

Felix had been awed to hear her singing from the kitchen, "Sweet little Jesus Boy. They made You be born in a manger. Sweet little Holy child. Didn't know who You was." On this day, he took it as another sign.

She lowered the cloth with which she was polishing the stainless steel refrigerator and leaned on the gleaming door.

"All night!"

"Oh, no. You must be exhausted."

"I am. And today of all days. I know Sam says we have to be careful, but can't we go to church, just today? It would help me so much. If I can't eat—"

"You didn't, did you?" he said.

"You told me not to after midnight, but you know that old saying: *If you can't sleep, eat. If you can't eat, sleep?* Well, I can't do either one, so at least let me soothe my soul."

Felix hadn't slept well, either. By this afternoon, they'd have a failed project on their hands, or pre-embryos of Christ in a culture dish. He went to Maggie and untied her apron, trying to smile encouragingly. She'd been cooperative and brave, but today would be difficult for her. He took her hand and they left by the kitchen door and walked in silence along Lawford Lane, hidden in the foggy morning.

They reached the main road where the church was, still holding hands like a couple because today in a way they were. Soon they stood on the semi-circular lawn in front of the Presbyterian Church, virtually unchanged since 1863 when it was built. To their right, an aged spruce spread its branches. To their left an old oak stood, its trunk scarred and strangely limbed in the spooky way of Hudson River Valley oaks. In his youth Felix had climbed it, pretending to be escaping from The Headless Horseman.

By way of the graveled driveway that circumscribed the lawn, parishioners would arrive in three hours for the first service. Felix rarely came here, but he loved this small white church, its oversized triangular gabled roof covered in slate shingles, four dormer windows on each side, the belfry's spire rising above the roof front on stilts. Original iron hinges, or decorative copies, supported the gothic arched double doors of the narthex. The doors were closed.

"Nobody's here," Maggie said.

"Oh, yes."

Felix led the way to a side door. As a boy, he'd come this way on many Sunday mornings to visit the Reverend Calvin Prickett, who became his friend by an embarrassing accident. Felix had let a local girl lure him under her dress in the summer he was fourteen, in spite of the guilt he felt. The minister caught them. He never told a soul, but invited them to come on Sunday mornings. In his office, he'd tell them wise and wonderful stories from the Bible.

Felix and Maggie entered a narrow carpeted hallway, calling, "Hello, hello?"

"Back here," a man's voice called.

They found old Cal at his office desk, looking the same as he had when Felix was young. Khaki pants, plaid shirt. The only difference was his wrinkles and gray hair. He stood when they entered.

"Felix, it's been thirty years since I've seen you come through my office door early on a Sunday morning. Come in."

"Thanks, Cal. We'd like to talk, if you have time."

"We'd like you to pray with us," Maggie added.

The minister nodded, looking only mildly surprised. "Of course, let's go into the church."

They followed him and entered via the chancel, the organ to their left, three rows of red-cushioned choir seats to their right. In the center was a simple wooden table with two candles flanking a silver cross. Faint light drifting in through stained-glass windows, left the nave's ten rows of cushioned wooden benches in shadows. Felix heard Cal flick a switch and the room was visible, the organ's pipes lit dramatically.

"Theater people in the congregation, you know," Cal said to Maggie. "It's quite nice, isn't it?"

Maggie nodded and sat on one of the chancel's cane-backed chairs, as Cal motioned Felix to a seat. They had remained friends like people did on the Landing—from a respectful distance, but with kindness. Felix hesitated, though the yearning on Maggie's face was plain. She needed to feel blessed and so did he.

"Feel free to tell me anything, Felix," Cal said with a pastor's insight. "It will never leave this room. You know that."

"Anything?" Maggie said.

Felix nodded and sat down.

"I've done something impossible, Cal. Something that would dazzle the world of science, guarantee me publication in its most prestigious journals, win me prizes and awards if I wanted them. I've achieved a 50 percent success rate in cloning healthy embryos of several different mammals. I've taken ancient DNA and successfully cultured it. I have the live cells at my place here in a lab."

They were silent.

"Congratulations, Felix. It sounds like you've made a real breakthrough. Am I surprised? No. All of us here at the Landing know you're brilliant."

Again there was a pause.

"It's human DNA, Cal. Today I'm going to harvest Maggie's eggs, remove the nucleus from each, and replace it with a cell containing the ancient DNA. I'll do several, in fact, hoping even one will survive five days. Then I'll transfer it to Maggie's womb. In another seven days, perhaps ten, we'll know if she's pregnant. If so, she'll be carrying a human clone."

Felix heard Cal let out his breath as he got to his feet. "I see. This is remarkable." He paced uncertainly in the chancel. "Just remarkable. Am I surprised? Yes, a little now." He stopped in front of Maggie. "You're going to mother the first clone of ... an ancient person? Remarkable." He looked at Felix. "It isn't risky, is it?"

"A little. We're prepared," Felix said.

Cal resumed his pacing. "This is extraordinary. Nevertheless we should obviously discuss the ... um, ethics involved, of course." Then he stopped. "How old is the DNA, did you say?"

"Very."

"Not Cro-Magnon man ancient or anything?"

"No, no. Not that."

Felix felt surer that Cal was the right person to confide in, if only because they needed spiritual comfort and his prayers. Since the first CNN story, Felix knew his window of opportunity had shrunk. He hadn't been named, but one day reporters would find him. He'd taken Sam's arrival as the first answer to his and Maggie's daily prayers. Perhaps Cal was the second.

"Cal, do you really believe in Jesus Christ?" He searched the minister's face. "Do you believe he lived, that he was born of a virgin, was crucified and briefly returned to life?"

"Ah," Cal said, as if comprehending though Felix knew he didn't. "Must we answer these questions to have the Christ experience in our hearts? Christ is also a paradigm."

"A paradigm?" Maggie said.

"Of love, community love. Of caring for the helpless and the poor, of sharing. Of loving others as we love ourselves."

"Christ was also a man," Felix said. "You believe that, don't you?"

"Yes. I believe he was. An extraordinarily loving man."

Felix clasped his hands, wanting to speak but fearing to. He looked at

Maggie, his courage gone, and whispered, "Tell him, if you like."

She gazed behind the altar at the stained-glass head of an angel. "Christ is coming back," she said.

Cal smiled. "Yes, he is. The Bible says—"

Felix interrupted. "I have DNA from the Shroud of Turin which is his burial cloth. It's from white blood cells that formed as Christ's body tried to heal itself during the Crucifixion. That's what I'm cloning. I will restore him from the wounds that caused his death. It's Christ she'll be the mother of."

Cal broke into anxious laughter. "Well, I'd better get on my white horse." When they didn't laugh, he stopped, perplexity in his eyes.

"It's true," Maggie said. "We're going to bring him back."

Cal put his hands to his head, his eyes widening. "Is this possible? This isn't possible."

"It is."

Cal slapped his thigh decisively. "Then you can't do it. You mustn't. It's … it's sacrilege. You can't artificially create a Second Coming. Is anyone sure the Shroud is real? Are you? Of course not."

Felix said, "It's real. I know."

"God can do anything he wants on this earth," Maggie said. "Why can't he use us to bring Jesus again?"

Cal stood. "What does your pope think of this? Isn't it his Shroud?"

"I'm in touch with a Catholic priest in Turin named Father Bartolo, but he doesn't know."

"Well, I imagine not," Cal said, "or he'd have something to say, we can be sure. Felix, if this is a joke—"

"No, it isn't. I wouldn't do that."

"Would you pray for us?" Maggie said. "Please, will you pray for us?" She knelt on the red carpet and held up her clasped hands. "Bless us, won't you, Cal?"

He only stared at them.

Felix sat at the organ and turned it on. It sighed as the pipes filled with air. He pulled out a flute stop and played a chord on the choir manual, the lowest keyboard. "You've known me a long time. I wouldn't lie."

Cal said, "Am I to understand I can't change your minds? Can't delay you so we can talk this through? You're doing this today no matter what?"

Felix played the opening notes of the *Ave Maria* then whispered, "Yes." He bent above the keyboard, touching it lightly, remembering his youth as an altar boy in New York. His heart filled as he played the *Ave Maria*. Hail Mary. *Ave Maria*. Hail Mary. No wonder it had come to his mind. He watched Cal go to Maggie, inexpressible worry on his face. He watched as Cal knelt with her and folded his hands to pray. *Ave Maria*. Hail Mary. *Ave Maria*.

When Cal walked them to the lawn the morning mists enveloped them, like the hallowed feeling that rose in the church while Cal and Maggie prayed. Felix knew Cal wasn't convinced, but he'd prayed in case it was true.

He shook Felix's hand. "What time will you do it?"

"At noon. If all goes well, a half hour later we'll have at least one pre-embryo."

Cal put a hand on Felix's shoulder. "I'll pray for you both and for us all until then."

Back at the house, Maggie and Frances scrubbed the obstetrics room while Felix sterilized his instruments and cleaned the lab. Frances had made one last effort to dissuade him. It hadn't worked.

By noon, he and his sister wore surgical scrubs, Maggie a clean white gown. They all had on masks and scrub caps to avoid infection and contamination. Felix cleansed his hands—a three-minute scrub with a brush, followed by a three-minute wash—then he put his arms through the clean surgical robe Frances held. He put his hands in the gloves she opened.

A pan had been fixed below the front of the birthing bed. Maggie lay down, looking anxiously at the speculum that would accomplish her request.

Felix was calm, ready, and he hoped she was. "Maggie, are you sure? I can try to manage with the virginal speculum if you're not."

"I'm sure. Get it out of the way."

"Frances, would you take her hand?"

Maggie laughed. "Thanks, Felix, but I can't see myself holding onto a woman when my hymen's broken, if you don't mind."

Felix wanted to laugh with her, but he knew it would be painful for a moment—perhaps longer. He put the speculum back on the tray. "Maggie, please let me make an incision first, won't you? It will be easier."

"No. I told you. Just do it. It's in the way. I'm ready. Go ahead. Go."

As Maggie's hands gripped the bed rails, he took a long, slow breath and inserted the speculum as far as it would easily go. Maggie flinched as he'd expected.

"Now take deep breaths, deep breaths. You'll feel a sharp pain then discomfort when you're dilated. Try to relax. It will be much easier, much less painful, if you can relax."

"Just go, I tell you," she said, sounding impatient with him, though he knew it was really fear.

She was far too tense, but they were running out of time. Felix checked the position of the speculum and pushed.

Maggie's cry was so pitiful Felix stopped. If Sam had been here, he would have barged in and shot someone. But Felix only hesitated a moment, knowing if he delayed it would only be worse. He inserted the speculum fully and released the spring to open its plastic jaws.

Maggie shrieked. It was done.

"God bless you, God bless you," he whispered and quickly bathed Maggie's insides as traces of her blood washed away into the pan. He saw her hands were trembling on the rails.

"Oh, Felix, can't you do something?" Frances begged.

"Hold on, Maggie, hold on," he said. "We're halfway there."

He picked up a needle and deadened her cervix with a shot of xylocaine. Then he took the vaginal ultrasound, a needle in its long port on the side, and inserted it. Watching the monitor, he guided the needle through the pink flesh of Maggie's upper vaginal wall, gritting his teeth when he heard her cry out again. She'd been right, of course. His work was easier now. With mild suction, he withdrew fluid from a swollen follicle, then another and another, overjoyed at the number of them he saw. He lay the syringe carefully on the tray and filled a second one.

"Are you ready, Maggie? I'm going to remove it, now."

He saw her grip the rails tighter and nod.

In one smooth motion he contracted the tongs and withdrew the speculum. This time Maggie trembled but didn't make a sound.

He picked up another needle. "Maggie, this is an antibiotic. Just a precaution against infection."

She cleared her throat. "I won't even feel it after that."

When he was done, he took Maggie's hand and emphatically kissed it. Her face was bathed in tears.

"Do you know how brave you are?"

"Nope," she said. "Just go ahead and get my eggs into that lab."

Nervously, they all laughed.

Felix said, "Push her bed closer, Frances. You two can watch on the monitor."

He went in the lab and in what felt like only moments separated Maggie's eggs from the fluid around them. She hadn't produced eight to twelve. There were easily twenty, which increased the chances of success. They were mature eggs, not underdeveloped. In another few hours she would have ovulated them.

Everything had worked.

Felix waved to them through the lab's glass windows. Working under the microscope, using its micromanipulator controls, he removed the nuclei from ten of Maggie's eggs. He saved ten for a second attempt should this one fail. Already waiting was a special sequential culture medium. It would simulate the nutritive environment a normally fertilized egg experiences in the womb.

He removed the cultured Shroud cells from their incubator and transferred one to a dish with one of Maggie's eggs. A tiny electrode had been fitted to the dish. He'd have to repeat the procedure for each egg.

This was it. This was the moment. This was why Maggie had just endured pain. If his previous success rate held, half the pre-embryos he was about to create would survive the necessary five days. Would he implant them all on the chance most would die and risk quintuplets if they didn't? Would he do a pregnancy reduction? Or would he use one and destroy the others? He hadn't discussed these things with Maggie, though Frances repeatedly brought them up. These were his moral burdens and he would bear them alone. What he did, Maggie would never know.

Felix looked up. Frances's nose was pressed to the window in worried suspense. Maggie had raised the head of her bed as far as it would go. She was watching the monitor, her palms together, her fingers extended and pressed to her lips.

For a moment Felix saw himself after the hit and run when he was nine, his body motionless on a hospital bed over which his mother cried. Nearby the most wonderful man he'd ever met, said, "Don't be afraid, Felix. I will bring you back to life."

He whispered, "In the name of the Son," held his breath, and energized the electrode. He looked up to the monitor on which the magnified cells were displayed. For an instant nothing happened. Then the cells began an incredible ballet. Felix felt a microbiologist's wonder as an egg cell and the Shroud cell approached each other. Their membranes opened as they converged. The cell from the Shroud joined with Maggie's enucleated egg. Then, the membranes closed.

For a moment, he was too stunned to comprehend. In spite of the obstacles still ahead, Felix raised both arms above his head and whispered, "He is risen!"

His arms still in the air, unexpected tears streaming down his face, he went to the glass and called to Maggie and Frances. "He is risen! He is risen!"

Again and again he said it, as the bell in the steeple of the Presbyterian Church began to toll. Cal had never rung the bell at twelve-thirty, but today it chimed and chimed and chimed.

Chapter 33

Sunday midday—Sam's apartment

Sam lay on his bed, newspapers and books spread out around him, thinking of what he'd learned from all the reading he'd done about Africa and Africans and about the black southern farmer.

As he thought about Maggie's story and the dead African kids he'd seen in the paper, they'd somehow grown linked in his mind.

It was troubling because Sam was no conspiracy buff. He didn't think a clandestine club of evildoers had secretly orchestrated history. Men like Brown had always existed, as far as Sam could tell, and for a while their power helped bring order—nicely or otherwise—before it was demolished by history's next big thing. A plague. A volcano. A bunch of guys with daggers stabbing you through your toga. The Russian winter. An airplane called Enola Gay, which blew up two of your cities. Sam didn't believe in history by conspiracy because big plans too often went hugely astray. Like the British aristocrats who at first supported Hitler then had to run from the bombs he dropped on London in The Blitz. Like our blindness to being hated by half the middle east. While terrorists were in training to hijack our airplanes and fly them like missiles into the heart of America, we were troubling our own house in Clinton-gate, getting ready to inherit the wind. Every MacArthur had his Truman, every Bill Clinton his Kenneth Starr and every unwise impeachment its Larry Flynt.

Even so, Sam knew what power could do, if only for a time. It could shift policy, sway events. It could kill.

He set aside his book about black farmers in the south. The U.S. Agriculture Department had set up a farmer's aid program supposedly designed to help them, but funds were passed out by local people still upset about civil rights. The government had turned the hen house over to the fox—those who didn't like blacks and coveted their land. The result? Ninety percent of black farmers lost their farms. One was Maggie's father.

A possible parallel to Brown's activities in Africa troubled Sam. CEO's of firms doing business in Africa often visited Brown. Had the U.S. Government, through the timid Secretary of State, turned another hen house over to the fox? A few of Brown's visitors probably wouldn't mind if African populations drastically declined, leaving more of Africa to them. Was Brown's slow extinction theory only a crazy belief or their goal? Sam had looked up information on the two warring countries. AIDS infection rates were as much as 35 percent—mostly young adults of childbearing age. Without exception, Sam's envelope deliveries for Brown to the consulate had been followed by carnage caused by the envelope's recipients. For neither AIDS nor the war was the cavalry on the way.

Sam knew his thinking had been affected by Maggie's peril. Because of it, weird explanations of Brown's behavior kept running through his mind: a powerful man might covet parts of Africa; the same man feared cloning of the great; an African-American woman planned to carry the clone of Christ. The rest of his speculations were equally bizarre.

Perhaps it was only wild supposition, but last night Sam couldn't sleep.

His ongoing woman problem didn't help. Right now, he simply had no time to find female companionship. Frances Rossi seemed to want to volunteer. Every time he saw her, she launched so many pheromones in his direction, he didn't know how much longer he could duck. She didn't mean to, he could tell; nature was taking over. Or maybe it was him launching the pheromones at her. Either way, it was the first time a society broad had lusted after his lower east side Irish behind. Even that hadn't stopped him from yearning for his dancer and a repeat of her stellar performance in the ballroom kitchen. As if that weren't enough, each time he walked with Maggie, he wanted to jump her bones, bust that cherry she'd had too long, have her sweet kiss again. Sam was a dog. He knew it and enjoyed it. But Maggie was a person he didn't want to hurt.

He'd also procrastinated getting back to Mr. Brown. It had been three days since he told Brown he'd found the reporter and put the screws on. If he delayed any longer, Brown would ask for explanations.

Sam got out of bed, showered and shaved. He picked up his usual cologne then put it down. He'd be going out to the Landing later and his pheromones were doing a good enough job without help. He dressed and took the elevator. Mr. Brown was in the library.

"What do you know?" Brown said without greeting him.

Sam sighed and sat down. "This one's been a lot harder to nail. I mean, how do you prove a guy is bluffing? The lawyers can't come up with a suit that will really scare the guy because he knows he'll win in the end and his family's rich enough to fight. He's decided to ignore us."

While Brown sat thinking, Sam decided this was the right time to casually cover the Rossis' absence, just in case. It should be easy. The sixth floor tenants had been gone two weeks. The fourth floor left after Christmas and wouldn't return until the spring. He'd thought of how to do it through the end of April. After that, he'd have to think of something else.

"Oh," he said, "I got so involved in the cloning thing I didn't say. The Amsterdams are off to Tahiti tomorrow. The Rossis went to Banff, Canada for skiing. They're buzzing about taking one of those round-the-world cruises afterward. That leaves only four floors in residence."

Brown looked up. "Good. Less to worry about. Sam, about the reporter?"
"Yes?"

"Why not get a little tougher?"

Sam sat up. Only once before had he gotten such an instruction from Brown, but it was for a creep who liked to hit his wife. Sam had been happy to deliver a roughing up to him. "Well, since I tried the law first, toughness could throw mud on my junior barrister's reputation, making him useless for future work."

Brown stood. "Make him useless, then."

Sam's stomach grew queasy. "You mean—"

"If you have to break the reporter's pencils, break them."

A few heartbeats later, Sam realized Brown was done and it was time to go. As he drove out to the Landing to check on Maggie and the Rossis, he wondered what the hell he was going to do. Brown trusted him. Sam couldn't let him become dissatisfied and turn elsewhere. Since Brown told his employees only what each needed to know, there could easily be some who were used to breaking people's pencils. Under direct physical persuasion, Newton would tell all. Sam's next report had to be convincing to get Brown off Newton's trail.

He pulled into the driveway then decided to park in the back from now on like Rossi did. He followed the path to Maggie's garden gate, remembering how he'd climbed the walls that first night. Her French doors were closed. He was pleased not to be able to see into her room this time. When he knocked, Maggie called, "Who is it?"

"It's me. Sam." He had to shout to be heard.

"Oh. I'm lying down. Please don't make me get up. Go around front and use your key to get in the house, okay?"

"What's the matter, Maggie, are you sick?" He put his face to the glass and saw a shadowy outline on the bed.

"Just go around front and use your key, Sam."

"All right, Maggie."

Sam hurried to the front door, entered and went downstairs. He tried her door from the laundry room under the stairs but it was locked.

"Sam, I said I'm lying down," Maggie called.

He tried the door to the obstetrics area, but it was locked. "It's Sam," he called and knocked.

He heard whispering, then Frances's voice. "You can't come in, Sam, we're working. We need to keep sterile conditions."

"Just let me in Maggie's room. Come around and open the door under the stairs."

"Would you wait a while? She's not feeling well," Felix said.

Sam walked back to the laundry room and called, "Maggie I'm coming in." He put his shoulder to the door, which flew open.

Maggie called out, "Frances, Felix, it's just Sam, breaking down the door and barging in like usual!"

"What's the matter with you?"

She didn't answer. She lay on her side, her hands pressed to her stomach.

"If you don't tell me, Maggie," he pointed to the obstetrics door, "I'll barge in there, too, and ask them."

Maggie closed her eyes. "Felix took my eggs a while ago. The needle made me sore from my waist down so I need to lie in bed, okay?"

"He did it already? I thought you were going to tell me. I thought—"

He knelt and rubbed her forehead. "They busted you, didn't they?"

Maggie looked away. Before she answered they were interrupted by a sound they rarely heard. The doorbell. It chimed intrusively, even in Maggie's room. He'd heard it only once, when Rossi's lawyer delivered papers to the house.

He heard doors opening in the lab, saw the surprise on Maggie's face.

"I'll be back," he said and went out to find Felix and Frances standing in surgical scrubs at the bottom of the stairs, looking up.

"Are you expecting anyone?" he asked.

Felix lowered his mask. "No, I'm not."

They followed Sam upstairs to the foyer. Through translucent glass panels on either side of the front door, they saw a man pacing. They all stared, Sam and Felix glancing at each as if they both had a terrible suspicion.

"Couldn't be," Sam said. He stepped forward and opened the door.

There stood Jerome Newton of London's *The Times*.

Chapter 34

"Well, if it isn't Mr. Hickock," Jerome Newton said. He slipped the camera from his shoulder and tried to look past Sam inside. "Any chance of afternoon tea?"

Sam sputtered, "There's a chance of my fist on your face!"

Felix stepped forward, taking off his scrub cap. "Come in, Mr. Newton."

"Felix! Why are you inviting him in?" Frances said.

He didn't answer.

Jerome Newton stepped into the foyer and swiftly snapped a photo, saying, "Dressed for a medical procedure, are we?"

Sam wrenched the camera from his hand.

"Give it back to him, Sam. Jerome, won't you come in the living room? Frances, could you arrange tea?"

Frances snatched her surgical mask down and strode away, looking as if she might put poison in Newton's cup. What Sam didn't understand was Rossi. Why be cordial to his enemy and give back his camera, of all things? Sam hoped Felix had something up his sleeve because at the moment he didn't. He felt stupid—checkmated by this measly piece of aristocratic trash. How had Newton found them?

As they entered the living room, he gazed dejectedly through the glass wall they'd gone to such expense to make opaque from the outside.

"How did you do it?" Sam asked Jerome.

Jerome went to the center of the cavernous room. "You shouldn't have given me back that five hundred dollars, Sam. That's your real name, is it? When you did that so readily, I knew you were protecting them. I followed you."

Sam felt a flush of mortification. "Nobody followed me."

"Not one body. Three. In three different cars, to make sure you didn't notice. Naturally, they don't know who they followed or why."

"Oh, crap," Sam said, grabbed a bottle of Macallan scotch from the teakwood bar and poured himself a shot. "Anybody else?" He held up the bottle, realizing Felix must be planning to make a deal. What else could they do?

"I'll join you," Jerome said.

Felix sat on a sofa. "Nothing for me, thanks."

Sam handed Jerome a glass. "I'd like to drink to your bad health, Newton."

Jerome laughed and downed half his drink.

Frances returned with a tray holding cookies, tea bags, and four cups of what had to be tepid water. She plunked the tray down on a coffee table and sat in an easy chair. Jerome Newton took the opposite easy chair. Sam sat across from Rossi.

Newton raised his glass to Frances. "Sorry. Found something in the interim."

Frances said to Felix. "You know this man?"

"Yes, I do. Jerome Newton and I collaborated once before on a news story. Newton, this is my sister, Frances."

"Delighted, madam."

Frances didn't respond.

"I assume that's what you want, now. Collaboration?" Felix asked.

Jerome smiled. "Quite right. I take it you need anonymity for at least nine months. Oh. Am I getting ahead of myself? How's it coming? Have you retrieved the DNA? Do we have a pregnancy?"

Felix and Frances looked at each other and said, "No."

"Then perhaps a bit more than nine months. It's still Christ you're doing, is it?"

They didn't answer, but a thought occurred to Sam. Maybe Newton showing up could end all this, make Felix or Maggie stop. Then he could get Maggie out of here.

"Right. Christ, it is. Second Coming. Here's my offer. I want to film the birth—with the usual discretion, of course. Close-ups of the mother's face as she labors; of yours, Felix; and of the child as it emerges so I can record its first cry. I want an exclusive. Photos of the pregnant mother against the sunset. Her first maternity outfit. The joy on her face when the child first moves. That sort of thing. Agree and you get your nine months. Who's the mother, by the way?"

"My sister," Felix answered. "Frances is."

Disappointed at Felix's fast thinking, Sam kept his face straight, and he saw Frances do the same. He thought of calling an anonymous tip into a local paper and revealing everything himself: their names, locations, everything. That would stop them. He didn't care how mad Felix got, and Brown would be satisfied. Then he thought of Maggie and what she'd given up today to bear the clone. He had to change her mind, not break her heart.

"Yes, I'm the mother," Frances said, giving Newton an indignant glance as if he were something disgusting underfoot.

Newton sat back and clapped his hands, his long-jawed face smiling. "A brother and sister act? Delightful. Who else is here with you?"

"Sam as our part-time guard, and our maid."

"Just the essentials, then? Protection and someone to cook and make the beds? May I meet this maid?"

"She's not here at the moment," Felix said.

Sam added, "She's a nice, kind black woman, just your cup of tea." Sam was counting on Newton's elitism to end his interest in Maggie.

"Doubtless. Well then." Newton sat forward. "Do we have an agreement?"

"No," Felix said.

Sam looked at him, realizing at last what Felix was doing.

"Your offer is worthless," Felix added.

"Perhaps you didn't understand it."

"I understood," Felix said and turned to Sam. "And I think you understood, didn't you Sam?"

"I did." Sam said, smiling.

"You must be daft, then," Newton said.

Sam stood. "As soon as you reveal who and where they are, you've lost your exclusive, Jerome. You'll get one story and that's all." Sam felt new respect for Felix.

Newton sputtered and went pale.

Felix said, "If you behave yourself, stop following us and making threats, I might give you an exclusive. I might give you a hundred stories for publication when I'm ready. I decide when, not you."

Newton stood, red-faced. "I might announce it just to take that smirk off your face."

They glared at each other. Felix had what Newton wanted. Newton could cause Felix trouble.

Sam said, "Gentlemen, how about a compromise?"

They both looked at him.

"If there's no pregnancy, you've got no story, Newton. Give Rossi time to see if it takes. What do you need? Two weeks?"

"Yes," Felix said.

"That cuts me out of the science," Newton said.

Sam said, "Oh, you want to try for contaminating the damn lab and messing everything up?"

Newton sniffed. "All right."

"Felix," Sam continued. "What say you give Newton an interview with Frances once a month on condition there's no publicity until after the birth?"

"Once a week!" Newton said, "starting now."

Sam leaned menacingly forward. "Every other week starting when the pregnancy's sure."

Newton rolled his eyes up in assent.

"How do we know we can trust him?" Frances said.

"As they said, Miss," Newton replied. "I want a great deal more for my exclusive than one story."

Frances nodded to Felix.

When Felix held out his hand, Newton shook it, saying, "You have a deal."

Once again, Newton smiled slyly, like a man with an ace up his sleeve.

Chapter 35

Friday, late afternoon—Cliffs Landing

In spite of Jerome Newton, the next five days at the Landing were serene. Sam didn't think Newton was a fool. He'd wait and he'd keep quiet. Otherwise he'd lose out.

Meanwhile, Sam delivered Brown's final 10 percent. He lied outright, said he'd put real pressure on the reporter who revealed the cloning story was fake. With Newton cooperating, no chance Brown could learn otherwise. After a couple more questions, Brown had stopped probing and accepted Sam's report with apparent relief. This left Sam free to spend his time at the Landing with one less worry.

He focused on two things: talking Maggie out of helping Felix, and making the house more and more secure in case he failed. One day Brown would learn the clone was real. One day the world would, assuming the pregnancy took.

After spending a day in bed, Maggie seemed herself again. Every day Sam walked with her, trying reason on the one hand and seduction on the other. She thought the clone's mother should be untouched. If he could interest her in sex, she might disqualify herself. However, all she did was sneak in questions about Brown.

Felix gave her daily shots. He and Sam didn't clash anymore. Instead, Sam learned a lot about in-vitro fertilization as Felix kept anxious watch on the incubator. More pre-embryos had died than he expected. Four remained. If even one reached the blastocyst stage, Felix would implant it tonight. Sam didn't ask what he'd do if they all lived. That was Felix's problem, not his.

Sam learned one thing more in these five days. If he and Frances didn't have a bed-thumping session and soon, the both of them would probably combust. He'd tried to ignore her but it hadn't worked.

At the present moment, she was walking in the woods near the cliff, and Sam was on the terrace. He knew Felix was in the lab and Maggie was taking a nap, resting for tonight. Sam couldn't help that his eyes followed Frances as she appeared and disappeared through the trees. Instead of her usual immobility, she'd stretch and breathe in the forest, lifting her face to the wind. She forgot her class and came alive outdoors. He walked to the near end of the terrace, climbed over the side and inched his way down, thinking this was nothing compared to scurrying over heaving companionways in heavy seas. He dropped four feet to the ground then walked to where she stood, her hands on her hips because she'd seen him.

He didn't know exactly what to say. Frances could do anything, have anything she wanted. She wasn't as gorgeous as his dancer, but she looked like the multimillion bucks she owned. She wore clothes in which everything matched everything, and the colors couldn't be found in stores. Her auburn hair shimmered in the afternoon sun. She smelled like the flowers she liked to grow. She stepped behind a large tree as he approached, gazing into his eyes as he gazed into hers.

"Sam," is all she said when he followed.

"Yep, it's me." He felt silly, but the pheromones were flying too thick to ignore.

When he reached out and stroked her hair, she went soft under his hand like a kitten, whispering, "Call me babe," in a reversal of what she'd yelled that first night.

He pulled her head to his chest, moaning, "Hello, babe." Their bodies locked, squirming into each other. She felt good then better, then close to great, but all Sam could see was Maggie's doe eyes in his mind. He tried to erase the image by kissing Frances, but all he could feel was Maggie's lips, sweet like summer berries. It was frustrating. His body wanted a woman, but his mind only saw the woman he couldn't have—one he frankly hadn't figured for the romantic interest of his life, only a good friend, a dear friend.

Sam told himself it was a typical male reaction. Men liked to chase what they didn't have. He could have Frances, not Maggie. That's all it was.

He tried to reach under Frances's sweater, sure that feeling a boob would get his mind where it belonged, but Frances pushed his hand away. He opened his eyes and saw anger in hers.

"I don't believe this!" she said. "What's happening to me? Here I am trying to kiss my doorman, and he's busy thinking about my maid!"

"I'm not!"

"Oh, Sam!" Frances pushed him. "It's not me you yearn for, Sam."

"Sure it is."

"You're not in love with me."

"Huh? Well, I didn't actually say I was, Frances. Not yet, I mean."

"You don't even lust after me much. I shouldn't lust after you at all. You're the doorman, for heaven's sake. I live in your building. You wouldn't break in someone's home and hold a gun to their head to save me from my folly—like you did for Maggie. You love her, Sam. It's been obvious from that first day."

"I don't!"

"Oh Sam!" Frances sighed and ran her eyes slowly up and down him as if he were a dessert she shouldn't have, then she turned toward the sparkling river. "You might not want me, but there happen to be many men who do. I don't know why I'm not with one of them right now. My brother's a mental defective, trying to clone Christ of all things. Yet I've felt the need to help him, no matter what. Why? I ask myself."

Sam put his hand on her shoulder. "Loyalty's a good trait, Frances. Don't knock yourself for it." He wondered why women generally did that. Most knocked themselves, even rich and beautiful ones. Men usually didn't. Maybe that was the key to his success with women. He always told them they were okay, because that's what he believed.

She turned around. "You don't want Maggie to do this, either, do you?"

"Not at all."

Frances shook his arm. "Why don't you do something then? Kidnap her and take her away. Break up Felix's lab. Something!"

Sam took her hand from his arm and kissed it, understanding exactly how she felt. "You could do it, too, you know. He lets you in the lab. You could have flushed the Shroud cells right down the toilet. You could go in there now and dump all his cultures out."

Frances slumped against Sam and covered her face.

"We're cowards, aren't we, Sam? Adeline would have intervened, but guess who talked her out of it? I love Felix and you love Maggie and though we think they're crazy, we can't destroy their dream."

"Frances, the truth is, we don't want them to get that mad at us."

She nodded.

Sam stroked her hair, then lifted her face and kissed her again—more in sympathy than passion. After a moment she pulled away and groaned, saying, "We'd better stop. Things are complicated enough."

"Yeah, guess you're right."

"Let's go back before somebody sees us."

They turned, his arm across her shoulder, and in swift punishment for his faithlessness, he saw Maggie going inside the terrace door.

"Oh, crap!" He let go of Frances and ran.

The terrace was too high to climb, so he ran to the front of the house, put his key in the door, and found it latched. He couldn't get in.

"Maggie, let me in!"

No one answered.

Frances rushed up the big round stones on the walk, puffing. "Here, I'll let us in."

"You can't. She's latched it."

"She can't latch my door!"

"It's not your door. It's hers, remember?"

"Oh, hell! Look what we've done. You'd think we could keep our hands to ourselves, knowing what she's facing."

"Maggie, let me in!" he shouted.

"Don't break anything. That's not going to help! Let's see if we can raise Felix."

Just then the door opened and Felix stood there. "What's all the shouting about? Why is Maggie crying?"

They walked in and Frances slumped against the wall. "You don't want to know, Flix."

"Of course I do. What's wrong with her?"

Sam rubbed the back of his neck. "I'm wrong with her, I guess."

"What did you do?"

When Sam hesitated, Frances flushed. "She saw us kissing."

Sam saw a shadow coming fast. His head jerked back when Felix's flying fist connected with his nose. Felix stood there, his hands clenched, while Sam bled on the foyer's hand-hooked rug.

Felix came at him again, while Frances started shrieking, apparently for Sam. "Stop, Felix! Stop!"

Then Maggie was there, like she'd been before, but this time she didn't hurry to throw herself between them. Sam saw her watch Felix punch him in the body, in the face, and knew she wasn't feeling sorry about it. Sam only tried to block the blows. He wouldn't fight back when he'd tried to screw the man's sister.

Maggie must have finally taken pity on him. She said to Frances. "Grab your brother, while I get Sam."

Frances looked confused then she bent and flung her arms around Felix's knees.

He stopped and looked down. "Get up, Frances."

"Not until you stop hitting Sam."

Maggie slipped past them and grabbed Sam by the arm. He stumbled after her to the hall bathroom. He knew better than to apologize right now. He sat on the closed commode and lowered his head. When Maggie smacked the back of his head with her hand, he didn't say a word. She smacked his head again. Then he heard water running in the sink.

He kept his head down until she told him to raise it. She took a wet cloth and wiped his bloody nose, while he touched his fingers to her cheek and brushed away tears.

"Don't get … it in your head … I'm crying for you, Sam Duffy."

"Maggie," he whispered. "Walk out of this house with me right now. Don't do it! For God's sake, for my sake, don't do it!"

Swallowing, she said, "It's for God's sake that I am."

He put his arms around her and pressed his face into her stomach, feeling her shudder back sobs. "You know what Frances said out there?"

"No! What did Miss Rossi say?"

"She said I'm in love with you, Maggie. She said I love you."

Maggie stepped out of his arms.

Chapter 36

Friday night—Cliffs Landing

It was an hour past the time Felix had planned for the implantation. He and Frances moved about the obstetrics room like ghosts, while Maggie lay on the birthing bed trying to relax.

Her blood pressure was high.

Even given the incident hours ago, it was too high.

The blastocysts had almost finished hatching from their membranes. They were ready to implant themselves in a uterus, and there was only so much time for delays. Maggie had filled and emptied her bladder, then drunk more water so it would be full again, straightening her uterus for the catheter. But Felix had to see if Maggie's blood pressure went down. Before, it had only flirted with the high normal range. In his professional opinion, her diet and exercise had worked. If so, why was he reading a pressure of 145/102, after she'd lain quietly for an hour?

He could kill Sam Duffy. Felix could just kill him.

He'd picked this day of all days to upset her, forcing Felix to guess. Was it only her emotions? Or had he failed to diagnose chronic hypertension in Maggie? If so, Felix couldn't proceed without knowingly risking her life.

When had all this passion happened anyway? Felix had missed it. Did subtle people—Sam, Maggie, his sister—surround him or was he dumb, deaf and blind? Who did or didn't love whom? Who was lusting and being lusted after? He couldn't believe the story Frances had poured into his ears. His own sister. Maggie, of all people.

Sam was no surprise. From the first, Felix sensed something irregular about Sam. Now he knew what it was. Behind Felix's back, Sam had tried to have sex with every woman in the house.

What about Sam appealed to them? Felix didn't know. All he knew was that Maggie was tense when he touched her and her blood pressure was sky high.

From the other side of the door to Maggie's room, Sam called. "How is it going in there? What's taking so long?"

"Shut up, Sam!" Felix shouted. "Let us work in peace."

Frances tiptoed up and asked. "Is she better?"

"No, she's not better. Go and try to calm her, Frances."

"I told you," Frances whispered. "She won't let me near her. I tried."

Felix glared at his sister. All these years he'd ignored her carnal nature. Now it had threatened the one thing he most cared about in life. He couldn't contain his anger. "Then you should make yourself useful by going in there and shutting up that loud mouth. Get in bed with him, that'll do it. Apparently, it's what you want."

"Why not?" she said. "I have no one else in my life. Did you ever notice that, Felix?"

He stared at her. She'd had loads of suitors. It was he who'd been alone, not her. He grew impatient. "No, I never noticed that. I noticed the reverse. If you didn't like your life you should have changed it!"

He watched Frances turn stone-faced and wondered how she could do that so easily whenever she liked.

"You owe it to me to try again to talk to Maggie. She's a reasonable woman. Try to reassure her, Frances. I'm at a loss, here. I don't know what to say."

"Felix?"

They turned around. Maggie stood there in her gown, slippers on her feet, her cap and mask on. She held out her wrist which had the blood pressure monitor attached. It read 139/87. Much better.

His hopes soared.

Maggie smiled. "Are we going to stand here and let four eggs with Christ's DNA just die?"

Frances touched her arm. "I didn't mean to hurt you. I don't know what happened, to tell the truth."

Maggie delivered a cool glance. "Don't apologize, Frances. You're grown. Sam's grown. You're both single. Sam's a lot of things, but I wouldn't have him. Take him, if you want."

"Maggie, it's not like that! It was just a moment."

Felix couldn't believe they were wasting time discussing Sam Duffy. "I'm ready, Maggie, if you are."

"I've been ready from the day I asked to be the one. That's why I'm here." Again she glanced at Frances. "Nothing else matters."

Maggie returned to the birthing bed. Frances folded her arms and leaned nearby against the wall. Felix rescrubbed, his heart drumming.

In the lab he pulled on surgical gloves then opened the incubator and removed the blastocysts. He placed them under the microscope. The last one was hatching from its thick transparent membrane, the zona pellucida, and the other three had already hatched. To Felix they were beautiful. Much more complex than an eight-celled three day embryo, these had passed an important milestone. They had activated their own genes and formed a fluid-filled inner cavity. They'd also produced two different cell types. Surface cells around the rim would become the placenta. An inner mass of stem cells clung to the cavity wall, ready to become a fetus.

Now he had to make a crucial decision. Should he implant them all, against the chance that most would die, and risk producing multiple clones of Christ? This was the standard practice in in-vitro fertilization, which is why it so often produced multiple births. If so, he could reduce the pregnancy later, which meant killing a clone of Jesus. Was that something he could do? He'd never destroyed an embryo in utero. He had to decide. Felix looked out at the cross hung above Maggie's bed.

He would risk failure and go with one.

Carefully, he examined the blastocysts under the microscope, grading them for quality. To him they were only potential life, incapable of sentience, regardless of what the Catholic Church said. They had no primitive streak, no means to think or feel or be. Two looked slightly fragmented. He separated them into another dish. He studied the final two, trying to decide and saying a prayer. He noticed a slight unevenness in cell size of one versus the other. He separated it, leaving the most perfect one.

Felix stared at the blastocyst. Its DNA had traveled through the centuries to fertilize a woman's egg and live again in a Petri dish. Would the tiny cluster of stem cells that clung to the cavity wall survive to become Jesus Christ? Should they? He closed his eyes and whispered the *Anima Christi:*

Soul of Christ, make me holy.
Body of Christ, save me.
Blood of Christ, fill me with love.
Water from Christ's side, wash me.
Passion of Christ, strengthen me.
Good Jesus, hear me.
Within your wounds, hide me. Never let me be parted from you.
From the evil enemy, protect me.
At the hour of my death, call me. And tell me to come to you.
That with your saints I may praise you. Through all eternity. Amen.

Felix opened his eyes, knowing he couldn't stop. He loaded the blastocyst into a sterilized catheter, put it on a tray, and took it out to Maggie's bedside.

Frances and Maggie watched as he lay it on the procedure tray.

"My baby's in there, isn't he?" Maggie asked.

That's what it came down to. Motherhood. Without it there could be no Christ.

She lay down and put her legs in the stirrups. This time, Frances didn't ask to hold her hand.

"Ready now?" he asked.

"Ready."

Felix inserted the speculum without stopping, aware that Sam was on the other side of the door. Though Sam had disgraced himself, though Felix had done his best to beat him to a pulp, Sam would probably still barge in if Maggie so much as whimpered.

She didn't.

Felix uncovered the catheter. He put it in Maggie's vagina, avoiding her torn but healing flesh, and inserted it up to and through the cervical opening to the top of her uterus. She didn't flinch.

"Well, here we go," he said.

Felix pushed the plunger and deposited the tiny blastocyst high into Maggie's womb.

Chapter 37

Saturday a.m., Late August—Turin, Italy

Seven months later in Italy's fourth largest city, where handsome townhouses flank tree-lined boulevards within sight of pre-Alpine hills, a boy on a bicycle rode past the first century Porta Palazzo, newspapers strapped to his bicycle. Father Bartolo had arranged these weekend deliveries to the priests, the nuns, and to some of the church's wealthy patrons. It helped augment the boy's family income.

Every Saturday he would stop here at the last Roman gate still standing in Turin, prop up his bicycle, climb the fence, and sit on the grass with his back against the statue of Cesare Augusto. He'd save his apple to eat here, as he looked at the ancient red brick walls, imagining what it was like to live in 28 B.C. when Augusta Taurinorum was founded—a date and name familiar to all Turinese children.

Dreaming of feathered helmets and fighting Gauls, the boy returned to his bicycle, and took a last luscious bite of apple. Some of the juice spilled from his mouth onto *The Times* of London he would deliver to Father Bartolo. The boy wiped the juice away, unable to read the smeared English word, only the letters c-l-o-n-e.

———

Saturday a.m.—Atlanta, Georgia

At 2:00 a.m. in Atlanta, Georgia, a woman reporter stumbled in the door of her town home and tried to make it to her powder room before she threw up. She didn't.

"Effing parties," she said between regurgitations. "Effing people!" Groggily, she wiped her mouth and, in spite of being Christian and conservative in her beliefs and politics, she toyed with the notion of saying the whole eff word.

"Effing parties," she repeated, then rinsed her mouth.

She went to the bedroom and fell onto her bed, crawled under the covers, realized she still had on heels and kicked them off under the sheets then pulled the cover up over her black sequined suit.

"Effing people!"

She fell asleep, dreaming of flat, perfect teeth instead of the bucked ones which made people call her names behind her back: the talking bunny, the panel hopper, the rabid red head. Last night she'd overheard them and the hurt caused her to drink.

The phone woke her from her flat teeth dreams. Angrily, she reached for it and answered, "What? What? Who the eff is this?"

A voice said, "Wake up and log onto *The Times* of London. Look for a cloning story. Dig around and have a feature ready for us at 7:00 a.m."

"What?"

"Just do it. G'night, bunny."

She slammed the phone down. "Effing people!" and dragged herself from bed.

———

Saturday a.m., Eagle Rock near Cliffs Landing

Maggie gripped Sam's hand for balance as they inched onto Eagle Rock, which crested the western brow of the hill a quarter mile from Skunk Hollow. Below them stretched the northern Hudson Valley in fertile grandeur. Other than the Cascade, Eagle Rock had become their favorite spot, though the climb here was harder on Maggie, now. Sam take out a wool blanket from his backpack and folded it into a small, thick square to give her a soft place to sit. Then he helped her down on it. Maggie leaned back on her arms, her stomach protruding, and inhaled the morning air.

"Take a good last look," Sam said and rubbed his hand across her stomach. "We're not coming back here until after the baby's born. The climb's too much for you."

She looked down at the river that flowed in two directions. Maggie called it by its Indian name, Shatemuc, because it felt like bad luck to recross it now and reverse direction like the river did.

She patted Sam's hand. "You only stopped trying to climb up me yourself a couple months ago, you know."

Sam grinned.

'You're a rascal, but you've got a good heart," she said.

He didn't seem to mind that she knew.

He'd been here every weekend since they were sure she was pregnant.

That day, Sam had held her hand while Felix ran the test, Frances pacing. When Felix made the announcement, Maggie had shouted hallelujahs. Frances had kissed Maggie on the cheek, apologized again for upsetting her, then drove off in her S-type Jaguar, saying she needed to get away for a bit. Maggie suspected that was code for, *I need to hook up with one of my old boyfriends.* Sam had popped the cork on a bottle of sparkling apple cider because Felix wouldn't permit Maggie even a sip of champagne. Felix declared her *the best woman in the world, and* Sam had agreed, adding they were both also crazy.

That had been seven months ago. Her due date was October 22, eight weeks and a day from now. If she had a molecule that hadn't been examined, sometimes twice daily, she couldn't say where it was.

Frances rarely stayed at the Landing all night anymore. She spent most nights at home. Maggie guessed disapproval had won out over brother love. Either that, or Frances wanted to stay away from Sam, who had instructed her to let neighbors think Felix was consulting overseas. Only every other Sunday was Frances sure to be around.

Without her or Adeline here, Felix seemed lonely in the rare hours he wasn't busy in the lab. Whenever Frances came he asked where Adeline was. Sometimes Frances knew and he'd try to call, but when he reached Adeline, they didn't seem to have much to say. He couldn't go where she was. She refused to come here. She said he didn't belong to her, but to the child.

It was Sam who was always there for Maggie. Usually he drove out after work during the week. Every other Sunday, he took her for a drive up to Nyack, a local tourist spot. Nothing strenuous. Just an easy afternoon stroll of its quaint art, craft, and antique shops, or along the waterfront, or through streets with Queen Ann, Victorian, and Carpenter Gothic architecture characteristic of the Hudson River Valley.

At one of the many restaurants, they would brunch—which is what everyone loved to do in Nyack on Sundays. Nothing fried. No extra salt.

She loved the outings, but after their third straight trip, Maggie knew Nyack had become a bore to Sam. He wouldn't admit it or stop the trips.

Maggie gazed to her left along the cliff toward the Ramapo Hills shining blue in the distance. A flock of sand martins rose from the riverbank and twirled crazily in the air, chirping their joyful song. "Oh, Sam, aren't they beautiful?" she said.

"Sure are."

Lazily he stroked the baby through her stomach, and she let him because his touch didn't arouse her like before. She was proud of her belly's protrusion. For almost five months her stomach had stayed flat, then it swelled like a new melon. Maggie had been thrilled when she first saw on the ultrasound, for herself, it was a boy. Being pregnant with Sam beside her, here in Cliffs Landing, Maggie was happier than she'd ever been. Most days she lazed like this in the sultry summer, her belly growing fat with the child.

As she gazed at the beauty of the landscape, aware of the beauty inside her, Maggie's feelings overflowed once more. Sam hugged her as she sobbed with joy. They were usually by the Cascade when it happened or at the river watching the sand martins fly. She knew Sam didn't understand, but he didn't pry or try to stop her. He just rubbed her forehead or her belly, whistled his Irish tune, and let her cry.

"There I go again," she said when the tears stopped.

He reached up to wipe her eyes with a tissue, and a streak of makeup came away on it. "Why do you wear this makeup stuff on your nose?"

She felt shocked, then embarrassed. How could he ask a woman such a thing? "It's … it's to balance my nose out."

He lay back and looked at the sky. "There's nothing wrong with your nose. By the way, I wish you'd let me eat with you when you have dinner in your room, or come in and watch TV. Felix isn't great company, you know. Why don't you, Maggie?"

She had asked him and Felix for privacy in her room to keep from feeling like a specimen in a jar—poked all day, watched day and night. And she'd rebelled against supervision of her every bite, so Felix made a special arrangement with Fabulous Food. If they'd create saltless meals and wouldn't fry anything, Maggie could order what she pleased. Many evenings FF delivered dinner to her garden door, and she ate alone. Felix had installed a small refrigerator in her room so she could satisfy her cravings. Carrots and fruit and such. Unless an emergency arose, her room was now off limits.

She opened her compact and tried to discreetly restore the nearly invisible streak of makeup down the center of her nose. Sam had never seen her without it, and she didn't want that to change.

"The only reason," she said gently, "is I need some time to myself."

Maggie sat Indian fashion as he rubbed her belly .

"Did I tell you the one about the Indian and old Charlie Lundstrom whose family used to live on the mountain in Skunk Hollow?"

"No, tell me."

"They were one of the white families here." Maggie pointed up. "The Indian lived way up this mountain in a cave. His name was Oddwad. He wore feathers and a bearskin robe. He lived off rabbits and birds he killed with his arrows, and he didn't bother anyone. Charlie Lundstrom gave him his first taste of bread and potato, or so Oddwad let Charlie believe. Oddwad liked the food so much, Charlie took him more. Oddwad always said, "Thank you, Charles, and thank you Ikas, I've got a friend."

"Ikas?"

"Mother earth."

"That's it?"

"Nice story, isn't it?"

"It could use a punch line."

Maggie nudged his shoulder. "It's got a punch line, Sam, if you look for it."

She'd picked wild tiger lilies and windflowers and twisted them into a bouquet. Now she raised it, and their perfume made her dizzy.

"What is it?" Sam asked, staring at her.

Maggie looked down at the Shatemuc feeling something terrible was there.

"What's the matter, are you feeling sick?"

She felt an urge, a sense, a woman's intuition rising to awareness. Maggie, in her faith, took them as taps on the shoulder from God—not something she could explain to Sam.

"I don't know," she said, but she did.

She'd imagined Sam in the Shatemuc, caught in dangerous tides made by fresh water flowing down from the Adirondacks and salt water up from the sea. As the sand martins whirled, she threw her arms around him. "Don't do anything crazy, Sam, all right? Be careful!"

He said he would and patted her back as she cried.

Chapter 38

Saturday midday—Fifth Avenue Lobby

Sam entered the ninth floor code into the elevator, speculating about what was so urgent that Brown's butler should call him on his day off. It could be for anything—a special envelope delivery, the kind of persuasion he'd tried on Jerome Newton, a private investigation. Brown took pains to check out new people before meeting with them, much less doing business. Sometimes he used Sam for this.

Sam had planned to stay the weekend out at the Landing with Maggie. Because of her, he'd had sex twice in seven months and both were pickups in local bars. No time for the Jersey docks. Fast in, fast out, use a condom or risk your pecker dropping off. Twice. Yet Sam was almost as happy as if he'd been screwing half the Rockettes chorus line.

He could picture himself in any number of life situations. Hung up on a pregnant black maid who wouldn't let him touch her? Who had let him near her once but no more? Just months ago he would have laughed at the idea. Maybe Frances was right and he loved her. Sam was certainly glued to Maggie Clarissa Johnson, lately of Harlem, New York—unwed mother and ex-maid.

When he wondered why out loud, Maggie said it was God. The child needed his protection, so God had made Sam her friend. Maybe so. Half the time he wasn't even horny. In Sam's experience, that was a miracle.

The elevator doors opened and there was Mr. Brown in the foyer. He'd been waiting and not happily. He had a folded newspaper in his hands. Sam recognized *The Times* of London.

Brown handed it to him. "Read this as we walk."

Sam followed to the library, seeing a circled feature. His pulse shot up. He felt sick as he read.

> *Cloning in America - Pssst! Get this!*
>
> *Anonymous sources are at it again. This time they've added a juicy, perhaps incredible, postscript to our earlier report that an American scientist is busily cloning someone not fully alive. Hear this, world! Our mad scientist has—through nefariously indirect, clandestine, and devious means—got hold of bits of one of those religious relics said to have been in contact with Jesus Christ. You know, bits of the True Cross, the Holy Manger, the Shroud, Veronica's Veil, the Nails, the Lance, the Crown of Thorns. That sort of thing. Anyhoo, sources say this mad American plans to extract DNA from the bits and clone them. Are you following me here? He plans to clone Jesus Christ and bring him back!*
>
> *Stay tuned to my features for more about the Second Coming!*
>
> *If you've been naughty of late, now might be a good time to repent.*

What had happened to their seven-month long deal with Jerome Newton? Now Sam had to explain why the same reporter was updating the same story, when Sam had said it was all a hoax. Worse still, Newton had identified the clone.

Sam read the article twice, verifying there was no hint of Rossi's identity, no allusion to where they were. This was still a deal breaker. Why didn't Newton fear losing the Sunday interviews?

Brown eased into his chair, working his jaw. He looked furious. "Talk. I'll listen," he said.

Sam gave him credit for self-control. Likewise, Sam steeled himself and smiled, his eyes on the newspaper.

"He's still playing his little game. Notice that he hasn't named anyone because, like I told you, there's no one to name."

Brown didn't speak until Sam looked up.

"He named the clone."

Sam chuckled. "Yeah, right. Cloning Jesus."

Brown kept staring at Sam and saying nothing.

After a while Sam asked, "What?"

"Did he pick the name Jesus out of a hat?"

"Maybe he was snorting something. You don't really think someone could—"

Brown interrupted. "Coulds are unimportant here. Does an American scientist believe he's cloning Jesus? That's what I want to know. It was your job to tell me that, Sam."

Sam slapped the paper with the back of his hand. "This proves it's a hoax, like I already said. Cloning Jesus? Incredible. In fact, it's impossible."

Brown stood and went to his shelves. He looked off like he was troubled. Then he withdrew a book. "I'm interested in beliefs, not possibilities." He held the book up to Sam. It was *War of the Worlds* by H. G. Wells. "You've read it?"

"Once. Martians landing in New Jersey and taking over?"

"Yes. Do you remember what was done with it?"

"Yeah. Orson Welles based a radio drama on it. He used realistic news announcements and scared everyone."

"A Martian landing was impossible." Brown put the book away. "Still there were riots in the street, traffic jams, wholesale panic up and down the east coast because people believed."

"But that was long ago, in the 1930s, I think. Who, today, would believe Jesus Christ could be cloned?"

"Human nature has changed in the last sixty-some years, in your opinion?"

"I think we're sophisticated enough to—"

"Stop, Sam." Brown returned to the desk, sat down and leaned forward. "Stop thinking."

Sam grew quiet.

"Do what I've asked."

"I will. That's a given, but try me once more. I'd like to understand."

Though he seemed upset, his benevolent scholar expression appeared. Sam had nudged him into full oracle mode. Brown pointed to the newspaper.

"This isn't a hoax. Something's behind these stories. This reporter's resistance to you itself is strange. You've never missed before, Sam. There's something here." Brown picked up a remote control, flicked a TV on then started a tape, saying, "This was on CNN after the news this morning."

Sam saw a woman with buckteeth, a regular guest panelist on CNN. She'd been unkindly nicknamed the rabid red head because she irritated both her enemies and her friends. She sat between a man wearing glasses and a bow tie, and another man conservatively suited. They were having an angry debate.

Brown turned the volume down and clasped his hands. "Cloning isn't a fantasy anymore. If a man wants to clone himself, his dog, his mother, father, fine. Great historical figures are another thing. They exist in the mind as potent symbols that can motivate mass behavior. Think what a clone of George Washington could convince people to do? Abraham Lincoln? Now think of what the Son of God could convince them of? Throughout history religions and religious figures have caused not only martyrdom and civil disobedience, but also the rise and fall of kings, murder, pillage, war, every kind of irrational behavior. Just two brief, cryptic articles in *The Times* and there are CNN panel discussions and spontaneous prayer vigils in parks."

Sam's knees felt weak.

"Beliefs are potent." Brown gazed down at his desk drawer. "Including superstitions. There are even those who think they see destiny in the stars."

"Are you one of them?" Sam ventured.

Brown's gaze drifted away. "I am Leo the king."

Sam thought of adding, *Well, I know I'm Taurus, or is it Aries? One of them, anyway,* but all he said was, "That fits."

He looked back. "Sam, the clone's real identity is unimportant. What matters is who he is believed to be."

"Pontius Pilate must have said something like that," Sam observed with a chuckle.

Brown ignored him. "A credible American scientist can't be allowed to produce a supposed clone of Jesus Christ from a credible—even a remotely credible—source of DNA."

They sat quietly, saying nothing, Sam aware that he was facing a man who felt he owned the new world order and didn't intend to let a has-been like Jesus Christ shake it up. Sam had seconds to decide what to do, but it was long enough. For seven months he'd explored scenarios in his mind in imagined hours, days, months. Do one thing and he'd have a particular stream of options. Do another and they'd disappear.

Quietly, Sam said. "I'm glad I asked. I didn't understand what you meant. This one's not for me."

Brown's searchlight glare fixed on Sam. "Oh?"

"I think it's nonsense, but if it isn't, you're saying clone but I'm hearing mother, baby. One you don't want to be born, if this is real. Am I right?"

Brown's gaze remained on Sam.

Sam paused, knowing the future turned on his next words. Brown was the most generous employer he'd ever had, but he expected unflinching loyalty in return. "I didn't sign on for anything like that. Count me out, okay?"

"I'll want you altogether out."

"Yeah, I know." Sam stood.

When Sam headed for the elevators, Brown rose and followed.

"I'll be out by midnight," Sam said when the elevator came. "I'll bring my keys, credit cards, access cards, passwords, everything, up before I go."

Sam faced Mr. Brown and pushed the button for the lobby.

As the elevator doors closed, Brown said, "Reconsider, Sam. You have two weeks."

Chapter 39

Saturday—Sam's apartment

As soon as Sam reached his apartment, he went to his refrigerator, pulled out a McSorley's *Black and Tan* and downed half of it. If he'd had hard liquor he would have drunk it. The things he knew about Brown were nerve-rattling enough; what scared Sam more were the things he didn't know. Was there such a thing as quitting Mr. Brown's operation? If not, what happened to those who tried?

Early in his eleven years with Brown, he'd sensed activities more hidden than his own. Once he bumped into a tall man in black, and another wearing a long leather coat, exiting quietly through Brown's garage. One look and Sam decided he'd be happier never knowing who they were or what they did.

Now their brutal faces were all Sam could think of. That and the question he had ignored for eleven years: did Brown's fall-back position for important projects include cutting little kids' heads open with machetes; did it include keeping AIDS drugs out of Africa; did it include murder? He'd especially ignored one question for a year. The wife of the Secretary of State had caught him in bed with her daughter from a previous marriage, and then wildly threatened to expose his dirty dealings. Sam had learned all this during a drunken crying jag when the Secretary collapsed in Brown's garage one night. Since then, Sam had tried not to wonder: had the wife really died from an auto accident, or had Brown killed her?

As Sam packed, he reviewed his decision to leave. He had no choice. If Brown learned who Maggie was and decided her child shouldn't be born, weekend visits wouldn't cut it. Maggie would need twenty-four hour armed protection by someone who couldn't be bought. Unfortunately, Brown had enough money to buy off half the disciples and the saints. Sam was all Maggie had.

He couldn't leave her unprotected while he stayed here and tried to outmaneuver Brown. Brown wasn't the outmaneuverable type.

So Sam had played his only ace: that Brown liked and trusted him, that he relied on the past, let it instruct his actions and his plans. In eleven years, Sam hadn't lied to him, or advanced a private agenda. Brown would never suspect Sam's involvement with the clone. Such a thing, to him, would be like Prometheus *not* stealing fire from heaven, and the east coast *not* panicking when they thought H. G. Wells's Martians were at hand. Sam had predictably steered the ship where he was told for eleven years. Mutiny wasn't in his makeup, as far as Brown was concerned. He'd think Sam was having scruples, like he said.

He decided to use the time Brown gave him and wait a week or so before making his resignation final. No point in hurrying things. For the moment, Sam had just one worry. Did Brown let key people quit?

Someone knocked on the door and he froze, listening. He grabbed his shoulder holster off its hook and took out his gun. The knock came again. Sam backed to the wall beside the door and called, "Who is it?"

"Sam, it's me," came a woman's voice.

He frowned. "Who's me?"

"Remember the ballroom kitchen?"

He looked up to the ceiling and whispered, "Oh, God! Why now?" He swung the door open, staying where he was. He heard her high heels before he saw her.

She came in, calling, "Sam?"

He kicked the door closed and there was his dancer. She turned, her glorious chestnut hair cascading over a slick red raincoat that she wore cinched at the waist. It matched her red stilettos and red fingernails.

"Mr. Brown said to tell you I'm the carrot."

Slowly, she untied her coat and opened it. She was naked, her skin shimmering like moon dust in the room's low light, baubles glistening like stars in her hair. As Sam stood there, taking her in, she started doing a funny roll with her belly, which made her amazing boobs rise a little and then bounce, and her pelvis move up and down. Not much. Just enough to set Sam on fire.

"Baby, what the hell is your name?" he said, his voice already hoarse.

"I'm Coral and you've got me for as long as you want."

He held his gun and walked around her.

"Keep doing what you're doing. Just drop that coat and kick it away."

She did and he felt the coat for weapons but found none, not that he'd expected to. She was a whore, not an assassin—a one of a kind, blue chip, make you pray for mercy whore. He laid his gun down and kept circling her, not touching, just looking as she moved. Slowly she raised her arms over her head and made the belly roll deeper, causing Sam to groan. Still he didn't touch her. He wanted to remember this sight. She smiled at him and poked her tongue out between her teeth, moving her belly, her hips, bouncing her boobs. When Sam was behind her, she looked back, winked, then spread her legs and bent over from the waist, her hair sweeping the ground as she gave him a full view of what had been hidden by more chestnut hair—the prettiest twat in the world.

A groan roared from Sam and he reached for her, tearing at his belt buckle with the other hand. Coral must have known he'd lost it. She whirled around and stroked him, held him, while Sam finished coming in his pants.

"Been a while, has it?" she said when he stopped shaking.

Sam thought of Maggie. Then it dawned on him that if he didn't screw Coral, Brown would suspect him for sure. There was no other way. He had to bang her. "Don't you worry, sweetheart, that was just an appetizer."

He took her to his bed and had carnal knowledge of Coral in every position he could think of for almost an hour. She was a pro and knew how to hold back, though sweat poured from him as he labored over her and they looked in each others' eyes. In the end Coral delivered his prize. Her nipples sat up, she flushed scarlet, and let go—screaming she was coming. Greedily he watched her, then followed.

As Coral lay drowsy beside him, he caught a bright hairpin that dangled from her hair and put it back.

"Diamonds, huh? Is that a mike?" he asked.

She looked cutely at him and said, "Nah."

"Would you tell me if it was?"

She dimpled and said, "Nah."

He chuckled, realizing he knew nothing about her. "Fair enough, but tell me how you got into this, okay?"

They had the lights off, the shades down. By the slant of the few sunrays escaping in, he guessed it was about 3:00 p.m.

"The whole truth and nothing but the truth?"

"Yeah, sure."

"I was a sweet young thing." She closed her eyes and stroked her fingers lazily down Sam's pecs. "Mr. Brown saw me in a musical. I wouldn't let him touch me, but for three months he put the world at my feet: clothes, money, private planes, opening night at La Scala in Milan."

"Then what?"

She snapped her fingers. "He vanished. Like that, I'm back in the chorus line, poor me. Another three months and one night his butler is backstage with a dress box. In it are a strapless black satin gown and black slippers. I put them on; he takes me out to a limo and there's Brown holding flowers that look like satin bells. He says they're black lisianthius, as rare as I am. Beside him is an actor who has his Oscar in his lap. Can't name him, but you know him. He makes us gals swoon. Al Hambra was the hot restaurant then. Remember the lotus pools?"

Sam remembered. For almost two years the Al Hambra drew elegant crowds. Limos from the building went there practically every other day. "Yeah, you had to know a guy who knew a guy who had the reservation number."

"Not us. Brown booked the whole place. In the next room, he had zithers playing. The chef-owner cooked and served the food himself. The President couldn't have gotten in that night."

"Then what?"

"We're sipping a brandy older than the country and Brown takes out a necklace—emeralds and diamonds. Big emeralds and diamonds. All I have to do is let the actor see my breasts."

'Well, well. Like that was all."

"It was. I cried a little so Brown told the guy if he laid a hand on me without my permission, he'd regret it until he died. I thought he meant it; the guy thought he meant it."

"So you did?"

"Brown did. Unzipped my dress, peeled it down slow, then draped the necklace on me while the guy gawked. The guy didn't say another word."

"He probably couldn't." Sam fondled a rosy nipple on a perfect breast. "When did you first—you know, go all the way?"

"Six months later. Same restaurant. Same guy gawking. More tears. He writes me a check for ten grand, twenty, fifty. I let him touch my breasts, but no more. Pretty soon he writes a check for a hundred grand. When the chef came back, the guy was on his knees doing me in the chair."

"Brown watched?"

"Sure did."

"Did he say anything?"

"He told me to come."

Sam patted her shoulder. "Should I feel sorry for you, baby?"

Her eyes still closed, Coral smiled. "Until just now, it was the best sex of my life."

He stroked her cheek. Again, Maggie crossed his mind.

"So what are your instructions? What did Brown tell you?"

Coral snuggled against him and opened one big hazel eye. "I told you. I'm the carrot. Did I work?"

"For me? You bet you did. For him?" He looked away. "You couldn't."

She sat up, not covering herself. If she was temptation and what they'd done was sin, Sam was bound for hellfire, couldn't avoid it if he tried. She had the worldliness the dock whores didn't and every bit of their brass.

"I guess you know what you're doing," she said. "He doesn't really get upset over little things, like our unapproved few minutes in the kitchen. It didn't bother him that much. You can't cross him on big things, you know. I'm guessing this is pretty big or I wouldn't be in the package." She stuck her tongue out and made a circle with it.

Sam smiled. "Oh yeah?"

"He had me scheduled for some deputy prime minister tonight."

He chucked her under the chin. "That figures."

"Yeah, that's why I'm guessing you're involved in something big. He likes you, you know."

Sam knew. He cupped her breasts thinking he would have paid a hundred grand just to touch them, too, like the actor. "How long do you get to persuade me?"

"Like I said, I stay until you tell me to go. Once I leave, no second helpings. But I have a feeling ..."

"What?"

"That if you do what Mr. Brown says, you might get a reward." Her nipples hardened and she moved against his hands. It felt like small branding irons in his palms. She was asking to stay longer, perhaps all night. He had to accept. He wanted to accept. It felt like his teenage hormones had returned.

"Give me a second, okay?"

He hopped from bed and, smiling at her, grabbed the cell phone he'd bought and took it with him to the kitchen. She couldn't listen in on his call. He turned on the tap full blast. Holding the phone close, he dialed Felix's number and when Felix answered, said he wouldn't be back tonight, but he'd better read the features section of *The Times* of London, and switch on CNN. As usual, Sam activated the security code when he hung up in case someone got hold of his phone.

When he returned to the bedroom, Coral had a surprise for him. She lay with her head at the foot of the bed, her upper body covered by sheets to the waist, leaving the bottom exposed, her fingers working between her thighs. Hell, she knew how to arrest a man's attention.

Sam dived onto the bed to join in.

Chapter 40

Sunday a.m.—Cliffs Landing

In his locked bedroom, the volume down, Felix watched the rabid red head attack another CNN guest opposed to cloning. He had a printout of Jerome Newton's feature, retrieved from *The Times'* website. Why had Newton chosen to up the stakes like this, announcing Jesus Christ was being cloned? Neither he nor Maggie had been named, but Felix sensed the outside world closing in on Cliffs Landing.

Maggie probably wouldn't see it unless it was brought to her attention, and he planned to keep her from watching TV when she came back from church. Cal held a private service for her now and then, though Felix knew Cliffs Landing must be buzzing about her pregnancy by now. Still, they had no reason to suspect the identity of her child.

What had gone wrong?

He needed time to talk this over with Sam, but Sam hadn't answered his cell phone. Surely he'd return in time to get Maggie out before Jerome Newton came for his interview. Would he make new demands of some kind, having frightened them with this second article?

To Felix's knowledge, Maggie had never heard of Newton, except briefly on CNN before they came to the Landing. They had Frances to thank for that. Felix could only be sure of seeing her every other Sunday when Sam and Maggie left for Nyack. Frances would put on the maternity body suit they'd purchased at a theatrical company and let Newton photograph her.

Felix flicked through the channels. Every major Sunday talk show was discussing Newton's article in *The Times*. Cloning itself was controversial enough, but cloning the dead?

He'd let too many things slip out of his control. Where was Frances? He didn't know. Where was Sam? He didn't know. He didn't know what Maggie ate every day. Felix had been in virtual isolation for seven long months, his usual work abandoned, semi-estranged from Frances, fully estranged from Adeline, Maggie spending her free time alone or with Sam.

In this isolation, old doubts had uselessly returned. Had he erred in his faith that the cells were still divine and the cloned child would be Christ? Clones were like identical twins who, studies revealed, matched 70 percent in intelligence and only 50 percent in personality traits. Like everyone, Jesus had been a product of his environment as well as his genes.

Had he properly handled the DNA? Cells were so minute a careless sneeze could have resulted in him having cloned himself. That's why police labs were always under fire in court trials: a sneeze, a skin cell falling, dandruff, could compromise a suspect's sample. Contamination could have occurred on the Shroud itself. Someone could have touched it with a cut finger, depositing the neutrophils. Conceivably, Maggie could be carrying a new Father Bartolo.

Even without such problems, the mitochondria in every cell of the clone's body came from Maggie. There were only fifty genes in its single-stranded DNA, but what effect would it have?

Maggie's confidence had steadily increased since he performed the implantation. In spite of Felix's prayers, his had declined.

He'd spent days, weeks studying the remaining DNA, experimenting with it, trying to reassure himself to no avail. There was only one indisputable fact. Maggie was carrying a clone from DNA on the Shroud of Turin. That was explosive, and it couldn't be undone.

He had created this situation and somehow must regain control. First, he decided to check their messages at home regularly. He couldn't be sure how often Frances did. If anyone learned his identity, they'd call there first. He dialed their number in New York and entered the pass code. Frances had agreed to take care of the mail, which meant bills were paid and replies to correspondence had been sent. There should be few messages.

They had six. A surprise.

One was from his tailor about a suit he'd forgotten. The next five were increasingly strident messages from someone named Sharmina. He replayed the last one twice:

"Dr. Rossi, you can keep ducking me all you want. I'm calling back here every day, twice a day, till I hear from Maggie Johnson. She said she was leaving with your family for a little while on vacation. Seven months ain't no little while. If you don't answer this phone by Monday, I'm calling the cops."

It must be Maggie's friend. Had Adeline forgotten to mail the postcards? He hadn't heard from her in so long. Where was Maggie, for that matter? She should have been back from church. He left a note in case Frances and Sam returned then climbed in the Range Rover and drove onto Lawford Lane, scanning the road in case Maggie was already walking back. He reached the church and was grateful to see no cars in the lot.

Felix parked and crossed the semi-circular lawn to the side entrance. Finding the door unlocked, he went in toward the minister's office. He stopped when he heard Cal praying and Maggie saying, "Amen."

They were praying with the TV on.

Felix tiptoed down the hall and peeped through the back of the half-open door. Maggie knelt on the carpet, Cal's hand on her head. On the TV screen, he saw a small crowd gathered on The Great Lawn in Central Park, just north of Turtle Pond. A spray-painted banner read JESUS LIVES.

"Don't be frightened," Cal said. " This must be God's will. All the changes, all the dreams are surely from God."

What changes? What dreams?

Upset that she should confide in Cal and not him or even Sam, Felix tiptoed away then came back, calling, "Maggie, are you here?"

He heard the TV click off as he entered. "Hi, Cal," he said. "Is anything wrong?"

Maggie didn't look at him.

"Ah, Felix," Cal said. "Just in time to take Maggie home."

"Good then let's go, Maggie."

He took her arm and said to Cal, "It can't be safe for her to come here anymore. People will notice and start wondering who the father is."

Cal and Maggie laughed.

"It's too late," Cal said. "Everyone in Cliffs Landing knows Maggie's pregnant. They know she's under your protection and mine."

"Then we should leave."

"No, no, I think you should stay. Am I sure? No, but my gut instinct is that you should. Whatever you decide, I hope God will bless you both."

"You believe?" Felix asked in surprise.

Cal closed his eyes as if seeking divine guidance. "Let's just say I don't disbelieve."

They gazed at each other, Felix envying Cal's simple faith. He wondered if it came from serving God or if belief came first and caused men like Cal and Bartolo to become ministers, rabbis, priests.

"What do you make of all this?" Maggie asked as they drove back. "Who is this reporter? How did he find out so much? Is it the one who tried to bribe Sam when you got back from Turin?"

"He's an acquaintance, that's all. Don't worry, we won't let him near you."

They walked the path of flat round stones to the house.

Felix said, "I thought I heard you mention strange dreams to Cal. Is anything troubling you?"

He opened the door for her.

Packed and standing in the entry were two pieces of Frances's luggage. It was 12:45 p.m. Newton would be here within an hour. Sam had yet to come.

"Maggie, if the doorbell rings, don't answer it. Understand?"

"With all this in the news? Don't worry, I'm not answering any doors."

He went to Frances's room, knocked, and opened the door. She was filling another suitcase.

"Frances, why are you doing this?"

Stubbornly, she kept packing as she replied. "Have you watched TV today, by any chance?"

"Yes, and?"

"Prayer vigils. Where did they come from? Sam warned us, didn't he. This has gotten dangerous. No, it's outrageous what you've done."

"I can't undo it, Fran."

She looked sharply at him. "Actually, yes you can. Before it's too late, you could simply put Maggie to sleep and do what you must. She need never know it wasn't a miscarriage. It's not like this is a real child. It's a laboratory fabrication. It's a freak."

Stunned, Felix sat down on the art deco chaise lounge by her bed. She was right. He still had a way out of his doubts and this growing madness. He sped through the logistics in his mind. He could give Maggie something to cause cramping then say the child was in trouble so he could perform a partial birth abortion. First he'd dilate her cervix then put her to sleep. Using forceps he would deliver the child feet first and, before the head was born, pierce its skull and suction out its brains.

The clearer he imagined it, the colder he felt, as if a glacier were forming inside him.

"I can't do it."

Frances had been watching his face. She resumed hurling clothes into the suitcase. "Adeline had the right idea. I'm joining her in Greece."

Eagerly Felix rose. "You know where she is? Why didn't you tell me? I need to talk with her."

"We're taking a Mediterranean cruise and you know what?" Frances straightened and gazed impassively at him. "I hear there'll be a number of eligible men aboard, not one of them a doorman. You should be worrying if your fiancée will fall in love and marry one of them."

"I love her. Adeline knows that, doesn't she?"

"How would she know that, Felix? How? I certainly might return as Mrs. Somebody, if I were her. If I do meet Mr. Right, I may very well have the captain marry us on board. When the cruise is over, we'll stop in Italy on our honeymoon to see Uncle Simone and meet the rest of our relatives. Shall I remind you why, Felix?"

Felix sat down. "I expect you're going to."

"Because that's where we belong. With our family, our relatives, our blood." She raised her voice. "Not our maid, Felix! Not our doorman! Because of you, I'm a guest in my own home!"

He didn't understand what had gotten her so angry. "Fran—"

"What were you thinking? What could you possibly have been thinking? Maggie owns you, now. She runs you. She and Sam. If you think you're in control, you're wrong. The moment you put that clone in her, she owned you!"

Felix sighed. "Control? Yes, that's laughable. A friend of hers is calling. Sharmina. I thought she was taken care of, but apparently not. She must think I kidnapped Maggie. Newton's up to something. Sam's not here. Something's happened to Maggie she hasn't told me about. I need you, Fran. Now more than ever. You can't leave me."

When her frosty expression didn't soften, Felix said. "I'm sure I'll love our relatives, too, when I get to know them. It's the timing that's bad. That's all."

"Felix!"

She reached into the suitcase.

"When were you going to tell me about this?" She picked up a photo. Her eyes filled with tears.

Felix recognized it right away. Two young lovers stood beneath a spectacular bower of roses. His father wore a yarmulke, his mother a scarf of black lace. He was handsome; she was beautiful. They were young and in love. Above them was their wedding gift: a small Italian villa of yellow stucco and brick. Below the villa Lake Maggiore shined. On its bank was a cottage with a wide deck on which they'd slept in the open, and a porticiollo for the little boat they sailed, a private shore where they lit fires and sat, arms entwined, under the stars.

"In exchange for this one picture, Flix, I would have given you my half of this whole house—assuming we ever get it back from Maggie! Or are you just going to let her keep it?" Frances was crying.

He'd forgotten to show her. He'd forgotten the photo was hers as well as his.

Chapter 41

Sunday p.m.—George Washington Bridge

Sam drove fast across the bridge, looking at his dashboard clock every other second. He couldn't believe it was already 1:00 p.m. He should have been in Cliffs Landing, should have left for Nyack with Maggie a half hour ago. Now, Newton would show up any minute and Maggie would be there. She must be worried about him. Felix must be pissed as hell.

Sam had no excuse. Last night he'd taken Coral out to dinner, after going to Bergdorf's and buying her a dress. If she went home to change, that was the end of the date, she'd said, and anyway she couldn't let him know where she lived. He'd bought a dress, shoes, earrings, and pantyhose. It was worth it. She looked great.

He'd liked knowing she was practically naked under that dress. After dinner, they'd gone to his favorite Irish pub. He loved how his cronies ogled her and then secretly congratulated him. None of them had ever had a broad like Coral. She was the most exciting thing ever to set foot in that bar. He let it be known theirs was no platonic acquaintance, by casually touching her knees, her hips, draping his arm around her shoulder so his hand could dangle near her breast. To make sure they understood, he kissed her twice.

He wanted them to know he was balling a babe, the best they'd ever laid eyes on in their lives.

He and Coral got back late, slept late this morning. Sam still woke in time, had dressed to go to Cliffs Landing. But when he tried to say goodbye to Coral at the door, she'd reminded him: no second helpings once she left. That meant he'd never see her again, because he had no intention of earning a second date as Brown's reward for coming back.

He couldn't help it. He'd opened the shirt he gave her to wear. Then he was gone again, lost between the hottest pair of thighs in New York. He was only a man, and he'd been fooling himself. He'd been horny for the better part of seven months. It had been humanly impossible to leave for Cliffs Landing. Who could blame him?

Sam sped up, knowing Maggie could.

Since Newton's three-car tailing trick, he took pains to make sure he wasn't being followed, even by a dozen cars, but when he turned into the Rossis' driveway, he saw a rental car already there. He hopped out and hotfooted it across the round stones of the walk, or tried to. He didn't have his usual pep. He started to open the door then saw a man come around the side of the house. Jerome Newton. Sam's energy returned.

"What the hell are you doing creeping around here?"

"Walter Hickock!" Jerome called sarcastically. "Good to see you. I have an appointment, as you no doubt recall. No one's answered the door. I went round the back. What do I see but two cars?"

"That doesn't mean they're here. People walk a lot of places in Cliffs Landing."

"Yes, so I've seen."

Jerome took a card from his wallet and pulled out a pen. "I'll return at the same time next Sunday. If no one's home, tell Rossi our deal is off."

"He might think it's off because of your new article in *The Times* yesterday."

"Once we talk, I'm sure he'll understand my position."

Sam snatched the card from Jerome's hand. "I'll see he gets it. Now get the hell out of here."

Jerome raised his eyebrows, went to his car, and drove away. Sam stayed at the door until he was sure Newton had left then he opened it with his key. There in the foyer were Felix, Frances, and Maggie peeping around a corner.

"He's gone, don't worry," Sam said.

Coming forward, Maggie said, "Felix won't tell me who it was. Will you, Sam?"

Sam sighed.

"Is it the reporter who's causing all the fuss?"

They stared at her.

"No, it isn't!" Felix said, "Just someone I know who's a pain and who shouldn't know you're here!" He turned to Sam, plainly irritated. "Where have you been?"

Maggie came closer as if she also wanted to hear. It was the first time in weeks he'd been gone all Saturday night. She had probably tried not to care, but he knew she did.

"I got tied up is all, but it worked out. I drove that fellow off. He left a card." Sam handed it to Felix.

Maggie's big doe eyes stared at Sam as if there were nothing else to look at in the world. Did she believe him? They weren't lovers, but he hoped she believed him. He wanted it to be true, though it wasn't. Still he wanted to reassure her, to reach out and touch her stomach. He wanted her to know he'd be there for her. She was so helpless and didn't know it, so vulnerable to her own misguided beliefs, here in this house with Felix the maniac. Sam didn't believe Felix really cared about Maggie, only what she could do for him.

"I just got tied up," he repeated, feeling regret, but not because he'd been with Coral—he couldn't avoid that—but because he'd enjoyed it so much.

He hoped Maggie believed him. He'd square the lie with God on judgment day, along with all the other wrongs he'd done. Today, he didn't want the fact he needed sex from sexy women to give Maggie any pain.

"You got tied up at work?" she asked.

"Here's my hand to G—" Sam stopped. In his eagerness not to hurt her, he hadn't realized what he was saying. Maggie would never forgive him for a lie sworn to the God she so fervently believed in.

He watched the brightness leave her eyes. The pause itself had given him away. Maggie knew. If he hadn't been with a woman, he'd have no reason to lie. As Felix and Frances watched them, Maggie quietly turned and headed for the downstairs door.

"I don't believe it," Frances said to Sam. "You've done it again."

A whispered argument followed. Then they went downstairs after Maggie. Sam headed toward the laundry room and Felix toward the obstetrics room. Both doors were locked.

"I've got to talk to her," Felix said under his breath. "Some woman she knows is threatening to call the police! And Maggie told the minister things she hasn't told me. Has she said anything to you about dreams, Sam?"

"Dreams? No, nothing."

"Well, we've got to make her talk to us. Why do you keep … keep—" Felix sputtered. "Upsetting her."

Sam sighed.

Frances unfolded her arms. "Well," she said. "I think you two deserve this, so I'll leave you to it. Goodbye, Sam. Goodbye, Felix, and good luck. As for me, I'm going to live a sane life."

She turned, but Felix grabbed her arm. "Take pity on Maggie's condition, at least. If she's under stress, she might need me. I'm her doctor, remember. Try to help us through this, won't you? "

Frances closed her eyes as if gathering patience, took a breath and yelled, "Maggie! Open the damned door! You're scaring the men-folk, if you can call them that." She lowered her voice a bit. "Idiots is what I'd call them, but please, won't you let us in? Felix is concerned for you. He says a woman is asking about you—"

"Sharmina," Felix whispered.

"Sharmina!" Frances yelled.

Felix whispered. "She says she's calling the police."

"She said she's calling the police," Frances shouted

Sam had a bad feeling, a growing hunch that something was wrong.

Felix looked at him. "What are you waiting for? Go ahead and break it down!"

"Again?"

"Again."

Sam did. He entered with Felix and Frances behind him. They didn't see Maggie, only neatly stacked boxes from Fabulous Food piled in a corner of the room. Practically every other surface held empty jars.

'Where are you, Maggie?" Felix called.

They looked in the bathroom, but she wasn't there. Sam opened the French doors, but she wasn't in the garden.

Then Sam heard Frances's frightened voice. "Flix, come here!"

They rushed in and saw Frances in the doorway to the powder-blue nursery.

Maggie was inside, sitting on the rug in a corner, holding an open jar to her chest. She reached in, pulled out a fistful of something, crammed it in her mouth and ate it. She seemed not to notice they were there.

Sam drew back and let Felix approach her, saying, "Maggie, Maggie?"

"What's she eating?" Frances asked.

Urgently, Felix said, "Get a blood pressure monitor, the EKG, oxygen. Get my stethoscope, Frances. Run!"

Sam tried to stay out of the way and not panic, but why was Maggie just staring?

"What was she eating?" he asked.

"Olives."

"Olives?"

He went back into the other room and quickly examined the jars. Every one had held olives. There were almost a dozen. No wonder she hadn't let him in her room of late. He went back and saw Felix wipe his eyes on his sleeve, then take her blood pressure.

"What's the matter with her? Did I do this?" Sam said.

Gently, Felix took the jar from Maggie, rolled her onto her side, and put a pillow under her head. "No, Sam. It's my fault. Keep control of yourself. She's seizing."

Frances returned with the equipment.

"Here, Maggie, I'm putting a mask on your face and a cuff on your wrist," Felix said, picking up the fetal stethoscope. "Now I'm listening to the baby."

He finished and sat beside her. "It will be over in a few more seconds. She's having what's called a complex partial seizure."

"I thought you were taking care of her."

"She's had every test that could have predicted this. Yes, her pressure was a little high, but only transiently. I thought we had it under control. There's been no edema, no proteinuria. I've been checking. I don't understand this. It can't be eclampsia, it can't be."

"What's eclampsia?" Sam said.

"I'd need to do a Cesarean."

They fell silent.

"What else might it be?" Sam said after a while.

"Perhaps brain or nervous system involvement, but I've checked her reflexes every day. I'll see she has an MRI. No need for a lumbar puncture. I know she doesn't have meningitis or encephalitis."

"Then what is it?"

"Most seizures are idiopathic, which means we don't know their cause. If she's had them before, she wouldn't know it. She couldn't tell us because she didn't remember."

Sam picked up the jar. "Why's she eating olives? Isn't there salt in the brine? You told her not to eat salt. Never heard of an olive craving, anyway, what happened to pickles?"

He realized Felix was fighting not to cry. " I wonder if she knows?"

"Knows what?"

"Olives were the most plentiful foodstuff in ancient Jerusalem."

Chapter 42

Saturday in September, a week later—Cliffs Landing

In his rented car, Jerome turned right on Lawford Lane in the early morning and drove to the very end, past all the houses. He'd devised a cunning plan to learn the truth before his next appointment with the Rossis.

Lately he'd been studying Ms. Frances Rossi's pregnant stomach. It had stayed the same size for a suspiciously long time, and then was suddenly larger.

On his last visit, he carefully watched her. It didn't seem to Jerome that she and her baby moved as one, so he did some research. He went to an obstetrician's office, pretending to be waiting for his wife, and observed genuinely pregnant women in the flesh. Then he watched movies in which actresses were padded to look pregnant, and voila!—a replica of Frances Rossi's pregnancy.

Of course they'd tried to fool him. It was in their interests to.

Jerome parked where his car would be obscured. He was dressed in the fashion of the less-wealthy locals, and wore dark glasses and a fisherman's cap to hide his bronze hair. Binoculars hung around his neck. He had a digital camera in his pocket. He wore his trusty earpiece and carried an inconspicuous box which could have been fishing gear, but a miniature parabolic dish was inside. It could pick up conversations a hundred feet away.

He was in search of the maid.

In all his Sunday visits he'd never seen her, nor had he seen Sam. Jerome sensed this was significant. Perhaps the maid was caring for the real mother elsewhere with Sam as bodyguard, while Rossi and his sister put on a show.

Jerome crept toward the cliff then turned left toward the Rossis' house, looking for a place where he could observe both front and back. He would wait. When she appeared, he would follow the maid. If this failed, he'd follow the Rossis.

The ground to the right of the Rossis' home sloped up to a small hill. Jerome lay behind a fence and settled in to watch. At about seven, he saw Frances Rossi leave the house, get in her Jaguar, and drive away. Miraculously, her pregnancy had disappeared.

A half hour later, she returned with groceries. Shortly afterward a van pulled up, marked with an attractive gold logo consisting of the words *Fabulous Food*, a lemon slice, a sprig of thyme and basil. It drove around to the back, and a young kid with a punk hairdo got out, carrying a food warmer. He went to the back gate and pushed a button. Soon French doors opened, and Sam came out to the gate. He and the kid went inside then the kid came out, carrying the food warmer.

That was strange. Why hadn't the kid gone through the front or the kitchen door? Were the Rossis having someone's meals catered for whom Sam was on guard? Maybe the mother had been downstairs all along with the maid.

Staying wide of the house, he made his way down the hill and crept to the rock walls surrounding the French doors. He climbed up, hidden by the ivy. The garden was in full bloom, summer flowers at its edges. Fish swam in a clear pool, dotted with water lilies. Two white wrought-iron benches and the white-pebbled ground completed the picture of a private space meant for a woman deeply cherished. But unless she was quite chummy with her bodyguard and doorman, it wasn't Frances Rossi's room behind those French doors.

Patiently Jerome waited, trying to see inside, but the treated windows resisted his binoculars. Now and then he glimpsed a shadowy figure, but he couldn't tell who it was. Then to Jerome's joy the French doors opened. Sam stepped out, stretching and yawning in the still-cool morning air. Someone else was at the door. Jerome held his breath. Sam turned and seemed to argue with the person.

Then out into the garden stepped an obviously pregnant black woman, blankets in her arms. Why would Rossi employ a pregnant maid?

Then it hit him with the force of a mugger. She was the mother, for Christ's sake! That was why he'd never met the maid. What kind of story would this make? Maybe none at all. A news story could get away with one bizarre element and be believed: someone's cloning a person. Actually, that wasn't bizarre. Human cloning was medically feasible, now.

A story could even have two bizarre elements, if handled well: someone's cloning a dead person. Add a third and credibility stretched: someone's cloning a dead two thousand year old person named Jesus Christ. This was why Jerome made his initial articles humorous and sarcastic. He'd wanted to simply get the idea out, get people used to the subject. Later he could turn it into serious articles and columns, then a documentary, then a book.

He hadn't known Rossi had a fourth bizarre element up his sleeve: the new Jesus is being born to a black maid. Did Rossi do it deliberately or was he just dumb as hell?

Jerome watched as the maid soldiered ahead on her own, Sam following as she waddled beyond the gate and toward the cliff. Jerome waited, then crept after them. They stopped near the cliff's edge. Jerome could hear the rushing of a waterfall.

He watched Sam spread blankets on the ground, refusing the maid's help. Then they sat, her back against a tree, and looked across the Hudson. Jerome crept closer, his mind groping for a workable headline.

He settled a good distance away behind a rock, took out his parabolic dish, and positioned it. As he listened, he snapped pictures with his soundless digital camera, a photojournalist's best friend. Hooked to his laptop, the camera's "film" could be sent anywhere in minutes.

"—ignoring me all week," he heard Sam say. "We're never going to be friends again?"

"Of course we're friends," she said. "I appreciate you watching over me, but it's not like you're my husband, Sam Duffy, so like I told you, I don't care what you did. Just drop it, Sam. Everything's fine."

"I care, Maggie."

What was this? Jerome thought. A love affair between Sam and the maid? If she was carrying Sam's child, Jerome was back to square one. Just in case, he wrote her name on a small notebook so he wouldn't forget it.

The pair weren't talking.

After a while, Sam said, "And you need to stay in bed like Felix said. At least tell him about the colors. They could be a symptom of something."

She snorted. "And have him put me on some medicine that could hurt the baby? Have him give me another test? As if I'm not full enough of needle holes already? I feel like a pincushion, Sam. He said the MRI came out negative and so did my neurological exam. I don't have toxemia. My blood pressure's down. He had me at Nyack Hospital for two days then on bed rest for four! I'm not going back to that hospital. I'm not sick. I don't need to be in bed."

That settles it, Jerome thought. Felix taking care of her meant it wasn't Sam's child.

"He said you're a pregnant woman with preeclampsia," Sam replied.

"No. I'm not. I've been reading about it ever since he said the word. He doesn't understand."

"He said seizures could cut off oxygen to the baby."

"Could, Sam. Could. He monitored me and said they didn't. They didn't find anything wrong with me. Besides, I know what the colors are. Felix won't believe me, just like you don't."

Sam sounded exasperated. "I don't remember the Bible saying Mary saw colors, Maggie, if that's what you're trying to say."

"They're like visions, but they're colors. Mary had visions, Sam."

Sam took her hand and held it though she tried to withdraw from him. "Maggie, I read about it, too. I looked it up. It's called visual seizures. They happen right before the ones where you can't remember what happened for a minute or two. It's a medical condition. Felix should know. If you don't tell him, I will when he comes back."

"You do and I'll see you're thrown out of the house. You know I can do that, Sam Duffy. I won't let you near me if you tell."

Again they were silent, Jerome taking pictures of Sam standing and looking at the river.

It took a while, but the maid finally said, "I wouldn't really do it, Sam. Come sit down again."

He did, saying, "Maggie I'm going to tell you what happened. I don't care if you don't want to hear." His hands sliced the air in obvious frustration. "I'm a man and not really a religious one. I could never go without sex all my life like you."

"Steady," Jerome whispered to himself, then frantically picked up the notebook and started writing—new possibilities exploding in his mind. She was a virgin? *Brilliant!* What were the chances of that? *Fantastic!* He had his headline, now: *The Black Virgin Mother*. This could work.

The maid said, "Nobody asked you to go without sex, Sam."

"I know, but haven't you wondered how I could stay out here all week?"

She looked at him, curiosity on her face. "You didn't quit, did you?"

"That's right. I quit."

"Sam, you didn't! Why?"

"For my own reasons. Anyway, Brown sent this woman … I told you about her once—"

"Your female mirror?" she snapped.

" … a naked woman to persuade me to change my mind—"

"I don't need the details, Sam. But if you're trying to tell me a naked woman hogtied your big behind and forced herself on you, I don't believe it. Not that it's any of my business and not that I care at all!"

Sam lay on the blanket and looked up at the sky. "No, she didn't, but one day, Maggie, after this baby's born, I hope you'll let me touch you again like before. I hope you'll let yourself feel what I know you did. Next time, there'll be no reason to stop. Then you'll understand."

Jerome stopped writing. Sam the Irish doorman wanted Maggie the black maid? He put down his notes and listened to them talk of other things.

How she called and reassured her friend, Sharmina. How Frances Rossi had decided not to take a Mediterranean cruise just yet, and Rossi, overjoyed, had called the Jewish Museum and commissioned a copy of a painting by Lesser Ury for her birthday. It was of a woman writing at a desk. Rossi had also commissioned its companion painting for himself—a man and some rocks. His sister's would arrive any time, now. The maid asked what Sam was going to do for money, now that he was out of a job. She said she had plenty in the bank so he didn't have to worry for the moment. Jerome made a note of it. Rossi must have paid her. A nice detail for the story.

Sam replied that the day he took money from a woman would be the day he'd lost his mind.

They kept talking as they sat in the forest, enjoying the day. After a while when the maid seemed less angry, their legs and arms would casually brush against the other's. They took no notice of it, as if they were related to each other. It was touching.

Listening to their small talk, Jerome grew drowsy. He didn't have to pay attention anymore. He had pictures. He already knew what his headline would read. Tomorrow he'd tell Rossi he knew the truth, would show the photos. Rossi would cooperate. He'd have no choice. Jerome would get to interview the real mother of the clone. He'd get to film the birth.

This story had already fostered worldwide interest and Jerome was going to cash in on it. In just one week, prayer vigils had become rampant. At night they went into parks, meadows, and fields, carrying candles and praying for Christ to come. It was starting to unnerve officialdom. Some countries sent riot police to disperse their praying citizens. A spokesman for the Christian right declared it all a hoax, since the Bible made no mention of Christ being cloned. Catholicism and Judaism remained silent. Jerome knew they wouldn't for long. What would leaders do if Jesus Christ really returned? Who would come to them for guidance anymore? Who would pay the least attention to a prime minister or a judge or the police, even the Queen, when the Son of God was on earth? Who would go to the churches if Jesus Christ was here? The faithful would go where he was, even to a rat hole or a sewer. They'd ask Jesus, not ministers or priests, how to live, how to pray, how to honor and worship the God they all believed in.

Which of their religions would he endorse? That's what was starting to scare them. Would a new Jesus tell the faithful to fill church coffers? Jerome laughed to himself. He had no sympathy for them. They deserved it for believing in a myth called God.

He was enjoying his thoughts so much, he almost missed it when the maid, said, "Sam, it's happening." Jerome turned the dish volume higher and picked up his binoculars.

Frantically, Sam rose. "Let me get you to the house." He tried to pull her to her feet.

"No," she said and pushed against his arms until he let her lie down on her side.

He kneeled beside her, saying, "Maggie, Maggie, don't." Then as if to himself, "One day I'm going to wring Rossi's neck, I swear." He patted both her cheeks. "Tell me what you're seeing."

"Colors, colors, beautiful. So beautiful, Sam. Colors. The brightest one is love, Sam. It's the brightest."

Sam Duffy lay on the blanket next to her and stroked her forehead while she moaned, mumbling about the colors. He said, "Maggie, stay with me. Focus. Stay here with me."

The maid looked away as Sam the doorman called her name. Then Sam slammed the blankets with his fist and rose to his knees. He looked up at the sky as if she weren't there anymore.

"God, if you're up there," he said, "Stop hurting her, or I swear, I swear—" He sighed and rubbed her stomach, whistling to himself, and then he sang, his voice breaking with emotion:

Over in Killarney
Many years ago,
Me Mither sang a song to me
In tones so sweet and low.

Just a simple little ditty,
In her good ould Irish way,
And I'd give the world if she could sing
That song to me this day.

Too-ra-loo-ra-loo-ral, Too-ra-loo-ra-li,
Too-ra-loo-ra-loo-ral, hush now, don't you cry!
Too-ra-loo-ra-loo-ral, Too-ra-loo-ra-li,
Too-ra-loo-ra-loo-ral, that's an Irish lullaby.

Jerome Newton watched as the maid lay still. Soon she groaned and looked at Sam, who pulled her into his arms.

Jerome put his notes away. He switched off the parabolic dish. He turned away from them and rested his back against the rock, aware of its hardness as if he and the stone were one, wishing it could embrace him like they embraced, wishing he were like them and less like the rock which had no one to tell it the color of love.

Chapter 43

Monday—Turin International Airport

Father Bartolo had never been on an airplane in his life. He taken the TGV bullet train from Turin and stood in the long boarding line for Air France Flight 1103 at Charles de Gaulle airport, amazed that people seemed so unconcerned about flying. Toddlers ran back and forth from their mothers' legs, teenagers listened to their portable CDs, men read their papers, as if everything were fine.

It had been hard enough to get permission for this trip. He had prayed before meeting with the bishop, and asked God what to say. If the bishop refused him, Bartolo would have had no recourse. Like all Catholic priests, he had taken a vow of obedience at his ordination. Appealing to the cardinal after a refusal by the bishop could only bring a Vatican inquisition. It would explore the cause of, and remedy for, Father Bartolo's unheard-of disobedience.

He'd said to the bishop, "I would like to travel to America to counsel a very devout Catholic I cannot name on a matter I cannot reveal."

The bishop had inquired into the weight of the matter and Bartolo gave assurance of its gravity. Then the bishop gave his consent, assuming—as

Bartolo knew he would—that a secret of the confessional was involved. Bartolo believed it would be when he arrived. Still, there'd been no guarantee that a simple priest would be allowed an unnamed mission, given the many other priests in every country of the world.

Twice he'd phoned Dr. Felix Rossi and received no answer. On the third try this morning, he left a message on the answering machine.

As Bartolo inched toward the flight attendants who were checking boarding passes, he prayed for bravery.

He smiled nervously at the one who tore off his stub, at the one inside who pointed him toward the far aisle of the enormous plane. The line moved slowly as passengers stowed their luggage in overhead bins and themselves in seats. Finally, Father Bartolo reached his row near the back of the plane, stored his carry-on bag, and took the window seat he'd requested. Out of curiosity, he'd scanned the secretary's airline schedule books when she was arranging his flight and had learned a troubling fact. Eight flights would be taking off at midday from Paris, Munich, and Zurich, intending to land in New York near 3:00 p.m. He couldn't guess how many more would simultaneously be taking off going elsewhere, or flying toward Europe from North and South American cities.

The afternoon sky across the Atlantic would be full of airplanes, trying not to collide. If he lived through takeoff, Bartolo planned to watch for them.

———

Monday a.m.—Washington, D. C.

A teenager who lived in the monied area west of Rock Creek Park and who fervently believed in Jesus Christ gave up, for the time being, trying to hack into the White House.

He crept down the hall and listened to his father, Congressman Dunlop, speaking to his guests, Congressmen Evermeyer and James, in the study. His father had just flown down from another mysterious meeting in New York.

"Has anybody ever thought of just calling his house? He lives in London, right?" the teenager heard Congressman James say.

Soon the boy heard his father's voice. "Yes, this is Congressman Dunlop for the director." There was a pause, then his father said, "Hi, remember that fella my committee's interested in? Can somebody just call his number in London? If he's not there, can you check with customs? See if he's here in the U.S. and where he entered? Get one of your boys on his trail, if he's here? I'll get the committee going in the meantime."

"You think we've got the votes?" Evermeyer said when Dunlop hung up.

"I know we do," Dunlop replied. "Officially, Congress opposes reproductive cloning because our constituents do, though a lot of us don't really give a damn. Our man wants the foot-dragging to end. He wants cloning the dead to be a felony."

"One day you're going to tell me just who our man really is," James added.

"His identity is on a need-to-know basis," Dunlop said. "If you ever need to know, you will."

"Suppose the Brits won't extradite this reporter?" Evermeyer said. "Suppose he's here and he tries to leave?"

"London doesn't want this any more than we do. If we ever get our hands on Jerome Newton, don't worry, he's not leaving." Dunlop sounded sure.

"Suppose it's real?" Evermeyer asked. "Suppose there's really a clone somewhere from Jesus Christ's DNA?"

The boy heard his father laugh. "Now you're sounding like that harebrained son of mine."

Evermeyer said, "I take that as a compliment since your boy, Zack, is smarter than me and you, too, Dunlop."

Zack's father continued, "I'd prefer if he'd been given common sense. He'd probably believe in a Second Coming since he already believes in UFOs and every conspiracy theory going. He's just a kid. You're a grown man, Evermeyer. What's your excuse? This is just some publicity stunt and a dangerous one. Maybe there's a clone, but of Jesus goddamned Christ?" His father laughed again.

Zack made a rude gesture with his upper arm, crept back to his room, opened a soda, and drank it, swinging the chain and cross he wore and surfing his favorite websites while he thought about what to do. First, www.izvestia.ru to see what the commies were up to. Putin making speeches, a Greenpeace protest that would be ignored, more former nuclear workers unemployed. Over to *China Daily*, the Chinese government's official English-language newspaper which he hacked into for its 100 percent good news: world leaders visiting, tourists touring. Nothing bad happening in China. Next, to *The Times* of London—more than two hundred years of studiously sarcastic, witty, bombastic or simply impolite reportage on Her Majesty's kingdoms.

He clicked on the features section and searched for the cloning stories.

Zack put down his soda and reread them. He opened his web-authoring program and stared at the blank page, tapping his fingers until inspiration came. He typed: "Our Lord In-Vitro Emerging," then emphasized the initial letters and swirled them into a logo that spelled out, OLIVE. He found a photo of an olive for the O and a way to underscore it with an olive branch.

He typed:

OLIVE is an organization of human beings from all nations who support the return of Jesus Christ. We believe in the Second Coming. We believe Jesus Christ can and would use modern technology to return. Therefore we believe in the clone. We oppose all laws and prohibitions against it. We urge you to lend your support by clicking here and signing the petition. Check below for a schedule of prayer vigils.

He translated the message into ten languages with only a little help from translation software. He designed a web page layout and a form for the petition then started it with two hundred made-up names, some foreign. He added a counter that showed there'd been almost a thousand visitors to date. He put it out on the web and submitted its keywords to major search engines. Then he visited the top five sites on the web and hacked on a link to OLIVE, planning to keep them active for only twenty-four hours. That's all it would take.

Later he planned to add Bible links and a few good pictures of Christ.

————

Monday a.m.—Meat Packing District, New York

In a warehouse that had once smelled of slaughtered beef, a woman closed the door to her chic loft apartment and left Jerome Newton sleeping in her bed. Braless under her thin black blouse; long, black-stockinged legs striding beneath a short black leather skirt, she rushed down to the cobbled streets of the Meat Packing District, the new *It* place in New York. She passed a store that sold candy and magazines beside a dive where prostitutes took their johns at night. At Ninth Avenue and Fourteenth she finally got a cab. Throwing the dangling end of a jungle brown watered Chinese silk scarf over her shoulder, she rode past the Heller Gallery on her way to work.

Jerome awoke in the loft's silence and scrambled, naked, from the bed, amazed at himself for delaying like this. He'd looked up the ravishingly cute American woman he'd once dated. More amazing was that she'd welcomed him back.

He opened his laptop computer which rested on her stylish butcher-block table, irises in an art nouveau vase on top.

Eagerly he connected his Nikon CoolPix to the computer and set his photographic software to view the pictures one at a time.

There they were.

Sam, the doorman, and Maggie, the maid. She as pregnant as a new day's dawn, he as smitten as a river with the banks in which it flowed. Yet the child inside her wasn't his. She was Mary. He was Joseph. They'd never done it. What a story.

He looked closer and saw the photo had an imperfection, the barest flaw, a smudge of some kind. It was in the next photo as well. Upset, Jerome scanned more photos and saw a similar smudge. A defect in the download. Had he erased the file on the camera? No, he hadn't. He downloaded it again and, while the software retrieved the pictures, grabbed his grundies and put them on so his backside wouldn't keep sticking to the fashionably retro chair.

He returned to the laptop and there it was again. Irritated, he zoomed in on it—a faint, flame-shaped streak of color against the tree or the bright blue sky. He lightened the photo, darkened it, and changed the contrast. Still the imperfection was there. He scanned even more of the photos. Each had the same flaw, a barely visible aura of color on the film—usually just above the maid's head, though in one it was around the doorman's hands where he touched her.

A defect in the camera. No problem. The photo-editing software would remove it.

From the pull-down menus he selected the computer version of a contact sheet, miniatures arranged in rows. Only then did he realize that, from photo to photo, the dim flaw was not the same.

Jerome stared at them, each a slightly dissimilarly hued version of the last. What in the world could it be? Sunlight glinting off the Hudson? Off someone's gold tooth? Sunspot activity interfering with his camera? Funny lightning? What was this color phenomenon, undetectable in a single photograph?

Feeling like he was wading through suddenly heavy space, Jerome rose and searched for the taped conversation. It took him a while to find what the maid had said.

"Colors, colors, beautiful. So beautiful, Sam. Colors. The brightest one is love, Sam. It's the brightest."

Jerome returned to the computer, selected the flame-like shape then instructed the software to erase all else. Photo-by-photo, a spectrum of unimaginable colors unfolded like a rainbow on the screen.

Chapter 44

Monday evening—Cliffs Landing

Sam stood in the foyer saying goodbye to Maggie. Yesterday they'd gone to Nyack, as usual. Felix had revealed he was nervous about the trips now, because of the seizures, though they were mild. Usually he tried to keep Maggie in her bed, but on Sundays they had no choice. Yet yesterday Jerome hadn't come. They'd all hidden their anxiety from her.

Sam knew Maggie was upset with him so he took it as a good sign that she'd voluntarily walked him to the door.

In these months, everything about her had changed. He could see it mostly in her eyes, which shone more brightly than before, revealing her self-consciousness had gone. She no longer moved along the sides of the Rossis' rooms, keeping out of the way. Maggie entered rooms like they did. At first she'd put away the beautiful shawl Adeline gave her. Now on cool nights she wore it. She was bidding him goodbye as if this were her home. They couldn't tell her what to do anymore. She cooperated only when she chose.

"How long will you be gone?" Maggie asked. She might as well have said, *Are you planning another romp with Coral?*

"Just the time it takes to get there and back. Brown gave me two weeks to reconsider. I figure it's been time enough."

"Then he's really hoping you'll change your mind."

He touched Maggie's nose. "Yeah, I know. No dice."

Sam wanted to pat her stomach like always, but since he saw Maggie eating olives and describing the color of love, he'd become the self-conscious one.

All life was sacred, Sam told himself, which made the life she carried precious, but not more so than the next. He often found himself thinking about this baby. What would it become and how, with Felix as a father and Maggie, his mother, believing what she did? He saw a warped life ahead, unless the child was who they thought, which was impossible.

Still, Sam didn't touch her stomach quite as freely as before.

She moved the shawl aside. "You can rub the baby."

He shook his head. She was always picking up his thoughts. "Nah, that's all right."

Maggie took one of his hands and put it on her stomach, and Sam felt so strange he almost snatched it away, but she held it there, smiling. He waited a decent interval, withdrew his hand, and headed out the door.

Maggie called, "He loves you," making Sam felt weird. If she'd said, *I love you*, he could have dealt with that. *He* loves you was a little too squirrely.

He said, "Yeah. See you later," got in his car, and pulled onto Lawford Lane. For a week, she'd been talking like that.

Even in winter, the drive down the Palisades across the GW Bridge and down the Hudson Parkway was something else. In summer and early fall it was glorious. Sam frequently drove this route just to clear his mind. Usually he'd stop at the Soldiers' and Sailors' Monument. This time he was coming in from the north. He'd have to turn off before getting there, but Sam was tempted to keep driving.

When he arrived at the building, he was glad he hadn't detoured. No sooner had he parked in an empty space out front, than his temporary replacement called, "Hey, Sam. Lucky you came by. Do you know where the Rossis are? There's somebody waiting to see them, and he says he won't leave until—"

"What?" Sam said going up to him, "Didn't I teach you guys anything? You know better than to let just anybody in to wait—"

"Sam, it's a priest!"

"What?"

Sam opened the door, saw an old man dressed in black and hurried down the stairs, saying, "Father?"

The priest turned, smiling, held out his hand, and in a thick Italian accent said, "I am Father Bartolo."

As he shook the priest's hand, Sam started walking him toward the door. He'd been a good Irish Catholic boy and felt he could recognize a real priest. To him, men who had deliberately renounced their own balls had an unmistakable otherworldly air.

"Yes, yes, if you'll come with me, Father, I can help you. Just come with me."

Father Bartolo looked surprised and gestured toward a black suitcase in the corner. Sam rushed back and grabbed it, then continued walking Bartolo toward the door. Once outside, they turned right toward his apartment, Sam saying, "I live here. I'm sure I can help you, just come in, Father, and we'll talk."

Sam opened his door and the priest followed him inside. He put the suitcase down. "Wait here for just a second, Father, just a second. I'll be right back."

The priest nodded, looking confused. Sam closed the door and walked back to his stand-in, making up a story as he went.

He said, "Don't you remember me telling you Frances Rossi wanted us to look out for this guy and call up to The Church of St. Thomas More when he came? You know how they're into the church and all?"

"Oh, yeah."

"Listen," Sam put his hand on the man's shoulder and leaned close. "I know you probably don't want them to know you kept the priest cooling his heels in the lobby."

"Damn right. I sure won't tell if you won't. Where is Dr. Rossi, anyway? On vacation?"

"No. No," Sam had no choice but to keep lying. "He's still on that research thing overseas, but he visited the other day, didn't you see him?"

"No."

"Yeah, he did. So who else came through while the priest was here?"

"Let's see. Brown's butler came down."

Sam's heart almost stopped.

"No. That was before the priest came. Let me see. The Robinsons on the fourth floor. Mr. Geer and his daughter on the second. Other than that, just Mrs. Amsterdam, coming back from lunch at the River Cafe."

Sam sighed in relief. He didn't like that all the tenants were back in residence except Felix, but Brown still had no reason to focus on him. He patted the man a final time and gave him his car keys saying, "You're home free. Watch my ride for a sec. Just don't mention it to anybody else."

When Sam reentered his apartment, he smiled. The priest rose and smiled back. He had an Italian name to go with his thick accent. Sam would bet anything he'd flown here from Turin because he'd figured it all out. Rossi had stolen something sacred that belonged to them and, without consulting priest or pope, planned to bring back the head of their church.

Sam put a finger to his mouth, indicating they shouldn't speak. Brown might have installed bugs if only to find out why Sam quit. As the priest watched, Sam retrieved equipment from the locked and hidden room behind the kitchen pantry and did a sweep. No bugs.

When he finished, he sat down across from the priest, who said, "Che cosa vi chiamate?"

"Beg pardon?"

"Scusatemi. Who are you?"

"Oh, sorry. I'm Sam Duffy. I work here, more or less."

The priest clapped his hands. "Buono! I look for Dr. Felix Rossi. I am Bartolo. You know when he returns?"

"Did you come from Italy?" Sam ventured.

The priest's eyebrows rose. "Si. Italy. I know Dr. Rossi. You must only tell him I am here."

"Did you come from Turin, by any chance?"

Bartolo's gaze locked on Sam's. "Why do you ask if I come from Turin?"

"Let's just say I guessed."

"Signor Duffy, can you help me contact Dr. Felix Rossi? That is all I want."

Sam decided to stop dancing. "Maybe I can. If you'll tell me why you need to see him—"

Bartolo stood. "Our business is private, Signor Duffy. As Bartolo picked up his suitcase, Sam positioned himself between the priest and the door.

"Permesso, Signor Duffy?"

Sam couldn't let a priest in a Roman collar wander around loudly asking for Rossi. Nor could Sam confide in a stranger. Then he had an inspiration.

"Father Bartolo. Would you hear my confession?"

"Perdonatemi signore? Non capisco." Bartolo looked bewildered. "You are Catholic?"

"More or less. I haven't been to church in a lot of years, but yes, I guess I'm still Catholic."

"But you live in New York, a big city with many, many churches. I am not your pastor, my son. Why confess to me?"

"Would you believe God just told me to?"

The priest put down his suitcase. "Signor Duffy, I cannot misuse the sacrament of confession. You must intend by your confession to return to the Father from whom you have strayed by sin. You must want to make a good confession, my son, or I cannot hear it."

"A good confession?"

They sat down, watching each other.

"There are five things for a good confession. First, recall all sins since your last confession. Next feel true sorrow for these sins."

"That I do."

Bartolo continued, "You must decide to avoid sin in the future. Also the people and places that lead you to sin."

That was simple enough, Sam thought. All he had to do was stay away from the docks and stick to Maggie, who would be glad to keep him straight. It was unlikely he'd ever see Coral—a good thing, because she had a 100 percent chance of leading him to sin.

"Next confess all sins to a priest. Last do penance. For this, I will give you prayers."

"If you'll hear my confession, I'm ready to give it," Sam said.

Bartolo opened his suitcase and retrieved a missal, a rosary, and his priest's stole. It was a long piece of silk perhaps three inches wide with a cross embroidered in the center and at each end. He kissed the center cross and drew the stole around his neck, its ends hanging down his chest. In this vestment he could intercede between Catholic mankind and God, perform sacraments, forgive sins, and purify Sam's soul. Bartolo picked up the missal, handed the rosary to Sam, then sat in a straight-back chair.

"Kneel or sit as you prefer, my son."

Sam's mouth went dry at the thought of what he'd have to tell Bartolo. For this, he shouldn't be sitting. Crawling, maybe. He knelt before the priest.

"Bless me, Father, for I have sinned."

"How long since your last confession?"

"Maybe nineteen years?"

"That is a long time. We had better start."

They were silent then Sam said, "Father, I'm not sure I remember all the sins."

"Allow me to guide your memory."

Bartolo closed his eyes and rattled off sins of thought, word, and deed. When he finished, he'd named thirty-nine confessable sins, and Sam was guilty of all but thirteen. Three didn't apply only because he'd never been married. Six had to do with sex and he'd done all but one of them multiple times.

"It would be easier to tell you what I'm not guilty of," he joked.

Bartolo crossed himself. "You may begin."

"How about lying?" Sam asked. "Can I start with lying?"

Bartolo opened one eye and peered at Sam, then closed it. "You may start with lying."

"I've lied about Felix Rossi to everyone for almost seven months."

Bartolo opened his eyes and folded his hands in his lap. Sam told him the whole story, studying Bartolo's impassive face.

He concluded, "They're hiding on Cliffs Landing in a house Rossi put in the maid's name. This is my confession, Father Bartolo."

Bartolo rose from the chair and walked across the room in silence. Sam stayed on his knees and this time genuinely asked to be forgiven. He'd used the priest's vows against him.

"Do you make a true confession, Sam Duffy? Are you sorry for these lies?"

"Not yet, but Father I promise I will be when they're safe."

"Can they ever be?" Bartolo said.

Sam didn't reply.

"What other sins have you committed, my son?"

"I've told lots of lies, but never to hurt or cheat anyone. I've been in more brawls than I can count. I've had carnal knowledge of some of the best ladies in the world, in my opinion. One in particular I'll never forget. I've had impure thoughts since the day I was born, and I've frequently abused myself."

"Are you sorry for these sins?"

"I'm sorry I wasn't able to resist. I'll try now, Father. I will."

Bartolo sounded troubled. "Say the Act of Confitier."

"Will you help me, Father? I don't remember it all."

Together, they said:

O my God, I am heartily sorry for having offended Thee, and I detest all my sins, because I dread the loss of heaven and the pains of hell, but most of all because they offend Thee, my God, Who art all good and deserving of all my love. I firmly resolve, with the help of Thy grace, to confess my sins, to do penance, and to amend my life. Amen.

"Say the rosary for your penance, my son. You confirmed my fears. I have come on the matter you confessed. Do not worry. I cannot break the seal of the confessional or make use of what you have told me, even to save my own life. It is as if I had not heard you."

"Yes, Father, I know. Forgive me. I did it because their lives could be at stake.

You see how the world is reacting. I'll take you to see Felix Rossi, now."

The priest reached out and made the sign of the cross on Sam's brow. "Egote absolve, Sam Duffy. I absolve you in the name of the Father, and of the Son, and of the Holy Spirit. Amen."

Chapter 45

Tuesday a.m.—JFK Airport, New York

Jerome Newton pulled the strap of his camera bag up higher on his shoulder and handed his passport, ticket, and driver's license to the agent at a British Airways check-in counter in Terminal Seven. His lady friend with the loft had gone ahead of him to London, while he covered a quick gallery opening here—the fashionable guests a greater attraction than the art. Today he'd drive his American lady out to Newton Hall to see what kith and kin thought of her. If they approved, he knew just what ancient family bauble would become her engagement ring.

It felt good to be reformed.

He knew it had happened as he crouched behind that rock.

As the agent typed away, searching for his reservation, Jerome cast a fond look up to the national flags hanging from the ceiling. Only now did it strike him he liked seeing them there, much the way he'd liked the United Nations when he toured it. Jerome felt a distant affection for the truly absurd notion that people could be on genuinely equal footing in the world. Any English aristocrat knew it was nonsense; still he vaguely liked the idea.

He also liked the photographs he'd taken of Sam, the doorman, and Maggie, the maid, and had looked at them for hours, wanting to share them with his woman friend but knowing he should not. One day soon, they would have fetched a fortune, made him a multizillionaire, and—he finally concluded—earned him a seat next to Satan in hell. He was no Faust, offering his soul to Mephistopheles on a dare, no fool making bargains with the devil for Daniel Webster to debate. On the outside chance J.C. himself might really be involved, Jerome had destroyed each photograph and then erased the camera file. He would never publish them, or be the cause of others doing so. He'd destroyed them. Now he was going home to meet his lady. He was leaving the story of the century behind in Cliffs Landing and going home to England, where he belonged.

"Mr. Newton?"

Jerome looked up saw a tall man holding his wallet open. On it was a gold badge that read: Deputy U.S. Marshal. Jerome glanced back at the agent's red face and knew she was responsible for the marshal's presence. What did they think he'd done?

"May I help you?"

"Yeah," the man said. "You can take this." He put an envelope in Jerome's hand.

"What is it?"

"It's a subpoena, Mr. Newton, to appear as a witness before the Special Investigative Subcommittee on Human Cloning of the House Science Committee."

"House?" Jerome said, not yet grasping what the subpoena meant.

"Congress, sir. You've been called to testify before Congress."

"Congress?" Hiding his alarm, Jerome handed the envelope back to the man. Already, they'd drawn the attention of those in nearby lines.

"Thank you ever so much for the invitation, Mr. Deputy Marshal, but I'm actually not an American citizen, in fact. Your Congress can't compel me to testify, and I was just leaving, so if you'll excuse me—"

He turned to retrieve his papers from the agent, but the marshal was quicker. He took Jerome's ticket, boarding card, and British passport from her hand.

"These are his?" the marshal asked.

As she nodded, a second marshal arrived.

"I'm afraid you can't leave, Mr. Newton," the first marshal said. "You see, we have the power to detain a foreign citizen for any of a whole bunch of reasons—"

Swiftly, the second marshal slid the camera bag from Jerome's shoulder. As Jerome whirled to grab it, the man clapped handcuffs on him.

The first marshal continued, "So we need to take you into protective custody, for now."

Jerome rattled the handcuffs and shouted, "I don't require protection! I have no testimony! I insist you contact the British consulate!"

The other marshal retrieved Jerome's suitcase. One on either side, they led him from the counters as the airport crowd stared.

The first marshal said, "We did contact the British consulate before we came here, sir, just so they'd know you're all right."

———

Tuesday evening—Cliffs Landing

Maggie was in the library when the doorbell rang. It was an open room just up the carpeted steps at the far end of the living room beside the baby grand. It had floor-to-ceiling bookshelves on all but one wall and comfortable seating in the center.

Felix was trying to keep her on complete bed rest, but when she tired of her own room, he let her sit here with her feet up. She read her Bible and books about birth and newborns.

Today it was the Bible and Galatians, in particular, about how the fruit of the Spirit is love, joy, peace, patience, kindness, goodness, faithfulness. Lately, she was having trouble with the patience part again.

She put the Bible down and peeped out the window, trying to see who was at the door.

Again the doorbell rang and she heard, "Hello? It's Cal."

She heard the door open and Frances say, "Hi, Cal. Come on in. Maggie's in the library. Felix is tied up with a priest Sam brought here."

Then Cal was at the low steps, looking up at her. "Hello, Maggie. There's a priest here about your baby?"

"Hi, Cal. Why he's here and where he came from, don't ask me. I'm not allowed to know things."

Cal said to Frances. "Go get them. I'll turn on TV. They have to see this."

When Frances returned, Felix, Sam, and Father Bartolo were behind her.

"Cal, what is it?" Felix said.

Cal had turned the living room television to CNN and Maggie had come down to watch. They all watched, transfixed. CNN had interrupted regular programming in favor of continuous coverage of unfolding events.

This time there was no panel of experts, only an anchor. The news was speaking for itself. Not dozens, but thousands of people crowded Central Park's Great Lawn. Thousands had gathered on Washington, D.C.'s mall. Maggie watched as CNN switched to other vigils around the world: Gethsemane Church in the former East Berlin, Place de la Concorde in Paris, Amsterdam's Dam Square, Tokyo's Ueno Park beneath the cherry trees, Vatican square in Rome, even some in Peking's Tianamen Square. Hordes of people. All over the world.

People lighting candles, people getting on their knees to pray. Every group had signs and banners reading: OLIVE, Our Lord in Vitro Emerging. The reporter didn't know where it had come from.

Maggie did. OLIVE came from God.

God was sending her a message in their numbers and their name. She craved olives. She feared crowds—ever since leaving Macon, Georgia. There'd been a crowd outside the bank when it auctioned off her father's farm; a crowd at their house throwing stones through the windows, shouting what they'd do to his ugly nigger daughter if her father kept talking about fraud; and, when he didn't stop, a crowd on their lawn for two nights straight, shouting the Johnsons didn't belong in Macon, Georgia, anymore.

She'd confided all her fears to Cal. He said, "Remember, Maggie, don't be afraid."

She barely heard him. "Sam, take me into town. I need to go to Central Park."

"Absolutely not!" Felix said. "You need to stay off your feet!"

Maggie went to him and put her hand on his chest. "Felix, I need to be there."

He stepped back. "No! It's far too dangerous. I can't let you go into a crowd like that when you're this far into your pregnancy. And what if you have a seizure?"

Maggie agreed with him, but not for the reasons he gave. She hadn't planned to recross the Shatemuc before her baby was born. On this side of the river she felt safe. Somehow, there was danger on the other side, but she had to go where God had called her.

"Then come with me, Felix. I've done every single thing you asked. Do this one thing for me. I need to go."

"Come now, Maggie. Listen to Felix," Frances said. "You shouldn't go. I'd worry about you every second."

"Then you come, too. We could take the Range Rover. What could happen if we all go? I'll be all right if everyone's there. Sam, tell them."

When Sam came to her, she took his hand and put it on her belly, whispering. "He wants me to go. I can feel it."

Sam cleared his throat. "I don't know, Maggie."

"Be my friend, Sam. I need to go."

He looked around. "Well, the medical part's up to Felix, but I guess together we could watch out for her. In a crowd at night, who would notice us?"

"Well, if it's all right with Felix that she go, may I tag along, too?" Cal asked. "I'll drive my car."

Maggie smiled at him. Cal believed, like she did, that she wasn't really sick.

Bartolo, who stood nearest to the entry, broadly grinned. "May a priest also go?"

They all laughed, except Felix. "Maggie, I forbid this!"

She ignored him and went to Father Bartolo, holding out her hand. "Father, I'm Maggie Johnson. It's probably me you came about. Glad to meet you. I'd love for you to come."

"Piacere! Lieto di conoscerla," Bartolo said. "It is my great pleasure to meet you, Signora Johnson." He blessed her when she stopped shaking hands.

She looked back at Sam. "I'm coming," he said. Frances said, "Well, then, so am I." Cal turned off the TV and followed.

Felix didn't budge until Sam said, "Felix, just this once, let her do it. She's been okay."

"Hang on," Felix said, glowering at them, "Let me get my medical bag."

Maggie reached into the hall closet and got Adeline's shahtoosh. Why she was going, Maggie couldn't explain. The shock of the name, OLIVE, and the sight of the frightening crowds had produced an impulse she couldn't resist— an urgency from her center, where the baby was.

Father Bartolo asked to sit beside her in the Rover. Frances rode with Cal. As they drove toward town, Maggie and the priest in back, she could feel Bartolo watching her in the dark. He'd talked to Felix, but had hardly said a word to her. She was trying to have patience like the Bible said: Sam avoiding her questions about Brown; he and Felix keeping things from her; a priest here about her baby but ignoring her.

"Maggie," Father Bartolo said. "May I baptize the child when it's time?"

Was that what he and Felix had discussed? She glared at the back of Felix's head. "I'll have to think about that, Father. I was raised Baptist. I'd have a heck of a time raising a child in a religion I don't know."

In the driver's seat, Felix cleared his throat and said nothing.

Father Bartolo seemed sad. "Yes, of course. You must think about it. Would you … would you send me a picture of him?"

That's when Maggie understood Bartolo. How he'd learned about them, she didn't know, but he'd come because he wanted to see Jesus. He wanted to know Jesus was real.

"I promise. And Father, you can visit him if you like."

His eyes hardly left her. "Thank you. I will come like the shepherds."

"Would you like to touch my baby?" she whispered.

"I am waiting for God to speak to me about your baby," he whispered back.

"How does he speak to you?"

Bartolo leaned closer. "In my heart. He puts a feeling in my heart."

"Me, too," she said.

"Shall we pray?" he said.

She nodded.

O God, our Creator, all life is in your hands from conception until death. Help us to cherish our children and to reverence the awesome privilege of our share in creation. May all people live and die in dignity and love. Bless all those who defend the rights of the unborn, the handicapped and the aged. Enlighten and be merciful toward those who fail to love, and give them peace. Let freedom be tempered by responsibility, integrity, and morality.

Maggie said, "Amen," thinking Catholic prayers were more like literature.

She didn't look out at the river when they crossed it. Instead, she and Bartolo sat whispering about the things God had told them, until Maggie saw they'd reached Central Park West. Her fear returned.

People everywhere—running to the park, leaving it. Couples holding hands with infants in their backpacks, men with toddlers on their shoulders, old women strolling in groups, youngsters in choir uniforms, others with shaved heads and pierced lips. White and Black and Hispanic and Asian people. Traffic stalled because of the people everywhere.

Maggie powered down the window and raised her eight-way adjustable seat so she could see the crowds. In the September night air, she shivered, though not a fist was raised in her direction, though no one called her names and the song, *Awesome God*, drifted to her from the park.

"Maggie, are you sure you want to get out in this?" Sam said.

Felix said, "Let's leave."

"No, please, please. I saw another pregnant woman. She seemed all right."

"I'm your doctor. I can't let you out in this!"

Maggie grasped the door handle, desperately hoping Felix hadn't engaged the rear safety door lock. He hadn't. The door opened and she stepped into stopped traffic as Felix and Sam yelled for her to come back. Pulling her shawl around her, she hurried between the cars to the sidewalk by the park, Sam following behind, calling, "Maggie!"

They'd stopped at Eighty-First street, just up from the Museum of National History. She could see the statue of Theodore Roosevelt on horseback. An Indian walked on one side of his horse, a Black man on the other. It was the first statue she'd noticed when she came here from Macon, Georgia. To her it represented the racial dominance that took away their farm: whites above, minorities below. Maggie had hated the statue with all her heart. Glimpsing it now she felt panicked, then Sam was there.

"Maggie Johnson, don't *do* that again!" he said as he reached her side.

She put on a brave face. "Stop fussing, I'm all right."

Sam walked her closer to the wall that surrounded Central Park. "We'll wait here for them," he said and put his arm around her.

"Don't do that again, Maggie," he repeated. "Promise."

"I promise, Sam."

They stood there, people passing, Maggie knowing she was safe with Sam, but staring at the statue, noticing each white face in the crowd. How would they react if they knew? What would they do if they knew she was the one?

Chapter 46

Tuesday evening—Central Park

"There they are," Sam said.

She watched him climb up on the bench where they were sitting and wave. Moments later, everyone was there.

Felix hurried to her. "Maggie, don't you ever—"

"Yeah, I told her, I told her," Sam said. "Let's go so we can see it, then get out." He helped Maggie up from the bench.

Felix took her arm. "Stay between us, Maggie. All right? Sam, hold onto her other arm, will you? The whole time?" He looked down at her. "We'll walk behind the others."

Ordinarily, Maggie would have laughed at Felix, but she hooked her arms through theirs without complaint. Even then she didn't feel protected when they joined the stream of people entering what Felix said was Hunter's Gate. In all these years, she'd never attended a performance or concert in the park, though they were usually free. She'd wanted to, but year after year she had missed everything that happened, here or anywhere, if it drew a big crowd. She'd missed James Brown and Sun Ra when they came to SummerStage. She'd missed every performance of Shakespeare in the Park at the Delacorte Theater, just south of where they were going. Maggie wasn't really into Shakespeare, but she would have tried it once if she hadn't been afraid.

"So now I will see your great Central Park," Bartolo said. He walked next to Cal in front of them.

"Yes, Father," Felix replied.

As Felix began to describe things for Bartolo, Maggie drifted into her own world. She didn't know what footpath they'd taken into the park. It diverged from the brighter-lit main road and sloped down. Before them, lanterns on the park's winding footpaths dotted the night like fallen stars. The pools of light they cast made Maggie more aware of the surrounding darkness, the shadowed trees, and outcroppings of ancient bedrock, the park's many bridges and arches—rustic and romantic in daylight, but sinister now.

Ahead of her and around her, people streamed into and out of the lantern light and Maggie shuddered, growing more and more afraid. They passed a playground. Up ahead, Felix was saying, loomed Winterdale Arch. They would walk under East Drive, which was really on the west side of the park, here. Maggie slowed, not wanting to go under the arch.

Then she heard the singing.

It started faintly and slowly grew like someone had piped up a human organ. They were singing *Amazing Grace*, her favorite hymn.

The people on the footpath rushed forward and they followed.

"Let's take a shortcut," Felix said.

They veered from the lit walkway onto an expanse of lawn and plunged into darkness. Maggie's terror would have been unendurable but for the music. Suddenly they were there. She let go of their arms and went to the four-foot wire fence around the Great Lawn. In the center, on the thick Kentucky bluegrass between the lawn's baseball fields, light shone from thousands of candles while the people sang *Amazing Grace*.

"Let's go in one of the gates," Sam said.

Maggie didn't move. She watched and listened, thankful as she clung to the fence. Behind it she felt safe, still she could see them, hear their sacred music. All kinds of people were gathered there. She recognized the green uniforms and silver and blue badges of PEP, the Park Enforcement Patrol. Half the officers from the park police precinct on 85th seemed to have come.

"Will the police stop it, do you think?" she asked Felix.

"No laws are being broken. This isn't a commercial activity, and it doesn't sound like they have amplifiers out there, just a CD player."

Maggie saw a policeman bend and pat his horse's neck. His lips moved, as if he were singing, too.

"Well, I guess this is the place," Frances said and spread out the blankets she'd brought. "Come, Maggie. You can lie down here and listen."

"In just a minute," Maggie said.

Felix sighed, joined his sister, and lay on his back, looking up at the night sky. Cal and Father Bartolo sat beside them on a bench. Sam stayed at the fence with her.

Beneath the music she heard children laugh, babies cry. The sound felt wonderful. It was like breathing love in with the air. Maggie let it sweep over her. Amazing the grace that saved. She touched her baby whom this love had called.

"Go over to the blanket and lie down, Maggie," Sam said.

"Let me stay here, Sam."

"It can't be good for you, hanging on the fence like that."

"I'm fine."

She heard whispering behind her. They did that a lot, these days. Maggie tried not to mind. They all wanted to help her, and they were all afraid. Sam brought her a blanket.

The song ended and the crowd applauded themselves. Then a grandmotherly woman rose above them, as if she'd stood on a box. She held her hands up for quiet. Maggie made out a little of what she said, something about the New York and Washington, D. C. branches of OLIVE monitoring something Congress would do.

Then another head popped above the crowd. It was a young man dressed in black, his shirt open. He shouted, "Listen to me! Listen!"

"Why?" a voice called. Someone else shouted, "Who are you?"

The crowd buzzed, drowning him out, and Maggie closed her eyes, disturbed by these new sounds. Felix, Sam and the others must have heard, too, because they rose and came to the fence.

"What's happening?" Felix asked.

As the crowd subsided, the young man's voice broke through, "—almost in sight of the richest synagogue in the world, Temple Emmanuel, in the very heart of our great city! How can you sing? How will you explain this to Jesus when He returns? We must cast out these Jewish demons who infect us with their money and their lies, these murderers of Christ! Good Christians, this is why He is returning, to give us courage to finish what Germany began!"

For whole heartbeats, the night was still. Maggie turned to Felix and saw his eyes become wounds, his face so shattered he looked naked as he stood there. In those heartbeats, Frances moved close to him and took his hand, and Father Bartolo and Cal began to pray. Sam looked at Felix with the kind of gentle pity Maggie had seen at funerals when someone died.

In those heartbeats, fear rose and swept love from the city's great park.

Like an enraged animal, the crowd roared. On their horses, the police began to gallop. The young man raised his fist in suicidal triumph, his black shirt blowing behind him in the breeze, as the crowd became a mob. He had desecrated their prayer vigil with words of hate. He'd taken their love away. If someone, something didn't reach him, Maggie thought they'd kill him in front of their babies and their children. They'd stomp him to death to make the love return.

Through the fence, she screamed, "No!"

She felt Sam's arms around her, his hands pulling her fingers from the fence. "Let's get out of here, Maggie!"

She held on, her eyes on the wild young man as he toppled from his box. She pleaded, "Help us, help us, help us." Then, for one heartbeat, silence fell. From her place behind the fence, Sam trying to pull her away, Maggie began to sing like she did in the 131st Street Baptist Church. She sang from deep within her heart and she sang loud.

"I want Jesuuuuuus ... to walk with me."

The people moved in slow motion, but the police seemed to race.

"Yes, I want my Jeeeeeesus, to wa-alk with me."

The notes formed and emerged from her throat as if the song had a will of its own. For a second heartbeat, the silence stayed.

"All along this … looooonesome jouuuurney."

She felt Sam let go of her hands.

"Well, I want my Jeeeeeesus to walk with me."

In a third heartbeat the grandmotherly woman got back on her box and joined Maggie's song.

"I want Jesussssss."

Another joined.

"I want Jesussssss."

Then another and another and half the crowd began to sing the old spiritual Maggie loved, and the police reached the man and it was over.

Jubilant, Maggie turned and saw the hurt still on Felix's face.

Felix went to Father Bartolo. "I haven't told you what started all this. I haven't told you the most important thing."

Bartolo reached for the crucifix hanging on his chest.

"The church has honored me in every conceivable way," Felix continued, "made my dreams come true by allowing me to examine the Shroud and I desecrated it. I did it for a reason, though it is one you may not understand. I'd imagined cloning Jesus for years, had even planned it, but that morning I found a reason to carry out the plan. Frances and I learned our parents were Jews."

Bartolo clasped his hands as if in prayer. "Be consoled, my son. This is not a new thing. It has happened before."

"That's why I stole the threads. If a Jew brings him back, those who believe Jews killed him might stop persecuting our people. Well, what do you think, now that you know I'm a Jew?"

Frances watched, Cal's arm around her.

Bartolo clasped Felix's hands, seeming even older in that moment. "You are right. I do not understand your act. This is not the way to fight prejudice. We cannot bring Jesus back. He must come when he chooses. Has he chosen you? Did he choose our Maggie? Perhaps. Perhaps not. What I see is your suffering. That is what I see. To me it is like the suffering of the cross, a sign of God's love for us. We do not understand this suffering, so we must bear it in faith. God has a plan, though we do not see it."

Maggie wanted to cry for Felix, for the young man full of hate, for the crowd that would have killed him. Bartolo was right. Somewhere in it was God's plan, but at the moment it burdened her, made her remember her heavy belly, her aching back, and that whether because of fear or yearning for God, she'd only lived half a life.

She turned to Sam and whispered, "Didn't you say you wanted to play darts at Molly Malone's, Sam Duffy?"

He frowned at her.

"A long time ago, in the elevator? Remember? You said you wanted to play darts at Molly Malone's and I said no? I've changed my mind."

He responded in his Irish brogue. "You didn't have Jesus in your belly, then, now did you?"

On the verge of tears, Maggie thought of the wild young man and wondered what would have happened if she hadn't been there. She lowered her head and wearily covered her face.

"Ah, Lassie. Do you really feel up to it then?"

She looked up. "Yes, Sam."

"Felix will never permit it."

"I know."

Sam took her arm. As they slipped into the darkness away from the others, he whispered, "I asked for a game of darts, Maggie my girl. That, I did."

Chapter 47

Tuesday evening—Molly Malone's Irish Pub

Sam opened the wooden door to Molly Malone's, knowing his cronies would be there, knowing in a moment they'd see pregnant Maggie, so different from the last woman he brought here. Did Maggie know what some of them might think? Sam did. His friends were civilized, though. They would treat her right. They would treat her like a queen. If not, he might damn well break open a bottle of McSorley's and put it to somebody's throat.

"Samuel Duffy, there you are, lad!" the bartender called as soon as they entered.

Heads turned and others called, "Hey, Sam!"

"Hi, Sam!"

"Sam, we were just planning your funeral, boy. We thought you'd died!"

"Hi, Pat," Sam said and put his arm around Maggie, waving at his cronies with the other.

Pat raised his eyebrows and gave a broad smile. "And who is this little mother you're bringing to us?" He turned toward the room and shouted, "You two blokes put those cigarettes out! We've got a pregnant mother visiting." He pointed to the nearest empty table. "Bring the girl here and sit her down, man."

"This is Maggie, Pat."

"Hi, Pat," she said and pulled her shawl closer as she sat down, looking around.

Sam remained standing as Pat came from behind the bar.

"There, that's better, isn't it?" he said to Maggie. "I don't know why you've come with this one, lass. He doesn't have a bit of sense. So if you need anything while you're here, just come tell Pat. I'll see to it."

She laughed. "Thank you. That's real nice of you."

Pat leaned down, his knuckles on the table. "Now what can I get you? A cup of tea? A glass of milk? What about a Guinness stout? It's good for a mother."

"I'll have milk."

"Milk it is." He pointed to Sam. "I don't have to ask what this one wants. He sucked McSorley's in his first baby bottle."

Sam slapped Pat's shoulder, grinning, and straddled a chair as he sat down.

Maggie leaned toward him. "This place isn't so bad. It's nice and cozy. I sort of wish I'd come before. The walls are even Kelly green. Are most Irish pubs like this?"

"A lot of them, I guess."

"By the way," Pat called from the bar. "Come here when you get a minute, Sam. I've got a message for you."

Sam started to rise then he saw three of his cronies approaching with their beers. He met each gaze, wondering why their eyes were twinkling. They surrounded the table. One—Charlie—put his foot on an empty chair and leaned on his knee. When there was trouble at Molly Malone's, Charlie usually started it.

"Get your foot off the chair, Charlie," Sam said, his voice barroom loud.

Charlie took his foot down and raised his hands. "No offense, no offense. We just came to ask the little lady something."

Sam stood. "Ask me, Charlie. She doesn't want to talk to you."

He felt Maggie's hand on his arm. "I can speak for myself, Sam Duffy." He turned to look at her, but she was gazing into Charlie's eyes, saying, "Charlie, you go right ahead and ask me what you want."

Charlie smirked at Sam. The room grew quiet as he put his foot back in the chair. "Miss, we've only come to ask if Sam's the one what done it. Was it him who popped your belly? Tell us true, and if he won't do right and care for your babe, we'll drag the money out of him, for ya."

Maggie burst out laughing and clapped her hands in glee. The customers and Charlie laughed, too. Not Sam.

Maggie said, "He's not the father, he's my friend, but I appreciate that." She looked up at Sam. "Charlie, I wouldn't be surprised, though, if some day some woman could use your help."

Grinning, Charlie grabbed Sam by the back of the neck then draped his arm across his shoulder. "She knows you, Sam. This girl knows you."

"My name's Maggie."

Charlie reached down and shook her hand. "Glad to meet you, Maggie, glad to meet you. I'm Charlie. Don't bother with the rest of their names. I'm the only one that matters around here, except Pat. And he only matters because he pours the beers."

She said, "Sam tells me you have darts here?"

At least ten different voices said, "Darts?"

"She plays darts, Sam?" Charlie said.

"I do," she replied.

"Come with us." Charlie pulled out Maggie's chair amid a general scraping of chairs on the sawdust-covered floor.

Sam joined the procession to the back room. Someone flicked a switch and illuminated Molly Malone's wall of dartboards. One had a picture of the Queen. Black score boards were mounted between them; league plaques and tournament trophies sat high above. Three toe lines had been painted on the floor.

Maggie gave the biggest smile Sam had seen on her in weeks. As Pat arrived with the drinks, she placed her shawl on the railing between the dart area and the stools.

"Steel tip or soft tip?" she asked Sam and drank some of her milk.

"Steel, of course."

Charlie brought the darts. Maggie took one. She rolled it in her fingers and stepped to the standard toe line.

"Just for practice," she said. "My balance is a little different than it used to be."

Everyone laughed.

Sam loved what he was seeing.

Maggie eyed the target. She put her left hand on her stomach as if to brace herself and, with a twist of her arm and a flick of her wrist, let the feathered dart fly. It landed in the dime-sized circle at the center.

"Double bull!" Pat shouted while Sam and his friends roared.

Sam went to her. "Maggie, what'll it be? 301? 501? Cricket?"

"Any one you want, but there's a game we play at my church. Would you like to try it?"

"They play darts in your church?" someone said. "I may convert."

"We call it fifteen seconds. Anybody have a stopwatch?"

Pat said, "I'll get one."

"What happens in these fifteen seconds?" Sam asked.

"You get a handful of darts and let fly with them as fast as you can.

Whoever's racked up the highest score when time is up, wins."

"I love it!" Sam shouted. He unbuttoned his cuffs and rolled up his sleeves. "Where's that stopwatch?" he called to Pat.

Pat appeared and handed it to Charlie. Then he flicked another switch, saying, "In honor of our guest." An Irish reel began to play. Pat had picked *Sleepy Maggie*. Sam's cronies started clapping.

Charlie shouted, "On your mark, set, go!"

Side-by-side they stood and hurled their darts, Maggie screeching in excited glee as Charlie counted down the seconds, as the room clapped and *Sleepy Maggie* played. Sam tried to be serious, to aim at the bull, but Maggie's squeals and frantic hurls were too joyful a sight. She was winning. He was doing terribly and having the time of his life as Maggie laughed, his cronies clapped, and the Irish reel played.

"Stop!" Charlie shouted.

Maggie raised her arms above her head in glee. "I won!"

"Don't jump!" Pat shouted. "You've got a baby in you, girl."

Sam couldn't help it. He went to Maggie and took her in his arms. The music played. His friends clapped. He bent and kissed her and they whistled.

"Should you be doing that, now, Sam?" Charlie said and walked around them. "Maggie, you didn't lie to us, did you?"

Laughing, she pushed Sam away. His arm across her shoulder, he turned her carefully to the Irish reel, its joyful music racing in his blood. They faced the door. Sam looked up. His feet stopped. His heart froze.

In the doorway leaned Coral in her slick red raincoat, staring at them.

Chapter 48

Tuesday evening—West of Rock Creek Park, D. C.

Congressman Dunlop's teenaged son opened the front door and saw a tall man holding his wallet open. On it was a gold badge that read: Deputy U.S. Marshal.

"I'm here to see the congressman, Son, he's expecting me," the man said.

Zack lingered outside the study as the U.S. marshal talked to his dad.

"So far, he won't cooperate. Says he won't give a deposition to the subcommittee staff."

"We can't hold him in contempt of Congress for not complying with a subpoena for a staff deposition."

"Maybe he found that out."

"Guess I'll have to up the stakes, take his testimony in executive session. The records will still be private, and he can't wiggle out of the subpoena then."

"I don't know what you're after, sir," the Deputy Marshal said, "but when we frisked him I saw this in his jacket pocket. I sort of slipped it out, just in case. He'll probably think he dropped it at the airport."

"A notebook?" the boy's father said. "Thanks. Good job."

Zack dashed from the hall and hid inside a closet. He heard footsteps, heard the front door open. Then he heard footsteps returning to the study. He crept from the closet and listened again.

For a long while, he heard nothing, then, "May I speak to Congressman James? This is Congressman Dunlop."

A pause, then, he heard, "James? Dunlop. Well, we're making progress."

Another pause.

"They found his notebook. He wrote this down: *Threads? From where? Shroud of Turin?*

Another pause.

"You know that thing, that cloth. It's supposed to have an image of Christ? Yeah, that one. Well, get this. He put a big circle around it later in pencil and on top he penciled in the word, 'clone'."

Another pause.

"Hell, how do I know if there's anything on it they could clone, but it sure sounds like what we're looking for. I'll let our man know. One of his people will check."

Another pause.

"Well, two things. First, from the other notes, it looks like he originally wrote this down in January. Now it's September. If this crap is for real, somebody could be seven or eight months pregnant with the damned thing. But this should help Brown find his scientist. Meanwhile, get going on a subpoena to make this reporter testify in executive session."

A final pause.

"Don't tell Evermeyer yet. If it gets out that the Shroud was the source, these Jesus fanatics will only multiply. A lot of them already think the damned Shroud's real."

Zack Dunlop crept from the hall outside his father's study and back to the computer in his room.

Chapter 49

"Hi, Sam, long time no touch," Coral said and walked in, the clicking of her heels suddenly loud as the Irish reel ended.

In a billion years, Sam wouldn't have expected Coral to show up here. She'd seen Maggie, and Coral worked for Mr. Brown. He found himself praying that Coral and Maggie had never met as they came and went from the building.

Coral stopped and looked Maggie up and down. "Introduce me to your little friend, Sam."

For an instant, no one moved then Sam watched in disbelief as Charlie stepped forward and took Maggie's hand, gazing down at her. When she didn't pull away, Charlie picked her shahtoosh off the rail and said, "Let's buy you that Guinness Stout, now, Maggie."

Sam held his breath, desperately hoping she would go quietly with Charlie who, for the first time in his raucous life, was doing Sam a real favor. Charlie couldn't know he might be saving Maggie, too.

"I'll just have a sip or two, Charlie," Maggie said.

She and Charlie walked past Coral into the pub's main room.

The others quickly followed, Sam's cronies ogling Coral as they left.

When they were alone, Coral started undoing her belt.

"No, babe," he said, irritated with himself for remembering the last time she did that. Maggie was right in the next room. Father Bartolo had absolved him of his sins and Sam was trying not to rack more up.

"Don't be silly, Sam, I've got clothes on." She let her coat drop to the floor. Coral had on clothes, all right, technically speaking—one of those rag dresses with strategically placed rips and shreds hanging provocatively where usually there was a lot more cloth. It was red, too. She looked sensational.

While Sam watched, half his mind trying to figure out what to do, and the other half worrying what Maggie must be thinking, Coral swayed herself over to the dartboard, pulled out a dart and twirled the shaft against her bottom lip.

"Ooo, sharp!" she whispered.

"Damn, Coral, stop it, would you? You came to find me, right? Why?"

"I did," she said and stuck the dart back in the center of the board. "Are you going to tell me who she is?"

"She who?"

Coral folded her arms and batted her hazel eyes at him.

"The girl I was dancing with? She's Charlie's friend, remember Charlie?"

Coral laughed. "Tell me another one, Sam."

Pat came to the door. "How about drinks back here? Scotch, right Coral?"

"Yes, but not here, Pat," she said. "We're joining the others. Would you get my coat, Sam?" She winked at him and left the dart room.

Pat whispered to Sam. "Sorry. It was her what left the message."

Sam picked up her coat, keeping his gaze off her lovely behind as they went in the main room. In the next life, Sam thought, if there was one, he was definitely going to ask to be a tree, a rock, anything but a man. He watched Coral sit at a table close enough to Maggie's and Charlie's that Maggie could plainly see them.

He sat down and said, "Coral, tell me what you came here for."

She made a face. "Sam, tell me who your pregnant friend is."

If he were the type of man who roughed women up, Sam thought he'd probably be doing it now—forcibly dragging Coral out of Molly Malone's so this wouldn't be happening. Maggie's face was as immobile as concrete, but her eyes were vulnerable and pained like Felix's in the park. She'd probably guessed who Coral was—the woman who'd tried to change his mind about working for Mr. Brown. Common sense, and maybe the instincts of a mother carrying a child, must be telling Maggie Coral was trouble.

"No," he said and looked at Coral unsmilingly. "The ball's in your court."

"Sounds nice."

He felt something under the table and realized it was Coral's foot. She was caressing his thigh. It should have felt great, but it didn't. He knew Maggie was watching, knew what it was doing to her. He'd had enough.

Sam stood and draped Coral's coat on her shoulders. "You're leaving," he said and pulled her up by her arm.

She glared at him, whispering, "Take your hands off me, Sam. You want to get yourself killed?"

"What the hell do you want?" he whispered back.

Coral jerked her arm away. "I came to find you, to tell you you're in trouble, asshole. I've been here twice, looking for you. Ask Pat."

Again Sam took her arm and walked her to the door out of earshot. "Before you leave, tell me why you think I'm in trouble."

"Brown thinks you're up to something. He got real mad when I gave him the details of our—" she cleared her throat "our date."

"What made him mad, exactly?"

"Hell if I know. Maybe the part where you said I couldn't change your mind.

All I know is two days ago he asked me to tell him, word for word, what you said when I was with you. Apparently, he expected you back by now. When I told him, he got a leather folder out and started poring over it. Then he asked if I believed in astrology and whether I think you're capable of murder."

"Me?"

"You."

"What did you say?"

"No and no. Was I right?"

Sam didn't answer. It would take something specific to make Brown suspect him and nothing had happened in the ten days since he quit. Nothing but the appearance of OLIVE. Brown would know Sam had nothing to do with that. And murder? Had some astrologer told Brown he'd be murdered?

"When did this conversation happen?" he asked.

"At a tender moment. When I'm not busy and he's not busy, we screw each other, Sam. Didn't you guess? He lets the butler watch sometimes."

So this was what Brown called stewardship? Sam had never cared who else Coral slept with, but now he felt jealous. Maybe Brown had felt the same. Sam couldn't picture it, though.

"Then what are you doing here, warning me, then?" he asked.

"He's just a paycheck and a friend." She flicked her fingernail under his chin. "You? You I really like."

Sam saw Maggie look quickly away. He had to end this. "Thanks, Coral. It's time for you to go."

"Would you kill him?" she asked.

Sam didn't reply, though he knew the answer.

Coral put her arms through her red raincoat as all the men watched. He didn't try to help. Touching her was just too dangerous.

She looked over at Maggie once more. "Is it her, Sam?"

"If we'd met a year ago, babe—" he began, then stopped and reached for the doorknob. "It's too late, now."

She reached out to touch his cheek, but he caught her hand then patted it whispering, "It was great, Coral, but it's over."

Coral sighed. "I expected to hear that line sooner or later, just not from you."

Briefly they gazed in each other's eyes.

"Bye, Pat," she called and let her red-tipped fingers slide off the door's edge as she left.

Sam didn't think Pat heard her goodbye, because Pat was busy staring at something on TV.

After the front door closed, Maggie rose, saying, "Take me home, Sam."

He went to her. "Okay, but we can't just walk out the door."

"Why not?"

"Trust me."

Sam didn't know what to make of Coral's warning, but if she was right and Brown now feared him, there was a chance she'd been tailed. Anyone who did wouldn't try to come in because this was a neighborhood pub. A stranger would stand out. If someone followed, they'd be waiting outside.

"Bloody hell!" Pat shouted.

"Did the Yankees lose again?" Charlie called.

"God, no, man." Pat turned the TV up. "Listen you here to what they're saying. You remember all that cloning malarkey? How they were saying somebody's bringing back J.C. Himself? It says here on the news the clone came from DNA on the Shroud of Turin, mates. I'm beginning to think this bloody cloning business could be real!"

Sam stared in shock. How had anyone found out the Shroud was the source unless Jerome betrayed them again? Brown had connections at the Vatican. How long could it take him to identify Rossi, now, realize his hunch was right and Sam must be involved? Or had it already happened?

First he had to get Maggie home. He went to Pat and whispered in his ear, went to Charlie and did the same. Then he made a phone call, while Pat and Charlie moved about the room.

A few minutes later, Sam was at the front window peeping out. He nodded to Charlie, who took the cue to approach a pal of theirs.

"I've been meaning to give you a piece of my mind," Charlie said, loud enough for the whole room to hear.

The other man replied, "Have you, now?"

"I have." Charlie put his hands on his hips, swaggering, and gazed around the room. "I figure a little of mine is better than none at all."

Everyone laughed as the man and Charlie rolled up their sleeves. Some customers stood on their chairs for a better view. Others moved closer and circled the men.

"Charlie, a sharp tongue and a sharp mind are never found in the same head. Didn't your mother tell you that, lad?"

The people whistled and applauded.

"Mothers?" Charlie looked puzzled. "Don't you have to be a life form to know about mothers?"

More laughter.

Sam took Maggie's hand. "Come with me." They eased by the crowd around Charlie.

"Such a mouth you have on you, Charlie. Your mother must have had a loud bark."

The customers cheered.

As the man raised his arms in victory, Charlie's fist reached back then sped forward. Pat flicked a switch and the joyful reel, *Sleepy Maggie*, began to play again.

When Sam and Maggie reached the dart room's door, Molly Malone's had erupted in a melee of swinging fists. Pat opened the front door and, as if on signal, the loud fight spilled out onto the street.

Sam rushed Maggie through the back door, out to an alley, and into a waiting cab.

Chapter 50

Tuesday night—Palisades Parkway

Sam leaned against the railing outside the service station's glass doors. Headlights approached and sped past on both sides of the divided highway. No point in risking a strange taxi driver taking them to Cliffs Landing. He'd phoned Felix to pick them up. As expected, Felix had sounded pretty pissed.

He saw a car pull in from the northbound lane and stop under the yellow lights. It was the Range Rover. It drove up and parked across from him. Felix got out, slamming the door, and rushing forward.

"I can't believe you pulled a stunt like that!" he shouted. "We looked all over Central Park for you two. Where's Maggie?"

Sam pointed. She was standing just inside the glass door, drinking a small carton of chocolate milk. "She's fine. She needed a break."

Felix stared at him. "It's time we talked about whether you need to stay involved, Sam." He'd obviously prepared this speech.

Sam folded his arms. "Guess you haven't heard the news."

"What news?"

"They know the DNA's from the Shroud."

Even in the bad light, Sam saw color drain from Rossi's face.

"Who? How?"

"Anonymous sources, again. Maybe it's Newton, in fact I hope it's Newton."

"Why?" Felix asked.

"You've got another problem. It's time you knew."

Felix looked more angry than before. "What problem?"

"There's somebody who might get serious about preventing the birth. That's why I'm here."

"Who? You mean someone who'd harm Maggie?"

"Maybe. I'm not sure. It's Mr. Brown back at the building. He could have people out looking for me. I'll need to keep my car hidden at your place and not drive it. We need a Plan B and we need it now. "

Felix gripped the railing. "Brown?"

"It'll take too long to explain, but I think he's dangerous."

"All right, Sam. What do we do?"

Sam looked at him. "How long will it take the Shroud people to figure out it's you?"

"Well, I'm certainly not the only American scientist who's had access to the Shroud."

"Anything special that would make them focus on you?"

Felix nodded. "Yes. I'm a microbiologist."

"Oh, right. But—"

"The equipment for cloning is in every microbiology lab, but only a few of us have had access to the Shroud. When the church realizes I not only left Turin after the first day's work, but I also have a second degree in obstetrics, they'll know it's me, even if they can't prove it. They'll have to say something, do something."

"Why?"

"The church owns the Shroud, for one thing. For another, they care what one billion Catholics believe."

Sam rubbed his neck, not liking Rossi's report. Still, it might take Brown time to get names of scientists from the church.

"What would the church gain by publicly naming you?" Sam asked.

"I don't know. Maybe they wouldn't. We should ask Bartolo."

Felix patted Sam's back. "I shouldn't have lost my temper. It's you I have to thank for preventing Bartolo from reporting us." He sat down on the concrete steps and looked at the traffic going by. "What a mess we're in." Then he glanced back toward the convenience store's glass doors. Maggie was munching on an apple.

"She's hungry," Sam said.

"I did hope you'd taken her to dinner."

"Not exactly. What about the other scientists? If the church can figure it out, can't they?

"Yes, several could."

Sam clapped his hands. "That's it, then, we need to get busy. Here's the plan. Tomorrow I'm buying us four new identities, including passports. Then you're buying another place with a doctor's office already installed. Not a glass house this time. Last, we get a plain, white Mendon leasing van, load it ourselves, shut up shop here, and drive away. Meanwhile, you need to nail down every route to get from Lawford Lane to the Palisades Parkway and from there to every Metro-North, Amtrak, Long Island Railroad, or New Jersey Transit train within

100 miles, every airport in the area: Teterboro, JFK, La Guardia, Newark, Westchester, Stewart up in New Windsor. We need the number of every taxi or limo company in the area, booking for any train or plane, commercial or charter. Hell, even the schedule for the Tappan ZEExpress from the Palisades Center Park and Ride."

"Well if it came to that, I could charter a plane at Teterboro to take us anywhere we want."

"Yeah, we'd just need a pilot who couldn't be bought."

Felix sighed. "You're talking money for the house, you know."

"How much can you get your hands on?" Sam asked.

"Enough. I'll have our lawyer—"

"Have him bring the money for the house, the new identities. Everything. When we cut loose, nobody can know where we are."

"You're talking a million or two for a house and incidentals," Felix said. "How much for the IDs?"

"Twenty grand."

"For what?" Sam heard Maggie say.

He turned to see her watching him from the steps, no expression on her face. She'd been like that since they left Molly Malone's.

Chapter 51

Tuesday night—Cliffs Landing

As soon as they reached the house and got to the living room, Maggie turned and faced Sam. She'd made a decision as she watched him with Coral at Molly Malone's. She'd watched carefully—each expression, every gesture—so the pain would make her wake up and see the light. Sam would never look at her like that.

On her best day, in her best makeup, in her finest clothes, she couldn't compete with a woman like that. Stand them next to each other and no man alive would pick her over Coral, not in America. Maybe in some far-off land she'd never seen except on TV and in *National Geographic*.

She stood looking at Sam, aware of their differences as she imagined Africa. Elephants, red earth, huts beneath a green, green hill. Somewhere there was a tribe in which the village beauty looked like her: lavish lips, wide nose, her backside not too large, but glorious to the men. Maggie longed for her lost village where she might have had the chance to be what Coral was. As she watched Coral and Sam she'd grown angry—first at America, then at herself, then with Sam. He only wanted to help "the best woman in the world." That was all. But Maggie wouldn't accept his sacrifice. She'd overheard the plans they'd made and wouldn't accept the Rossis fleeing because of her.

"I've made a decision," she said.

She saw Sam and Felix both frown, as if they'd forgotten she had a mind that could decide things.

"What decision?" Felix said.

"You'd better sit down."

They sat in chairs. Maggie remained standing.

"I'm leaving."

Instantly they were on their feet.

"No, you're not," Sam said.

"Please sit down, you two, and listen to me."

They sat down, staring at her.

"Felix, you and Frances are in danger because of me. Me and my baby are in danger because of you. I know you've got some kind of legal rights, Felix. But you've also got the right to stay alive. So does my baby. Only me leaving can help, now."

"That's nonsense, Maggie," Sam said.

"No, listen. I'll just call Piermont Taxi & Limo and go home in one of their nice Lincoln Town Cars. I'll pack, check into a hotel and when the time comes, have my baby at Harlem Hospital, nobody the wiser."

"No, you won't," Sam said.

Maggie ignored him.

It was thrilling, this decision. She felt unburdened and alive, felt life's possibilities reopening for her baby and for her. She should be grateful to Sam and she was. But the thought of missing him didn't alter her determination. She was going to leave Sam—her only love, who didn't love her—leave Felix who had indirectly fathered her child, but she knew joy would follow her.

It was the baby.

Maggie caressed her stomach in happiness as they stared. It was the baby.

She wanted to laugh, to shout, to lean forward and kiss their stunned faces. Maggie closed her eyes and felt the glow inside her. He was coming back, bringing joy. All the world could celebrate, lay down its woes. He was coming back to give us peace and jubilation. He'd come to save us. Hallelujah! Glory, glory be.

"What if someone discovered you?" Felix asked.

At least he hadn't ordered her to stay. Maggie gazed on Felix like the child of God he was. "I'll just be another unwed mother, giving birth to what they'll assume is another mixed child—don't you see?"

230 J R LANKFORD

Sam stood, an odd expression on his face. She didn't have long to wonder what it meant. He shouted, "You can't go!"

Maggie's joy disappeared as she remembered how he'd looked at Coral, how Coral had run her foot up his leg.

Quietly, Maggie said, "I'm my own woman, Sam. Nobody owns me."

Neither of them replied, as if her words had cast a spell.

Maggie turned to go. She reached the basement stairs before she heard Sam shout, "Maggie, I love you!"

She heard his footsteps, the sounds of a scuffle, and Felix saying, "Give her a moment, for heaven's sake."

Maggie sped up because for some reason Sam was making her cry. Down in her room she buried her face in her pillow and dug her hands in the mattress, wishing it were baked earth like the Serengeti Plain she'd seen in pictures.

She heard Frances's voice at the top of the stairs, asking what was wrong. Maggie hadn't bothered to lock the door. Sam would just kick it in again, but she didn't want to hear him say he loved her anymore.

She rose to go out to the garden, then Sam was at the door, Felix trying to pull him back.

"Sam Duffy, for once would you listen to me—"

That was all Felix got out before Sam crossed the room and his hands cupped her face, before his mouth found hers, kissing her as if she'd risen from the grave. In front of Felix and Frances, Sam kissed her.

At the feel of his lips, Maggie remembered Coral's pouting lips and how he must have kissed them passionately.

Angrily, she pulled away. "Don't you dare touch me, Sam Duffy!"

Her words moved Felix, who'd been watching, open-mouthed. "Sam!"

But Sam said, "Damn it, Maggie, I love you! I love you!"

"Tell that to your female mirror!" Maggie snapped and backed away, desperate to be away from him or she'd go mad.

"Damn it, Maggie!" Sam said.

Frances ushered Felix out to the garden, pushing at his shoulders. Sam closed the garden door behind them, drew the drapes and they were alone.

In the silence, Maggie could hear their heavy breathing—his through nostrils thin and white like sand and hers dark like fertile earth and wide.

He said nothing until she looked into his eyes, then Sam fixed his gaze on hers and said, "Maggie Clarissa Johnson, I love you!"

Maggie burst out crying, wishing it were true.

He sat on the bed with her and let her cry like he had all summer by the Cascade, by Eagle Rock, by the river when sand martins chirped and made her weep. Repeatedly he said, "I love you!" It changed from a declaration to a whispered chant, a fevered vow, "I love you, I love you. Maggie, darling, darling

Maggie, sweetheart, I love you."

When she couldn't stand it and shook with loud sobs, he took her in his arms. Outside, she could hear Frances and Felix arguing. Felix called, "What are you doing to her, Sam?"

"Only this," Sam whispered. He put his face to Maggie's and his beard scraped her cheek once more. He breathed his vow of love into the hair she thought ugly, but he stroked it like a baby's until her tears finally stopped, then he breathed his vow before the lips she thought too wide until he sealed them with his own.

Maggie grew weak in his endless kiss. It seemed to reach back and fill the empty years. It looked forward into her days and promised they wouldn't be lonely anymore.

"What's happening?" Felix shouted, but to Maggie his voice might have come from another galaxy. She was too lost in Sam to worry about Felix and Frances. Sam obviously was lost too, his breath hot on her neck, his hands all over her.

He raised his head and Maggie saw the yearning in his eyes, but he didn't try to make love.

"I'll wait, Maggie, as long as it takes. Please don't go away."

Maggie looked at his strong shoulders, the old scars on his neck from brawls, the devilish, knowing twinkle always in his eyes. It, more than anything, brought women like Coral under his spell. Sam didn't need to be here. He didn't need to beg a woman for anything. He could have beautiful women, have jobs, have a life. The only explanation for Sam's ever being here was that he loved her.

"All right, then, Samuel," she whispered.

He lifted her chin. "You won't go?"

She nodded.

"I want you to marry me, Maggie Johnson. Understand?"

She laughed and kissed his hand. "You do, do you? Well, I accept your proposal, Sam Duffy. We'll get married when the baby comes."

He smiled.

She let his hands caress her, because his hands were love and couldn't hurt the baby. She let his lips take control of her, let Sam's body rub against her side and his breath grow ragged as if she were the last woman and he were the last man and this was the last moment on earth.

Felix called, "Sam, don't you dare—bother her!"

Sam moaned, "Touch me, Maggie."

And Maggie touched the man who loved her, not caring that in the middle of it her pants somehow grew damp. She wished they could stay like this forever, Sam gazing down like he adored her. It didn't even last two minutes.

She heard knocking, then Felix angrily clearing his throat, saying, "Maggie, Sam?"

Maggie felt like she'd die of embarrassment. She said, "Just a minute, Felix."

They stepped out into the garden and the soft rays of a crescent moon, Sam casually announcing, "We're engaged!"

Chapter 52

Wednesday—Washington, D.C.

In the Chamber of the U.S. House of Representatives, as the Chaplain offered the day's prayer, Congressman Dunlop, head unbowed, thought of what had happened when he visited Brown last night. Dunlop had stopped in to deliver the reporter's notebook with the scribbling about threads, but Brown had already heard about it on TV. Brown accused Dunlop, or someone on his team, of the leak. Dunlop had to find out who.

Meanwhile, Brown had decided the Subcommittee should act. No later than next week, there should be a vote on the floor of the House of Representatives. No more wrangling like they'd done over other cloning legislation. Strings would be killed. A majority of them were indebted to Mr. Brown, whether they knew it or not. Dunlop certainly was. Without Brown, he couldn't finance his next campaign. He'd been in Brown's hip pocket too long to attract big donations from elsewhere.

Dunlop regarded the majestic backdrop of the Speaker's Rostrum. In black marble, its four ionic columns supported a white entablature against white marble walls. In the center hung Old Glory, stripes vertical, stars on top, and on either side the Bronze Fasces: axes bundled in rods entwined in ivy. They had been symbols of civic authority since Roman Consuls used them.

Dunlop's eyes traveled above the flag. Carved in marble were the words: *In God We Trust*. Sometimes Dunlop wished he did, but God wasn't here. Brown was. He'd strongly hinted he could ruin Dunlop's marriage as well as his career—with photos, no doubt, of his unplanned intimacy with Coral.

Ever present in the back of Dunlop's mind was something else: the dead wife of the Secretary of State. By an unfortunate coincidence, she'd belonged to his wife's bridge club. As her marriage fell apart, the woman drank and talked of things she shouldn't. Dunlop would never forget the day of her death. He'd arrived early at Brown's as a tall man dressed in black got in an Audi S4 and drove away, followed by an inconspicuous blue van. The police never found the

Audi or the blue van witnesses saw on the road when the Secretary of State's wife drove off a cliff. Though D.C. buzzed the incident faded, just like the death of Martha Mitchell in the '70s. She'd been the wife of John Mitchell, Nixon's Attorney General, who resigned to head the committee to reelect him. They lived in the Watergate. Martha drank too much, talked too much, and then she was dead. D.C. buzzed. Nothing happened.

He scanned the Gallery above the Rostrum, looking for his son. There he was, in the seating reserved for Members' families. Dunlop felt encouraged that the boy had asked to see this bill introduced when he'd learned about it at breakfast. Usually, Dunlop thought his son hated him. Why he'd taken an interest in cloning, Dunlop didn't know but he was glad. At least clones, unlike UFOs, were real possibilities.

The prayer ended and the Sergeant-at-Arms entered with The Mace—a bundle of ebony rods entwined in silver bands topped by a silver globe and an eagle. He placed it on a green pedestal to the Speaker's right and the Speaker called the House to order. A few minutes later, Dunlop rose and stood before his party's podium. Beneath the words, *In God We Trust*, he looked out at the nearly vacant chamber. He asked unanimous consent to introduce the bill Brown had angrily stuffed into his hands. It would be referred to the House Science Committee's Subcommittee on Human Cloning, which he chaired.

C-SPAN recorded the sessions, which would get Brown media coverage—a necessary step since, as Brown had anticipated, wall-to-wall TV coverage of the rumored Jesus clone resumed last night. Knowing his son listened, and that through a camera the world watched, Congressman Dunlop summoned oratorical power and read the bill to the virtually empty room with solemnity:

A BILL

To prohibit human cloning of the deceased.
  Be it enacted by the Senate and House of Representatives of the United States of America in Congress assembled,

SECTION 1. SHORT TITLE.
  This Act may be cited as the `Deceased Human Cloning Prohibition Act.'
SEC. 2. PROHIBITION.
  (a) GENERAL RULE- No person shall—
    (1) engage in cloning of deceased human beings or
    (2) aid and abet such cloning.
SEC. 3. DEFINITION.
  For purposes of this Act, the term `deceased human cloning' means the

use of somatic cell nuclear transfer, or any other means, to create a new individual human being with a genome identical, or substantially identical, to that of a deceased individual human being.

END

Dunlop left the podium and dropped the bill into the "hopper," the wooden box beside the Rostrum, provided for the purpose. The Clerk would give it an official HR number, and see it got in the Congressional Record along with the Speaker's referral to Dunlop's Subcommittee. Through the people and organizations Brown controlled, IOU's would be collected for this vote. Quick passage in the Senate was similarly assured. The President would sign it into law. Then the police and FBI could join the search for the scientist and the clone's mother.

Now Dunlop had to find whoever leaked the story about the Shroud. Given Brown's ire last night, Dunlop felt capable of not only firing, but also strangling the culprit himself.

He waved to his son, Zack, in the Gallery and headed for the hotel where the questioning of the reporter, Jerome Newton, was vigorously underway. It was all beginning to make sense. Newton had once written an article about Shroud scientists—not one, unfortunately, but a whole slew of them. As of this morning, Newton still hadn't cooperated, but it might not matter soon.

———

In the Gallery, Zack Dunlop waved back to his father and penned a message on the *ibook* in his lap, then translated it into ten languages. It began:

URGENT!
OLIVE TO MARCH IN PROTEST OF THE ANTI-CHRIST U.S.
CONGRESS

Today, Congressman Dunlop introduced legislation to ban the Second Coming of Jesus Christ.

Would all OLIVE members and sympathizers please assemble at the following locations at noon local time? Chapter leaders, please enter your pass codes to obtain the destination of each march.

Zack logged onto the Internet through a phone line meant for the press. He smiled as the counter showed he was OLIVE's five millionth, four hundred twenty seven thousandth, hundred twelfth visitor to date—only a thousand visits faked that first day. He posted his message, then scanned the many versions of Jesus he'd described on the OLIVE site: not only the familiar Jesus of Nazareth, but Yeshu the Jew, a rabbi; Metteyya, the next would-be buddha; the Muslim prophet Isa ibn Miryam whom the Qur'an called the Light and Fragrance of God; Jesus the guru and avatar who learned the secrets of divinity from the Hindus; as well as Jesus the Hindu God Prajapati himself.

He'd found hundreds of images: Jesus with blonde hair and a purple flaming heart, Persian-eyed Jesus posed artfully against a tree, Ethiopian Jesus with black silken hair, the colorful Ojibwe Indian Jesus of Morrisseau, Dali's surreal Jesus on a yellow cross, an African baby Jesus carved in olive wood, Chinese Jesus with a Mandarin moustache, a turbaned Jesus on a couch, Caraveggio's Jesus, Michelangelo's Jesus, a black *Jesus of the People* painted recently in New York, Jesus as Che Guevara.

The oldest was from the third century: a very swarthy *Jesus Enthroned with the Apostles*, a few of whom looked inexplicably Negroid. It was his favorite.

OLIVE's website recognized any Jesus anyone believed in, as long as it might make them pray, sing, march, and cause civil disturbance until the Son of God was safely back.

Chapter 53

Cliffs Landing

In his first spare moment the next morning, Felix tried to find Adeline. He learned that madam, Adeline Hamilton, had checked out of The Savoy on The Strand in London long ago. Backtracking, Felix discovered madam was not in residence at the Hotel Hassler Villa Medici at the top of the Spanish Steps in Rome, nor at The Bristol on Paris's rue du Faubourg Saint Honore. Where was she? When Frances canceled out of the Mediterranean cruise, Adeline did, too. Now that they were about to drop from sight, Felix realized he would lose touch with the woman he still loved.

Father Bartolo had already left, upgraded to the Concorde by Felix. The attorney had come and gone, leaving packets of money. Thousand dollar bills didn't take up much space. Frances had taken most of it to buy them a house. To keep from attracting attention, she planned to let it be thought she was a mob wife. She could pull off the accent, she said. They'd get the house. No one would pry.

Sam had gone to Chelsea to rent a truck. At a shop on Amsterdam Avenue he'd buy false licenses, passports, birth certificates, and social security cards in the names they'd chosen: Daniel and Agnes Crawford, Chuck O'Malley their driver and bodyguard, and Hetta Price, their maid.

Felix went back to packing up essentials and wondering if his relationship with Adeline was damaged beyond repair.

Maggie was on bed rest in her room but Felix could hear her say her morning prayers. As he tiptoed to the door, he heard her whisper to the baby, "Don't you hurry, sugar. Listen to your mama, do you hear? No matter what's going on out here in this world, take your time. Let the grownups worry about it all for now, okay? If you need to come out, I'll see you do. Right now you just keep on growing. Can you hear your mama, sweetheart? I love you more than anybody does—okay, except your real father—so you listen and stay in there."

Felix felt upset with her.

He had asked his lawyer to discourage stepfathers of the clone. It was obvious she didn't remember that if she married it would void her financial settlement in the contract. It would trigger a custody suit, one that Felix with his greater resources would win. The lawyer warned that a family court would actually consider the best interests of the child, but Felix had wanted to give Maggie pause about marrying. He knew and trusted her, but a husband, especially Sam?

One look at Maggie's glowing face last night and Felix knew he couldn't tell her.

She looked up, saw Felix at the door, and sighed. "I'm just talking to my baby, everything's fine."

"You're sure?"

"I'm sure."

He started into the room. "I need to check your—"

"Felix, I'm fine! Let me have a minute's peace!"

He stopped, feeling hurt, not understanding her bad mood. He thought she'd still be on cloud nine.

She sighed. "I'm sorry. I didn't mean to snap. Come in and sit with me for a minute. Let's see what they're saying about us now."

Felix turned on the TV then sat beside her. He stroked her belly, so large with the baby it seemed to offer itself for touch. He often forgot to ask her permission. Everyone did. Even Father Bartolo had finally touched her protruding belly and talked to her child as Maggie smiled.

Gently, Felix asked, "You haven't been having hallucinations? More seizures? You'd tell me, Maggie, wouldn't you?"

She didn't answer.

"It's very, very important that I know. It could … It could—"

"I told you!" Maggie snapped. "I don't care what happens to me. Take care of my child."

"You could become ill, very ill. This is the most dangerous time in a way. If you don't tell me everything—"

She rose up on her elbows. "You said the baby was old enough to live now since I'm thirty-three weeks."

"Yes. I started you on corticosteroid therapy a few weeks ago to mature his lungs, just in case, but—"

She sighed and lay down again. "I told you, already, Felix. I told you that first day! If something happens, save the baby. Cut me open. Right away."

Did Maggie think she might not live to marry Sam?

"Even if you can't get me to a hospital.," she continued, "cut me open." She gazed at him and spoke quietly. "Kill me if you have to, Felix. Save my baby. I don't care about anything else, I don't care!"

He stroked her arm. "We have everything we need to do a Cesarean, if necessary. I've told you that over and over. Why do you talk like this?"

Felix lowered his head to the mattress and stroked the child through Maggie's belly, not trying to look at her anymore. Lately she talked like that all the time out of Sam's hearing, "Cut me open, kill me, just save my baby," and Felix had ignored her, tried not to hear, because he knew it was his fault.

From the first, her pressure had been too high to be involved. It had always been too high. When she'd signed the papers, with her first injection, when he implanted the blastocyst from Maggie's egg and the Shroud cell, he'd consciously gambled her life. Never mind that the chance of real trouble seemed low. He shouldn't have let her take any risk at all.

He had no proof; still he knew her occasionally elevated pressure and the seizures and hallucinations were linked. She'd probably had them regularly and hadn't told him. Any day, any time, he expected her to develop edema, proteinuria, oliguria, for her visual disturbances to become severe. Why it hadn't already happened, he didn't know. It was a likely prognosis and he'd known it all along, though he'd lied to himself to get through the days with her.

Yet it didn't seem real. His life felt like it belonged to someone else—having to flee, Maggie engaged, Maggie's health now in such danger. Since last night when Sam told him about Brown, nothing had seemed real. He'd have to live with knowing he should have found someone else, instead of playing brinkmanship with Maggie's life. He'd have to live with her reminders to kill her and save the baby, because—if the situation arose—he knew that's what he'd do.

Of course, it wouldn't.

He was watching her, running the tests. At the first sign of trouble he'd institute seizure prophylaxis using magnesium sulfate, then perform a Cesarean when she was stable. Delivery was the cure for preeclampsia. It would take half an hour. She'd be fine.

Felix closed his eyes and listened to the baby's heartbeat, listened to it move in the fluids Maggie's body had made. Was the child who he hoped? The chance of that wasn't good. In these long months Felix had faced this truth. Still, he'd always known if there was any hope at all, he'd not only cut her open to take the baby, he'd go to jail, give up his money, sacrifice his reputation, he'd die himself for this child who might be Jesus. Nothing else mattered to him. Nothing in the world.

He didn't look up when a breaking news story was announced. He'd heard, but he didn't care what it was. He wanted to stay near Maggie, near the baby. He wanted to ponder the aberration he'd somehow become: a Moses who would kill this lamb to set his people free.

"Felix, Felix, look!" Maggie said.

She grabbed the remote and increased the sound. CNN had live coverage of a demonstration on D.C.'s Capitol Hill. Mounted policemen, concrete barriers, and ropes greeted the thousands estimated to be there, with more arriving.

Felix gazed at the TV.

The scene switched to Paris, where people had gathered on the Place de la Concorde, once the Place de la Guillotine, carrying crude signs of a baby's severed haloed head.

"Oh, how terrible!" Maggie cried and embraced her stomach.

Across a bloody dagger were the words Etats Unis.

"Etats Unis?" she said.

"The United States. Congress has introduced a bill to criminalize cloning of the dead. OLIVE is protesting."

The scene switched to a slugfest outside a church in Berlin. Why they were fighting, no one was sure.

"Can you believe it?" Felix took the remote and switched to another channel. "They're tear gassing an OLIVE group in Indonesia."

Maggie said, "It won't last long. When my baby comes—"

CNN broke in with an announcement that the Vatican had a message for the world.

Felix sat down on the floral sofa. TV evangelists had been thumping their bibles about the clone in Sunday sermons for weeks. Most threatened hellfire and damnation to any who dared believe in it. One claimed the clone spoke to him in a dream, advising the faithful to double their offerings because Judgment Day was near.

As the camera scanned the crowds in Rome's St. Peter's Square, Felix let the scene transport him to the past. At seventeen he'd stood alone there in the early morning, statues of saints looking down from Bernini's masterful surrounding colonnade. He had joined the scattered faithful heading for the "new" Basilica, only six hundred years old, erected on the spot where Constantine had built the first one. St. Peter the Apostle was buried here. His grave was under the shrine, which was under the high altar, over which Bernini's spiraled pillars soared, Michelangelo's dome above them. In the Gospel of St. Matthew, Jesus said, "You are Peter and on this rock I will build my church." An excavation beneath the altar in 1939 found ancient bones that were likely his. In the Basilica, Felix had dropped to his knees before Peter's grave, his heart open to Christ through His Apostle.

He remembered how he'd prayed to Peter, a poor fisherman, who in death was surrounded by the riches he'd eschewed. Above his tomb was a gilded throne, a baroque canopy of bronze, jeweled chalices upon a marble altar. Even at seventeen Felix noticed.

Now he watched as the wind blew the Pope's red and white banner hanging from St. Peter's central loggia. From there the Pope would tell the waiting world what he thought about the clone. Felix wondered what Peter, the fisherman, would think of his successors, the popes: the pious ones, the bloodthirsty ones. Even today, the Pope retained three roles: Bishop of Rome, head of the college of bishops, and monarch of Vatican City, the smallest state in the world, except in influence.

The Pope appeared on the balcony, the white skullcap called a zucchetto on his head. Only now did it strike Felix that a Catholic priest's zucchetto and the Jewish yarmulke were indistinguishable—a visible reminder that Jews founded Christianity.

"Brothers and Sisters," said his translated voice. "You have come to hear a message from Mother Church about the rumors of a clone. On this question, Our Saviour, Jesus Christ, has already spoken in Matthew's gospel, Chapter 24. *'And Jesus answering, said to them: Take heed that no man seduce you: For many will come in my name saying, I am Christ: and they will seduce many'.*"

Maggie rose on the bed. "Why's he saying that?" she cried. "He hasn't even met us."

"He can't meet us," Felix said, "It would be like an endorsement."

But if he'd been there in the square, Felix would have shouted, "No!" at the Successor of Peter who was simply quoting from the Bible in which all Christians believed. The Holy Father's voice was firm, but loving. It reminded him of his own father's voice. Felix could see his father in his mind, hear him speaking in the same firm and loving tones.

The Pope continued, "*And many false prophets shall rise, and shall seduce many. Then if any man shall say to you: Lo here is Christ, or there, do not believe him.*"

From a long-ago past, Felix heard his father, say, "Listen to me, Felix. Listen carefully."

The Pope held out his hands as if to embrace the gathered crowd. "*For there shall arise false Christs and false prophets, and shall show great signs and wonders, insomuch as to deceive (if possible) even the elect."*

Felix was looking at himself at age nine as the tape of his forgotten memories played. He saw his father's hands, heard his father's tearful words, "Repeat what I am saying, Felix, because you are not a Jew. Say: I am not a Jew."

"Behold I have told it to you, beforehand," the Pope was saying, though Felix no longer saw St. Peters Square. He saw a boy in a yarmulke run, crying, through Central Park while a group of boys chased him, calling, "Jew, Jew, show us your horns!" All his life, this image had been in his mind, but he'd never seen the boy's face.

"If therefore they shall say to you: Behold he is in the desert, go ye not out: Behold he is in the inner rooms, believe it not."

Felix whispered, "Turn around, little boy. Show me who you are."

"For as lightning cometh out of the east—"

The boy turned.

"and appeareth even into the west—"

Like in a movie of a long-ago scene, the boy smiled.

"so shall the coming of the Son of man be."

"Felix, why's he saying this?" Maggie pleaded.

Felix was looking at his own face at age nine. His mother had told him a secret story called the Haggadah about how the Jews had escaped from Pharaoh. She gave him a cap and said not to wear it in public, but in Central Park he proudly showed it and shared the story with a friend who told the others Felix was a Jew. They chased him. When his father found out, he did a terrible thing. He took Felix to the boy's home to persuade the family Felix wasn't a Jew.

"And immediately after the tribulation of those days, the sun shall be darkened and the moon shall not give her light—"

Felix had been embarrassed, humiliated. He'd begged his father not to visit any more of his friends' homes. When his pleas were ignored, Felix ran into the street.

"and the stars shall fall from heaven, and the powers of heaven shall be moved:—"

He never saw the car that hit him and dragged his body down the block. Until now, all Felix remembered was the ambulance, the hospital, and the face that years later Felix saw on the Shroud of Turin. He remembered being with Jesus. Ever since, Felix had wanted to be with Him again.

"And then shall appear the sign of the Son of man in heaven:

… But of that day and hour no one knoweth, not the angels of heaven, but the Father alone."

Felix went to Maggie and hugged her, sharing her disappointment and that of the people in St. Peter's Square, as if hope had been outlawed in the world.

Felix eased her down, sat on the bed beside her, and held her hand as the Pope, who must have felt the sadness, too, concluded.

"Brothers and sisters, The Shroud of Turin belongs to the Church which has kept it under careful guard. This guardian can confirm no theft from the Shroud. It remains intact."

Maggie lowered her head. In the square, you could hear the people sigh.

"However," the Pope continued. "If there is a woman who believes herself pregnant with the Son of man, I say to her—"

Maggie raised her eyes. "The Holy Mother was a mortal woman, too. She bore her child in pain, like you will. I offer this prayer for you and for mothers everywhere." The Pope crossed himself and began, *"Hail Mary, full of grace, the Lord art with thee …"*

Chapter 54

Charles de Gaulle Airport

When the Pope completed his message, Father Bartolo was alone in the Air France Concorde lounge, the other passengers departed, his connecting flight forgotten as he watched. He said, "Amen," at the end of the *Hail Mary*, his heart in deep despair. The Catholic Shepherd had done what he believed to be right: herded the faithful from false belief. From the Church's point of view, the Pope's speech was necessary because the Pope didn't know what Bartolo did: something had been stolen from the Shroud.

He reached into his briefcase and retrieved an unopened manila envelope, intended for persuasion had Felix Rossi balked. Sam Duffy's confession had intervened, preventing Bartolo from carrying out his plan. Once he'd met Maggie Johnson, Bartolo might not have, in any case. She was only a simple maid. She didn't belong to the True Church, but Maggie believed she was carrying Christ. He thought she would willingly die to save the child whose genes, Bartolo knew, had come from the Shroud of Turin.

What had surprised Bartolo about Maggie was her affliction. She had seizures, otherwise known as epilepsy, the sacred disease, though down through history some hadn't called it that. In the Jewish Cabala, two of the four angels of prostitution—Lilith and especially Naamah, the mother of demons and the devil—were said to inflict epilepsy. Medieval Christians, thinking epilepsy a sign of witchcraft or of demons fighting for control, had epileptics institutionalized, sterilized, killed. Jesuits forbade their ordination. Some said epileptic seizures, in the guise of divine rapture, appeared in both the Bible and the Qur'an as Paul's vision of Jesus on the road to Damascus, as the prophet Muhammad's trances, and his visitation by the archangel Gabriel. The Greeks and Romans thought epileptics had the gift of prophecy from a god that had jumped into their bodies.

Given this, Bartolo had found it awe-inspiring that Maggie Johnson was epileptic. He found it just as curious that she was black given that, prior to the Renaissance, most images of the Madonna were dark skinned. Hundreds of Black Madonnas still existed over the world, especially in Europe. He was particularly fond of the twelfth century Notre Dame de Rocamadour and had a copy on the mantle of his fireplace in Turin.

As he sat in the Air France lounge, staring at the televised waving Pope, he felt the sadness of the people in the square and remembered what Maggie had said this morning when he bade her goodbye. Bartolo had put his hand on her stomach and immediately felt a peace he'd never known. Seconds later, he realized Maggie had gone into a trance. When he couldn't rouse her, he'd started to call for help, but in her trance, she'd said, "Father Bartolo, help them believe." Then she awoke, saying she was fine.

In the Air France lounge, Bartolo removed the contents of the manila envelope: a photo of a scientist lifting his microscope off the Shroud. When rumors of a Christ clone first appeared in *The Times* of London, Bartolo had begun a systematic search. He'd scrutinized the hundreds of photos taken at the palace of the Dukes of Savoy when the Shroud was out of its casket. This one was a close-up taken with a wide lens, the scientist's face obscured by his microscope. The close up only needed to be slightly enlarged to see, dangling as plain as day from beneath the microscope, two blood-soaked threads from the Shroud. A second photo taken simultaneously—and now well hidden back in Turin—had revealed Felix Rossi performed this theft.

These photos proved the Pope was wrong. DNA from which a gifted scientist might produce a clone had indeed been stolen from the Shroud.

Now he looked at the desk, briefly vacated by the lounge attendant to assist another passenger. To Bartolo, this was the crucial moment of his priesthood. He already had this photo when Sam Duffy confessed, so Bartolo wouldn't be breaking the seal of the confessional. He wouldn't be committing the sin of disobedience, since he hadn't asked permission and been denied. He wasn't jeopardizing Maggie, because in the close up Felix's face was obscured.

Instead, Bartolo had a chance to fulfill Maggie's request which was, by a miracle, the greatest priestly yearning of his life: to help give a clear and certain sign that God lives. On His feet we walk. In His arms we fall. His is the wing by which Jesus Christ would rise.

Bartolo took out his priest's stole and kissed the cross on its back. He didn't know if this would be the Second Coming foretold, but he felt he had touched the pregnant mother of God. He should give these photos to the Pope, but how might Church bureaucracy react to a potential Jesus in the flesh? Bartolo preferred not to speculate on such things. He draped the stole around his neck and went to the empty desk where he picked up the phone and—since he was in France—asked the operator to connect him to Agence France-Presse, the leading French news and photo wire service, and one of the world's big three.

Chapter 55

Cliffs Landing

Maggie heard Sam coming before she saw him. What else but a moving van could rumble like a dinosaur as it careened down Lawford Lane? Tired of her room and of TV, she'd come up to the library to put her feet up and read a magazine. Felix wouldn't let her help pack.

Now she went down the open library's steps, past the glass living room wall, up the two steps to the foyer, and opened both sides of the front door, securing them. Sam climbed down from the driver's seat, came to her and hugged her. He took a passport from his pocket and showed it to her, saying, "There you are, Hetta Price."

Maggie looked at herself and laughed. "Let me see you."

He showed the passport of Chuck O'Malley who looked exactly like her Sam. All morning, Maggie had been practicing thinking of him as *her Sam*.

As if he'd read her thoughts, Sam kissed her again. She pulled away. "No more of that, now. We can wait."

He grinned and rubbed her shoulder then they heard a car. Frances's Jaguar appeared, Cal in the passenger seat. Sam had dropped him at the church, and Frances must have picked him right back up.

Frances lowered the window and as the Jaguar stopped, Felix arrived outside with George, the caretaker, come to help with the packing and loading.

"Frances, thank goodness. Tell us you got a house," Sam said.

"I did but, gentlemen, Maggie, did you know we're on the radio?"

As they listened to yet another breaking story on the clone, Sam resolved that in the next life, not only would he not be a human male—a monkey, maybe, since they seemed to have a lot of fun—he would pick a world that didn't have radio or TV.

"Should this photo be called: The Theft of Jesus?" a man's voice asked. He described a lab-coated scientist bending over the Shroud of Turin, his face obscured by a microscope, two threads dangling from it. The photo had just been published by Agence France-Presse who vouched for the reliability of its anonymous source.

Felix went pale. "How in the world did they get it?"

"At least he says they can't see your face," Frances said.

Felix reached in the Jaguar and turned off the ignition. "Brown may already be guessing it's me."

"Mr. Brown? Our Mr. Brown at the building?" Frances said, her voice rising. "He's the fearsome threat?"

Sam nodded.

"Isn't that wonderful! Will we all be killed now, Sam? Never mind. Let death surprise me. Did he give this photo to the press?"

"It had to be Bartolo or someone else in Turin. Bartolo, I bet. His flight connected in Paris," Felix said.

"Couldn't be," Sam said. "Remember my confession?"

Frances got out of the Jaguar. "It doesn't matter who. It's done. What are we going to do?"

"Will the other scientists know it's a photo of you?" Sam said.

"Probably."

"Then Brown will know. We're out of time. We've got to clear out of here."

"I agree. I'll get some things," Frances said, and started for the house.

"No!" Sam said. "Now! I've seen Brown work. Felix, grab your medical bag. We don't have time for anything else."

Maggie was stunned.

She listened to Sam tell Frances to leave her Jaguar. She watched him toss George the keys to the white Mendon Leasing truck, which in a pinch wouldn't be fast enough, he said. Felix told George to park it and close up the house until further notice. They climbed into the Range Rover, Felix at the wheel, Sam beside him, Frances in the back with Maggie. They drove onto Lawford Lane, a flock of sand martins from the riverbank twirling crazily overhead. As they sped by the Presbyterian Church and out of Cliffs Landing, Sam frantically scanned the road.

Maggie wondered if the house Frances had bought was on this side of the river. Given what happened the first time, she didn't want to cross the Shatemuc now.

Sam said all that mattered was to get as far away as possible before Brown's men got to the Landing, saw they were gone, then learned Rossi's maid owned the house, owned a Niagara Gray Range Rover and had fifty thousand in the bank.

Chapter 56

Washington, D.C.

Zack left his room and listened outside the office door as his father, Congressman Dunlop, and his two guests, Congressmen James and Evermeyer, watched a TV news interview with a young man who once made deliveries for Fabulous Food. He described the garden door of a pregnant woman who never let him see her. The meals were charged to the Rossi family's account.

"Well, the cat's out of the bag, now, that's for sure," Evermeyer said. "What's our man going to do?"

He heard his father clear his throat and, sounding a bit frightened, say, "Hell if I know. I just hope he knows we had nothing to do with this. But it's got to be easier now."

"How the hell could it be easier?" James said.

"If the mother has an accident, anyone could have caused it: that fanatic they arrested in the park during the OLIVE vigil, anyone."

"What about the reporter?"

"Jerome Newton's being released. What can he say?" Dunlop asked. "They're after this Felix Rossi guy and the mother now. He must have done it, must have cloned DNA off the Shroud. Can you beat that?"

"But suppose he—"

"Suppose what? James, you've never had any balls. There's nothing you can suppose that Our Man can't take care of."

Outside, Zack did something he'd never done. He reached for the knob and turned it. He opened the door to his father's office while a meeting was underway.

Dunlop looked at his son, confused. Why was he standing in the door like that? Why did he look triumphant?

"What's wrong, Son? I'm still in conference."

James and Evermeyer said hello to the boy, but he didn't answer. He only looked at his father, relishing his surprise.

"Your conference is over," said the boy.

His father reddened then he stood, planning to exert parental authority so he wouldn't be embarrassed in front of Evermeyer and James.

He ordered, "Go to your room!"

Zack didn't move. Instead he raised his hand over his head. In it was a miniature tape player. He flicked the switch. The tape began to play:

"*Now you're sounding like that scatterbrained son of mine. He'd believe in a Second Coming since he already believes in UFOs—*"

Zack switched the tape off and enjoyed seeing fear gradually replace his father's anger as he realized he'd heard his own voice.

"If you've been sneaking around taping—"

Again, he switched the tape on:

"*You think we've got the votes?*" Evermeyer's voice said.

"*I know we do,*" Dunlop's voice replied. "*It's our man's baby, after all.*"

Zack switched the tape off, watching James's and Evermeyer's faces turn pale.

"What do you want?" Evermeyer asked.

Zack said, "Every conversation held in this office about the clone is on tape. I have copies of the tapes in a train station locker. Not in D.C., somewhere else. I've mailed the key and directions to the locker to myself at a local address. If I'm not there tomorrow when the mail's delivered, someone in that house will open the directions and get the key."

Dunlop felt like he was waking from a dream to find a nightmare going on in his real life. All the leaks had come from his own son. He moved from behind the desk.

"Son, why have you done this?"

Zack backed up and pressed the tape again.

Dunlop heard his recorded voice.

"*If this crap is for real, somebody could be seven months pregnant with the damned thing. Our man's got to find this scientist.*"

Zack switched the tape off and asked, "What is Mr. Brown going to do when he finds the clone's mother? That's who your man is, by the way," he said to Evermeyer and James. "A Mr. Brown of Fifth Avenue, New York."

He watched James and Evermeyer exchange a "we're in trouble" glance. He watched his father close his eyes and groan.

"What will he do?" Zack said. "Tell me and I promise no one will ever know where I got my information."

Dunlop gazed at the stranger he'd called son. "Brown's a dangerous man."

"Tell me," Zack said and listened as his father described a hopped-up Audi S4 and an inconspicuous blue van—both of which were there when the wife of the Secretary of State drove off a cliff.

Chapter 57

Palisades Parkway

"First thing is we've got to ditch this car," Sam said, as they reached the Palisades. "It's in Maggie's name."

"How will we do that?" Felix asked.

"Easy! The airport. We'll rent something in one of our new names then we'll leave this in long-term parking. Brown'll find it and think we left town. Teterboro Airport's on the way. We'll do it there."

Felix drove down the Palisades toward I-95, settling his mind for a two-hour trip. He would take the Garden State Parkway to the New Jersey Turnpike, stop at Teterboro then go on to their new home, a secluded colonial on Barnegat Beach Island in Bay Head. He looked forward to quiet walks on grassy beaches and having the time to envision the lives of Daniel and Agnes Crawford and Hetta Price. Chuck O'Malley, the new version of Sam, would go about his business when he saw he had no future with them. In the rear view mirror he could see Frances in the back, looking resigned to having lost her identity. She couldn't be Frances Rossi ever again. He couldn't be Felix. The lives they'd lived were over. He only wished Adeline knew or was here.

Maggie was leaning sideways. He noticed she kept shifting against the armrest then back in the seat then on Frances. She asked Frances to rub her back. Then Felix heard her moan. It was low, but he heard it.

"What is it, Maggie?"

"Nothing, I'm all right."

She moaned again.

The Palisades Parkway had no real curb lanes. Felix slowed then pulled off the road onto the wide grassy shoulder. They were three miles from I-95.

He retrieved his medical bag then opened Maggie's door and climbed in, glaring at Sam and telling him to keep out of the way.

Sam did, watching Maggie. Eyes closed, she seemed intent on her breathing.

"What is it?" Felix asked, pulling out his fetal stethoscope. He slipped it beneath Maggie's long blouse and heard a strong fetal heartbeat. Then he felt Maggie's belly harden beneath his hand.

Without a word, they met each other's gaze, Maggie panting so lightly Felix wouldn't have known if he hadn't been right there.

"How long has this been happening?"

"What?" she said.

"You're having a contraction."

"I can't be. It's way too early. I just have a backache."

"Are you okay, Maggie?" Sam asked.

"You're having a contraction," Felix repeated.

"No, I—"

Maggie's doe eyes widened and Felix saw something in them no man would ever share. He reached for her, but Maggie pushed his hand away and got out, her mouth open. Felix followed. Sam and Frances quickly came. Maggie put her palms against the Range Rover and bent over, trembling. That's when Felix heard a gush of water on the grass.

He felt like a scared first-time father, not her doctor, gazing at the fluid until its meaning registered.

"Your water broke!"

Maggie leaned on Frances and moaned in the way only laboring women did.

"Hold on," Felix said to Maggie and grabbed Sam's arm. Hurriedly he walked him away. "Did you have sex with Maggie last night?"

Sam's face went pale. "No! Well, not her. Me. I swear. I just—" he patted his chest, "fooled around up here and kissed her, Felix. I swear."

"Idiot! Nipple stimulation releases oxytocin which can cause the uterus to contract!"

"Bull shit!" Sam pushed past him, saying, "How come all pregnant women don't—"

"Not all women, Sam, just some—like Maggie, for instance, who was at risk of preterm labor."

"Felix, you're handing me a bunch of crap—" He went back to Maggie.

"Sam, the baby's coming."

Looking like the criminal Felix considered him to be, Sam picked Maggie up and put her in the back. "Get in and take care of her!" he said to Felix. "I'll drive. We need to get to the house."

"House?" The doors slammed as they got back in. "We're not going to any house! We're going to the hospital!"

"No, we're not!" Sam said.

"I've got to stop her contractions, for God's sake! She's only thirty-three weeks! I can't risk treating her in an empty house!"

Sam's jaw trembled, but he turned on the ignition and pulled back onto the Palisades.

"You're ignoring me? I'm her doctor!"

Sam said, "Yeah, but I'm responsible for her safety. I've thought it through. In Brown's penthouse is a special computer. It can download troop strengths from the Pentagon, much less find pregnant women admitted to New York area hospitals. No, he won't know Hetta Price is Maggie Johnson, the Rossis' maid. He'll just know that Maggie Johnson disappeared seven months ago. And he'll know before the day's out. He'll check every pregnant black woman admitted to a New York hospital from now on. Understand? If she goes to one, the risk is 100 percent Brown will be suspicious, given the timing. He'll locate Maggie Johnson's photograph and check. Taking her to a hospital will be like delivering her to Brown's front door. Maggie's only chance is to disappear like we planned. No hospitals, Felix. Just check her out!"

Felix was so shocked, he did as he was told. For Maggie to go from nothing to membrane rupture, then immediately to full contractions was alarming. Sam must have traumatized her while having sex. The only other possibility was that Maggie had already been in silent preterm labor. Sidetracked by all the commotion and Maggie's protests, Felix hadn't performed a full morning exam. She could have been in labor for almost eighteen hours. Now Sam was saying he couldn't take her to a hospital.

"Idiots!" Felix whispered, expressing fury at both Sam and himself.

He had Maggie lie down on the seat, her knees bent. Kneeling on the carpet, he put the fetal stethoscope on her stomach. Her skin had been flawless that first day, now light brown stretch marks were prominent everywhere. Felix found the baby's heartbeat—still strong, if slightly faster.

"You have to keep the car steady for a minute," he said.

"Steady as she goes," Sam said and stopped changing lanes.

Felix snapped on sterile gloves. A post-rupture manual exam risked infection, but he had no choice. He had to know.

"How are you doing, Maggie?"

"I'm fine," she mumbled, not sounding like she was.

One hand on her stomach, Felix inserted his fingers between her labia, reaching for her cervix. If it hadn't changed, he had a chance of stopping or slowing her contractions by himself. He couldn't let Maggie labor without instituting seizure prophylaxis. The danger to her and the baby was too great. That meant a magnesium sulfate drip. He had to slow her labor, but all he had was a dose of terbutaline in his bag.

Maggie cried out before his fingers touched her cervix.

"What the hell are you doing?" Sam said.

"For once, would you shut up? I'm trying my best not to hurt her."

Maggie took deep breaths. "I'm all right, Sam."

Suddenly, Felix felt her stomach harden beneath his hand. She groaned deeper and looked terrified. "Felix, Felix! Oh no! I think I need to go to the bathroom! Real bad!"

Felix scanned her face. "What? No! It's not that. Your body wants to push. Don't! It's way too early. Don't push! Breathe, Maggie, breathe!"

Frances reached back and took her hand. She and Sam echoed in anxious voices, "Breathe, Maggie!"

Maggie's contraction had come far too quickly behind the last. Was she hypertonic, contracting too fast for the baby to tolerate? Felix waited and tried again, this time pushing toward her cervix until he reached it, but he didn't believe what he felt. She was fully effaced. In no time she'd be fully dilated.

"Maggie's in second stage labor," he announced, his voice trembling, as he hurriedly prepared to administer the terbutaline subcutaneously. It was a potentially risky drug for a preeclamptic woman, but the risks of not slowing her labor were as great. "We might not have time to get to Bay Head. If we can't go to a hospital and we can't go back to Cliffs Landing where my equipment is, what are we going to do, Sam?"

"I don't know!" Sam shouted. For the first time, he sounded afraid.

"Oh, think, would you?" Frances said. "Check into the nearest hotel, Felix. Call George and ask him to bring whatever you need."

As Felix found a blood pressure monitor and strapped it on Maggie's wrist, he thought of the University Club on Fifth Avenue and 54th, a marbled, gilded, wood-paneled Italian Renaissance palazzo, so rule bound it put a President's wife out for a small infraction. Jackets and ties were required, but not if you were checking into one of the guest rooms. He could sneak Maggie in a private entrance. George could send a few things up.

"They don't tell people whether a member is there or not. Isn't it worth a try, Sam?"

"I dunno. Half the membership could be in Brown's pocket."

Frances added. "And I can just picture Maggie's screams resounding through the marble halls. Are you crazy, Felix?"

"Something else is wrong, isn't it?" Maggie said, staring at Felix.

"No," Felix lied. "You're just in active labor. It's just a little early."

Felix was really watching her blood pressure, terrified. It was at 150/95. If it rose, she would seize, convulse. She and the baby could die. How would he treat a simultaneously eclamptic patient he should deliver at once and a hypertonic patient whose delivery he should slow?

"It's happening too fast, isn't it?" Maggie said. "Tell me the truth."

"Is it?" Sam asked.

Felix cleared his throat. "Yes, it's fast."

Sam was driving over the speed limit, there was traffic everywhere, but the car became hushed, as if the world had emptied of everyone but them.

"Can't you do something?" Sam said.

Felix reached into his bag, hoping magnesium sulfate solution would magically appear or at least a second dose of terbutaline. "I am. I'm hoping this terbutaline will slow her contractions, but it's way too late to stop her labor."

Maggie's eyes were huge with fear. "What happens if they don't slow down?"

Felix didn't answer right away.

"What happens if they don't?" Sam repeated.

"You could—" Felix began then he stopped, not wanting to go on. If she was hypertonic, if he couldn't control her pressure, a Cesarean would be the only way out.

"What?" Maggie whispered.

"You could have seizures—different from your other ones. You could convulse. It could cut off the baby's oxygen. His heartbeat could stop."

Maggie lifted the fetal stethoscope and put it in Felix's hand. "Listen to his heart. Take him out if he gets in trouble. You can do that, can't you?"

"Yes, but not safely for you."

"Forget me."

"Don't talk like that, Maggie," Sam said.

She didn't look at Sam. Maggie kept her eyes on Felix. "Is that everything? The whole truth?"

"No, Maggie. The seizures themselves could kill you, too."

Maggie didn't flinch. "If I die before he's born, he dies too?"

"It's very likely."

"You're sure he's old enough to live?"

"Yes. Remember, I matured his lungs."

"Then take him out!" Maggie cried. "Do it now before he gets in trouble!"

Sam careened onto the shoulder, brought the Rover to a stop, reached swiftly back and put Felix in a strangle hold.

"No one—not you, not God, not his Son—is going to take Maggie from me. Not even her. I'll kill you. I swear!"

When Felix nodded, Sam let go of his throat and pulled onto the road again. Gasping, Felix heard Frances softly cry in the front seat. He looked at Maggie, remembering how they'd both vowed to die for the child. Her eyes were shining into his.

As the Range Rover approached I-95, Felix put the fetal stethoscope on her belly and listened to the heartbeat of Christ.

Chapter 58

As the Palisades widened from a two-lane wooded road to three lanes heavy with traffic, Sam spotted a blue Volkswagen EuroVan and remembered he'd seen Brown's leather-coat man drive one. He felt sick as he watched it pull from the curb lane into traffic behind a Range Rover similar to theirs. The EuroVan drove up close behind the other Range Rover then pulled off to the side while Sam moved to the far left lane, trying not to speed and attract attention. The EuroVan had barely stopped when they passed it, Sam glancing fearfully over.

Then it started raining, though there hadn't been a cloud in the sky. Sam turned on the wipers, whispering, "Thank you God," hoping the rain would shield them as they sped away. As traffic slowed to a crawl, he watched in the rear view mirror, knowing a EuroVan was ideal for surveillance, given its tinted glass, folding table in back and rear bench that converted to a bed.

"What is it?" Frances said.

"I don't know yet."

Felix looked to see what Sam was watching. "Well, what do you think is out there?"

"Maybe nothing."

Visibility wasn't great—rain pouring in the last gray light of dusk—but Sam kept scanning the mirrors, hoping not to see the van. Then, one car behind in the right lane, he saw a flash of metallic blue. It was the EuroVan.

He might have been at sea with a man overboard, given the swiftness with which his mind cleared. "Frances, if you can shoot, open the glove compartment and get my extra gun."

Sam had bet she wouldn't panic, and she didn't.

"I can't shoot, Sam, but I can drive like hell."

"Good. You see the blue van behind us to your right?"

She looked back. "Yes."

"Don't try to outrun it, but keep us away from it."

Frances nodded and slipped her leg over the gearshift, looking determined. He let her take the wheel, her left foot slipping over his right and onto the gas pedal. In spite of the tight fit and awkwardness, she managed to hold the wheel steady, sliding over, as he slid under, until they'd traded places.

He looked back and saw Maggie was falling asleep. She hadn't seen. The shot

Felix gave her must have sedated her.

"I'll take that extra gun," Felix said.

Sam handed it to him, his eyes on the EuroVan. It was pacing them, not trying to close in. "Don't shoot at anything till I tell you to."

"Sam, let's forget Jersey," Felix said. "I don't know it. I know the city."

"So do I." Sam rose from the front passenger seat and squeezed through into the back next to Felix.

"George Washington Bridge, it is," Frances said, as Sam gazed on Maggie's face, then clambered into the rear cargo area. He looked for something to hold onto with his left hand, the gun poised in his right. He still hoped he was mistaken, and the blue van had innocently appeared.

They reached the bridge, paid the four-dollar toll, and drove over the Hudson River, rain obscuring the cliffs of the upper Jersey shore. Sam felt like he was back on the ocean during a storm, his bearings lost in the turmoil of sea and sky. Though he'd had a seaman's skills, only instinct had told him when to use them. He was relying on instinct now, on a presentiment of tragedy no one could avert but him. Felix had been unbelievably stupid—to have hauled two women into predictable danger when he couldn't even protect himself. If Brown's man was in the EuroVan, he was just a modern version of the folks who'd nailed the first guy up.

Sam tried to ignore these thoughts as he watched the EuroVan, aware of everything around him: water pouring on the windshields, tires thumping across the joinings of the bridge, rain falling on the river Maggie called the Shatemuc. He glanced at her, seeing her profile in the murky light, and for an instant imagined another setting: elephants, red earth, huts beneath a green, green hill. He hated that she thought herself ugly.

In his eyes, she was glorious as she slept.

Chapter 59

Two things happened when they reached the end of the bridge. They plunged back into relative darkness, and the rain became a deluge in which Frances slowed the car.

"Don't slow down, step on it, Frances! Now's the time to lose them," Sam said.

The Range Rover launched forward, its powerful V8 engine delivering high torque, its electronic four-wheel drive delivering traction, just as if the rain weren't there. Maggie awoke in the car's new motion, her eyes quickly fixing on

Felix's gun.

"What's wrong?" She rose up and looked at Sam in the cargo area. He had his back to them, staring at the road behind.

Felix pressed on her shoulder, saying, "Lie down, now," trying to keep his voice calm. He could see from the wrist monitor that her blood pressure and pulse had risen. He hoped it was simply the shock of seeing the guns.

Sam called, "Keep going! We're losing them."

Felix heard Maggie whisper and realized she was probably saying a prayer.

"Move!" Frances yelled at whatever she was seeing through the windshield.

On open road, they would have quickly lost the EuroVan, but traffic diminished the Range Rover's speed advantage. Still they moved down the Henry Hudson Parkway, throwing sheets of rain onto slower cars.

"We need to get off this! Where do I get off this?" Frances said.

Sam answered, but Felix didn't pay attention. He was watching the blood pressure monitor and Maggie, who closed her eyes and slipped her hands onto her stomach under her blouse. Felix briefly shined the flashlight on her face to see if she was straining. Her eyelids were pressed shut.

"Maggie, are you having a contraction?"

"Ssshh," she murmured. "I'm trying to relax myself back to sleep."

Felix looked up and noticed the rain had lessened. He heard tires splash in the rain, heard Maggie breathing deeply, like he'd taught her. Her first two contractions had been less than three minutes apart, but there hadn't been a third in almost twenty minutes. She wasn't hypertonic anymore. Their pursuers were nowhere in sight. Perhaps Sam had only imagined the EuroVan was after them. Felix sighed and stretched his legs out on the floor, resting against the seat, holding Maggie's wrist so he could keep an eye on her monitor. Maybe they'd get to Bay Head after all. He'd have time to get some magnesium sulfate, purchase urgently needed supplies. The rest he'd replace in a matter of days.

He felt hopeful until Maggie opened her eyes. They passed under a streetlight, and he saw her gaze was turned inward. For her, the outside world didn't exist anymore. He watched her belly visibly contract. And now the tires and the rain were drowned out by her moan. Felix gripped her hand, trying to organize his thoughts. What was her Bishop's score? Where was she on the Friedman Curve, or had she fallen completely off it? She had an anthropoid pelvis, like many black women: narrow in front, wide in back, narrow from side to side, but the side walls flared. Once the baby was deep in her pelvis, labor would be faster, easier. In Maggie's case, that was good unless she became hypertonic again.

He watched her writhe, Felix doing nothing—like an incompetent, an obstetrics student awed by his first labor, like a panicked father helpless though he feared the loss of wife and child.

"He didn't move until Maggie whispered, "Felix, I can't help it. I'm having another hard contraction!"

Then Felix sprang into action, his voice authoritative.

"All right, Maggie. Try to relax below your waist. Breathe shallow up in your chest and pant, pant, pant, blow! Wonderful. Do it again."

There was silence in the car except for Felix's voice. She lay back when the contraction eased.

"I'm going to listen to the baby's heartbeat now."

He put the fetal stethoscope to her stomach and counted the beats of a tiny heart, knowing its mother would deliver in an hour at the longest, come what may. If she seized in the process, the child might not survive. It could experience severe fetal distress, could suffocate, experience cardiac arrest. Maggie could convulse, her blood pressure soaring. In less than an hour, she could bleed to death. Felix listened, counting as he looked at his watch, then he saw her blood pressure rise. Now it was 150/110. Far too high. Maybe it was just the juggling of the car, the fear of being chased, the fear of giving birth. If it wasn't he could lose her, lose the child. He pictured the scalpels that lay ready in their sterile bundle in his bag. If he tried to use them, Sam would interfere. That was a given. Felix's only recourse was to make the first incision irreparably deep, so he could instantly extract the child.

Ordinarily, he'd first make a Pfannenstiel incision down to the fascia. He should extend it with Mayo scissors he didn't have and open it with Kocher clamps he didn't have. Next, he would separate the rectus muscles, tent up the peritoneum, and incise it with Metzenbaum scissors he didn't have. As it was, he'd have to butcher Maggie to get the baby, just like she'd urged him over and over: *Cut me open, kill me, save my baby.* Had she had a premonition?

"How is she?" Sam asked.

Felix didn't answer. He was listening to the baby's heartbeat. It had almost risen to a reassuring rate. Then he felt Maggie's stomach harden and heard her moan again.

Stunned, Felix said, "She's in active labor. She's going to deliver."

"Take the next exit, then, Frances," Sam said. "We'll find a hotel."

Frances said, "It's 96th Street—"

"Yes, go that way!" Felix urged, having made a decision.

"Why so close to home?" Sam demanded.

Felix didn't answer, because Sam would only argue. When they got off the exit, he'd tell Frances to take the 96th street transverse through Central Park. Frances was still his sister; she'd do what he said. They would emerge two blocks from Mount Sinai where he still had privileges, could admit Maggie, and care for her himself. He'd tell Frances to stop the car. He'd tell her to back up two blocks to the hospital. What could the men in the EuroVan do, shoot them on Fifth Avenue? What could Sam do? Then Felix would hire armed guards. He'd keep them at her door around the clock.

What Felix wouldn't do was risk Maggie and the baby out here in the rain anymore. Her uterus was hypertonic. She was eclamptic. He had no medicines to treat her. Any trained physician could predict the calamity ahead.

"Where are you taking us, Felix?" Sam said.

Again, Felix didn't answer. As if approving of his decision, the rain stopped. Traffic sped up and they flew past other cars.

"Fine! Don't tell me! That's dandy!" Sam growled.

Felix coached Maggie through the contractions, Sam and Frances silent and looking back for the EuroVan.

Night had fallen.

Across the river, low lights shimmered along the Jersey shore. Lights studded a parking lot that paralleled the road along the riverbank. Frances moved the Range Ranger into the far right lane, preparing to take the 95th-96th exit.

"What's that?" Sam said, rising up in back.

Felix looked up, but through the wet window he only saw a low wall between the road and the parking lot beyond. He rolled the window down. Suddenly the wall ended. Across the guardrail, in the riverside parking lot, he glimpsed a dark vehicle moving parallel to them, followed by a smaller car. They came into view under the lights. It was a blue Volkswagen EuroVan and an Audi S4, merging beside them toward the exit.

"Sam!" Frances screamed. "Look, look!"

"Hell!" Sam shouted. "They used the parking lot!"

Then Felix heard a whine, followed by a thud. Instantly, the moon roof exploded, sending glass chunks down on Frances. Somehow she kept control of the wheel, screaming, blood running down her arm.

"They're fucking shooting at us!" Sam yelled and shattered the back glass, returning fire.

Felix started to roll up the window where the bullet must have entered, but Frances cried, "Get back! Both of you!" She looked fierce and stepped on the gas. Divining her intention, Felix got to his knees, bending over Maggie. He gripped the seatback and braced his feet.

He heard Maggie praying about being in the valley of the shadow of death.

Sam yelled, "Geroni-fucking-mo!" then Frances rammed the van.

They felt the jar of the crash, heard the EuroVan's side crumble, and its tires screech to a halt, heard the Audi crash into it, but Felix stayed put, Maggie beneath him. The Rover entered the single lane for the 96th street exit, alone and seemingly unscathed.

"Step on it, babe!" Sam shouted. "Maggie, are you all right?"

She didn't answer because she was talking to God.

"She's praying," Felix said and turned to bandage Frances's arm. The Rover hurtled down the sloping exit, careening left as it turned, then back up toward the road. He stanched the blood flow as she drove. He opened antiseptic, unrolled gauze. Why did her blood seem the color of the carpet in the Lesser Ury painting he'd bought for her?

"95th or 96th?" she asked.

"Just get in the city," Sam said. "Okay, 96th is faster. Is that why you want to take it, Felix?" He reached over the back seat to stroke Maggie's brow. She was having another contraction, and Felix could hear her desperate panting.

"Sam, NYPD will respond if we get off shots in the city," Felix said.

"Cops?" Sam snorted and looked up. "Yeah, with Brown right behind them. We can't depend on cops. We've got to lose them permanently. Gotta get out of this Rover and beg, borrow or steal another car. We'll be safe, then."

When Felix finished, Frances said, "Thanks, Flix."

She sounded just like she used to when they spent Sundays together, he reading, she writing letters to her college friends, just like in the Ury painting. She'd finish and he'd hand her the front section of the paper and she'd say, *Thanks, Flix,* just like that.

Felix returned to listening to the baby's heart. It sounded like a rapid, muffled drum. He grew more alarmed when he looked at Maggie. Her pressure was holding at 150/110, a dangerous level, but it was holding. How strained and tired she seemed in so short a time. He should open his bag. He should take out his scalpels. He should save the child she'd begged him to save.

"Hang on, Maggie," he whispered. "I'm getting you help."

Maggie's big eyes pleaded. She looked sorry, as if she'd failed.

"What is it?" he whispered.

"I can't stop. The baby's coming down."

Only after she repeated it, did Felix understand. Still, he didn't believe her. He felt her stomach, using the third Leopold Maneuver. The baby's head had started to descend and he hadn't noticed.

"I've got to push!" Her voice was strangled. "Let me push!"

"No, Maggie!" Felix said, thinking of the shape of her pelvis and that she might now labor faster, and he had no way to decrease her risk of seizing.

She took deep, gasping breaths and gripped the seatback, twisting and panting. Felix panted with her, helping time the breaths, watching as she fought not to push. He was looking in her eyes when she lost.

Crying, Maggie put her chin to her chest.

"All right, then," Felix said, sweat on his brow, beneath his gloves, drenching his shirt. He eased her knees up and watched, hoping the baby wouldn't crown. "Don't hurry. Just a gentle push. Now stop. Take a breath. Hold it. Another?"

She nodded.

"All right. A gentle one. Stop when the contraction stops."

Maggie lay back and sighed. "It's over. I'm sorry. I couldn't help it."

Felix didn't answer because he was listening to the baby through the fetal stethoscope. His little heart had slowed. He was in distress. Felix should take him. He should do it now.

"Is he all right?" Maggie asked, sounding worried.

Felix didn't look at her. He reached for his scalpels. If he didn't do it now, the child might die. His hand slipped inside the bag, found the bundle, and undid it. He held cold steel in one hand. With the other, he exposed her belly fully. It was huge with new life, though she'd never known a man. He remembered how he'd said he'd deflower her if the baby weren't Christ and how she'd laughed. When he caught her gaze, Maggie's eyes were shining into his. Silently, she nodded. He nodded in reply.

He saw her skin move up and down as she breathed, saw it shift with the movement of her baby. Felix held his breath and picked the site, imagined the depth of his cut.

"What are you doing?" Sam shouted and Felix jumped, dropping the knife.

"Sam, do your job! I'll do mine."

He couldn't C-section her with Sam watching. Instead, he gripped Maggie's hand and looked ahead into the night, his heart drumming, too, his pulse as fast as hers. They were on 96th street, speeding up the right lane past cars stopped on the left. Sam was shouting instructions and Frances was shouting back, but Felix didn't hear them. All he heard and felt was the beating of three hearts. He looked back at Maggie and her eyes were pleading still. Her baby was in trouble and she knew. She wanted him to kill her. That's what they'd agreed. If he did, the child might save the world.

"Take the 96th street transverse!" Felix said as they approached Amsterdam.

"What? No!" Sam objected from the back. "We're not going back into Brown's own territory!"

"Listen—"

"Wait! They're here again, for God's sake!" Sam called.

"Take the transverse!" Felix repeated. "Take it, Frances."

Frances didn't answer. She was busy driving through a red light. Felix looked back and saw the EuroVan run the light as well.

Then something exploded beside them and the street grew darker. A shot had missed them and taken out a Don't Walk sign, which apparently shorted out the streetlight.

"They're not going to stop. You've got to get out of here," " Sam said as Frances swerved back and forth between the lanes.

"Who?"

"All of you." Sam said, his voice tense. "They'll follow me! They'll follow the Range Rover! All of you get out of here. When we cross Central Park West, Frances stop, and all of you jump off in the park by the playground. They won't see you if you're quick."

"No, not you," Frances said. "Me! I'll stay in the Rover. Sam, you need to go with Flix and Maggie to protect them."

"Hell, Frances," Sam said. "You're fabulous."

"No! We're going to the hospital!" Felix said.

Sam said, "Felix, listen to her! We're not going to the hospital. We're going to be dead if you don't do exactly what Frances says. She's right. I need to stay with you and Maggie. Get ready to get out."

No one spoke as they careened through the streets, frightened, desperate. Felix's mind rushed through a kaleidoscope of options, searching for another way out and finding none. Sam was right. If they got out at Mount Sinai, the EuroVan would drive by and shoot them. It had already tried.

Frances amazed him. But it had always been like this between them. What he wouldn't do, she wouldn't do. Once committed, they were in all the way.

"Oh God, Frances." Felix said. "Forgive me."

"Bring us Jesus," she said. "Or whoever it is."

They reached Central Park West and Frances shot into the intersection at the end of a yellow light, the EuroVan only seconds behind. Sam had climbed into the back, carrying blankets, his hand on the door as Maggie sat up, gasping, and Felix closed his bag.

"No, they'll catch us," Frances said, putting on brakes and veering left at the last minute. She raced up Central Park West, the EuroVan screeching and spinning behind them as it tried to brake and turn. When they reached 101st, Frances ran a red light and drove into the park through Boy's Gate. She drove around the sawhorse across the right side of the road. Signs on the sawhorse said: *Stop, Do Not Enter, Park Drives Closed*. Had the road been open, they would have faced oncoming traffic, but at this time of night, Central Park's north quadrant was deserted of both people and cars. Felix knew it well and so did Frances. Blindfolded they could find their way around it.

"Meet you under London Plane, like always," Frances said to Felix, her voice breaking

"Frances, noooo!" Felix began to openly cry.

"God is going to watch over you, Frances," Maggie said.

The Range Rover stopped. Sam opened the door and reached back for Maggie, carrying her out, saying to Frances, "Don't let 'em get you, babe."

Felix lingered another second, stroked his sister's hair, gave her his gun, said, "I love you, Fran," and disappeared with Sam and Maggie into the dark.

Chapter 60

They hid in the shadows of the playground, Felix hoping the blue van hadn't seen them enter the park and would pass by on Central Park West. His hopes vanished when the EuroVan smashed into the sawhorse as it came into the park, followed by the Audi. The van paused for a moment then the duo drove on, the Audi darting ahead like a MIG searching for a dogfight. Overcome with dread, Felix left Sam and Maggie and, in the dark beside the road, ran behind the EuroVan. What had he been thinking to let Frances go? What would happen to her? How would she elude them? Would she think to leave the park's West Drive and go among its endless paths and driveways?

He crossed to the other side, trying to see beyond the bend in the road. The rain had created mists that gathered here and there like thin clouds. Then Sam was beside him, grabbing his arm.

"Felix, we don't have time for this! We've got to take Maggie where she can have this baby! You need to be helping her."

Felix kept his eyes on the misty darkness into which Frances had disappeared. "I know, I know. All right. Where? Where do we take her?"

"There's a tourist hotel a couple blocks down on 101st. Sink in the room, bathroom down the hall, but it's the closest, except for that huge youth hostel over on Amsterdam. It's not the place for us."

Angrily, Felix said, "Yes, and there's a police station between Amsterdam and Columbus!"

Sam sounded impatient, "I already told you—we can't do that."

Felix shook his head as they started back. "She can't walk, for God's sake."

"Hell, we'll carry her. No, I'll find a cab and have it drive in. Get her, Felix." Sam sprinted back toward Central Park West.

Felix went to Maggie and, in the dark between two lanterns, eased her to the ground and put her in his lap. He held the fetal stethoscope to her belly so he could hear the baby's heart. It seemed surreal that they were here on this moonless night, Maggie trying to have her baby in the open, on the ground. He couldn't see her, but he could feel her, knew the baby was lower still. She was courageously holding back so it could rest between contractions, holding back until they found a safe place for the birth.

Minutes ago, she'd offered him her life and he'd tried to take it. Again, Felix had the eerie thought he was a spectator in a life other than his own. Dr. Felix

Rossi couldn't think and do such things, couldn't let his sister drive off alone, pursued. He'd become someone else.

Maggie gripped his arm, whimpering quietly, and he took her pulse. He couldn't read her pressure because it was too dark to see. Her pulse was rapid. He felt a new contraction harden her stomach. Was the baby crowning? Even if it was, he couldn't see. Where were the blankets, where was his bag with the flashlight and supplies? He held her in his lap, not wanting to put her on the hard ground and search for them.

He whispered, "Can you tell where the baby's head is? I can't check. These gloves aren't sterile anymore. Can you hold on, Maggie?"

"I can't tell, not exactly," she said between pants, "but it feels like I can make it a little longer. Not much longer, Felix," she groaned. "Not much."

Felix let her grip his hands until the contraction eased.

"How do you feel?"

Maggie sounded exhausted, "Like a bowling ball is trying to come out of me!"

"Yes, of course."

"But you know what, Felix?" He could feel her body shift as she looked around, though there was nothing to see but scattered lanterns, casting solitary globes of light.

"Doesn't it look like all the constellations came down in this park tonight? It's like he's being born in the sky."

Felix had often thought the park's lanterns looked like fallen stars. As he gazed at them, something began to change inside him. It was his fear for Frances, his fear for Maggie. It was a dawning awareness that he, Felix, had caused their lives to be in danger and no one else. In pain and guilt, he watched Maggie's earthbound constellations shine.

He heard hurried footsteps and prayed it was Sam because, if not, he and Maggie couldn't escape. Whoever, whatever, tried to harm them now would succeed—and the fault was entirely his.

"Felix! Felix! Where are you?"

It was Sam.

"Sam, we're here," Maggie called.

"There's a van sitting at Boy's Gate," Sam said when he found them. "I saw another Audi S4 going north. I think there are two. I think they're patrolling the exits. They must know we're here. We can't get out. We've got to hide."

Felix lost control and sobbed. If what Sam said was true, the Range Rover would be stopped.

"Damn it, Felix! We don't have time!"

In his mind, he saw Frances dying. He heard her cries.

"You said you know the park better than me, Felix! Help us!"

Maggie whispered, "Sam, find his medical bag, get the blankets. He left them by the playground."

When Sam left, Maggie took Felix by the chin like he was a child and said, "Hush, now. Hush, now. God's watching over your sister. It's me and this baby who are in your hands. I don't have nobody else. My baby's coming, Felix, and he has nobody else. Hush, now."

Felix wiped away tears though more replaced them. Still, he helped Maggie stand then he lifted her in his arms. Keeping to the grass and the darkness, he struggled toward the stairs near Boy's Gate, stepping briefly under a lantern so Sam could see where they were. A siren wailed and Felix imagined Frances in a racing ambulance as her life ebbed away.

Sam came, tucked his gun in his pocket, gave Maggie the blankets and Felix his medical bag. Then he helped Felix carry her. Together they managed to hurry across the grass. Felix avoided the stairs as well as the footpath where the lanterns were as he tried to decide where they should go. They passed a large outcropping of the ancient bedrock that underlay most of Manhattan. He thought of climbing the grayish stone to search for a hiding place.

Then he remembered Glen Span Arch. "I know where."

They stayed near the footpath until they reached a rustic bridge and heard the sound of falling water. Two lanterns lit the bridge and the path. In their light, Felix saw the north end of a small lake called The Pool. On endless summer days, he and Frances had floated their boats there and waded in when the grownups weren't around. Weeping willows lined its banks and dropped their limbs over the dark water. Ducks and geese and city birds visited or made it their home. One was softly quacking, disturbed by their approach.

Felix pointed behind the farther lantern.

"Down there?" Sam asked.

"Yes. Glen Span Arch. West Drive crosses over it like a bridge. That's the waterfall in front of it you hear. It's rocky, like a cavern. Homeless people sleep there at times."

Sam kissed Maggie and said, "Here, take her. Let me go in first." When Felix did, Sam pulled out his gun. "Let's go."

They found the path that led to the bottom of the waterfall and there was Glen Span Arch. It looked like the huge open door of a rocky cathedral, except the roof, high above, was actually a road and the other side was open, just like this. Water flowed next to the walkway beneath the arch. On the other side, it emptied into a larger stream named The Loch. Beyond was the North Woods and wilderness.

Sam took out the flashlight so they could find their way.

To Felix, Glen Span Arch felt the same as in his childhood—like a majestic grotto in which ancient spirits dwelled. Even playing children whispered here beneath its boulders. At Glen Span Arch, only the waterfall raised its voice.

Felix watched as Sam went beneath the arch and found a small recess along the right wall. He picked up what seemed a pile of rags, and tossed them out the other side then spread blankets on the ground.

"Here, Maggie, my girl. Here's a nice, soft place to lie."

He helped Felix lower her then stood and looked around.

"This is a great place, Felix. One entrance, one exit. I can cover both sides with no trouble. All you have to do is take care of her, now."

Sam took out his gun and went back toward the waterfall.

Felix knelt next to Maggie, and in the ambient light from lanterns on the bridge above, he opened his bag. He spread out the sterile pads he'd brought. He laid out the instruments in his delivery kit. As he did, Maggie lay so quietly on her back, she seemed not to be laboring anymore. He slid a sterile pad beneath her, took the flashlight and looked between her thighs. To his relief, he didn't see the baby's head. She had held back. How, he didn't know.

"Maggie?"

Her answer was a groan of pain.

Felix retrieved the fetal stethoscope and listened, searching everywhere on her stomach for the heartbeat he didn't hear.

He shined the flashlight on her blood pressure monitor and grew frantic. It read 160/115. "Maggie, I can't hear the baby!"

When she opened her eyes, he saw deep circles around them.

"I'm tired, now. He is, too. Go on and take him from me, Felix. I can't help him anymore."

Instantly, Sam was there. "We're having none of that, Maggie. You've got to try for Frances, try for me! Please, sweetheart." He raised her upper body so she could brace herself against him. "Take a deep breath, Maggie, and push!"

"Sam, I can't."

He kissed her. "Yes, you can. Now push!"

"It's all right to try," Felix said, knowing he should do a Cesarean. "If it doesn't work, I'll take him. I promise."

Sam compressed his lips, but didn't say a word.

They waited for her, Felix too numb to pray for the child. Somewhere in these long months it had become Maggie's baby, not just a clone of Jesus. He watched Maggie take a breath, hold it, grit her teeth and bear down, trembling. She took in air and pushed again, then Felix saw the head briefly crown.

"He's coming, Maggie!" Felix whispered. His sorrow turned to wild, exuberant joy. "He's coming!"

Maggie grimaced in pain and Sam knelt beside her, trying to hug and coach her at once. "Push, Maggie, push!"

"No! Don't listen to Sam! Pause, Maggie," Felix said and they laughed at themselves, Maggie panting. It reminded Felix that childbirth was at once a beautiful miracle and a terrifying, painful, bloody roller coaster that not even the doctor could control. When life renewed itself, nature was in charge.

"Take another deep breath," Felix began, but other sounds interrupted.

Voices above the waterfall.

Sam and Felix exchanged a glance. Then Sam eased Maggie down to her elbows. He took her face in his hands, said, "Remember I love you," kissed her and was gone.

Maggie looked frightened as Sam tiptoed by, still she was relentless. She pushed because her baby was in trouble, though its first cry could mean their deaths.

Felix spread a second sterile cloth beneath her and watched, dumbfounded, as a red stain spread on it. Maggie was bleeding. That's why she'd been hypertonic. He lifted the cloth, aimed the flashlight at the dark blanket, and saw the blood had soaked through. He touched it in horror, not believing what it was. Then Felix realized whose life he had been leading tonight. It was his father's. Maggie's blood was his mother's blood. Their flight in the Range Rover and into Central Park was his parents' desperate escape into the Alps. Their infant son that died was this child, both born in the open. His mother had survived.

Would Maggie?

Her placenta was abrupting and tearing her apart. He looked down at the blood on his hand and in that moment chose Maggie above the child.

"No, Maggie, stop!"

She pushed again, her head bending to her chest. Maggie was delivering this baby to the world, finding strength when strength was gone, in silence pushing her life out with the child.

"Stop, Maggie, stop!"

Frantically, he pressed a sterile gauze pad against her perineum and checked her pressure. It had risen sharply to 170/120. He checked her peripheral reflexes at the ankle. They were over responsive. It was happening. She was going to convulse.

"Maggie! God, no!"

Maggie didn't answer. She grew quiet and still. He lifted the flashlight to her face and saw her gaze was fixed. He had to get the baby out or neither mother nor child would survive. But the head had slipped back into the birth canal.

There was no time to do it right.

Felix grasped his scissors and performed a deep episiotomy, cutting nearly to her rectum. He stripped the sterile covering from his forceps and inserted them in Maggie … killing the child, the mother or both, he had no way to know. The forceps touched the head and he nudged them into position behind the ears. He felt the forceps snap on and, gently but insistently, Felix pulled. At first the baby didn't budge so he used both hands and pulled hard until the head slipped and crowned. Then he put one hand on the baby and helped the shoulders emerge. The rest of the body quickly came, followed by the entire placenta and an awful gush of blood.

"Oh, God, what have I done?"

He had to stop Maggie's bleeding or she'd die in moments. He had to help the baby breathe. Tears filled his eyes as he lay it down. Swiftly he suctioned the throat, nose and clamped the cord, urging in a desperate cry, "Hold on Maggie. Please, please hold on!"

The child didn't move. It made no sound. Praying, Felix turned his attention to saving Maggie. He ground his fist down on her uterus, desperately trying to make it contract and staunch the river of blood. He kneaded it, pushed on it, to make the blood vessels close, pausing only long enough to thread a needle with suture and make fast stitches in her torn flesh. He dumped his bag's remaining contents on sterile cloths, planning to use the bag to elevate her feet before he rushed back to the child.

Then shots rang out—so loudly Maggie stirred, the seizure over.

One shot. A rush of wings as birds in The Pool took flight. A second shot, a third, then silence.

Maggie's gaze, full of terror, met his then traveled to the baby. Felix tried to hold her down, but she struggled until he had to release her. She picked up the baby. It lay limp in her weak arms.

"Oh, help him, help him," she said.

Felix held the baby upside down and flicked its feet, then vigorously rubbed it. It made a sharp, plaintive cry, which echoed in this grotto where ancient spirits dwelled. Avoiding its eyes, he gave the baby to Maggie and immediately rose to his feet, listening for approaching footsteps, for voices and not knowing what he'd do if they came. He thought of Frances and the shots they'd heard. He looked down and saw Maggie hug the baby, cradle it, kiss its tiny cheek, touch it everywhere, though it was covered in her blood and screaming—like any human, its death inherent in its birth. She raised her blouse and tried to nurse it, swaying as she sat, and the baby quieted.

"Lie down, Maggie. Let me help you." He'd only slowed her bleeding. It hadn't stopped.

She sat there, murmuring words of love to the baby at her breast and saying, "Sam's going to be all right. Don't you worry."

"Maggie, please! You've got to let me help you."

He pushed gently on her shoulder but she resisted and held the baby tighter, ignoring him. She bent and kissed its tiny hand, as if her life wasn't important anymore.

Wretched with sorrow, praying for his sister and that Sam would return, Felix watched her nurse her baby. If he didn't get help, she wouldn't survive. Her pulse was rapid, her breathing shallow. Mount Sinai was down this path, through these woods and across a meadow, but she'd never make it there.

"For God's sake let me help you!" he cried.

She didn't answer, only looked at him and smiled. Then, with the baby on her stomach, she fell back on the blankets Sam had laid. Felix worked like a madman, doing all he could.

Desperately he kneaded her uterus as the last truth dawned. His parents had no choice. Nazis forced the risks they took. Nothing had been forced on Felix. Instead of being a Moses, he'd been a plague on those who trusted him. He had always had a choice not to do this—not to abandon his sister to killers in the night, not to use Maggie's faith, take her virtue for his ends, risk her life. Not to spend Sam's great heart in an egoistic cause, as if God needed help from Felix to put someone in the world. Tonight, Felix was his father in all but one respect. Felix willfully endangered those around him—including those his father would have done anything to save.

Now he couldn't feel Maggie's pulse. This was no holy event, not the birth of quiet awe he had imagined. It was a violent, horrible disaster. He wished he could close his eyes. He didn't want to see her die.

When the monitor recorded no pressure or pulse, Felix stopped. Maggie was gone.

He had no right to hold her child but he had to find Frances. He had to care for the baby. He looked down at the blood on his hands and cried out The Salve Regina:

> Hail Holy Queen, Mother of Mercy,
> our life our sweetness and our hope.
> To thee do we cry, poor banished children of Eve;
> To thee do we send up our sighs, mourning and
> weeping in this valley of tears.

Gazing on Maggie's body, Felix shuddered and choked down sobs to complete his prayer. "Turn then, most gracious advocate, thine eyes of mercy on … on …" Felix changed the words, "on this woman I have killed and will mourn forever."

He saw a movement. Had Maggie stirred? To his wild joy and disbelief, her eyes opened.

"Lie still, Maggie," he said.

"Something's wrong with me, Felix!" she whispered. "I can feel it! What is it?"

Felix shined the flashlight on Maggie. She was right. Something was happening. Something inconceivable. Still he saw it. He saw the first tear the baby made in Maggie's body close. He saw the episiotomy he'd stitched only minutes ago, heal. He saw her blood flow stop and her flesh transform to what it was when he first examined her.

Felix grew speechless at the enormity of his sin, if he had harmed a woman God would choose to make a miracle for. Or perhaps God had planned this all along. But how could it be happening? Surely in the darkness, he'd misjudged her injuries. She'd only seemed to be dying, only seemed to be miraculously cured.

Maggie said, "Where's Sam?"

Felix was at first too stunned to respond. Then he scrambled forward and hugged her, crying, "Maggie, Maggie! You're all right! You're alive! Thank you, Maggie, thank you for what you did."

She held the baby in one arm and him in the other, whispering, "You're a big ole cry baby, Felix Rossi, you know that? Now sit up and tell me where Sam is."

Felix kneeled back on his heels, remembering the gunshots. "He's not back, Maggie. Can you stand? Can you walk? I've got to find Frances, but I can't leave you alone."

Maggie looked toward the waterfall, then back to the other exit from Glen Span Arch. "But isn't somebody else here? I could have sworn I heard somebody talking to Sam."

"No, Maggie. No one's here."

"I could have sworn—" Maggie's eyes opened, her hand went to her ear as if she were listening. "I thought I heard someone. I did. Sam was calling me, calling me, and then ... and then."

"What?"

She looked down at the child in her arms. "Clear as day I heard a voice say to Sam, *'I am he who has come in all ages. She is well. Do not be afraid.'*"

Chapter 61

Felix held the baby while Maggie wept and sang *Amazing Grace*—to tell the angels Sam Duffy was coming, she said. Felix worried she'd be heard, but the rocks from Glen Span Arch seemed to conspire otherwise and trapped the sounds.

He couldn't convince her Sam might be alive. Maggie said she felt him too deep in her soul for him to still be in the world. Anxiously, Felix gazed out toward the waterfall as she mourned, then down at the baby whose eyes hadn't opened. Was it Jesus? Wouldn't the Son of God have cured her from within her womb—stopped her seizure before she bled and almost died? It didn't matter anymore. It was her child. Felix was glad it had survived.

He touched her shoulder. "Maggie, we're not safe here. We've got to go. I've got to find Frances. You must try to get up."

He helped her stand and she leaned on him, weak from the birth. Together they hesitated at the opening through which they'd come. On any path this way out of the grotto, they might be seen. The other direction was dominated by forest. His arm around Maggie, they turned and went the other way. They crept along the footpath by the stream toward two rustic bridges beyond. He could hear Maggie's voice shaking as she hummed, *I once was lost but now I'm found.*

Even in the dark he knew his way. They reached an oval clearing and made out two old red oaks against the sky. He heard the cascade that ran beneath a log bridge and he turned right. When he reached a second bridge—a creek trickling beneath it—he turned right again.

In this way, they came unnoticed to Springbanks Arch, one of the park's most secluded spots. Lovers walked beneath it in the daytime. Dope addicts, muggers, and worse might huddle there at night. A moment ago, Felix wouldn't have cared if he died. Now he had to live to find Frances, get Maggie and her baby to safety. He had to be like his father, had to be their Sam, in case Sam had died.

He gathered courage and they went into the blackness beneath Springbanks Arch. No sooner had he entered than he stumbled over something in the dark. He heard a man's voice grumble—someone harmless taking shelter? Then a powerful hand gripped his, and brought him to his knees, though he struggled, holding the baby, and Maggie screamed.

"You could say excuse me, buddy," someone breathed in his face and Felix's stomach heaved from the smell.

Gut instinct told him not to fight. "Yes. Excuse me. Now please let us go."

Another voice grumbled, "It's a family, leave them alone," and Felix was released, was clear of the arch, he and Maggie clambering up the rocks that lined the steep banks beyond, his heart pounding, Maggie breathing hard from the climb. They gained the fence and ducked behind a tree as a light shone and passed, probably a park police cruiser looking for the source of the three shots.

He gave the baby to Maggie and lifted her over the fence, then climbed over it. They stood on the path that would take them past North Meadow to London Plane.

"I'm so tired," Maggie said. "I've got to rest. Let me hide in those dark trees there while you find Frances."

"But—"

Maggie was already heading for the trees. "You can't make time with me and the baby."

He helped her under the trees, made sure they couldn't be seen then returned to the path. As children, he and Frances had timed distances in the park. Walking, it would take twelve minutes to reach London Plane.

Felix ran.

Into North Meadow, past its baseball fields and soccer fields, the lights of New York shining around him in the distance—the twin towers of the San Remo to his right, Mount Sinai Hospital to his left. By a grace he couldn't comprehend, Maggie didn't need a hospital anymore. Felix sensed all else was in his hands.

He ran, gulping when breath was gone, to North Meadow's Recreation Center on the grass, onto the walkways that surrounded it, and the wide bridle path that wound through Central Park. He kicked up pebbles from the dirt and his feet raised dust where Frances and Adeline once rode their horses side-by-side—Moonless, the Arabian, and the Andalusian, King.

How he'd loved watching them ride. How he'd adored them without knowing all that mattered was them. He should have proposed marriage, not cloning, to Adeline. Frances had been trying to help him see.

On the bridle path, a dark, massive shape loomed before him and his despair turned to hope. It could only be London Plane. Like a rooted giant, its limbs stretched high. They stretched wide and spanned the bridle path, stretched back toward the Reservoir behind.

Where was his sister? If she wasn't here, how would he find her?

"Frances!" Felix called. He slumped against the huge trunk. It was like a graceful Doric column, its fluted depressions big enough to stand in.

"Frances, Frances!"

Felix circled the tree, distressed by the silence. What would he do if she didn't come? How would he find her? He had no street smarts like Sam. All Felix knew was to get to a phone, call his lawyer, have him buy private detectives, cops, commandos to scour Manhattan until they found her.

"Frances!"

He heard a rustle of leaves and saw a dark shape fall.

"Flix, sssshhhh, for goodness sake!"

She'd climbed the trunk and crawled out on the limb, just like when they were children.

Felix stumbled toward her on the grass, dropped to his knees and cried as he hugged the sister he adored.

"Flix, Oh, Flix. I've never seen you cry like this in your whole life. How's Maggie and the baby?"

"You wouldn't believe how well they are."

"Oh, wonderful! I thought I'd lost those creeps and I was trying to get to you. I knew you'd go to Glen Span Arch. I just knew it. You always loved it so. They must have doubled back and found me. Sam shot at them so I could get away."

Felix hugged her tighter.

"Sam's okay? He's with Maggie?"

"No. Sam didn't come back, Fran. Maggie thinks—"

He couldn't finish, but Frances understood. Then it was the same as when they were children, hiding in the shadows of London Plane, pretending they were in Camelot escaping Sir Modred and crying because King Arthur was dead.

"Poor Sam. Poor, brave Sam," she said. "We're going home now, Flix."

"What? Where on God's earth is home?"

"Come on. Get up, now." Frances stood and pulled his arm. "We're getting Maggie and the baby and going home."

"How? Maggie's covered in blood. We can't drive the Range Rover so we don't even have a car! And they're still out there." Felix stared toward the faint lights of Fifth Avenue.

"Ssssh! Come on, Flix."

She led him down the bridle path to East Drive and past the playground at 96th. They exited the park a block from the building where they lived, Felix protesting all the way. But instead of turning right toward home, she went left and stopped at an old Buick. The window rolled down when she approached. A young couple looked out. They looked in love, like his parents had, in the only photo they had of them when they were young.

Frances bent to the woman, "Any more news?"

"OLIVE chased a blue van away from the park and two S4s. We've got the park surrounded, but they might come back."

"OLIVE?" Felix said. "But how did you know?"

"It's right on the website to look out for a blue van and an Audi, especially if they seem to be chasing anyone," the woman said.

Frances chuckled. "How much for your dress as well as the car?"

Felix looked at his sister in surprise, then opened his wallet and peeled off bills. He had all the money with him. They turned their backs while the woman took off the dress and put on her husband's jacket. Then he reached in his pocket to find a particular name Sam gave him in case of emergency.

Two hours later, Daniel and Agnes Crawford, along with their maid, Hetta Price, and an as-yet unnamed child, boarded a Gulfstream V jet plane which revved its engines, taxied to the runway, and took off from Teterboro airport in New Jersey, piloted by a friend of Sam's.

Chapter 62

At Mach 0.87 forty thousand feet above the Atlantic Ocean, the pilot radioed their estimated time of arrival ahead. They'd had no way to search for Sam. He wouldn't have wanted them to. He wanted Maggie and her baby safe. They landed at Turin International Airport at six o'clock, less than two hours from sunset and the start of shabbat, the Jewish sabbath, but true to his word, Uncle Simone was there. Frances had called him on the cell phone that belonged to the couple in the Buick and said they were in danger. Uncle Simone had replied, "Come home."

When their uncle saw them, he clasped his hands and exclaimed, "Baruch Atah Adonai Eloheinu Melech ha-olam, shehecheyanu v'kiyamanu, v'higiyanu la'zman hazeh."

In Italian he told Felix it was the *Shehecheyanu*, a blessing recited in praise and thanksgiving. It meant, "Blessed are you, Lord our God, king of the universe who has protected us and sustained us and brought us through to this great day."

Now Felix sat next to his uncle as he drove through Turin's streets—Frances and Maggie in back with the baby. Maggie was physically well, as if she'd never carried a child, but she'd wept the whole flight. As for her baby, he resembled her in no respect but one. Maggie had a birthmark shaped like a crescent moon beneath her chin. The child did, too. Otherwise, to Felix's eye, it could have been any middle eastern woman's child. They would never be sure who he really was. Still Felix had the urge to whisper near the baby.

They drove into the vast arcaded Piazza Vittorio, the dome of the church of Gran Madre di Dio looming on the green hill beyond. They crossed the River Po and ascended behind the church to the Strada Sei Ville, a private road of homes perched on the emerald hillside.

Uncle Simone stopped before the black iron gates their father's letter had described and inserted a card in the lock. Down a short drive, they came to the large three-story villa of stucco, stone and brick where their father had been born.

Felix felt transported back in time to a world that had awaited their return. They ascended the double stone staircase and a smiling woman met them. When she held out her arms, Maggie let her take the baby and she cooed to it in Italian. It was Silvia, Uncle Simone's wife. Cousin Letizia and another woman came and fussed over him, and Maggie smiled a little for the first time since they'd left.

Frances stood among them. Felix had never seen such happiness on her face. "There's someone else here, Flix," she said. "I told her to come when I saw trouble starting."

Silhouetted in a doorway, he saw a familiar shape. At first he didn't believe she could be real. It was Adeline.

"Will you forgive me?" Adeline said to Felix, "I just couldn't bear it."

"It's me who needs forgiveness," Felix said.

She asked to see the baby, looked down on his face, then hugged Maggie. Then Felix took Adeline in his arms, her spirit that had loved him so, returned.

The Fubinis applauded as they kissed, as if seeing the completion of a love story begun in this house long ago.

When Uncle Simone announced they must prepare for shabbat, they went to bathe and change clothes, so that eighteen minutes before sunset, the sabbath service could begin. Adeline came to Felix's room. This time, she didn't have to persuade him to make love.

Once the family gathered in the dining room, Uncle Simone brought two tissue-wrapped packages and opened them. One held a midnight blue yarmulke with fine embroidery at its edge. It had been his father's. The other held a scarf of delicate black lace, his mother's.

"Felix, Frances, if you would like to wear them tonight," Simone said, "you may. They are yours to keep as remembrances."

Felix gazed at the garment of his lost faith, at the uncle who resembled his father: the same salt and pepper beard, the same kind round eyes. He didn't care anymore whether he was Catholic or Jewish. Family was family. God was God.

"I'll wear it, Uncle."

Silvia should have lit the candles, but she stood aside and motioned to Frances. For the first time in her life, Frances lit the shabbat candles, her eyes shining.

The next morning, in the cellar of Turin's Great Synagogue, in a dazzling little *Tiempietto* used for daily worship, Felix stood among the men, wearing the blue yarmulke, a prayer shawl called the tallit around his shoulders. The rabbi stood in the lavishly Baroque golden Tevah at the center of the little amphitheater. Another man in the Tevah held the huge ornate scrolls of the Torah, taken from the temple's golden Ark.

Adeline, Frances and Maggie were in the women's galleries above, where they could come and go as they pleased. Only men had a duty to pray in temple, Uncle Simone had explained. How could God compel a woman to come to temple, when she might have to tend a sick child? Still it seemed that most of Turin's thousand Jews were there.

No part of the room seemed forbidden to the children. As the men's deep voices rose in chant and song, the children climbed up and down the amphitheater's steps between their mothers and their fathers. One climbed on the Tevah and pulled on the rabbi's robe. During the service, men took their children under their prayer shawls and said blessings over them.

The ceremony was stunning, ancient, wondrous. Whenever Felix glanced up to the women's galleries, Frances's face was wet with tears and Adeline was radiant, gazing at the children. She'd been in his arms all night. Whenever he saw Maggie, another woman was beside her, holding the baby.

Back at the house, it all ended.

No sooner had they returned, than the telephone rang. Felix paid no attention until it kept ringing and no one answered. Simone, Silvia and Letizia continued with what they were doing as if they hadn't heard.

"Shouldn't you answer it?" Felix asked.

Simone smiled. "Oh no. We can't break shabbat. They will call back tomorrow."

From across the room, Silvia added in a cheerful voice. "Felix, it is probably one of his Christian friends. He has friends everywhere. I suppose people love him, because he loves them. Your uncle knows everyone!"

Simone shrugged, as if he enjoyed this chiding from his wife.

The phone rang again. Two rings, then it stopped.

This time, both Simone and Silvia paused and glanced at the phone.

It rang again once and stopped. Silvia put down the tray of small sandwiches she carried and moved close to her husband.

Again the phone rang and this time Simone strode purposefully toward it, Silvia beside him, and answered.

"Pronto," he said. His expression grew serious as he listened.

He hung up, went to Maggie and tenderly stroked the baby's head. "Yesterday when I received the call from Frances about a mother and a baby needing to be hidden from pursuers, I was not surprised. You must tell me now, if you will. This is the child they speak of on the news? Your baby is the clone?" He looked at Felix. "And my nephew has produced it?"

When Felix translated, Maggie nodded.

Uncle Simone sighed. "Well, then, so it is true. Our people will not believe in your son, Maggie, in the same way others may. You realize that?"

"It doesn't matter," she said. "I know God sent him, just like he sent Moses and all the rest. The Buddha. Confucius. Others, too. Jesus said there were many mansions in his father's house. Couldn't that be what he meant? There are probably other special people here on earth right now. Angels, good spirits.

Whatever you want to call them."

She looked down at her baby. "He's one of them."

Uncle Simone listened to Felix translate, then he smiled. "As you say, it doesn't matter. He turned to Felix. "Nephew, I am sorry. You must take up your hat."

Felix wondered where he'd heard that expression before, then he remembered. It was how his parents had been warned that the Nazis were near. Alarmed, Felix asked, "Who was on the phone?"

"One of those I have asked to help me observe. You have Adeline to thank. She did not keep your secret. We are prepared." Felix pulled Adeline close as Simone continued. "We watched before when the Nazis were here. Italians are good at it. Someone has learned you have family here. Someone has inquired after you."

"Oh Lord!" Maggie cried when she understood what Simone had said. "Am I going to be on the run forever? Haven't I lost enough? Why can't I just be left alone with my baby?"

Uncle Simone patted Maggie's hand. "If you will let us, we will offer you a haven. We will hide you and protect you. Our people know how to do this. There is a place, if Felix and Frances are willing. A perfect place."

"Of course we are," Frances said.

In the cellar of the house, Uncle Simone opened a hidden door and led them down a dusty corridor, pointing out that it was permitted to break the sabbath if lives were at stake. He said the corridor hadn't been used since the Nazi occupation. At the end of it, Simone knocked on a wooden wall. It opened and he shook hands with a man and his family who lived in another house on the hillside. They handed Simone a set of keys, then entered the corridor going toward Simone's home. A few moments later Felix and the others were in the neighbor's van, driving down Strada Sei Ville. As they passed Simone's house, Felix glimpsed the shabbat candles through a window and a family sitting down to the shabbat meal. To all appearances, the Fubinis were still at home.

At five o'clock that afternoon, Maggie was in her new home in a village seventy-two miles away from Turin. A woman from the village was already up at the house, thanks to Simone, and orders had been placed for the things Maggie would need. Felix gave her his remaining money, keeping only enough to return to New York. He arranged with Uncle Simone to disguise future transfers from his bank in New York to one in the village.

"Will she be safe?" Frances asked.

"Count upon us," Simone said. "Count upon the Italians. In time they will realize someone is here in hiding with a child, but should a stranger come and ask after her, they will say, 'You are mistaken. There are no black women here.'

Should the stranger insist, they will say, 'Yes, you are right. There was once a black woman here, but she is gone and we don't know where she is.' Meanwhile they will have called us, told us to, *Take up her hat.* Do not worry, niece. Ninety percent of Italy's Jews survived the Nazis. In this country, we know how to save a life."

The baby nearby in a basket, Felix and Maggie spent the final moments alone, holding hands, finding it almost impossible to speak. Though physically he knew her as intimately as a physician could, he felt awkward now. She was different. She seemed less a part of the world, whether because of Sam's death or the child's birth, he didn't know.

"Sam's not blaming you," she said. "He's safe. He's right here in my heart." She put her head on Felix's shoulder and cried while he held her.

"I can't believe I'm leaving you and the baby, Maggie, but I've got to go. I have to go back and convince them a clone never existed. Afterward, I can't be anywhere near you and the child. Not soon, anyway. Neither can Frances."

He saw the same courage settle on Maggie's face that was there the day she asked to be the one.

"You think you can convince them?" was all she asked.

"Whatever it takes, I'll do."

They didn't talk anymore, only hugged by the beautiful lake.

Then Simone, Silvia and Letizia drove south toward Turin while Felix, Frances and Adeline drove north in the taxi they had hired. They were fortunate in their driver. His name was Piero. He spoke English. He knew the route they asked to travel. He paid little attention to *Keep Out* signs and managed to cheer them with his jokes.

He drove them straight to Domodossola and helped them find the priest's house and the woods behind it where Felix and Frances's parents hid from the Germans on otto settembre over fifty years ago. He drove them into the beautiful Valley Vigezzo their parents traveled in a hay wagon, watching slopes become hills and hills become mountains, their peaks obscured by clouds. They reached a small town called Re only miles from the Swiss border, and he found the local inn where their parents had been sleeping when the Germans came.

After searching, he took them to the low woodshed across the tracks where their parents had fled.

Back in the car, they followed the railroad tracks over hills and valleys and streams. Piero stopped, as they asked him to, only a few kilometers from the Swiss border, where the railroad crossed the top of a small hill. On either side, trestles rose from the valley floor to support the tracks. They heard the rush of water over jagged rocks.

It was Felix who climbed down to the little clearing as Adeline and Frances watched from the road above. He found the tallest tree and kneeled before it. He planted a Star of David where the infant body of his brother lay and said the Kaddish Uncle Simone had taught him. Then he went back to Adeline and Frances and they drove across the border to the town where his parents had stayed that awful night, their child dead, his father's face turned from all they'd known.

They had lunch in a restaurant Piero found and Felix wondered if his parents had eaten there, too, making desperate plans like them.

Chapter 63

September 12—New York

Dr. Felix Rossi, microbiologist, MD, former head of a scientific team—got out of a taxi before The University Club on its famous corner at Fifth Avenue and 54th. Like The Harvard Club to which Felix also belonged, The University Club had been designed by the great architects McKim, Meade & White. Nothing but the best for the world's premier private gathering spot.

Frances came from the taxi and gripped his hand. She wore mannish slacks under a double-breasted jacket, its collar turned aggressively up. She'd slicked back her auburn hair to look as fierce as possible, but he could feel the perspiration on her palm.

Adeline got out of the taxi behind her and held his other hand with a serenity created by her belief in God.

"Ready now?" he whispered to them.

"Yes," Adeline whispered back. "It's perfect, you know. It's the most irredeemably stuffy place in New York. People will believe you just because you're here."

Unnoticed they made their way through pedestrians on the sidewalk until they reached the granite steps. Leaving wouldn't be this easy.

They ascended under a royal blue canopy and were let in by a dour-looking man uniformed in green. He guarded the club from his podium just inside the door.

Opposite them in the first floor lobby was a Terrazzo wall, framed by a cortile of eight Connemara marble pillars. Above the fireplace, a carved panel of white statuary marble depicted full-armored Athena, the goddess of wisdom, next to a young Greek holding a torch—probably Phidippides, the ancient messenger who ran twenty-six miles in about three hours. Repeating the run to tell of Athens's victory at the Battle of Marathon, Phidippides was said to have dropped dead on the spot.

Felix didn't enjoy the thought of death following delivery of a message, given the task before him.

Through a wide Numidian marble doorway, an old man stared at them, then up at the gold-coffered ceiling in the Reading Room where he stood. Behind him, gilded pilasters, set into red velvet walls, framed high arched windows draped in gold. The club outdid Italian Renaissance architecture in its imitation of it.

The man looked lost in the palatial room. He looked small and tweedy and bookish, as if his eyes had focused on nothing but words all day. He looked harmless. Was he?

Felix stared at the old man, then convinced himself everything was fine. He said, "We have a little time. Would you like to go to the tea service at the Theodore Dwight Room? "

"Not that old paneled, woody place," Frances said.

Felix shook his head. "No, not the dining room, The Dwight Lounge, remember? The yellow room?"

Frances made an impudent sister face. If he'd listened to her warnings, they wouldn't be in such danger now. They turned left down the marble hall and entered the yellow room, full of people sipping tea, eating scones and such.

As soon as they entered, a long-jawed, bronze-haired Englishman turned, as if he'd felt Felix's gaze. The imperious stare was gone. Felix saw remorse on Jerome Newton's aristocratic face.

Newton came forward, his hand extended. "Dr. Rossi. How can I apologize for … I mean I wish I'd never—"

Felix delivered a cold glare. "You weren't invited."

"Flix—" Frances began.

Felix ignored her. "Leave or I'll have you thrown out."

Jerome looked resigned. "Sorry, you can't. I'm a non-resident member of the club, though I've not had much occasion to use it. Too many rules, a bit stuffy, don't you think?" He gazed around. "Even castles hundreds of years more ancient in Merry Ol' are done up a bit cheerier than this."

Felix wasn't yet able to forgive Jerome. "What do you want?"

Jerome Newton looked haunted for a moment. "I just wondered if you could direct me to Sam Duffy. I owe him an apology as well."

Frances quietly said, "Read the obituaries in the newspapers you help write."

They left Jerome Newton in the yellow Dwight Lounge, slumped in a chair and staring at a half-eaten scone.

In the lobby, reporters were arriving and being escorted upstairs to prevent them from taking unauthorized photographs in the world's premier private club. The invitations had been personal, reserved for a handful of press elite on condition of secrecy until after the event. Still Jerome Newton had heard.

They took the elevator up to the ninth floor Cathedral Rooms and entered the one reserved for them. Reporters were already there, filling their plates from two long tables that groaned with lobster, caviar, prime rib canapes, and wine from the club's outstanding cellars. Tasteful floral arrangements accented the room. Under original plaster ceilings, television cables ran across the floor.

The world was ready for the news.

A waiter offered him champagne. Felix gulped it. Then he seated Adeline and Frances and went to the podium.

The media's upper crust took their seats and fell politely silent. These were no paparazzi.

"Good afternoon," he said, his eyes adjusting to the glare of klieg lights training on him. "Most of you already know me. I'm Dr. Felix Rossi, a microbiologist and a physician. I organized the third scientific investigation of the Shroud of Turin."

"Louder, please."

"Yes, of course."

Felix felt his throat begin to close, his palms sweat. He'd once been a devout and respected man. At minimum, this press conference would ruin his career. Financially he wouldn't suffer, but neither the Church nor his colleagues would ever trust him again. He didn't care.

"You've heard reports that I stole threads from the Shroud of Turin."

The room subtly buzzed.

Felix looked into the cameras. "The reports are true."

Instant silence.

"Last January I stole two blood-soaked threads and extracted the DNA. I apologize to the Catholic Church for my breach of their trust and will accept whatever censure they impose." He paused, swallowing. "From the stolen threads I obtained a large cluster of neutrophils—white blood cells found in new wounds." Again he paused, knowing it would take a moment to sink in that these must have formed in Christ's wounds as he was dying on the cross. "From these neutrophils I extracted the DNA of a human male."

The calm ended.

Photographers scrambled to the podium. In blinding eruptions of light, they snapped pictures of the mad scientist confessing his success. A TV camera zoomed in on his face. Felix barely noticed. His thoughts were on a pair of piercing eyes he couldn't see, the face large like an idol's and framed by platinum hair.

He cleared his throat. "Using Nuclear Transfer, I replaced the DNA in a donor egg with DNA from the Shroud and caused the egg to multiply. Then I re-implanted the egg in the woman who donated it—" He looked down, whispering a prayer for her then he gazed into the camera and the unseen eyes. "Maggie Johnson, a thirty-five-year old black woman from Harlem who'd been my housekeeper for five years. At approximately midnight on September 6th, she gave birth to a male child."

Everyone still seated rose to their feet in a total lack of decorum. The room exploded with shouted questions. Felix raised his voice, calling, "He was premature! Premature!"

In the pandemonium, those few who heard him shouted to their neighbors to be quiet. Eventually, silence was restored.

Felix stared into the camera at the intimidating eyes he couldn't see. "I couldn't save him. I tried. He was two months premature. We never made it to the hospital. The mother bled to death during delivery."

From the second row, Jerome Newton asked, "Are you saying that after … all this—"

Jerome faltered and Felix knew he was thinking of Sam.

"The Jesus clone is dead," Felix said.

In the ninth floor Cathedral Room of the world's premiere private club, those who had been standing sat down, or lowered their heads, or sadly leaned on the velvet walls.

————

Fifth Avenue

Felix Rossi, Frances Rossi, and Adeline Hamilton stood on the red carpet in front of the Fifth Avenue building where the Rossis lived, and where they had never expected to return.

Aware that eyes no doubt watched from above, Felix gazed across the wide sidewalk. The building's heavy glass front door with its bronze handle seemed miles away. He heard the neigh of a horse being ridden in Central Park and the din of New York traffic going by.

"Flix," Frances said. "I feel we're standing at the gates of hell."

He let go of her hand, put his arm across her shoulder and Adeline's, resisting the urge to look up toward the penthouse. "We are."

A strange man appeared behind the glass door and slowly opened it. He wore a long green coat and black-brimmed hat. Felix knew he was more than a doorman, just like Sam whom he'd replaced. In secret he worked for the penthouse occupant.

"Not exactly Sam Duffy, your friendly Irish doorman," Frances whispered as they started to walk.

"Ssshhh," Felix said, though she was right. This doorman was nothing like good natured, loyal Sam … loyal to the death. This man was sullen, wiry, furtive … had soulful puppy eyes on a haunted and haunting face—a newborn's gaze above skeletal cheeks.

The man came out and stood with his back to the door, blocking the way. He tipped his hat. "Good morning, sir. Ladies. He nodded to each of them. "Who are you visiting?"

Felix flipped straight black hair off his face and extended his hand, putting on deliberate charm in a way he'd never done.

"You must be new. I'm Dr. Rossi. I live on the eighth floor."

As the doorman returned the handshake, his eyes registered no surprise

"Excuse me, Dr. Rossi. I started working here since you've been gone. I'm Rave."

"Hello, Rave. Let me introduce my sister, Frances Rossi."

"Hello, Miss Rossi."

Frances only nodded, but Adeline held out a steady, dry palm for him to shake and casually said, "Hello, Rave. We've been traveling."

The puppy eyes smiled and Rave opened the door.

Briefly Felix glanced to his left and saw another, smaller door—the entrance to Sam's old apartment. Sam had revealed what was in a hidden room behind the kitchen pantry: monitors for pinhole cameras, receivers for mikes.

Now the new doorman lived there and had access to the hidden room Sam had never really used.

Rave preceded them down into the lobby, a domed chandelier above their heads. Frances had been on the tenants' committee that helped pick it out.

As Rave pushed the button for the elevator, Felix stared at the back of his head, feeling hatred.

"You have luggage?" the doorman asked, turning around.

"Soon," Felix said. "It's being shipped."

Felix saw interest in Rave's eyes at the prospect of learning from where the luggage would come. Norway, as it happened. They'd flown from Turin to Oslo to London, covering their tracks with the fake passports on the Oslo/London leg. Felix had their luggage sent to Norway from Cliffs Landing. It would be shipped home to Fifth Avenue from a yacht moored in the Oslo fjord.

The elevator came. When they stepped inside and the doors closed, Felix knew in moments they wouldn't be alone. He knew Rave had rushed to the monitors in the hidden room, to spy on them for Mr. Brown.

Felix squeezed his sister's now-trembling hand, hugged Adeline, proud of their unconcerned expressions. No one would ever guess they knew they were being watched.

They stepped from the elevator into their private eighth floor lobby. In recesses on either side of the double doors were two blue and yellow vases intricately patterned in the majolica style—just where they'd been eight months ago.

Felix unlocked the doors and switched on the soft hall light, then stood back so Adeline and Frances could enter. They walked the corridor's long carpet and stopped, as planned, before the seventeenth century silver crucifix that hung above the ebony prie dieu in the hall.

Felix knelt on its red cushion and clasped his hands, the religious turmoil in which he'd produced the clone burned away in the agony of that night in Central Park. Never again would he care whether he worshiped in synagogue or church—as long as those he loved were safe and happy.

Behind him, Adeline and Frances made the sign of the cross on their brows, over their hearts, on their shoulders. They could light no sabbath candles here.

Felix prayed aloud. "Father, forgive me for not listening to my sister, who predicted the calamity that occurred."

He felt Frances touch his shoulder.

"Forgive me for not listening to Adeline, who in her love tried to save us."

Felix bowed his head and real tears came. "Forgive me, if you can, for Sam Duffy and Maggie Johnson's deaths."

He heard Adeline breathe sadly and Frances begin to cry.

"Most of all, forgive me, forgive me …" Felix thought of Sam dying to save Frances, Maggie and the child. He needed to be crying to speak these lies in prayer to God. "Forgive my incompetence. At my hands Your Son died a second time."

He thought of the questions asked at the press conference. *Where are they buried?* Felix said he'd had them cremated to avoid disturbance to their graves. He was spending a fortune to credibly back up his story for those who might check. Maggie had no family, just her friend Sharmina. When Maggie phoned her, Sharmina swore on the sacred heart of Jesus she would never say a word. He knew the press would besiege him here at the building, but Brown would see the Rossis weren't kicked out as a result—not until Brown learned what he wanted to know.

Behind him, Adeline sobbed.

Frances knelt and hugged him. "Sam and Maggie forgive you, Flix, I know they do."

They said the Our Father together then Felix rose.

As planned, Frances walked ahead of them to her room. She pulled her collar ominously up as Adeline lingered and buried her face in his neck. She clung to Felix—the altar boy who'd wanted to become a priest.

Together they walked into the guest room where she often stayed. He kissed her, held her to him, put his lips to her ear, and whispered, "Courage, darling," then he sat down, loosening his tie, unbuttoning his cuffs. He watched the woman he loved take off her gray jacket, kick off her shoes, unbutton her slim pink skirt from around a tiny waist, knowing his sister in her bedroom was undressing, too.

He hoped Rave the doorman would mistake for passion the rage that shivered through him, knowing they were watched and would be night and day—as they showered, as they slept. They were going to let it happen. They were going to let Rave devour Frances's and Adeline's undressed bodies until they'd convinced him of three lies. First, that the Rossis didn't know about the hidden room. Next, that they didn't know who Sam had really worked for. Most of all, they had to convince Rave they didn't know that their neighbor, Mr. Brown—who lived in the penthouse on the floor above their heads—was the one who'd tried to kill them and the clone.

His heart pounding, Felix said *The Universal Prayer* in his mind.

> Lord, I believe, increase my faith.
> I trust in you; strengthen my trust.
> I love you: let me love you more and more.
> I am sorry for my sins: deepen my sorrow …

Trembling, he took Adeline in his arms.

———

Arona, Italy

"No, Signora, resti, resti!"

The woman stood in the doorway of a little yellow villa two kilometers outside of Arona on Lake Maggiore's vast and beautiful shore. The villa had brick and stucco walls, arched windows, a tiled overhanging roof, and a small front balcony supported by spiraled columns. Above its garden wall, a bower of roses grew. There a young Jewish couple who'd looked barely old enough to wed had been photographed, ignoring the sunshine, the birds, the glorious lake beyond—having eyes for one another alone.

Maggie stood on the spiral-columned porch of her new home and stared at the woman she'd known for less than forty-eight hours, who was trying to make her stay inside. Her name was Antonella. She lived in the village. She could be trusted. That's all Maggie had been told.

Antonella's thin arms stretched out to take the baby Maggie cradled.

Firmly, Maggie said, "Antonella! Grazie! No, okay?"

From the pocket of her print dress, Antonella pulled out the dictionary she'd been consulting all day then she looked up and said, "Nurse bambino. Nurse!"

Maggie's eyes filled with tears. That's what she'd been trying to do, but he wouldn't take her breast, and Maggie's milk seemed to be drying up in response. She knew it was just anxiety from the movers who'd been tromping in and out all day, bringing in God-knows-what that Felix had ordered—and everybody speaking a language she didn't understand. It was the piles of boxes Antonella had been unpacking, like a sharp-eyed female eagle foraging for things to feather Maggie's new nest. It was the Black Madonna statue that had mysteriously arrived, an elegant, long-waisted woman, seated with a child on her lap—a breathtaking work of art, done in walnut, except for the virgin's necklace and the jeweled gold crowns on their heads. They had wide noses, like Maggie did. The note had said it was a copy of the Notre Dame De Rocamadour from twelfth century France, but there was no signature or card, saying who sent it.

Maggie couldn't communicate and tell Antonella and the movers to stop all this fuss and check to see if the back doors were locked, pick up the phone and make sure it still worked, test the strength of the filigreed ironwork at the arched front windows—side by side and still uncovered because the house had been empty before she came. She'd been made to lie down when what she really wanted was to explore the villa's grounds to find the best way out, get a knife, get a gun, stand watch because those who killed Sam would kill her child if they found him.

Wondering how she'd ever be safe in a place that felt so foreign, Maggie had realized where she wanted to go.

"I'll be back, Antonella," Maggie said and hurriedly descended the stairs, the child she'd named Jess in her arms. She walked beneath the roses, crossed the driveway, the short lawn. She came to the stone steps that descended on right and left. They were nearly overgrown with pink and purple hortensia bushes, the flowers fat and densely petaled. Climbing down, she reached the villa's shore-side property. The lake house was to the left, tucked under overhanging tree limbs. The concrete porticiollo with its white railings stretched into the lake in the center. Two white crow's nests with lanterns in them, guarded either side of its far opening. Once a boat must have sailed between them, coming in and going out. To the right of the porticiollo, a Weeping Willow dropped its tendrils into the lake as if it had wept too long.

Maggie went to the lake house and out onto its wide deck over the water where she'd said goodbye to Felix. No one would look for her here. They'd first go to the villa, giving her time to hide on the pebble-covered bank beneath the deck.

Feeling safe, now, she kneeled with Jess on the wooden planks and whispered Jesus' words on Gethsemane, " 'Abba, Father, everything is possible for you! Take this cup from me!' "

She waited for God to answer her prayer by putting a feeling in her heart, like always, but all she felt was a soft wind blowing from the hills behind her. All she saw were small whitecaps being churned up on the bright waters. Air dense with the smell of lake water, rich earth, and flowers filled her lungs and she let the wind dry her tears.

"I know I'm supposed to thank you, Lord," Maggie said aloud, "and I do. Thank you for restoring my body. Thank you for giving me this place where I can raise Jess. Help me keep him safe. Thank you for Uncle Simone and the people at the synagogue in Turin who have hidden us and who will teach him as he grows. Help me show my gratitude to them."

She bent in pain. It was physical. It was the memory of a kiss, of a body whose weight she'd never feel on her own.

"Sam Duffy loved me," she whispered to the lake.

She gazed north to the gola. Felix had told her it was Italian for throat. There Lake Maggiore narrowed and gentle slopes rose on either side, defining the south basin. Beyond it lay the distant Alps, shrouded in smoky haze. Across the lake, the stark green hills of Angera looked primeval against the chalky cliff and haunting sky.

"Jess, look," she said. "This is your home, darling." She uncovered his face a little but he was still sleeping, like a darkly beautiful cherub who'd stumbled to earth and lost his wings.

Maggie slipped her little finger into his hand but he barely gripped it. Why wouldn't he wake? Had she and Felix done right to bring him back into the world?

"Wake up, sweetheart, wake up!" she urged, touching his cheek. "It's your mama calling. You've got to wake up. There's a whole world, here, waiting for you darling, especially me. Do you know how much I yearned for you? Wanted a baby all my life, but never had a man, no one took a second look, so I figured God was saving me for something. It turned out to be you."

Maggie unbuttoned her dress, rubbed his cheek, put her breast to his mouth, trying to start the rooting reflex that, according to the baby books, should make him latch on.

When he didn't, she lifted her face to the sky. "Oh God, why did you let him come if you plan to take him? Don't do that, don't! Please, please. You've already taken Sam, don't take Jess from me."

She cried, rocking him in her arms, and through her tears, saw swans in a corner of the porticiollo. Their necks curled down, two adults surrounded a poor little baby who was obviously deformed. A black webbed foot grew on its little back. She moved closer to the beautiful creatures, grateful for Jess's perfect body, as if God had revealed her blessings, then wrapped his arms around her and asked her to be strong.

"I'll try. I'll believe, no matter what. Even if you take him," she murmured, "Not my will, but thine."

Maggie closed her eyes, lifted her face to the wind, and sang the tune Sam Duffy had always whistled: Too-ra-loo-ra-loo-ral, Too-ra-loo-ra-li. She sang in a rich contralto, like she'd sung gospels back in the 131st Street Baptist Church, its neon cross a talisman against sin in Harlem nights. In the distance thunder rolled, as if heavenly drums beat an accompaniment to her song.

Still singing, Maggie opened her eyes and slowly realized some of the branches extending above her head were from a dogwood. According to legend, Jesus' cross came from a dogwood tree. It would drop its white blossoms on the deck in the spring, thorny crowns at their centers, edges spotted brown-red like blood. She drew in her breath, lowered her eyes, and prayed.

In the silence she heard Jess begin to cry. She felt her milk come in response.

Eagerly, tremblingly she put him to the breast and this time felt him suck. Maggie settled onto the deck's wooden planks and nursed her baby, feeling her milk flow into him, feeling as if life itself was being gathered from every part of her and going into him. She wept with joy, but silently, her eyes gazing down in adoration on her child—amazed to be the woman who'd given birth to the Lamb of God.

The End

About the Author

J R Lankford is the author of the mystery/thriller *The Crowning Circle*, which was selected by BookBrowse.com for its 2001 *Best of the Year* list. She lives with her husband in Texas where she is at work on her next novel.

My research for this novel was greatly assisted by the remarkable website, http://www.shroud.com, maintained by Barrie M. Schwortz, photographer for the 1978 Shroud of Turin Research Project. Barrie kindly answered several of my questions concerning the Shroud, for which I thank him.

This book has also benefited from the expert contributions of the following: Lynn Hoffman, who gave information on Judaism and whose PhD dissertation in Anthropology, *The Myth of the Maritime Culture*, suggested details of Sam's background to me; Professor Levi Raffaello who gave so generously of his knowledge of Turin's history; Silvia Raffaello who suggested Arona and Domodossola as locations for the novel; Piero Giachino, the excellent driver and translator during the trip in which I fell in love with northern Italy; Raffaello Lampronti and the gracious staff at Turin's Great Synagogue for their help and welcome; Dr. Bernard Glick who explained a few fundamental concepts in microbiology to me; Scott Kimbrell, M.D., who corrected several of my emergency medicine mistakes as did Sue Asher, M.D.; Mildred Crosby, R.N. BSN, RDMS, who provided information on obstetrics; Alan Carter who commented on merchant marine aspects of the story; Garth Stein, who made several helpful suggestions; Nancy Klistner whose personal guided tour of Central Park led me to Glen Span Arch; my brother, John Rhines, who told me about *One if by land, Two if by sea* and shared his knowledge of Catholicism; and my brother Dr. Jesse Rhines who showed me his New York and suggested several details of Maggie's background.

Any remaining errors in specifics are due to a writer's imagination at work on their advice. None are guilty of the fanciful use to which I have put their expertise. Nevertheless, I am indebted to each of them.

Thanks to my sister, Julie Lee, who discussed the novel with me and read and commented on each chapter as I produced it. Her belief in me and in this book was pivotal. Thanks to my sister, Jennifer Barbour, whose help in Turin was an asset and a joy.

Thanks to NovelDoc, the online list I founded, for the support of its members, especially those who read the manuscript in whole or in part and gave comments.

Thanks to my mother, poet Julia Watson Barbour, for filling our home with books and loving me.

I am forever devotedly grateful to my husband, Frank Lankford, who for years has read out loud or listened to every word I wrote, supplied me with the latest computers and equipment, purchased the reference materials I needed, and financed my domestic and overseas research—all before I had published a single line.

Thank you, darling.